TEMPTED INNOCE

BY
MAYA BANKS

Published in Great Britain 2012
by Mills & Boon, an imprint of Harlequin (UK) Limited,
Eton House, 18-24 Paradise Road, Richmond, Surrey TW9 1SR

© Maya Banks 2012

ISBN: 978 0 263 89199 7
ebook ISBN: 978 1 408 97194 9

51-0812

Harlequin (UK) policy is to use papers that are natural, renewable and recyclable products and made from wood grown in sustainable forests. The logging and manufacturing processes conform to the legal environmental regulations of the country of origin.

Printed and bound in Spain
by Blackprint CPI, Barcelona

Maya Banks has loved romance novels from a very, *very* early age, and almost from the start, she dreamed of writing them, as well. In her teens she filled countless notebooks with overdramatic stories of love and passion. Today her stories are only slightly less dramatic, but no less romantic.

She lives in Texas with her husband and three children and wouldn't contemplate living anywhere other than the South. When she's not writing, she's usually hunting, fishing or playing poker. She loves to hear from her readers, and she can be found on Facebook or you can follow her on Twitter (@maya_banks). Her website, www.mayabanks.com, is where you can find up-to-date information on all of Maya's current and upcoming releases.

One

There came a time in a man's life when he knew he was well and truly caught. Devon Carter stared down at the brilliant diamond solitaire ring nestled in velvet and acknowledged that this was one such time. He snapped the lid closed and shoved the box into the breast pocket of his suit.

He had two choices. He could marry Ashley Copeland and fulfill his goal of merging his company with Copeland Hotels, thus creating the largest, most exclusive line of resorts in the world, or he could refuse and lose it all.

Put in that light, there wasn't much he could do except pop the question.

The doorman to his Manhattan high-rise hurried to open the door as Devon strode toward the street, where his driver waited. He took a deep breath before ducking into the car, and the driver pulled into traffic.

Tonight was the night. All of his careful wooing—the countless dinners, kisses that started brief and casual and became more breathless—was a lead-up to tonight. Tonight his seduction of Ashley Copeland would be complete, and then he'd ask her to marry him.

He shook his head as the absurdity of the situation hit him for the hundredth time. Personally he thought William Copeland was crazy for forcing his daughter down Devon's throat. He'd tried everything to sway the older man from his aim to see his daughter married off…to Devon.

Ashley was a sweet enough girl, but Devon had no desire to marry anyone. Not yet. Maybe in five years. Then he'd select a wife, have two-point-five children and have it all.

William had other plans. From the moment Devon had approached him, William held a calculated gleam in his eye. He'd told Devon that Ashley had no head for business. She was too soft-hearted, too naive, too…everything to ever take an active role in the family business. He was convinced that any man who showed interest in her would only be seeking to ingratiate himself into the Copeland fold—and the fortune that went with her. William wanted her taken care of and for whatever reason, he thought Devon was the best choice.

And so he'd made Ashley part and parcel of the deal. The catch? Ashley wasn't to learn of it. The old man might be willing to barter his daughter, but he damn sure didn't want her to know about it. Which meant that Devon was stuck playing stupid games. He winced at the things he'd said, the patience he'd exerted in his courting of Ashley. He was a blunt, straightforward person, and this whole mess made him grit his teeth.

If she was part of the deal, he'd rather all parties know that from the outset so there would be no misunderstandings, no hurt feelings and no misconceptions.

Ashley was going to think this was a grand love match. She was a starry-eyed, soft-hearted woman who preferred to spend time with her animal rescue foundation over board meetings, charts and financials for Copeland Hotels.

If she ever found out the truth, she wasn't going to take it well. And hell, he couldn't blame her. Devon hated manipulation, and he'd be pissed if someone was doing to him what he was doing to her.

"Stupid old fool," Devon muttered.

His driver pulled up to the apartment building that was home to the entire Copeland clan. William and his wife occupied a penthouse on the top floor, but Ashley had moved to a smaller apartment on a lower floor. Various other family members, from cousins to aunts and uncles, lived in all places in between.

The Copeland family was an anomaly to Devon. He'd been on his own since he was eighteen, and the only thing he remembered of his parents was the occasional reminder not to "screw up."

All this devotion William showered on his children was alien and it made Devon uncomfortable. Especially since William seemed determined to treat Devon like a son now that he was marrying Ashley.

Devon started to get out when he saw Ashley fly through the door, a wide smile on her face, her eyes sparkling as she saw him.

What the hell?

He hurried toward her, a frown on his face.

"Ashley, you should have stayed inside. I would have come for you."

In response, she laughed, the sound vibrant and fresh among the sounds of traffic. Her long blond hair hung free tonight instead of being pulled up by a clip in her usual careless manner. She reached for his hands and squeezed as she smiled up at him.

"Really, Devon, what could happen to me? Alex is right here, and he watches over me worse than my father does."

Alex, the doorman, smiled indulgently in Ashley's direction. It was a smile most people wore around her. Patient, somewhat bemused, but nearly everyone who met her was enchanted by her effervescence.

Devon sighed and pulled Ashley's hands up to his waist. "You should wait inside where it's safe and let me come in for you. Alex can't protect you. He has other duties to attend to."

Her eyes sparkled merrily, and she flung her arms around his neck, startling him with the unexpected show of affection.

"That's what you're for, silly. I can't imagine anyone ever hurting me when you're around."

Before he could respond, she fused her lips hungrily to his. For God's sake the woman had no sense of self-control. She was making a spectacle here in the doorway to her apartment building.

Still, his body reacted to the hunger in her kiss. She tasted sweet and so damn innocent. He felt like an ogre for the deception he was carrying out.

But then he remembered that Copeland Hotels would finally be his—or at least under his control. He would be a force to be reckoned with worldwide. Not bad for a man who had been told that his sole ambition should be not to "screw up."

Carefully, he pulled her away and gently offered a reprimand.

"This isn't the place, Ashley. We should be going. Carl is waiting for us."

Her lips turned down into a momentary frown before she looked beyond him to Carl, and once again she rushed forward, a bright smile on her face.

He shook his head as she greeted his chauffeur, her hands flying everywhere as she spoke in rapid tones. Carl grinned. The man actually *grinned* as he handed Ashley into the car. By the time Devon made it over, Carl had already reverted back to his somber countenance.

Devon slid into the backseat with Ashley, and she immediately moved over to nestle into his side.

"Where are we eating tonight?" she asked.

"I planned something special."

As expected she all but pounced on him, her eyes shining with excitement.

"What?" she demanded.

He smiled. "You'll see."

He felt more than heard her faint huff of exasperation and his smile broadened. One thing in Ashley's favor was that she was extraordinarily easy to please. He was unused to women who didn't wheedle, pout or complain when their expectations weren't met. And unfortunately, the women he usually spent time with had high expectations. *Expensive* expectations. Ashley seemed happy no matter what he presented her with. He had every confidence that the ring he'd chosen would meet with her approval.

She nestled closer to him and laid her head on his shoulder. Her spontaneous demonstrations of affection still unbalanced him. He wasn't used to people who were so…unreserved.

William Copeland felt that Ashley needed someone who understood and accepted her nature. Why he thought Devon fit the bill Devon would never know.

When they married, he would work on getting her to restrain some of her enthusiasm. She couldn't go through her entire life with her emotions on her sleeve. It would only get her hurt.

A few minutes later, Carl pulled up to Devon's building and got out to open the door. Devon stepped out and then extended his hand to help Ashley from the car.

Her brow was creased in a thoughtful expression as she stared up at the building.

"This is your place."

He chuckled at her statement of the obvious. "So it is. Come, our dinner awaits."

He ushered her through the open door and into a waiting elevator. It soared to the top and opened into the foyer of his apartment. To his satisfaction, everything was just as he'd arranged.

The lighting was low and romantic. Soft jazz played in the background and the table by the window overlooking the city had been set for two.

"Oh, Devon, this is perfect!"

Once again she threw herself into his arms and gave him a squeeze worthy of someone much larger than herself. It did funny things to his chest every time she hugged him.

Extricating himself from her hold, he guided her toward the table. He pulled her chair out for her and then reached for a bottle of wine to pour them both a glass.

"The food is still hot!" she exclaimed as she touched the plate in front of her. "How did you manage it?"

He chuckled. "My super powers?"

"Mmm, I like the idea of a man with super cooking powers."

"I had someone in while I was gone to collect you."

She wrinkled her nose. "You're horribly old-fashioned, Dev. There was no reason to collect me if we were spending the evening at your apartment. I could have gotten a cab or had my father's driver run me over."

He blinked in surprise. Old-fashioned? He'd been accused of a lot of things, but never of being old-fashioned. Then he scowled.

"A man should see to his woman's needs. All of them. It was my pleasure to pick you up."

Her cheeks pinkened in the candlelight, and her eyes shone like he'd just handed her the keys to a brand-new car.

"Am I?" she asked huskily.

He cocked his head to the side as he set his wineglass down. "Are you what?"

"Your woman."

Something unfurled inside him. He wouldn't have considered himself a possessive man, but now that he'd decided that she would be his wife, he discovered he felt very possessive where she was concerned.

"Yes," he said softly. "And before the night is over, you'll have no doubts that you belong to me."

A full body shiver took over Ashley. How was she supposed to concentrate on dinner after a statement like that? Devon stared at her across the table like he was going to pounce at any moment.

He had the most arresting eyes. Not really brown, but a warm shade of amber. In the sunlight they looked golden and in the candlelight they looked like a mountain lion's. She felt like prey, but it was a delicious feeling, not at all threatening. She'd been waiting for the moment when Devon would take their relationship a step further.

She'd longed for it and dreaded it with equal intensity. How could she possibly keep pace with a man who could seduce a woman with nothing more than a touch and a glance?

He'd been a consummate gentleman during the time they'd been dating. At first he'd only given her gentle, nonthreatening kisses, but over time they'd become more passionate and she'd gotten a glimpse of the powerfully sensual man under the protective armor.

She had a feeling that once those layers were peeled back, the man behind them was ferocious, possessive and...savage.

Another shiver overtook her at the direction of her thoughts. They were fanciful, yes, but she truly believed her assessment. Would she find out tonight? Did he plan to make her his?

"Aren't you going to eat?" Devon prompted.

She stared down at her plate again. What was it anyway? She wasn't sure she could eat a bite. Her mouth felt as if it was full of sawdust, and her entire body trembled with anticipation.

She moved the shrimp with her fork so that it gathered some of the sauce and slowly raised it to her lips.

"You aren't a vegetarian, are you?"

She laughed at the look on his face, as if the idea had just occurred to him.

"Tell me I haven't been serving you food you won't eat all

this time," Devon said with a grimace. "You would have said something, wouldn't you have?"

She put the shrimp into her mouth and chewed as she put the fork down. When she'd swallowed she reached over to touch his hand.

"You worry too much. I would have told you if I was a vegetarian. A lot of people assume since I'm so active in my animal rescue organization that I refuse to eat meat of any kind."

The relief on his face made her laugh again.

"I'll eat chicken and most seafood. I'm not crazy about pork or the more uppity stuff like veal, foie gras and stuff like that."

A shudder worked over her shoulders.

"There's something about eating duck liver that just turns my stomach."

Devon chuckled. "It's actually quite good. Have you tried it?"

She wrinkled her nose in distaste. "Sorry. I have a thing about eating any sort of innard."

"Ah, so no cow's tongue for you then."

She held up her hands and shook her head back and forth. "Don't say it. Just don't say it. That's beyond disgusting."

"I'll make a note of your food preferences so that I never serve you animal guts," he said solemnly.

She grinned over at him. "You know, Devon, you're not as stiff as everyone thinks you are. You actually have quite a sense of humor."

One finely arched eyebrow shot upward. "Stiff? Who thinks I'm stiff?"

Realizing she'd put her foot solidly in her mouth, she stuffed another shrimp in to keep the foot company.

"Nobody," she mumbled around her food. "Forget I said anything."

"Has someone been warning you off of me?"

The sudden tension in his voice sent a prickle of unease over her.

"My family worries for me," she said simply. "They're very protective. Too protective," she finished with a mutter.

"Your *family* is warning you about me?"

He acted as though it was the very last thing he expected. Was he so sure that her entire family was pushing for a match between them?

"Well no, not exactly. Definitely not Daddy. He thinks you hung the moon. Mama approves but I'm sure it's because Daddy does. She thinks he can do nothing wrong so if you have his stamp of approval you have hers."

He seemed to relax in his chair. "Who then?"

She shrugged. "My brother wants me to be careful, but you have to understand he's been saying the same thing about all the guys I've ever dated."

Again that eyebrow went up as he raised the glass of wine to his lips. "Oh?"

"Yeah, you know, you're a philanderer, a player. Different woman on your arm every week. You aren't serious. You just want to get me into bed."

A blast of heat surged into her cheeks and she ducked her head. Stupid thing to blurt out. Stupid!

"Sounds like a typical older brother," Devon said blandly. "But he's right about one thing. I do want you in my bed. The difference is, once you're there, you're going to stay."

Her lips popped into an *O*.

He smiled, a lazy, self-assured smile that oozed male confidence.

"Finish eating, Ashley. I want you to enjoy your meal. We'll enjoy…each other…later."

She ate mechanically. She didn't register the taste. For all she knew she *was* eating cow's tongue.

What did women do in situations like these? Here was a man obviously determined to take her to bed. Did she play it cool? Did she go on the offensive? Did she offer to undress for him?

A bubble of laughter bounced into her throat. Oh, Lord, but she was in way over her head.

Firm hands rested on her shoulders and squeezed reassuringly. She yanked her head up to see Devon behind her. How had he gotten there?

"Relax, Ash," he said gently. "You're wound tighter than a spring. Come here."

On shaking legs, she rose to stand in front of him. He touched her cheek with one finger then raised it to her temple to push at a tendril of her hair. He traced a line over her face and down to her lips before finally moving in, his body crowding hers.

He wrapped one arm around her waist, and cupped her nape with his other hand. This time when he kissed her there was none of the restraint she'd seen in the past. It was like kissing an inferno.

Hot, breathless, so overwhelming that her senses shattered. How could one kiss do this to her?

His tongue brushed over her lips, softly at first and then more firmly as he forced her mouth to open under his gentle pressure.

She relaxed and melted into his embrace. Her body hummed. Her pulse thudded against her temples, at her neck and deep in her body at her very core. She wanted this man. Sometimes she felt like she'd been waiting for him forever. He was so…right.

"Devon," she whispered.

He pushed far enough away that he could see her, but he still held her firm in his embrace.

"Yes, sweetheart?"

Her heart fluttered at the endearment.

"There's something I need to tell you. Something you should know."

His brow furrowed, and he searched her eyes as if gauging her mood.

"Go ahead. You can tell me anything."

She swallowed but felt the knot grow bigger in her throat. She hadn't imagined it being this difficult to say, but she felt suddenly silly. Maybe she shouldn't say anything at all. Maybe she should just let things happen. But no, this was a special night. It needed to be special. He deserved to know.

"I—I've never done this." She gripped his upper arm with nervous fingers. "What I mean is that I've never made love with a man before. You...you'd be the first."

Something dark and primitive sparked in his eyes. His grip tightened around her waist. At first he didn't say anything. He kissed her hungrily, his lips devouring hers.

Then he pulled away, savage satisfaction written on every facet of his face.

"I'm glad. After tonight you'll be mine, Ashley. I'm glad I'm the first."

"Me, too," she whispered.

Some of the fierceness in his expression eased. He leaned forward and kissed her on the brow and held his lips there for a long moment.

His hands ran soothingly up and down her arms, stopping to squeeze her shoulders. "I don't want you to be afraid. I'll be very gentle with you, sweetheart. I'll make sure you enjoy every moment of it."

She reached up on tiptoe to wrap both arms around his neck. "Then make love to me, Devon. I've waited so long for you."

Two

Ashley stared up at Devon, unsure of what to do now. He didn't suffer any such problem. Dropping another kiss on her brow, he bent and lifted her into his arms and carried her to the large master bedroom in the corner of the apartment.

She sighed as she laid her head on his chest. "I've always dreamed of being carried to bed when the big moment came. I probably sound silly."

Soft laughter rumbled from his chest. "Glad I could fulfill one of your fantasies before I even get you naked."

She blushed but felt a giddy thrill at the idea of him undressing her. That was number two on her fantasy list for when she lost her virginity.

After listening to so many girls in high school and college talk about how utterly unremarkable their first times were, Ashley had vowed that her experience would be different. Perhaps she'd been too picky as a result, but she'd been determined to choose the right man and the right moment. So she was feeling pretty damn smug because it didn't get any more perfect than Devon Carter right here, right now.

He set her down just inside the doorway and she glanced nervously around his enormous bedroom. A person could get swallowed up in here. And the bed was equally huge. It looked custom-made. Who needed a bed that big anyway? Unless he regularly hosted orgies and slept with ten women.

"I'm going to undress you, sweetheart," he said in a husky voice. "I'll go slow and you stop me if you feel uncomfortable at any time. We have all night. There's no rush."

Her heart melted at the tenderness in his voice. He seemed so patient, and she warred with appreciating this unerringly patient side of him and being frustrated because she wanted to be ravished.

It's your first time only once.

She could hear herself issue the reprimand. And she was right. She had plenty of time for down-and-dirty, hot monkey sex. But she would only have this night once and she wanted it to be a night she'd always remember.

"Turn around so I can unzip your dress."

Slowly she turned and closed her eyes when he gently moved her hair over one shoulder so he could reach the zip. A moment later, the light rasp of the zipper filled the room and the dress loosened precariously around her bust.

She slapped her hands over the strapless neckline just before it took the plunge down her body.

Devon's hands closed around her bare shoulders and he kissed the curve of her neck. "Relax."

Easy for him to say. He'd probably done this a hundred times. That thought depressed her and she made herself swear not to dwell on how many bed partners he may have had.

He turned her back around, his smile tender enough to melt her insides. Carefully he pried her fingers away from their death grip on her dress until it fell down her body, leaving her in only her panties.

She flushed scarlet. Why, oh, why hadn't she just worn the strapless bra? She felt like a hussy for not wearing anything but it wasn't as if she had a huge amount of cleavage and the dress fit tightly over her chest so she hadn't been in danger of flopping out of it.

And it wasn't as if she knew she was going to be seduced tonight.

She'd hoped. But then she'd hoped every time Devon took her out. She'd given up on trying to predict when or if the day might come.

"Very sexy," Devon breathed out as his gaze raked up and down her body.

Thank goodness she'd worn the lacy, sexy panties and not the plain white cotton ones she sometimes wore when she was feeling particularly uninspired or just didn't give a damn whether she felt girly and pretty or not.

"You're beautiful, Ash. So damn beautiful."

Some of her trembling stopped as she absorbed the look in his eyes. The eyes didn't lie and she could read arousal and appreciation in those golden depths.

He took her shoulders, gently pulled her to him and kissed her again. Hot. Forceful. In turns fierce and then gentler as though he had to remind himself not to overwhelm her.

She wanted to be overwhelmed.

She may be a virgin but she was no stranger to lust, desire and extreme arousal. She wanted Devon with a force that bordered on obsession. He'd fired many a fantasy that had kept her up at night.

And it wasn't as if she hadn't been tempted in the past. She'd been courted by other men. Some she felt absolutely no desire for but with others she'd experienced a kernel of interest and had wondered if she should pursue a sexual relationship. In the end, she hadn't been sure and if she wasn't absolutely sure, she'd promised herself she wouldn't take the plunge.

Not so with Devon. She'd known from the moment he introduced himself to her in that husky, sexy-as-hell voice that she was a goner. She'd spent the last weeks breathless in anticipation of this night. Now that it was here, her entire body ached for him to take her.

He pulled away for a moment and she stared at him with glazed eyes. He touched her cheek, tracing a path down her face with his fingertip. Then he kissed her again. And again.

Hot. Breathless. His tongue slid between her lips and feathered over her own. Warm and decadent, his taste seeped over her tongue and she drank him in hungrily, wanting more.

His harsh groan exploded into her mouth and the rush of his exhalation blew over her face. "You make me crazy."

She smiled, some of her nervousness abating. That she had this effect on this gorgeous, perfect man infused her with a sudden rush of feminine confidence.

He fastened his mouth to her jaw and kissed a line down to her neck. He pressed his lips just over her pulse point and then lightly grazed his teeth over the sensitive flesh.

Shivers of delight danced over her shoulders. His hands glided up her arms and then gripped her just above the elbows. He held her in place as his mouth continued its downward trek. Over the curve of her shoulder and then down the front.

He went to his knees in front of her so that his mouth was barely an inch from her nipple. She sucked in her breath, afraid to move, wanting so badly for him to touch her there. His mouth, lips, tongue… She didn't care. She just knew she'd die if he didn't touch her.

He lowered his head and kissed her belly instead. Just above her navel. She sucked in her breath, causing her stomach to cave in. He moved up an inch and kissed her again, tracing a path between her breasts until finally he pressed a kiss directly over where her heart beat.

A slow smile turned his lips upward, the movement light against her skin.

"Your heart's racing," he murmured.

She remained silent. It didn't require acknowledgement from her—her heart *was* beyond racing. It was damn near about to explode out of her chest.

But her hands wouldn't remain still. Drawn to the light brown wash of his hair, she threaded her fingers through the short strands. In a certain light, she could see the shades of his eyes. Amber. Golden. That warm, liquid brown.

Her fingers moved easily through his hair. No styling products stiffened the strands. A little mussed. Never quite the same from day to day. He paid as little attention to his hair as he did to the other things he deemed inconsequential.

He glanced up, her fingers still thrust into his hair. "Are you afraid?"

"Terrified," she admitted.

His gaze softened and he wrapped his arms around her body, pulling her into his embrace. The shock of her naked body against his still fully clothed one sent shivers up her spine.

"I'd feel less afraid if you were naked, though."

He blinked in surprise and then he threw back his head and laughed. "You little tease." He pushed upward to his feet until he towered over her. "I'm happy to accommodate you. *More* than happy to accommodate you."

She licked over suddenly dry lips as he pulled away and began unbuttoning his shirt. He tugged the ends from his slacks and unfastened his cuffs before shrugging out of the sleeves.

She swayed precariously because oh, Lord, was the man mouthwateringly gorgeous. He was lean in an "I work out" way but he wasn't so muscled that he looked like he got carried away with the fitness regimen. He was hard in all the right places without being a neckless, snarling, swollen, knuckles-dragging-the-ground caveman type.

A smattering of light brown hair collected in a whorl in the center of his chest and then tapered to a fine line that drifted down his abdomen and disappeared into the waist of his pants.

She wanted to touch him. Had to touch him. She curled her fingers until they dug into her palms and then she frowned. There weren't rules to seduction, right? She could touch. No reason for her to stand here like a statue or an automaton while he did all the work. While taking things slow did have its good points, there was simply too much she wanted to experience to stand idly by while seduction *happened*. She wanted to take an active part.

He'd only began to undo his pants, when she slid her hands over his chest and up to his shoulders. He went still and for a moment closed his eyes.

His response fascinated her. Did her touch bring him as much pleasure as his touch brought her? A sudden rush of power bolted through her veins, awakening the feminine roar inside her.

She moved in closer, wanting to feel his naked flesh against hers. Hot. She gasped when her breasts pressed against his chest. It was an electric sensation that was wildly intoxicating. She wanted more. So much more.

"What are you doing?" he asked hoarsely.

"Enjoying myself."

He smiled at that and remained still, his hands still gripping the fly of his pants. She ran her palms openly over his chest, exploring each muscled ridge, enjoying the rugged contrast between his hardness and the softness of her own body.

"Take them off," she whispered when her hands drifted perilously close to where his hands were positioned.

"Has the blushing virgin turned temptress?"

On cue, she flushed but he smiled and then let go of his pants to frame her face in his palms. He kissed her, nearly scorching her lips off with the sudden heat. "You take them off me," he murmured into her mouth.

Sudden nerves made her fingers clumsy as she fumbled

with his pants, but he stood there patiently, his hands caressing her face, gaze locked with hers as she pushed his pants down his legs.

Swallowing, she chanced a look down to see his erection straining hard against the cotton of his briefs. Plain, boxer briefs. Somehow she'd imagined something a little more... She wasn't sure. She just knew she hadn't imagined plain boxer briefs but then he was a no-fuss kind of guy. Yes, he wore expensive clothing, but it was comfortable expensive clothing. The kind you only knew was expensive because you recognized the label. Not because it looked terribly pricey.

Simply put, Devon Carter looked like a man who'd made money but wasn't overly concerned with appearing as though he was wealthy. It wasn't as if he couldn't look the part. She'd seen him in full business attire with the sleek designer labels and the polished, arrogant look to match. But she'd spent much more time with him privately. When he was relaxed. Less guarded. That was the word. In public situations, he was intensely guarded at all times. Almost as if he was determined to let no one in. It thrilled her that he trusted her enough to see his more casual side.

"Put your hand around me," he coaxed in that low husky tone that had her melting.

Tentatively she slid her fingers beyond the waistband of his underwear and delved lower until she encountered the velvety hardness of his erection. Emboldened by the immediate darkening of his eyes, she curled her fingers around the base and slowly slid upward, lightly skimming along his length.

His hands left her face and he impatiently pushed his underwear down until he was completely nude, cupped in her hands as she gently caressed him.

Having nothing but stolen glimpses of elicit photos to compare him to, he seemed to measure up adequately in the size department. At least he didn't look so huge that she feared compatibility issues.

He gently took her wrists and pulled her hands away from his erection. Then he pulled her hands up until they were trapped between them against his chest. His thumb lightly caressed the inside of her palm as he stared into her eyes.

"You, my love, are driving me slowly insane. It was me who was supposed to do the seducing and yet you utterly enslave me with every touch."

She flushed with pleasure, her skin growing warm under the intense desire blazing in his eyes.

He kissed her again, and he pressed in close until he walked her backward toward the bed. He stopped when the backs of her legs brushed against the sumptuous comforter.

He wrapped his arm around her waist and lowered her back until she was lying on the mattress, him hovering above her.

His expression grew serious and he brushed her hair from her forehead in a tender gesture. "If at any time I do something that frightens you, tell me and I'll stop. If at any time you simply want to slow down, just let me know."

"Oh," she breathed out. Because it was impossible to say anything else around the tightness in her throat.

She reached for him, pulled him down to meet her kiss. She felt clumsy and inept but it didn't seem to matter to him. She wished she was more artful. More practiced. But she couldn't wish for experience because more than anything she was glad she'd waited for this moment. For him.

"I love you," she whispered, unable to hold back the words that swelled and finally broke free.

He went still and for a moment she was terrified that she'd effectively thrown a wet blanket over a fire. She drew away, eyes wide as she searched his face for something. Some reaction. Some indication that she'd breached some forbidden barrier.

Trust her to ruin what would have been the most exciting, wonderful, splendiferous moment of her life by opening her

big mouth. She'd never been able to restrain herself. She tried.
Most of the time.

"Devon?"

His name came out in a near croak. Her lips shook and she
started to withdraw, already feeling the heat of embarrassment
lick over her with painful precision.

Instead of answering her, he moved over her in a powerful rush. He took her mouth roughly, devouring her lips as his
tongue plunged inside, tangling with hers.

Her body surged to life, arching up into his. She wrapped
her arms around his neck as he gathered her tightly against
him. Their bodies were as fused as their mouths. Between her
legs, she could feel him so hard. Hot.

His hips jerked, almost as if he could barely contain the urge
to push inside her. She gasped for air, partly out of excitement,
partly out of sudden, delicious fear and anticipation.

His hands and mouth were everywhere. A sensual assault on
her senses. Magic. Gentle caresses mixed with firmer, rougher
touches. He slid down her body until his mouth hovered over
one taut nipple. And then he flicked his tongue out and licked
the tip.

She cried out, nearly undone by the shock of such a simple
touch. Pleasure rocked over her and she shuddered violently,
her fingers suddenly digging into his flesh, marking him.

Not satisfied with the intensity of her reaction, he closed
his mouth over the rigid peak and sucked strongly.

Her vision blurred. She gasped but couldn't seem to draw
air into her lungs. Oh, but it was heaven. So edgy. She couldn't
even find the words to describe such a decadent sensation as
his mouth sucking at her breast.

But then his hand slid between them, over the softness of
her belly and lower.

She held her breath as his fingers tentatively brushed
through her sensitive folds and then he found her heat, teasing, touching. He knew better than she knew herself exactly

how to pleasure her. Where to touch her. *How* to touch her. Each stroke brought her to greater heights.

It was as though she was being wound tighter and tighter. Tension coiled in her belly. Low. Humming through her pelvis. She wasn't ignorant of orgasms, but this was nothing like she'd ever experienced before. It was powerful. Relentless. Nearly frightening in its intensity.

His fingers left her and he carefully parted her legs. His hand glided soothingly up the inside of her thigh and then he stroked her intimately again as he positioned himself above her.

His mouth left her breasts and she moaned her protest. He covered her lips once more with his own and then whispered softly to her.

"Hold on to me, love. Touch me. I'm going to go inside you now. I'll be gentle. There's nothing to be afraid of."

She trembled from head to toe. Not in fear or trepidation. She was so close to release that she feared the moment he pushed inside her the barest inch that she'd go over the edge, and she wanted it to last. She wanted to enjoy every single moment of what was to come.

"Wait," she choked out.

He went still, the tip of his erection just touching the mouth of her opening. Strain was evident in his face as he stared down at her, but he held himself in check.

"Are you all right? Did I frighten you?" he asked urgently.

She shook her head. "No. No, I'm fine. I just needed a second. I'm so close. Just need to catch up."

He smiled then, his eyes gleaming with a predatory light. "Tell me when."

She reached up once more, feathering her hands over his shoulders and to the bunched muscles of his back. Her gaze met his and she drowned in those beautiful amber eyes. "When."

He swallowed hard and his lips tightened into a harsh line.

Then he closed his eyes and flexed his hips, pushing into her inch by delicious inch.

At one point he stopped and she stirred restlessly, a protest forming.

"Shh," he murmured as he kissed the corner of her mouth. "Give me just a moment. I don't want to hurt you. Better to have done with it quickly."

She nodded her agreement just as he surged forward, burying himself to the hilt.

Her eyes widened and a strangled sound escaped her throat as she sought to process the sudden wash of conflicting sensations that bombarded her from every angle.

He was deep. Impossibly deep. She surrounded him. He surrounded her. Their hips were flush against each other. His body covered hers possessively. There was a burning ache deep inside her, and she couldn't discern whether it was pleasure or pain.

She just knew she wanted—needed—more.

She whimpered lightly and struggled, not against him, not in protest. She wanted something she couldn't name. She wanted…him. All of him.

"Easy," he soothed.

He kissed her, stroked his tongue over hers and then deepened the kiss just as he began to move inside her. Gently. He was so gentle and reverent. He lifted his body off of her and arched his hips, pushing deep then retreating.

Then he levered himself down, resting on his forearms, never breaking away from her eyes.

"Okay?"

She smiled. "Very okay."

"You're beautiful, Ash. So very beautiful. So innocent and perfect and mine."

His. The possessive growl in his voice thrilled her and sent another cascade of pleasure through her body.

"Yes, yours," she whispered.

"Tell me how close you are. I want to make sure you're with me. I can't hold off much longer."

"Then don't." Her voice shook. She was nearly beyond the ability to think much less speak. Her body was taut. Her senses were shattered and she was so very close to losing all control. Just one touch. One more touch…

He gathered her close and thrust again. And then again. He forced her thighs farther apart, plunged deeper and she lost all sense of herself.

She cried out his name. Heard him murmur close to her ear. Soothing. Comforting. Telling her beautiful things she could barely make sense of. She was spiraling at a dizzying speed, faster and faster until she closed her eyes.

It was the single most beautiful, spectacular sensation she could imagine. She'd wanted wonderful, but this far surpassed even her most erotic fantasies.

When she regained at least a modicum of sanity, she was firmly wrapped in Devon's embrace and his mouth was moving lightly over her neck. For that matter she was on top of him. Her hair was flung to one side while he nuzzled at the curve of her shoulder, moving up and down to just below her ear and back to her shoulder.

She raised her head to stare down at him, still feeling a little fuzzy around the edges. "How did I get here?"

He smiled and slid his hands over her naked body. They stopped at her behind and he squeezed affectionately. "I put you here. I like you covering me. I could get used to it."

"Oh."

He raised one eyebrow. "Speechless? You?"

She sent him a disgruntled look but was too wasted to follow up with any sort of admonishment. Okay, so obviously she was speechless.

He chuckled and pulled her down against him. She settled over him with a sigh and he rubbed his palm over her back, stroking and caressing as she lay draped over him like a wet noodle.

"Did I hurt you?"

She smiled at the concern in his voice. "No. It was perfect, Dev. So perfect I can't even find the words to describe it. Thank you."

He lifted a strand of hair and lazily twined his fingers around it. "Thank you? I don't think I've ever been thanked by a woman after sex."

"You made my first time special," she said quietly. "It was perfect. You were perfect."

He kissed the top of her head. "I'm glad."

She yawned against his chest and cuddled deeper into his hold.

"Go to sleep," he murmured. "I want you to sleep here tonight."

Her eyes were incredibly heavy, and she was already drifting off when his directive registered in her consciousness.

"Want to sleep here, too," she mumbled.

His fingers stilled in her hair and then his hands wandered down her body, bold and possessive. "That's good, Ash, because from now on, you'll sleep every night in my bed."

Three

Devon woke to the odd sensation of a female body wrapped around him. Not just wrapped but completely and utterly surrounding him.

Ashley was draped across him, her legs tangled with his, her breasts flattened against his chest, her arm thrown across his body and her face burrowed into his neck.

He…liked it.

He lay there a long while watching the soft rise and fall of her body as she slept soundly across him. She was really quite beautiful in an unsophisticated, effervescent way. She lit up a room when she walked in. You could always pick her out of a crowd. She was extremely…natural. Perhaps a bit too exuberant and unrestrained but in time with the proper guidance, she'd be an excellent wife and mother.

He ran the tips of his finger lightly up her arm. She was pale. Not so pale she looked unhealthy, but it was obvious she wasn't a sun bunny, nor did she indulge in salon tanning. Perhaps what he liked most about her was that she looked the same no matter when he saw her. Though she wore makeup, she didn't wear so much that she was transformed into some-one completely different when they went out.

Glossy lips and a touch of coal to already long, lush lashes seemed to be all she did, but then he was hardly an expert on women's gunk.

But she didn't seem fake. At least not that he could tell. Yet. Who knew what the future would bring. He liked to think she wasn't an accomplice in this ridiculous plan of her father's even when he knew it was best for all parties involved to know the entire story from the start.

The selfish bastard in him liked the idea that she felt af-fection for him, free of machinations. If her words from the night before weren't merely a result of being overwhelmed in the moment, *affection* was perhaps the wrong term. She'd said she loved him.

It both complicated the matter and gave him a certain amount of satisfaction.

While he may approach the marriage as a matter of neces-sity, convenience and a chance at a successful business ven-ture, the idea that she would be coming into the marriage for the same reasons bothered him immensely.

It made him a flaming hypocrite but he was happy for her to want him because she desired him and yes, even loved him.

First, however, he had to get the preliminaries out of the way. One of which was making their upcoming nuptials offi-cial. She didn't know it yet, but she would become Mrs. Devon Carter.

He carefully extricated himself from the tangle of arms and legs, but he needn't have worried because she slept soundly, only wrinkling her nose and mumbling something in her sleep when he slipped away completely.

He pulled on his robe and glanced back at the bed. For a moment he was transfixed by the image she presented. The sun streamed through the window across the room and bathed her in its warm glow.

Her blond hair was tousled and spread out over his pillow. One arm shielded most of her breasts from view, but there, just below her elbow, one nipple peeked out. The sheet slid to just over her buttocks but bared the dimple just below the small of her back.

She was indeed beautiful. And now she was his.

He dug into the pocket of the jacket he'd discarded the night before to retrieve the box with the ring in it and then quietly left the room. When she awoke, he'd put into place the next part of his carefully orchestrated plan.

Ashley stirred and stretched lazily, blinking when the sun momentarily blinded her. She kept her eyes shut for a moment, simply enjoying the warmth and comfort of the sumptuous bed. Devon's bed.

She sighed in contentment. As virginal deflowering went, that had to top the list of all-time most awesome. How could it possibly have been any better? A wonderful night. Romantic dinner for two. Devon staring at her with those gorgeous eyes and murmuring that she would now be his. Oh, yeah, perfect.

Then she realized that he was no longer in bed with her and she opened her eyes with a frown. Only to see him standing just across the room. Staring at her.

He was clad in a robe, though it dangled loosely, open just enough that she could see his bare chest. He was leaning against the doorway to the bathroom and he was simply watching her. For some reason that sent a giddy thrill up her spine.

Then a flash of color caught her eye and she glanced downward to see a lush red rose lying on the sheet next to her. But it was the tiny card propped next to a dazzling, truly spectacular diamond ring that took her breath away.

Blood rushed to her head and she stared openmouthed at the items before her. She pushed to her elbow and reached for the ring, hands shaking so badly that she was clumsy, nearly dropping the small velvet box where the ring rested.

Then she glanced at the note again, sure she'd misunderstood. But no, there it was. In his neat, distinctive scrawl.

Will you marry me?

"Oh, God," she croaked out.

She looked at the ring, looked at the note and then back up to him, almost afraid that he'd be gone and that she'd imagined this whole thing.

But he was still there, an indulgent smile carving those handsome features.

"Really?" she whispered.

He nodded and smiled more broadly. "Really."

She dropped the rose, the ring, the note—everything—and flew out of bed, across the room, and launched herself into his arms.

He stepped back and laughed as she kissed his face, his brow, his cheek and then his lips. "Yes, oh, yes! Oh, my God, Devon, yes!"

He made a grab for her behind before she could slide down him and land on the floor. Then he hoisted her up so they were eye level. "You know it's customary to actually put the ring on."

She glanced down at her hand and then over her shoulder to the bed. "Oh, my God! Where is it?"

Shaking his head, he carried her over to the bed then set her on the edge while he reached behind her.

A moment later, he took her hand and slid the diamond onto her ring finger. She sucked in her breath as the sun caught the stone and it sparkled brilliantly in the light.

"Oh, Dev, it's beautiful," she breathed.

She threw her arms around his neck and hugged him tightly. "I love you so much. I can't believe you planned all this."

He gently pulled her arms down and then collected her

hands in her lap as he stared into her eyes. "I don't want a long engagement."

Was this supposed to worry her? She beamed back at him. "Neither do I."

"In fact, I'd prefer to get married right away," he added, watching her all the while.

She frowned and chewed at her bottom lip. "I wouldn't mind. I mean if it was just me, but I don't know how my family would take that. Mama will want to plan a big wedding. I'm her only daughter. It's not that I care about a big fuss—I don't. But it would hurt her if she wasn't able to give us a big wedding."

He touched her cheek. "Leave your family to me. I assure you, they'll be on board with my plans. You and I will have the best wedding—one that your mother will be more than satisfied with. I think you'll find they won't object to our plans at all."

Excitement hurtled through her veins until it was nearly impossible to sit still. "I can't wait to tell everyone! Won't this just be amazing? Everyone will be so thrilled for me. I know Daddy despaired of me ever finding a suitable man and settling down. He always says I'm too unsettled, but really, I'm still young."

He gave her an amused smile. "Are you saying you don't want to get married?"

She stared at him in shock. "No! That's not at all what I was saying. I was merely going to say that I was waiting for the right man. In this case, you."

"That's what I like to hear," he murmured.

He leaned forward to kiss her brow. "How about you take a long bubble bath to recover from last night's activities and then we'll have breakfast together."

She flushed red. She had to be flaming. But she nodded, eager to discuss their future.

Mrs. Devon Carter. It had such a nice ring to it. And speaking of rings… She glanced down, transfixed by the radiance of the diamond that adorned her finger.

"Like it?" he asked in a teasing voice.

She looked back up at him, suddenly serious. "I love it, Dev. It's absolutely gorgeous. But you didn't need to get me something so expensive. I would have loved anything you gave me."

He smiled. "I know you would. But I wanted something special."

Her heart did a little dance in her chest. "Thank you. It's just perfect. Everything is perfect."

He kissed her again, long and leisurely. When he pulled away, his eyes were half-lidded and they were glowing with desire.

"Go draw your bath before I forget all about breakfast and make love to you again."

"Breakfast?" she whispered. "Were we planning to eat?"

He made a sound in his throat that was part growl, part resignation.

"I don't want to hurt you, Ash. As much as you tempt me, I'd rather wait until you're fully healed from last night."

She pushed out her bottom lip.

"As adorable as you are when you pout, it won't move me this time. Now get your pretty behind out of bed and hit the bathroom. Breakfast will be served in forty-five minutes. Plenty of time for you to soak."

She sighed. "Okay, okay. I'm going."

She got up and walked toward the bathroom but just as she got to the doorway, something he'd said the night before came back to her. She paused and turned around, her head cocked to the side.

"Dev, what did you mean last night when you said I'd be sleeping here with you every night from now on?"

He rose and pulled his robe tighter around his waist. He stared back at her, his gaze intense and serious.

"Exactly what I said. I'll want you to move in as soon as

possible. I'll arrange to have what you need transferred from your apartment. You're mine, Ash. From now on, you'll spend every night in my bed."

Four

"Well, you finally took the leap," Cameron Hollingsworth said as he stared across the room to where Ashley stood with a group of women.

Devon took a sip of the wine, though the taste went unappreciated. He was too distracted. Still, he forced some of it down, hoping it would at least take the edge off.

The official announcement would be made in a few moments. By Devon himself. Ashley's father had wanted to do the honors, but Devon had preferred to do it himself. William Copeland had already orchestrated entirely too much of Devon's relationship with Ashley. From now on, things would be done his way.

Though everyone in attendance was well aware it was an engagement party they had been invited to, Ashley had insisted on waiting until all the guests had arrived before their engagement was announced.

"Cold feet already?" Cam asked dryly. "You haven't said two words since I got here."

Devon grimaced. "No. It's done. No backing out now. Cope-land has all but signed off on the deal. After the ceremony he'll fax the final documents and we'll move forward with the merger. I'll want to meet with you, Ryan and Rafe as soon as I return from the honeymoon."

Cam arched an eyebrow. "Honeymoon? You're actually going on one?"

"Just because this marriage is part and parcel of a business deal doesn't mean Ashley has to have any less of a marriage or honeymoon," Devon murmured.

Cam shrugged. "Good idea. Keep her happy. If she's happy, Daddy's happy. You know what they say about Daddy's girls."

Devon frowned. "Don't be an ass. She's…"

"She's what?" Cam prompted.

"Look, she has no idea what her father's done. She thinks this is a wildly romantic courtship that culminated in an equally romantic marriage proposal. If I don't take her on a honeymoon, it's going to look strange."

Cam groaned. "This can't end well. Mark my words. You're screwed, my friend."

"Anyone ever tell you what a ball of joy you are?"

Cam held his hands up in surrender. "Look, I'm just trying to warn you here. You should tell her the truth. No woman likes being made a fool of."

"And have her tell me to go to hell and take my proposal with me?" Devon demanded.

He sighed and shook his head. Yeah, he knew Cam had been through the wringer in the past. He couldn't blame his friend for his cynicism. But he wasn't in the mood to hear it right now.

"This deal is important to all of us. Not just me," he con-tinued when Cam remained silent. "Marriage isn't my first choice, but Ash is a sweet girl. She'll make a good wife and a good mother. Everyone gets what they want. You, me, Ryan and Rafe. Ashley, her father. Everyone's happy."

"Whatever floats your boat, man. You know I'm behind you all the way. But remember this. You don't have to marry her to make this work. We'll find another company. We've suffered setbacks before. Not one of us expects you to martyr yourself for the cause. Rafe and Ryan are deliriously happy. There's no reason you shouldn't hold out for the same."

Devon snorted. "Turning into quite the rah-rah man. I'm fine, Cam. There is no love of my life. No other woman in the picture. No one I'd rather marry. I'll be content with Ashley. Stop worrying."

Cam checked his watch. "Your intended bride is looking this way. I think you're on."

Devon glanced over to where Ashley stood surrounded by friends and relatives. He could never sort out who was who because there were so many. She smiled and waved and then motioned him over.

He handed Cam his wineglass and made his way through the throng of people until he reached Ashley.

She sparkled tonight. She wore a radiant smile that seemed to captivate the room. But then she always drew people. She'd talk to anyone at all about anything at all.

As soon as he approached, she all but pounced on him, took his hand and dragged him into her circle. He smiled at each of the women in turn, but their names and faces kind of blended. After a moment he bent to murmur in Ashley's ear. "It's time, don't you think?"

She all but quivered in excitement. Her eyes lit up and she smiled as she squeezed his hand.

"Excuse us, ladies," he said smoothly as he drew Ashley away and back in Cam's direction. There wasn't anyone standing around Cam. Cam had that effect on people. It was the perfect place to call for attention and announce their engagement.

"Hi, Cam," Ashley sang out as they walked up to his friend. She let go of Devon's hand and threw her arms around

Cam's neck. Cam grinned and shook his head as he attempted to extricate himself from her embrace.

"Hello, Ash," he said before dropping an affectionate kiss on her cheek. "Come stand by me while Devon makes a fool of himself."

Devon sent a glare Cam's way before taking Ashley's hand and pulling her to his side. Laughing, Cam handed him a fresh wineglass and a spoon.

"What, are you kidding me?" Devon asked. "You want me to bang on a wineglass to get attention?"

Cam shrugged then tossed the spoon aside. Then he put his fingers to his lips and emitted a shrill whistle. "Everyone, I'd like your attention please. Devon here has an announcement for us."

"Thanks, Cam," Devon said dryly. Then he turned to face the room filled with Ashley's friends and relatives. And they were all staring at him expectantly. All wanting him to make this moment perfect for Ashley. Hell. No pressure or anything.

He cleared his throat and hoped like hell that he'd manage to get through it without sticking his foot in his mouth.

"Ashley and I invited you all here tonight to join us in celebrating a very special occasion." He glanced fondly down at Ashley and squeezed her hand. "Ashley has made me the happiest of men by consenting to marry me."

The room erupted in cheers and applause. To the right, Ashley's mom and dad stood beaming at their youngest child. William nodded approvingly at Devon while Ashley's mother wiped at her eyes as she smiled at her daughter.

"It's our wish that you'll all attend our wedding to take place four weeks from today and help us celebrate as we embark on our journey together as man and wife."

He held up his wineglass and turned again to Ashley whose entire face was lit up with a breathtaking smile. "To Ashley, who's made me the luckiest man alive."

Everyone raised their glasses and noisy cheers rang out again as everyone toasted Devon and Ashley.

"Quite an eloquent speech there," Cam murmured in Devon's ear. "One would almost think you meant every word."

Devon ignored Cam and slid an arm around Ashley as they braced for the onslaught of well-wishers pushing forward.

His head was spinning as he processed face after face. Bright smiles. Slaps on the back. Admonishments to take care of "their girl" as everyone in the family seemed to have a claim on Ashley.

She was everyone's younger sister, daughter, best friend or person in need of protection. It bewildered him and annoyed him in equal parts that everyone in Ashley's family seemed to think she was incapable of taking care of herself. Nothing in his relationship with Ashley had led him to believe this was an accurate assessment.

Yes, she was flighty. She was too trusting, definitely. She was a bit naive. He grimaced. He supposed he could understand that in a family of business sharks she was an anomaly, and perhaps they were right to worry that she'd be swallowed up.

But it didn't mean she was totally incapable of taking care of herself. It just meant she needed someone who'd look out for her best interests and occasionally protect her from herself. Someone like him.

Her hand feathered over his arm and she leaned up on tiptoe. He immediately lowered his head, realizing she wanted to tell him something.

"We can leave anytime," she whispered. "I know my family is a lot to take."

He almost laughed. Here he'd been thinking of how she needed his protection and she was busy protecting him from her overwhelming family.

"I'm fine. I want you to enjoy yourself. This is your night."

Her brow furrowed and her eyebrows pushed together as she stared up at him. "And not yours?"

"Of course it is. I only meant that you're surrounded by your family and friends and I want you to enjoy yourself."

She smiled, kissed him on the cheek and then settled back at his side as they were besieged my more congratulations.

"Ashley! Ashley!"

Devon turned to see a young woman barreling through the crowd practically dragging a man in her wake. He looked a bit harried but wore an indulgent smile. Devon stared a moment and then realized that whomever the woman was, she bore a striking resemblance to Ashley and she had every appearance of sharing many of the same personality traits. Probably one of her many cousins.

"Brooke!" Ashley cried. She put out her hands just as Brooke careened to a halt and Brooke grabbed hold, beaming from ear to ear.

"Guess what, guess what?" Brooke said breathlessly.

"Oh, don't make me guess. You know I'm horrible at it!" Ashley exclaimed.

"I'm pregnant! Paul and I are going to have a baby!"

Ashley's shriek of excitement could be heard over the entire room. Devon winced then quickly glanced around as everyone stared their way.

"Oh, my God, Brooke! I'm so excited for you! When? How far along are you?"

"Just ten weeks. I had to tell you as soon as I found out, but then you've been so busy with Devon and then I heard you guys were getting married and I didn't want to intrude—"

"You should have texted me at least," Ashley said. "Oh, Brooke, I'm so thrilled for you. I can only imagine how excited I'll be when I become pregnant. I hope our babies are close together and can be playmates!"

Ashley had grown louder and louder, her exuberance drawing the attention of the others, who cast indulgent smiles in Ashley's direction.

She was animated and talking a mile a minute, throwing her hands this way and that, and nearly crashed into a passing waiter. Only Devon's and Cam's quick lunge for the tray of drinks prevented complete disaster. Ashley continued, oblivious to the chaos around her.

Then she impulsively hugged Brooke again. For the third time. Then she hugged Paul. Then she hugged Brooke again, the entire time wringing her hands in excitement.

Cam chuckled and shook his head. "You've got quite the chore on your hands, Dev. Keeping up with her is going to wear your stick-in-the-mud ass out."

"Don't you have somewhere else to be and someone else to torture?" Devon muttered.

Cam glanced Ashley's way once more and Devon swore he saw genuine affection in his friend's eyes.

"She's cute," Cam said as he put his wineglass aside.

"Cute?"

Cam shifted uncomfortably. "She's sweet, okay? She seems… genuine and you can't ask for more than that."

Devon stared agape at his friend. "You like her."

Cam scowled darkly.

Devon laughed. "You like her. You, who doesn't like anyone, actually like her."

"She's nice," Cam muttered.

"But you don't think I should marry her," Devon prompted.

"Shh, she's going to hear you," Cam hissed.

But Ashley had already drifted away from Devon and was solidly ensconced in a squeal-fest with Brooke as others had heard the news and had descended. She wasn't going to hear an earthquake if a fault suddenly opened up under the building and sucked everyone in.

"If you think she's so cute and nice, why the big speech

about not being a martyr and getting married, et cetera?"
Devon persisted.

Cam sighed. "Look, I just hate to see her get hurt and that's
what's going to happen if you aren't straight with her. Women
have a way of knowing when men aren't that into them."

"Who the hell says I'm not into her?"

Cam arched an eyebrow. "Are you saying you are? Because
you don't act like a man who's into his future bride."

Devon frowned and looked around, making sure they
weren't overheard. By anyone. Least of all Ashley's overpro-
tective family. "What do you mean by that? You, Rafe and
Ryan know the real circumstances of my relationship with
Ashley but no one else does. I've given no one reason to suspect that I'm marrying her for any other reason than I want
to."

Once again Cam shrugged. "Maybe you're right. Maybe
because I know the real story it's easier for me to see that you
aren't as excited as your lovely bride to be is over your impending nuptials."

"Damn it," Devon swore. "Now you're going to have me
paranoid that I'm broadcasting disinterest."

"Look, forget I said anything. I'm sure it'll be fine. It's none
of my business anyway. She just seems like a sweet girl and I
hate to see her get hurt."

"I'm not going to hurt her," Devon gritted out. "I'm going
to marry her and I'm damn sure going to take care of her."

"And you're being summoned again," Cam said, nodding in
Ashley's direction. "I'm going to take off. I'll walk with you
over to Ashley so I can offer my congratulations again and say
good night."

Devon started in Ashley's direction then listened attentively while she introduced him to one of her cousins—one of
the many in attendance—and then waited while Cam said his
goodbyes and kissed her on both cheeks.

But the entire time, his mind was racing as he processed

his conversation with Cam. Was he coming across as someone who was less than enthused about his upcoming marriage? The very last thing he needed to do was drop the ball when everything was so close to being in his grasp. Finally.

He'd worked too damn hard and long to allow any slips now. If he had to wed Satan himself to seal this deal, he'd don the fire retardant suit and pucker up.

Five

No matter how many nights she'd already spent in Devon's apartment, she still got butterflies when she entered his bedroom to get ready for bed. Granted she'd only been here a week and it was still a little uncomfortable and awkward because she still didn't feel any sense of ownership when it came to his home.

She was pulling on her satin nightgown when Devon's chuckle broke the silence in the room. She turned quickly, her brow furrowed as he regarded her in amusement.

"What's so funny?"

"You. Every night you spend so much time putting on that lovely nightgown only for me to promptly take it off you when you come to bed. By now one would think you wouldn't bother."

She flushed. "It seems…presumptuous…to think you want…I mean to assume you'd want…"

"Sex?" he finished for her.

She nodded, her cheeks flaming.

He grinned and pulled her toward the bed. "I think it's a safe presumption that I'll always want sex with you. Feel free to assume all you want. I assure you…" He bent and kissed her lingeringly. "That I'll never ever…" He slid his mouth down her jaw to her neck and nibbled at her ear. "*Not* want…" He licked the pulse point at her neck, and her knees buckled. "To have sex with you. Unless I'm in a body cast and even then I'll be thinking about it."

Her nose crinkled and she shook with silent laughter. "It's true then. That sex is all a man ever thinks about?"

"We occasionally think about food."

She laughed aloud this time. "My mother is scandalized that I've practically moved in with you."

"Not practically," he said as he slid one strap over her shoulder. "You *have* moved in with me."

She shrugged. "Well she was aghast. My father told her to stop being such a worrywart, that you and I were getting married and it was only natural that we'd want time together before the big day to see if we were compatible. Eric, on the other hand, seemed pretty ticked. He thinks Daddy's nuts to *allow* me to move in with a man who's boned half the city— his words, not mine."

Devon straightened his stance and stared at her with an open mouth. "Do you *always* do that?"

She sent him a perplexed frown. "Do what?"

He shook his head. "Blurt out whatever comes to mind."

Her frown grew deeper. "Well, I guess. I mean I haven't really thought about it. It *is* what he said. I mean I didn't really pay any attention to him. He's just really protective of me and he always gets snarly when a guy starts paying attention to me."

"I hardly think me asking you to marry me can be compared to some random guy paying attention to you," he drawled.

"Well, but I'm living with you now so he obviously knows

we're having sex and he doesn't like to imagine his little sister having sex. With anyone."

Devon shuddered. "Who would?"

She grinned. "My point is, he's just being Eric and he had to get his two cents in."

"For the record, I have not *boned* half the city."

She wrapped her arms around his neck and pulled him down to kiss her. "As long as I'm the only one you'll…well, you know, in the future? I don't really care about the past."

"The future? Oh, yeah. And the present. Like right now."

She shivered as he lowered her to the bed. For having been a virgin a mere week ago, her education was no longer sorely lacking. Every night he'd taken her to places she'd only halfway imagined, and others she hadn't even known existed.

If this was a precursor to how life with him was going to be, she was going to be one very happy woman.

"Joining our meeting via video conference call this morning are Ryan Beardsley and Rafael de Luca," Devon said as his two friends' faces flashed up on the monitor on the wall. "Ryan is on location at our site build on St. Angelo Island, where our flagship resort is in its first stage of development. When completed, this resort will be the standard for every new Copeland property. Good morning, Ryan. Perhaps you could give us a progress report on the construction."

Devon tuned out Ryan and glanced over at Cam, who was slouched in a chair. Devon knew well the progress on construction. He got daily and sometimes hourly reports. Though Ryan was on site, his focus was on his very pregnant wife, who could deliver at any moment. To that end, Devon kept in contact with the foreman so that any issues that arose could be swiftly dealt with.

Cam hadn't dressed for the occasion. He'd never quite bought in to the idea that image is everything in the business world. But then he didn't really care what others thought or didn't think. It was easier for Cam, though. He'd been born to this world, while Devon had to claw and dig his way in, one torn fingernail at a time.

Cam looked like a man who could be heading to the beach for the day or at the very least planning to spend the day kicked back with a beer in one hand and a cigar in the other. But then Cam didn't drink or smoke. The man had no vices. He was disgustingly perfect in his imperfection.

Members of Tricorp's staff listened attentively to Ryan's report. Jotted down appropriate notes. The secretary took detailed minutes. There was an air of expectancy in the room. Everyone knew it was a matter of time before the big merger was announced.

Devon thought it kinder to wait. Maybe he was getting old and soft. Maybe he didn't even deserve to be on the verge of the biggest coup of his career. Because at the very moment when he stood to gain everything he'd ever wanted, he'd actually gone to William Copeland and suggested that they postpone the announcement for six months. He thought it would be kinder to Ashley if she were to think that business had nothing to do with their marriage and that the merger came after. William wouldn't have it, however. He insisted that things proceed as planned.

He thought Devon worried too much about Ashley's potential reaction. She loved him, wasn't that enough? It had made Devon cringe that apparently the whole world knew she was madly in love with her husband to be.

Besides, William pointed out that as disinterested in the family business as Ashley was, the chances of her actually putting it all together were slim. William's advice to Devon? Keep her busy and happy.

Suddenly in the midst of Ryan's report, a sound jangled over the room. There was a series of starts as his employees looked down and then around. Devon frowned. What the hell was it? It sounded like a ring tone, but it wasn't one he'd ever heard before.

Then slowly everyone's gaze turned to him and it was then he realized it was his phone going off in his pocket.

"What the hell?" he muttered.

Cam snickered.

Devon yanked his phone out of his pocket to see Ashley's name on the LCD. He nearly groaned aloud.

"Excuse me a moment," he said as he rose. "I'll take this outside."

He hurried out the door, irritated by Cam's look of amusement. He knew damn well who was calling Devon.

As soon as he was outside the conference room he punched the answer button and brought the phone to his ear. "Carter," he said tersely.

Ashley wasn't even remotely put off by his greeting. Or lack of one.

"Oh, hi, Dev! How's your day going?"

"Uh, it's good. Look, was there something you needed? I'm kind of in the middle of something here."

"Oh, nothing important," she said cheerfully. "I just wanted to call and tell you I love you."

An uncomfortable knot formed in his stomach. What was he supposed to say to that? He cleared his throat. "Ash, did you change the ring tone on my phone?"

"Oh, yeah. I did. I downloaded one so you'd know when I'm calling. Neat, huh?"

Devon closed his eyes. The cheerful cascade of noise that sounded like a cross between Tinker Bell sneezing fairy dust and a waltz at some damn princess ball would make him the laughingstock of the office in short order. Not to mention that Cam would never, ever let him live this down.

"Neat," he lamely agreed. "Look, I'll see you tonight, okay? We still on for dinner at nine?"

"Yes, that's perfect. I'm at the shelter until eight so if it's okay I'll just meet you at the restaurant."

He frowned. "Do you have a ride?"

"I'll get a cab."

He shook his head. "I'll send a car for you. Stay put at the shelter until it arrives. I'll arrange it for eight."

She sighed but didn't argue further. "Have a good day, Dev. Can't wait until tonight!"

"Thanks. You, too," Devon said but she'd already hung up.

He stared at his phone for a long moment and then punched a series of buttons. How did you even change the ring tone? He'd never designated a special ring tone for a person. His phone rang, the contact showed up, and if he wanted to answer he did. If he didn't, he let it go to voice mail. No way he wanted sparkly Tinker Bell music to play every time Ashley called him. What if she made a regular habit of it?

To his never-ending grief, she called him every single day. It baffled him that her timing was utterly impeccable. She always managed to catch him right in the middle of a meeting or when he was with a group of people.

After the second instance, he began silencing his phone and putting it on vibrate, but on two occasions, he simply forgot and his entire meeting was treated to Tinker Bell on crack.

After two weeks, he began to get amused, indulgent looks from some. Sympathy from others. Delighted grins from the women personnel. And Cam laughed his fool head off.

Ashley simply called whenever the mood struck, and unfortunately for him, he could never be sure when she would be moved to call him. Sometimes she wanted advice on wedding details. Like flowers. How the hell did he know what the difference between a tulip and a gardenia was? And invitations. Elopement to Vegas had never looked so enticing as it did right now.

Rafael and Ryan hadn't gone through all of this for their

weddings. They'd both had exceedingly simple affairs. Devon was in hell. A wedding that was being planned by the entire Copeland clan.

He was ready to throw his cell in the Hudson.

Six

"Dev?"

Devon stuck his head out of the bathroom then proceeded toward the bed, rubbing his hair with a towel. She was laying stomach down on the bed, feet dangling in the air as her jaw rested in her palm.

There was a slight frown marring her delicate features, which told him she was thinking about something. He almost didn't want to ask because he'd quickly learned that Ashley's thoughts ran the gamut.

He sat on the edge of the bed and rubbed his hand over her back. "What's up?"

She turned slightly so she could stare up at him. "Where are we going to live? I mean after we get married. We haven't really talked about it."

"I assumed we'd live here."

Her lips turned down just a bit and her brow wrinkled. "Oh."

"That doesn't sound like a good 'oh.' Do you not like the

apartment? It's bigger than yours so I naturally thought it would accommodate us better."

She scrambled up and sat cross-legged beside him. "I do like it. This is a great apartment. It's a little manly-looking. More like a bachelor pad. It's not really appropriate for children or pets."

"Pets?" he croaked out. "Uh, Ash, I don't know about pets."

Her frown deepened, which he found distressing. Ashley rarely pouted about anything, which was good, because it was damn hard to resist her when she looked unhappy. Maybe it was because she was rarely ever anything but happy.

"I've always wanted a house in the country. A place for kids and pets to run and play. The city isn't a good place to raise a family."

"Lots of people raise families here," Devon pointed out. "You were raised here."

She shook her head. "Not always, no. We didn't move to the city until I was ten. Before that we lived on this really great farm. Or at least it was a farm before my father bought it. It was such a beautiful place to live."

The wistful note in her voice was a shot to the gut.

"It's something we can discuss when the time comes," Devon said by way of appeasement. "Right now, my focus is on making you my wife, having a week of uninterrupted time with you on our honeymoon and getting you permanently moved into my apartment."

She smiled and leaned up to brush her lips across his jaw. "I love it when you talk like that."

He raised a brow as she drew back. "Like what?"

"Like you can't wait for us to be together."

She snuggled against him and wrapped her arms around his waist. And again he was assailed by an unfamiliar nagging sensation in his chest. It wasn't comfortable. He wasn't sure he liked it even as he didn't want it to go away.

"It won't be long now," he said. And then some strange urge

to continue on and at least make a token effort to lift her spirits pushed stubbornly at him. He stroked a hand over her silky hair and pressed a kiss to the top of her head. "We can always revisit the issue of where to live later. Right now, though, I want our concentration to be on each other."

She squeezed him tighter and then pulled away as she'd done before to stare up at him, her blue eyes shining. "Can we talk about one other thing?"

"Of course."

"When you say you want our concentration to be on each other, does that mean you'd prefer to wait to start a family? We've talked casually about children. I've made it no secret that I'd love to become pregnant right away but you haven't said what you want in that regard."

A sudden picture of her swollen with his child and her radiant, beautiful smile flashed through his mind. It shocked him just how gratifying the image was. He was assailed by a surge of longing and possessiveness that baffled him.

He'd always viewed marriage, a wife and eventual children with clinical detachment. Almost as if they were components of a to do list. And maybe they had been. Right underneath his goals of business success.

Now that he was suddenly faced with all of the above, he had a hard time thinking rationally about what he wanted. It was a very damn good question.

At some point he'd stopped looking at marriage to Ashley as the chore it had begun as. He'd resigned himself to the inevitability and honestly, he could do so much worse. She was intelligent, good to her core, sweet, affectionate and tenderhearted. She'd make a perfect mother. Much better than his own had ever been. But would he make a good father?

"Dev?"

He glanced down to see her staring at him with worry in her eyes. It was instinctual to want to immediately soothe the concern away. He kissed her brow. "I was just thinking."

"If it's too soon to be having this conversation, I'm sorry. Daddy always says I get too far ahead of myself. I just can't help it. I get excited about something and I just want to reach out and grab it."

He couldn't help but smile. It was such an apt description of her. She embraced life wholeheartedly. And she didn't seem to much care if she stumbled along the way. He wondered if anything ever got her down at all. People like her were a puzzle to him. He didn't understand them. Couldn't relate to them.

He pulled her onto his lap until she was astride him. "What I think is that you'll be a perfect mother. I was just imagining you pregnant with my child and decided I quite liked the image. I also had the thought that I've never used protection, which is hugely irresponsible of me even given the fact that we both have clean histories and are safe, which makes me wonder if subconsciously I was hoping to get you pregnant all along."

She sighed and went soft, melting into his chest as she leaned toward him. "I was hoping you'd say that. I mean about wanting children. It's not that I *have* to have them right away. A small part of me realizes it would probably be better to wait but I've always wanted a large family and I don't want to be old when they're graduating high school."

"You realize we've done nothing to prevent pregnancy so far," he said in a low voice.

"Do you mind?" she asked anxiously. "I mean would you be upset if I was actually pregnant before we got married?"

He chuckled. "It would be the height of hypocrisy for me to be upset over something I could have very well prevented."

"I just want to be sure. I don't want us to have a bad start. I want everything to be…perfect."

He touched her nose and then traced a path underneath her eye and down the side of her face. "Do you suspect that you're already pregnant, Ash? Is that why you're bringing this up tonight? I don't want you to be afraid to tell me anything. I'd never be angry with you for something that is equally my responsibility, if not more so. You were an innocent when I made love to you. Birth control absolutely should have been my responsibility."

She shook her head. "No. I mean I don't know. I don't think so anyway."

He rested his forehead on hers and thought for a moment that they already acted like a married couple who were at ease in their relationship. Strangely, he trusted Ashley and felt comfortable with her. There was a sense of rightness that he couldn't deny. Maybe William Copeland had known what he was doing after all.

"Well, if you are, then fantastic. Really. I want you to tell me if you even suspect you could be. And if you aren't? We'll work on remedying that. Deal?"

She grinned and a delicate blush stained her soft cheeks. "Deal."

"Now what do you say we go to bed so you can have your evil way with me?"

Her cheeks grew even redder and he smiled at the shy way she ducked her head.

He leaned in to nibble at her ear and then he whispered so the words blew gently over her skin. "I'll do my very best to make you pregnant."

To his surprise, she shoved him forward. He landed on his back on the mattress with her looming over him, a mischievous grin dimpling her cheeks. Then her expression grew more serious and her eyes darkened. "I love you so much, Devon. I'm the luckiest woman on earth. I can't wait until we're married and I'm officially yours."

As she lowered her mouth to his, he was gripped by the feeling that she was completely and utterly wrong. It wasn't she who was the lucky one.

Seven

"Ashley, if you don't sit still we're never going to get your hair and makeup right," Pippa said in exasperation.

"I still think she should have just called in a stylist," Sylvia said as she eyed the progress Tabitha was making on Ashley's hair.

"Tabitha *is* a stylist, silly," Ashley said. "She's the best and who doesn't want the best on their wedding day? And who knows more about makeup than Carly?"

Pippa snorted. "That's so true. I'm convinced cosmetic companies should just pay her to endorse their products."

"Close your eyes, Ash," Carly said. "Time for mascara. Just a bit, though. Don't want you looking clumpy on the big day."

Ashley frowned. "Definitely not clumpy."

"Darling, are you almost done?" Ashley's mother sang out from the doorway. "You're on in ten minutes."

"Ten minutes?" Tabitha shrieked. "No way. Can you stall them, Mrs. C.?"

"I'm not going to be late to my own wedding," Ashley said

firmly. "Just hurry faster, Tab. My hair will be fine. Just put the veil over the knot."

"Just put the veil over the knot," Tabitha grumbled. "As if it's that easy."

Sylvia rolled her eyes, pushed between Tabitha and Ashley and quickly affixed the veil to the elegant chignon. "There, Ashley. You look beautiful."

"Lip gloss and we're done," Carly announced. "Make a kissy face."

Ashley smacked her lips and a moment later, Carly pulled away to allow Ashley to see herself in the mirror.

"Oh, you guys," she whispered.

Her best friends beamed back at her in the mirror.

"You look beautiful," Pippa said, her eyes bright with tears. "The most beautiful bride I've ever seen."

"Absolutely you do," Tabitha said.

The four women crowded in to hug her.

"Girls, time for you to go. Your escorts are waiting. We don't want to make the bride late," Ashley's mother called.

Her friends scrambled toward the door, bouquets in hand.

"Your father is coming to get you now," her mother said as she walked over. She paused when she got to Ashley and then smiled, tears glittering in her eyes. "My baby, all grown up. You look so beautiful. I'm so proud of you."

"Don't make me cry, Mom. You know I have no willpower."

Her mom laughed and reached for her hands. She squeezed them and then helped her to her feet.

"Let me fix your gown. Your father will be pacing outside the door. You know how he hates to be late for anything."

She fussed with Ashley's dress and then there was a knock on the dressing room door.

"That will be him now. Are you ready, darling?"

Sudden nerves gripped Ashley and her palms went sweaty. But she nodded. Oh, God, this was really it. She was about to walk down the aisle and become Mrs. Devon Carter.

She threw her arms around her mom and hugged her tight. "Love you, Mom."

Her mother squeezed her back. "Love you, too, baby. Now let's go before your father wears a hole in the floor."

She went ahead of Ashley to open the door and sure enough, her father was outside checking his watch. He looked up when he heard them and his expression softened. A glimmer of emotion welled in his eyes and he held out his hand to take hers.

"I can't believe you're getting married," he said in a tight voice. "It seems like only yesterday you were learning to walk and talk. You look beautiful, Ash. Devon is a lucky man."

She leaned up to kiss his wrinkled cheek. "Thank you, Daddy. You look pretty spiffy yourself."

The wedding coordinator hurried up to them and motioned with rapid flying hands. She shooed them toward the entrance to the aisle and then spent a few seconds arranging the train of her dress.

Ashley's mom was escorted down the aisle and seated, which only left Ashley to be walked down the aisle with her father.

The music began, the doors swung open and every eye in the church turned to watch as Ashley took her first step.

Her bouquet shook in her hands and she prayed her knees would hold up. The dress suddenly seemed to weigh a ton and despite the cold outside, the church felt like a sauna.

But then she caught sight of Tabitha, Carly, Sylvia and Pippa all standing at the front of the church, their smiles wide and encouraging. Pippa winked and held a thumbs-up then pointed toward Devon and made a motion like she was fanning herself.

And finally her gaze locked on to Devon and she forgot about everyone else. Forgot about her nervousness, her sudden doubt. Nothing but the fact that he awaited her at the front of the church and that from now on, she'd belong to him.

It gave her a warm, mushy feeling from head to toe.

And then her dad was handing her over to Devon. Devon

smiled reassuringly down at her as they took the step toward the priest and the ceremony began.

It pained her to later admit that she didn't remember most of the ceremony. What she did remember was Devon's eyes and the warmth that enveloped her standing next to him as she pledged her love, loyalty and devotion. And the kiss he gave her after they were pronounced husband and wife scorched her to her toes.

Suddenly they were walking back down the aisle, this time together, as a married couple. They ducked into an alcove to await the others and Devon pulled her close into his side.

"You look absolutely stunning."

He kissed her again. This time slower. More intense. Long and lingering. He took his time exploring her mouth, and when he pulled away, she swayed and caught his arm to steady herself.

Around her, the noise of well-wishers grew and she realized that guests were coming out of the church.

"Darling, they need you back inside the church for pictures," her mother called as she hurried towards Ashley and Devon. "All your attendants are already gathered. The others are going ahead to the reception. The car is waiting to take you and Devon after you're finished with all the photos."

Devon looked less than happy at the idea of posing for so many photographs but he gave a resigned sigh and took Ashley's hand to lead her back into the sanctuary.

"It'll be over soon," she whispered. "Then we can be off on our honeymoon."

He smiled down at her and squeezed her hand. "It's the only thing making the next few hours bearable for me. The idea of you and me locked in a hotel suite for days."

She flushed but shivered in delight at the images his words invoked. She too couldn't wait for them to be alone.

But at the same time, this was her day and she was going to enjoy every single moment of it. She smiled as she was swarmed by her friends. She was surrounded by countless cousins, her uncles and aunts, her parents, her brother, distant relatives, friends.

It was truly the happiest day of her life.

Devon collected a glass of wine while Ashley's brother took his turn on the dance floor with her. Devon should probably be dancing with one of her family members but she had so many female relatives that he couldn't keep track.

Cam immediately found him and Devon whistled appreciatively to mock the formal tuxedo his friend wore.

"Only for you would I wear this getup," Cam said darkly. "I didn't wear this for Rafe's wedding and Ryan married Kelly so fast we were lucky to get a phone call saying the deed was done."

"You weren't *required* to wear one for Rafe's wedding," Devon pointed out.

Cam shrugged. "True, but then I wasn't required to wear one for yours, either. I didn't want to disappoint Ash. She thinks I look hot."

Devon shook his head. "I can't believe you've stuck around this long. Not like you to be out of your cave for such an extended period of time."

Cam made a rude noise. "I'm supposed to convey my congratulations or commiserations, whichever you need or prefer, from Rafe and Ryan. They were both sorry they couldn't make it but with wives about to drop the package at any moment, they understandably remained at home by their sides."

"You have to cut it out," Devon said. "My getting married isn't the end of the world. You didn't give Rafe and Ryan this much grief."

"Oh I did," Cam said with a grin. "I totally did. But they deserved it. They were both total douche bags."

"Like you're a shining example of chivalry, Mr. I-hate-everyone-and-women-in-particular."

Cam sobered. "Don't hate women at all. I like them too much if anything. Kind of sucks if you ask me. Besides, it's fun to give you hell. I think Ashley is perfect for a stuffy stick-in-the-mud like yourself."

"I didn't mean that, man," Devon said wearily. "I'm just on edge. I'll be glad when this is all over with. Too much stress. I've worried on a daily basis that she'd find out the truth and tell me to go to hell. The sooner we can get the hell out of here and on the plane to St. Angelo, the better I'll feel."

"For what it's worth, I wish you well," Cam said. "I think you made a huge mistake marrying someone over a business deal, but she's a sweet girl and you could certainly do worse. It's not you I worry about anyway. It's her."

"Gee, thanks," Devon said dryly. "Glad you've got my back on this one."

Cam's gaze found Ashley on the dance floor as her brother spun her around. She laughed and her smile lit up the entire room. It was clear she was having the time of her life.

"At least you won't suffer a broken heart," Cam said in a low voice. "Can you say the same for Ashley?"

"I'm not going to break her heart, damn it. Can we drop this? The last thing I need is for someone to overhear us."

"Yeah, sure. Think I'll go cut in on Ashley's brother, pay my respects to the bride before I head back to the cave you accuse me of crawling out of."

Devon watched as Cam sauntered onto the dance floor. A moment later, Eric relinquished Ashley into Cam's arms.

"You've made my little girl very happy," William Copeland said.

Devon turned around to see his father-in-law come up behind him. William smiled broadly and clapped Devon affectionately on the back. "Welcome to the family, son."

"Thank you, sir. It's an honor."

"You take Ashley and you two have a good time. Don't

worry a thing about the business. We'll have plenty of time to focus on what needs to be done when you get back."

Devon nodded. "Of course."

"Ashley's mother wanted me to tell you that the car taking you and Ashley to the airport is waiting outside. Now tradition is that you stick around, do silly stuff like cut the cake and stuff it into each other's faces, but if it were me and I'd just married one of the sweetest girls in New York City, I'd duck and make a run for it. You could be to the airport before anyone notices you're gone."

Devon smiled. "That sounds like the best plan I've heard all night. You'll cover my exit?"

William smiled back conspiratorially. "That I will, son. Go on now. Go collect your bride. Everyone here will be more than happy to eat the cake for you. No groom I ever knew gave a damn about cake anyway."

Devon laughed and then waded into the crowd to go retrieve Ashley from Cam.

Eight

The sun was sinking over the horizon when Devon carried Ashley through the doorway of their suite. As soon as he put her down, she ran to the terrace doors, flung them wide and gasped in pleasure at the burst of color splashed across the sky.

"Oh Devon, it's beautiful!"

He came up behind her, slipped his arms around her body and pulled her into his chest. He nibbled at her ear and she sighed in pleasure.

"I can't believe this is our view for the next week. Do you know how long it's been since I've been to the beach? I was a little girl."

"What?" he asked in mock horror. "You don't go to the beach?"

"I know. Terrible, isn't it? I don't know why. It's just not where our family ever went on vacation and my friends aren't really beachgoers. I just haven't made it a point to go and yet here we are and it's so fabulously gorgeous that I don't even have the words to describe it," she said breathlessly.

He chuckled. "Sounds to me like you have plenty of words. But I'm glad you like it."

She turned in his arms, allowing his hands to drop to her waist as he held her there. "How on earth did you find this place? I'd never heard of St. Angelo."

"We're constructing a resort here. We broke ground several weeks ago. Ryan and Kelly live here, remember?"

Her nose wrinkled. "Oh yes, you told me about them. I remember now. I've never met them. I've only met Cam."

"A situation I'll remedy soon. Bryony and Kelly are both very near to their due dates and so they aren't able to travel. We'll have dinner with Ryan and Kelly while we're here and I'm sure we'll have the occasion to meet Rafe and Bryony before long."

"I can't wait."

"I couldn't care less about them at the moment," Devon murmured. "I'm more interested in our wedding night."

Heat exploded in her cheeks at the same time a delicious shiver wracked her spine. "I have to get ready," she said in a low voice. "I have something special. It's a surprise."

"Mmm, what kind of surprise?"

"Umm, well, it was a gift from my girlfriends. They assured me no man alive would be able to resist me in it."

"Oh hell, remind me to thank them."

She raised an eyebrow. "You haven't seen me in it yet."

"I'll like it. I'm sure I'll like it. I'd like you in sackcloth. Whatever it is they bought you, I'm sure I'll appreciate it. Right before I peel it off your delectable body."

She all but wiggled in excitement. She was barely able to contain herself. "Okay, you wait here. Give me fifteen minutes at least. I want to look perfect. And no peeking!"

He held up his hands. "Would I do such a thing?"

Her eyes narrowed. "Promise me."

He sighed. "Okay, okay. But get moving. I'm going to go down and arrange for a very good bottle of wine and also give them our breakfast order for the morning. You have until I get back to do your thing."

She went up on tiptoe, kissed him and brushed past him into the suite. She waited just until he walked by and out of the bedroom before she hurriedly retrieved the bright pink, totally girly gift box from her suitcase.

At her lingerie shower, her girlfriends had delighted in making her eyes grow wide at all the things they'd bought her. The gifts had ranged from totally classy and elegant to absolutely outrageous and daring.

For her wedding night, she'd chosen a gown that was the perfect blend of elegant and sensual. It was sexy without being over-the-top siren material, although Ashley had no objection over the siren part. Being a seductive temptress for an evening had its merits and she was determined that she'd eventually work up the nerve to pull that one off.

She hurriedly changed and then went to survey herself in the mirror in the corner. The gown was beautiful. She felt like a princess and she liked that feeling very much. A pampered, cherished princess.

She reached for the clip holding her hair up and let the strands tumble down onto her shoulders. She fluffed it a bit, ran her fingers through the ends to straighten it and then took another step back to survey her reflection.

The bodice plunged deep between her breasts and offered just a hint of a view of the swells. If she turned just right, her nipple was almost bared. Almost, but not quite.

The skirt of the gown was sheer and it shimmered over her legs like a dream. Maybe she'd underestimated the siren quality of the lingerie. It seemed innocent enough in the box, but on her…? It took on a more seductive air and made her look less innocent and more brazen.

Not a bad look to achieve on one's wedding night.

She flashed herself an impish grin and turned away from

the mirror. Impulsively, she swirled around, outstretching her arms as she pretended to dance with an imaginary partner.

Humming lightly she twirled again, sighing dreamily as she performed the steps to the waltz she and Devon had danced at her reception. He was a good dancer. He didn't seem entirely comfortable with dancing as a rule, but he'd been more than adept at it. He moved like a dream. Commanding. Graceful with a hint of arrogance that made her all giddy inside.

She closed her eyes and whirled again. Her outstretched hand smacked against something hard and pain flashed over her knuckles at the same time a crash jolted her out of her fantasy.

Devon's laptop that had been resting on the mantel of the fireplace along with his wallet, keys and the contents of his pockets, was now lying on the floor in pieces.

She dropped to the floor, groaning her dismay. It looked as if the battery had just popped out but how could she be sure? What if she'd broken it? Who knew what all-important, irreplaceable things he had on his laptop. If he was anything like her father and brother and countless other family members, his entire life was in the damn thing.

Okay, she knew her way around computers. She may not spend her life on one, but she was capable of working one. Or determining whether or not she'd just broken her husband's.

She put the battery back in, checked for further damage and then pressed the power button, praying that it would come on. After a moment, the black screen of death remained and she let out another groan.

In frustration, she punched several buttons on the keyboard, willing something—anything—to come to life. The problem was, as soon as she began pressing the keys, the monitor blinked and she was treated to a dozen programs opening and flashing in rapid succession.

At least the damn thing worked.

She bit her lip in consternation and began closing the programs down. There were lots of Excel spreadsheets, countless charts and graphs that made her head swim. Halfway through she was struck by the fear that none of these were saved or that she was losing valuable information.

As much as she didn't want to ruin the moment, she'd be better off telling Devon what happened and let him sort out his laptop. That way tomorrow when he opened it up, there would be no nasty surprises.

She downsized the pdf that looked to be more a mammoth-sized report when her name caught her eye. She slowed down to read, her fingers pausing on the keyboard. It was an email from her father and she smiled as she saw the reference to her as his baby. But what she read next halted her in her tracks.

I've had time to consider your reservations in regard to Ashley and perhaps you were right to be concerned. I don't want you to think I discounted your intuition, but rather I want you to understand that I want her protected at all costs. Her knowing the truth of our arrangement isn't necessary even as I understand why perhaps you're uncomfortable with it. She's my only daughter and I love her dearly. The truth is, I'd rather she never know that the marriage is a condition of the merger. You are a welcome addition to this family and I trust that you'll always act in her best interests, which is why I implore you to remain silent as to our agreement.

Stunned, Ashley stared at the screen, sure that she couldn't have understood this correctly. She was jumping to conclusions, something her mother had always accused her of.

She admonished herself to remain calm even though her pulse was racing so hard that she could literally feel it jumping in her neck and in her temples.

She returned to the email, forcing the blurry words to focus. "Ashley?"

She yanked her head up, startled as Devon suddenly loomed over her.

"It fell," she croaked out. "Off the mantel. I was afraid it was broken. The battery fell out of it. When I put it back together and started it back up, all these programs opened and I was trying to shut them all down."

He reached down to take the laptop, but she held onto it, with bloodless fingers.

He swore when he caught sight of what she was reading and he wrested the computer from her grip.

"Give it back, Devon. I want to know what it says."

He closed it with a sharp snap and tucked it underneath his arm. "There's nothing you need to see."

"Don't lie to me," she grit out. "I read most of it. Or at least the important parts. I want to know what the hell it means."

Devon stared back at her, his lips drawn in a thin line. He looked as though he'd rather be anywhere but here, doing anything but having this conversation with her. Too bad. She wasn't about to back down.

"Nothing good can come of it, Ash. Just forget it, okay?"

She gaped at him. "Forget it? You want me to just forget I saw an email from my father basically admitting he bought me a husband? Or at least manipulated you somehow into marrying me? This is my wedding night, Devon. Am I supposed to pretend I didn't see that email?"

Devon cursed and ran his hand through his hair. "Damn it, Ashley, why the hell did you open the laptop?"

"I didn't mean to! Believe me I'd give anything not to have knocked the damn thing down. But the fact is I did and now I want to know what's going on. What kind of a deal did you strike with my father? Tell me the truth or I swear I'm walking out of here right now."

"This is precisely why you're your own worst enemy at times, Ash. You're too impulsive. You don't think before you act. You just go around wading into situations and you end up getting hurt. If it enters your mind, you simply do it. That quickly. At some point you have to learn some control."

She gaped at him, openmouthed, as his frustrated, angry words bit into her. How was she the bad guy here? What the hell had she done? This wasn't her fault. She hadn't entered this marriage under false pretenses. Devon knew precisely where she stood. God knew she'd told him enough times.

His eyes flashed and he turned his back. He walked across the room to the dresser and slapped the laptop down on it. For a long moment, he stood there, not facing her, silent. Tension rose sharp and so thick it was uncomfortable. Fear struck a deep chord within her because she realized that she was about to learn something truly terrible about her life. Her fate. Her marriage.

"Devon?" she whispered.

She thought back on their relationship. The whirlwind courtship. Suddenly the blinders were off and she began to analyze every date. Everything he'd said to her. How much of it had been a lie? Was any of it true?

She didn't want to ask. She wasn't sure she could bear to know the answer to her most burning question, but she also realized she had no choice.

He turned around and his eyes were shuttered. His expression was impassive almost as if he hoped to quell any further discussion.

Suddenly the circumstances of her marriage didn't matter to her. There was only one thing she absolutely had to know. The most important thing. The one thing that would determine her future. And whether she had one with him.

"Just answer me one question," she said faintly. "Do you love me?"

Nine

Dread had a two-fisted grip around Devon's throat. He stared at Ashley's pale, stricken face and he knew his time had come. Maybe he'd always known that this moment would come. He'd never really believed that it was possible to prevent Ashley from finding out the truth and furthermore it was stupid to try to keep it from her.

Damn fool of an old man. William Copeland didn't want his precious daughter hurt and yet he'd set her up for the biggest fall of her life. Nice. And now Devon was going to look like the biggest bastard of all time.

"I care for you a great deal," he said evenly.

Anger and fear warred with one another in her eyes. His answer sounded lame even to his own ears but he couldn't bring himself to destroy her even further. Hadn't she endured enough already?

"Let's have the truth," she demanded. "Don't patronize me or pat me on the head while whispering pretty words to pacify me. It's a very simple question, Devon. Do you love me?"

His nostrils flared. "The truth isn't always a pretty thing, Ash. The truth isn't always pleasant to hear. Be careful when you ask for the truth because it can hurt far more than not knowing."

If possible she went even paler. Her eyes were stricken and all the light vanished from their depths as if someone had extinguished a flame. For a moment he thought she'd let it go, but then she squared her shoulders and said in a low, dead voice, "The truth, Dev. I want the truth. I need to hear it."

He bit out another curse and thrust his hand into his hair. "All right, Ashley, no, I don't love you. I care about you a great deal. I like and respect you. But if you want to know if I love you, then no."

She made a broken sound of pain that was like a knife right through his chest. Why couldn't he have just lied to her? Because she would have known the truth whether he admitted it or not and she'd already been deceived enough.

And maybe now they could finally go forward with complete and utter honesty and he could stop feeling like the worst sort of bastard at every turn.

She started to step backward, but she swayed precariously and flailed out one arm to catch herself on the mantel. He bolted forward, caught her shoulders and then guided her to the bed, forcing her down into a sitting position.

He took one step back and then heaved out a breath. Before he could launch into what he wanted to say, she found his gaze and he flinched at the raw vulnerability reflected in those eyes.

"What a fool I've made of myself," she whispered. "How stupid and naive. How you must have laughed."

"Damn it, Ash, I've never laughed at you. Never!"

"I loved you," she said painfully. "Thought you loved me. Thought we were getting married because you wanted me, not my father's business or whatever it was he offered you. How much did I cost you, Dev? Or should I ask how much my father offered you to marry me?"

Furious at the senseless direction this was heading, he yanked the chair out from the desk, turned it around and sat so he faced her.

"Listen to me. There's no reason we can't have an enjoyable marriage. We're compatible. We get along well together. We're good in bed. Those are three things many married couples don't have going for them."

She closed her eyes.

"Look at me, Ash. This may be painful to hear but maybe it's for the best if we get it all out in the open. You're far too emotional. You wear your feelings and your heart on your sleeve and it's only going to get you hurt. Maybe it's time for you to grow up and face the fact that life isn't a fairy tale. You're too impulsive. You dash about with no caution and no sense of self-preservation. That's only going to cause you further pain down the road."

She shook her head in utter confusion. Her eyes were cloudy and it was clear she was battling tears. "How could I possibly ever hurt as much as I do now? How can you be so…so… *cold* and calm and so matter-of-fact as if this is nothing more than a business meeting where you're discussing figures and projections and sales and a whole host of other things I don't understand?"

His gut twisted into a knot. He'd never felt so damn helpless in his life. He wished to hell it was as simple as telling her to be harder and for her not to let this destroy her, but he knew it was pointless because Ashley was one of the most tenderhearted people he knew and he was an ass to sit here and tell her to get over it.

She covered her face in her hands and he could see her throat working convulsively as she tried to keep her sobs silent. But they spilled out, harsh and brittle in the quiet.

He lifted his hand to touch her hair but left it in the air before finally pulling it back. She wouldn't welcome comfort from him, of all people. If it were any other woman, she'd have already come after his nuts and he'd deserve everything she dished out and more.

"Ash, please don't cry."

She lifted her ravaged face and pushed angrily at her hair. "Don't cry? What the hell else do you suggest I do? How could you do this? How could my father? Tell me, Devon, what was the price put on my future? What do you get out of the bargain?"

He stared at her in silence.

"Tell me, damn it! I think I deserve to know what my happiness was traded for."

"Your father wanted me to marry you as part of the merger between Tricorp Investments and Copeland Hotels," he bit out. "Happy now? Can you tell me what possible good it does for you to know that?"

"It doesn't make me happy but I damn well want to know what I've gotten myself into, or rather what my father got me into. Did I ever even have a chance? Did you study up on all the ways to worm your way into my heart?"

"Christ, no. Look, it was all real. It's not like I faked an attraction to you. It wasn't exactly a hardship to pursue you. If I hadn't wanted to marry you, no merger or deal would have persuaded me differently. I thought and still think that we'd make a solid marriage. I don't see why love has to be the be-all and end-all in this equation. Mutual respect and friendship are far more important aspects of a relationship."

"Maybe you can tell me how the hell I'm supposed to respect a man who doesn't love me and who manipulated me into a marriage based on deception. Does everyone think I'm a brainless twit who should be pathetically grateful that a man sweeps into my life and offers to take care of me? I've got news for you and my family. I hadn't married yet because it was my choice. I hadn't had sex with a man yet because I had enough respect for myself that I wasn't going to be pressured into something I wasn't ready for. It's not like I haven't had men interested in me. I'm not pathetically needy nor was I going to waste away if I wasn't married by the ripe old age of twenty-three. I was happy. I had a good life."

"Ashley, listen to me."

He leaned forward, caught her hands and stared until she quieted and returned his gaze.

"Right now you're upset and you're hurting. But don't discount the possibility that we could enjoy a comfortable, lasting marriage. Don't make a snap decision you may regret later. Take some time to think about it when you've calmed down. When you're not so volatile, you'll be able to look at the situation more objectively."

"Oh screw off," she snapped. "Could you be any more patronizing? 'Don't be so high-strung, Ashley. Don't be so stupid and naive. Don't expect ridiculous things like love and affection in a marriage. How perfectly absurd would that be?'"

"I don't think we should have this conversation any longer," he said tightly. "Not until you've had time to calm down and think about what you're saying." He stood abruptly and she looked hastily away but not before he saw the silver trail of her tears streaking down her cheeks.

He wanted more than anything to pull her into his arms and let her cry on his shoulder. He wanted to comfort her, hold her, soothe her fears and tell her it would be all right. But how could he when he was the sole reason she was devastated?

"I'm sorry, Ash," he said hoarsely. "I know you don't believe that, but I'm more sorry than you'll ever know. I would have done anything at all to spare you this pain."

"Please, just go away and leave me alone," she choked out. "I can't even look at you right now."

He hesitated a moment and then sighed in resignation. "I'll take the couch in the living area. We'll talk more in the morning."

It took every ounce of his willpower to turn around and walk out of the bedroom. His instincts screamed at him not to leave her alone. To take her in his arms and force the issue. Make her listen to him. To not relent until she agreed that their marriage could and would work if only they could set aside the emotional volatility that always seemed to accompany declarations of love.

He had only to point at his friends to know this was an inevitable truth. Their lives were emotional messes brought on by the letter *L*.

All that angst and suffering in the name of love. Rafe and Ryan had spent more time in abject misery and all because they'd been ripped to shreds by…love.

Devon grimaced and sank onto the couch in the dark living room. What a wedding night this had turned out to be. Maybe he'd always known that it was inevitable that she learn the truth. How could she not? But he'd hoped they'd have a lot more mileage behind them. Then she could see that their marriage wasn't defined by love or emotion, volatility or vulnerability.

Friendship, companionship, trust, respect.

Those were all things he was on board with.

Love? Not so much. It was a messy, raw emotion he had no desire to embroil himself with.

Ten

Ashley sat on the private veranda and stared over the ocean as the sun began its hesitant rise. She felt empty. Rung out. She felt stupid and so horribly naive that she cringed. It still baffled her that a life she'd thought was so perfect just hours before was a complete facade.

All night she'd sat huddled in an uncomfortable chair trying to come to grips with the fact that she'd been lied to at every turn. She'd been used and manipulated, not just by Devon, but by her own father. And all over a business deal.

She couldn't wrap her head around it.

Why? Why had it been so important for Devon to marry her? Was her father so unconvinced of Ashley's ability to manage her own life that he'd all but hired a man to be her husband? She winced at the thought, but it was appropriate. At the very least, she'd been used as a bargaining chip.

She rubbed at eyes that felt full of sand. She'd cried all that she was going to allow herself to cry. She be damned if she shed another single tear over her husband.

A dry laugh escaped her. Her husband. What was she going to do about her marriage? Her complete and utter farce of a marriage.

She closed her eyes against the humiliation of it all. What a fool she'd made of herself over the last month. She wanted to die from it.

Had he laughed at her the entire time? Had he joked with his friends about what a gullible idiot she was? She didn't like to imagine he could be so cruel, but the man she'd faced down the night before and demanded the truth from had been brutally honest. At her insistence, but crushingly forthright all the same.

"It's time you had the cold hard truth, Ashley," she whispered. She'd been living a fantasy.

She rubbed at her temples, willing the vicious ache to go away. But the pain in her head was nothing compared to the unbearable ache in her heart.

Should she leave him? Should she ask for a divorce? They could have the shortest marriage on record. She could go back home. Chalk it up to a lesson learned the hard way. It was doubtful at this point that her father would pull the plug on the deal because Devon had lived up to his end of the bargain. It wasn't Devon who was unhappy with the result. It was her. Everyone had evidently thought she was the very last person who should be consulted about her life.

But the idea of divorcing Devon held as little appeal as living in the cold, sterile state her marriage now existed in. She deeply loved him and love wasn't something you could switch off at will. She was hurt beyond belief. She was angry and she felt horribly betrayed. But she still loved him and she still wished that they could go back to the way things had been before she'd found out the damnable truth.

It was true what they said about ignorance being bliss. She'd give anything at all to go back to being that innocent little girl who still believed in happily ever after with Prince Charming.

For just a little while Devon had been that prince. He'd been perfect. She'd built him into something he wasn't, and that wasn't entirely his fault. He couldn't be blamed for her utter stupidity.

No, she didn't want a divorce. But neither did she want to live a life with a man who didn't love her.

She thought back to all the things he'd said to her the night before. His criticisms had stung. They'd stunned her. She'd never imagined that he'd thought of her in such a negative way. But maybe he was right.

Maybe she was too impulsive, too flighty, too exuberant. Perhaps she should be more controlled, more guarded, show more of a knack for self-preservation.

It was evident that he didn't want the person she was. It was evident he didn't love flighty, impulsive, tender-hearted, animal-loving Ashley Copeland, who called him at work just to say she loved him.

If he didn't want or love that person, then the only two options left to her were to walk away and get a divorce or to *become* someone he could love.

Could she make him fall in love with her? Her family always worried that she was too trusting. Too naive. Too everything. Apparently they were right.

The only person who didn't seem to think anything was wrong with who Ashley Copeland was, was Ashley herself. And it was becoming increasingly clearer that her judgment stank.

It was time for one hell of a makeover.

But the idea didn't excite her. It didn't infuse enthusiasm into her flagging spirits. It was a bleak thought and she dimly wondered if Devon was worth such an effort.

Would his love be enough, provided she could even make him fall in love with her?

A voice in the back of her mind whispered that it was time for her to grow up. It was a voice that sounded precariously close to Devon's. He thought she should grow up. Her father evidently thought the same. Maybe they were both right.

She stiffened when she heard a sound on the terrace. She knew it was Devon but she wasn't ready to face him yet.

"Have you been out here all night?" he asked quietly.

She nodded wordlessly and continued to stare over the water.

He walked to the thick stone railing that enclosed the private viewing area, shoved his hands in his pockets and for a moment stared over the water as she was doing. Then he turned to face her and leaned back against the stone.

He looked as bad as she felt, though she had no sympathy. His hair was rumpled. He was still in the same clothes as the night before.

"Ash, don't torture yourself over this. There's no reason we can't have a perfectly good marriage, no matter the circumstances of *how* we came to be married."

He was starting to repeat his arguments from the previous night and the truth was, she couldn't stomach hearing again how she was naive and impulsive and whatever else it was he'd said when he outlined all her faults.

She bit her lip to keep the angry flood from rushing out because at this point it did her no good and she didn't have the emotional energy to spare.

She held up a hand to stop him and cursed at how it trembled. She put it back down and tucked it into her gown, blinking as she realized she was still in her sexy, lacy lingerie that she'd so painstakingly picked out for her wedding night.

Unbidden tears welled again in her eyes as she realized just what a disaster her wedding night had been. What should have been the most special night of her entire life would forever be a black hole in her past no matter what happened in the future.

"I agree," she said before he could launch into another list of her shortcomings.

He promptly shut his mouth and then stared at her, his brows drawn together in confusion. "You do?"

She nodded again because the words seemed to stick in her throat. Almost as if they were rebelling. It took her a few moments to force out what she wanted to say.

"You're absolutely right. I was being silly. I had unrealistic expectations and I shouldn't allow them to get in the way of marriage."

He winced but remained quiet.

"I am agreeable to at least a period of time in which we see how things progress."

He frowned at that but she looked up with dead eyes. "Be glad I'm not on a plane home with an appointment to see a divorce lawyer."

He pushed out a breath and then slowly nodded. "All right. How long do you think this test period will last?"

She shrugged. "How would I know? I can't exactly put a time frame on when I can give up all hope of having a happy marriage."

"Ash."

The low growl in which he said her name only served to make her angrier. She curled her fingers into tight balls, determined not to give in to the urge to scream at him. She was determined to get through this, no matter how excruciating it was.

"I'm not trying to punish you, Devon. I'm trying to get through this without losing what little pride I have left."

He went pale and pain flickered in his eyes. And shame. Though that hadn't been her intention, either. She wasn't trying to make digs at him because that wouldn't make this go away. It wouldn't give her back her happiness. It would only make her more miserable than she already was.

"You seem to think we can have an enjoyable marriage. I personally find no joy in being married to a man who doesn't love me, but I'm willing to try. You're probably right in that I shouldn't allow something so silly as love to enter the equation."

"Damn it, I care a lot for you—"

"Please," she bit out, halting his words in midsentence. "Just don't. Don't try to make it better by offering me platitudes. It was hard to hear your assessment of my faults. Does anyone ever like to hear that about themselves? But I'm willing to work on not being so impulsive and exuberant or whatever else it was that you mentioned. I'll try to be the best wife I can be and not disappoint you."

He bit out a sharp curse but she ignored him and plunged ahead before she lost all her courage and fled.

"I just have one thing to ask in return," she whispered.

She was trying valiantly not to break down again. She'd already made such an idiot of herself in front of him. She was forever making a total cake of herself with him.

His lips were thin. His eyes were dark with raw emotion. At least he wasn't totally unaffected by her distress.

"I find the situation I'm in immensely humiliating. I'll make every effort to be a wife you'll be proud of. All I ask is that you please not embarrass me in front of my family by making our issues known to anyone. What I'm asking you to do is pretend. At least with them."

"God, Ash. You act as though I despise you. I'd never embarrass you."

"I just don't want them to know you don't love me," she choked out. "If you could just act like—like a real husband in front of them. You don't have to go overboard. Just don't treat me with indifference now that you don't have to pretend in order to get me to marry you anymore."

And then another thought occurred to her that very nearly had her leaning over to empty the contents of her stomach.

"Are you all right?" Devon asked sharply. Then he swore. "Of course you aren't all right. You look as if you're going to be ill."

"Is there someone else?" she croaked out. "I mean did you ever plan to be faithful? I won't stay married to you if you're going to sleep around or if you have a mistress on tap somewhere."

This time the curses were more colorful and they didn't stop for several long seconds. He closed the distance between them, knelt down in front of the lounger she was curled up in and grasped her shoulders.

"Stop it, Ashley. You're torturing yourself needlessly. There is no other woman. There won't be another woman. I take my marriage vows very seriously. I don't have a mistress. There's been no other woman since well before you entered the picture. I have no desire to sleep around. I want *you*."

Her shoulders sagged in relief and she leaned away from him so that his hands slipped from her arms.

"Damn it, I wanted to tell you the truth from the very beginning but your father wouldn't hear of it. My mistake. I should have told you anyway. But it doesn't change anything. I still want to be married to you. If I found the idea so abhorrent, I'd simply wait until the deal was done and begin divorce proceedings. There wouldn't be a damn thing your father could do at that point."

She closed her eyes wearily and rubbed at her head. The sun's steady creep over the horizon was casting more light onto the terrace and each ray speared her eyeballs like a flaming pitchfork.

"Do you have one of your headaches?" he asked, his voice full of concern. "Did you bring your medicine?"

She opened her eyes again, wincing as she tried to refocus. "I want to go home."

Devon's expression darkened. "Don't be unreasonable. What you need is to take your medicine and get some sleep. You'll feel better once you rest and eat something."

"I won't stay here and pretend. It's pointless. You even brought me to the island where you're building a resort, I'm sure so you could keep up with the progress. So don't tell me I'm being unreasonable for wanting to dispense with the fairy-tale honeymoon. You and I both know at this point it's a joke and we'll just spend all week staring awkwardly at each other or you'll just spend most of the time at the job site."

His jaw ticked and he stood again, turning briefly away. Then he turned back, irritation evident in his gaze. "You wanted me to pretend in front of your family. Why can't you pretend now?"

"Because I'm miserable and it's going to take me a little time to get over this," she snapped. "Look, we can say I wasn't feeling well. Or you can make up some business emergency. It's not as if anyone in my capitalistic family would even lift an eyebrow at the idea of business coming first. Right now my head hurts so damn bad, we wouldn't even be lying."

Some of the anger left Devon's gaze. "Let me get you some medication for your headache. Then I want you to get some rest. If…" He sighed. "If you still want to leave when you wake up, I'll arrange our flight back to New York."

Eleven

She slept because the pill Devon gave her would allow her to do no less. She rarely resorted to taking the medication prescribed for her migraines for the reason that it made her insensible.

When she awoke, she was in bed by herself and it was nearly dusk. Her headache still hung on with tenacious claws and when she moved too suddenly to try to sit up, nausea welled in her stomach. Her head pounded and she put a hand to her forehead, sucking air through her nostrils to control the sudden wash of weakness.

The room was blanketed in darkness, the drapes drawn and no lights had been left on. Devon had made sure she had been left in comfort, only a sheet covering her and the air-conditioning turned down so it was nearly frigid in the room.

Before, his consideration would have been endearing. Now, she could only assume he was operating out of guilt.

She pushed herself from the bed and sat on the edge for a moment, holding her head while she got her bearings. After a moment, she got to her feet and wobbled unsteadily toward the luggage stand, where her still-packed suitcase lay open.

She ripped off the silky gown she'd so excitedly donned the night before and tossed it in the nearby garbage can. If she never saw it again, it would be too soon.

She dug through the suitcase, bypassing the chic outfits, the swimwear and the other sexy nightwear she'd purchased, and pulled out a faded pair of jeans and a T-shirt. She briefly contemplated shoes, but the idea had formed in her head to take a long walk on the beach. Maybe it would clear her head or at least stop the vile aching. For that, she wouldn't need shoes.

Having no idea where Devon was, or if he was even still in the suite, she opted to leave through the sliding glass doors to the veranda. The breeze lifted her hair as soon as she walked outside the room and she inhaled deeply as she took the steps leading down to the beach.

The night was warm and the wind coming off the water was comfortable, but she was cold to her bones and she shivered as her feet dug into the sand.

It was a perfect, glorious night. The sky was lit up like a million fireflies had taken wing and danced over the inky black canvas. In the distance the moon was just rising over the water and it shimmered like a splash of silver.

Drawn to the mesmerizing sight, she ventured closer to the water, hugging her arms around her waist as the incoming waves lapped precariously close to her toes.

At one point, she stopped and allowed the water to caress her feet and surround her ankles. There she stood, staring over the expanse of the ocean, stargazing like a dreamer. It would take a million wishes to fix the mess she was currently in. And maybe that was what had gotten her into this situation in the first place.

Stupid dreams. Stupid idealism. She'd been a fool to wait for the perfect guy to give her virginity to. She'd always been somewhat smug and a little holier-than-thou with her friends who'd given it up long ago. But they at least had gone into the situation with their eyes wide open. They hadn't confused sex for love. They weren't the ones on their honeymoon with the migraine from hell and a husband who didn't love them.

They were looking pretty damn smart for shopping around and Ashley was looking like a moron.

She pulled out her cell phone and stared down at her contacts list. She could use the comfort of a good friend right now but she wavered on whether to send a text. She was already humiliated enough. Could she bear to tell her friends or even one friend the truth about her marriage? Or would she go back home, live a lie and hope that Devon would pretend as agreed.

Could she ever make him love her?

She lowered the hand holding the phone and then she shoved it back into her pocket. What could she say anyway in the limited number of characters allowed by a text message? Or maybe she should just tweet everyone.

Marriage fail. Honeymoon fail.

That would get the message across with plenty of characters left over.

She shoved her hands into her pockets, closed her eyes and wished for just one minute that she could go back. That she would have asked more questions. That she would have picked up on the fact he'd never said he loved her even when Ashley made it a practice to tell him every day.

She'd just assumed he was a typical guy. Devon was reserved. He was somewhat forbidding. But she'd been wildly attracted to those qualities. Thought they were sexy. She'd been convinced that he quietly adored her and that his actions spoke louder than words.

She'd never considered even once that his actions were practiced, fake and manipulative.

Another shiver overtook her and she clamped her teeth together until pain shot through her head.

"Enough," she said.

She had beat herself up for the last twenty-four hours, but it was Devon who was the jackass here. Not her. She'd done nothing wrong. Naiveté wasn't a crime. Loving someone wasn't a crime. She wouldn't apologize for offering her love, trust and commitment to a man who didn't deserve any of it.

He was wrong. She wasn't.

The only thing she could control from here on out was what she did with the truth. It was no longer about what Devon wanted. If he could be a selfish jerk-wad, she could at least focus on what she wanted from this fiasco.

Then she laughed because what she wanted was the jerk-wad to love her. That might make her pathetic.

No, she couldn't text Sylvia or Carly or Tabitha. Definitely not Pippa. Pippa would have her in front of a lawyer in a matter of hours and then she'd likely take out a hit on Devon.

Plus her friends would tell her she was being stupid for wanting to stay in the marriage. And she may well be an idiot, but she didn't want people telling her that. She'd already made one mistake. It wouldn't be the first or last and well, if it didn't work out, at least then she could cite incompatibility and she wouldn't have to tell everyone that the marriage had fallen apart before it had ever gotten off the ground.

She had just enough of an ego to want to save face. Who could blame her?

Feeling only marginally better about taking control over a perfectly out-of-control situation, she turned to retrace her steps. She was hungry but the thought of food made her faintly nauseous and her head was hurting so badly she wasn't sure she could keep anything down anyway.

She was still a good distance from the steps leading to her and Devon's suite when she saw him striding toward her on the sand.

Even now after so much time to think and decide how she wanted to proceed, she wasn't prepared to face him. How could she just go on after finding out he was nothing like the man she'd thought she'd married? It was as if they were strangers. Intimate strangers who would now live together and pretend a loving existence to outsiders.

There weren't manuals for this. Certainly no one had ever given her advice on such a matter. She wasn't good at artifice. She hated lying. But it was what she'd asked him to do. It was what she herself had just decided to do with her friends and family. To the world.

"Where the hell have you been?" Devon demanded as he approached. "I was worried sick. I went in to check on you and you were gone."

Before she could answer, he put his hand around her elbow and pulled her toward the glow cast from the torches that lined the beach.

She flinched away from the burst of light and he muttered something under his breath.

"Your headache isn't any better, is it?"

She slowly shook her head.

"Damn it, Ash, why didn't you come to me? Or take another pill. You should be in bed. For that matter you've eaten nothing in twenty-four hours. You're as pale as death and your eyes are glazed with pain."

She braced herself as he reached for her again, but his touch was in direct contrast to the tone of his voice. He was infinitely gentle as he pulled her against his side and began leading her back to the suite.

Unable to resist the urge, she laid her head on his shoulder and closed her eyes, trusting him to at least get her safely up the steps. His hold tightened around her and then to her shock, he simply swung her into his arms and began carrying her back.

"Put your head on my shoulder," he said gruffly.

Relaxing against him, she did as he directed and for a few moments, basked in the tenderness of his hold.

Pretending was nice.

He carried her back into the suite, into the still-darkened bedroom, and carefully laid her on the bed.

"Would you be more comfortable out of your jeans?" he asked. But even as he asked, he was unfastening her fly and pulling the zipper down.

He efficiently pulled her pants down her legs, leaving her in her panties and T-shirt. She lay there, cheek resting on the firm, cool pillow, and willed the pain to go away. All of it.

He sat on the edge of the bed and then turned, sliding his leg over the mattress and bending it so he was perched next to her.

"I'll get you another pill, but I don't think you should take it on an empty stomach. It might make you ill. But neither do you look as though you could keep down much so I'll call down for some soup. Would you like something to drink? Could you handle some juice?"

As he spoke, he smoothed his hand over her hair, stroking gently, and she had to bite her lip to keep the hot tears from slipping down her cheeks again. This wasn't going to work if she broke down every time he was nice to her or took care of her.

And it wasn't as if he was doing anything different than he'd done all along. It was one of the things that had made her think he loved her to begin with, even absent of the actual words. He'd been so…good…to her. So caring. Protective. Possessive. A guy couldn't fake all of that, could he?

"Soup sounds good," she said faintly.

He continued to stroke her hair and then his hand went still and he frowned. "Is that bothering you? I wasn't thinking. I'm sure you must be supersensitive to any touch or sound."

"It was…nice."

"I'll be right back. Let me order your soup. You need to get something in your stomach. It might help with the headache, too."

She closed her eyes as he stood and walked across the room.

He stepped outside but she could just make out the low murmur of his voice as he ordered room service. A moment later, he returned and gently laid his hand over her forehead.

"It'll be here in a few minutes. I told them to put a rush on it."

"Thank you."

He was silent for a few seconds and then he said in a voice full of resignation, "I'll make arrangements for us to fly home in the morning. Perhaps it's best if you're back in familiar surroundings. I don't want you to suffer with a headache the entire week we were supposed to be here. At least at home, you'll have your family and your friends to surround you and…make you feel better."

She nodded, her chest heavy and aching with regret. It should have been different. They should have spent the week making love. Laughing. Spending every waking moment immersed in each other.

Instead they'd go back home to a very uncertain future in a world that was suddenly unfamiliar to Ashley. Where she'd have to guard every word, every action.

It frightened her. What if she failed? What if even after she removed the annoyances he still felt nothing more for her than he did now?

Then he doesn't deserve you, the voice inside her aching head whispered in her ear.

He didn't deserve her now. The intelligent side of her knew and accepted this. But she wanted him. Wanted his love, his approval. She wanted him to be proud of her.

If that made her an even bigger moron than she'd already been, she could live with that. What she couldn't live with was just walking away without seeing if their marriage could be salvaged.

"It will be better when we get home," she whispered.

His hand stilled on her hair but he remained silent as he

seemed to contemplate her words. His expression was grim and tension radiated from his body in waves.

Then there was a distant knock and he rose once more. "That'll be the food. Just stay here. I'll wheel the cart in and we'll get you a comfortable spot made up so you can eat in bed."

He strode out of the room and Ashley lay there a moment mentally recovering from what felt like a barrage of emotional turmoil. Finally she pushed herself upward and sat cross-legged on the bed, with pillows pushed behind her back to keep her propped up.

Devon returned with the rolling table and parked it at the end of the bed. As soon as he uncovered the bowl of soup, the aroma wafted through the air and her mouth watered. On cue, her stomach protested sharply and sweat broke out on her forehead.

"You okay?" Devon asked as he positioned the tray in front of her.

His gaze was focused sharply on her face, his forehead creased with concern. She nodded and reached for the napkin and utensils with shaking hands.

When she would have slid the bowl closer, Devon gently took her hand away.

"Perhaps it would be better if I ladled the soup into a mug so you could sip at it. Less chance of spilling it that way."

She nodded her agreement and watched as he filled one of the cups on the table with the delicious-smelling broth.

"Here. Careful now, it's hot."

She brought the steaming mug to her lips and inhaled, closing her eyes as she tentatively took the first sip.

It was heaven in a coffee cup. The warmth from the soup traveled all the way down to her stomach and settled there comfortably.

"Good?" he asked as he edged his way onto the bed beside her.

"Wonderful."

He watched as she downed a significant amount of the soup and then he took her medicine bottle from the nightstand and shook out another pill.

"Here. Take this. Once you're finished you can lie down and hopefully sleep until morning. I'll wake you up in time to catch the flight. Don't worry about your things. I'll lay out something for you to wear on the plane and I'll pack everything else and have it all ready to go. All you'll have to do is get dressed and head out to the car when it's time."

Even though she was still devastated and angry, she couldn't be so much of a bitch not to recognize or acknowledge that he was taking absolute care of her.

She leaned back against the pillows, cup in hand, and glanced his way.

"Thank you," she said quietly.

A flash of pain entered his eyes. "I know you don't believe this right now, but maybe in time you will, Ash. I never meant to hurt you. I never wanted this to happen. I wouldn't have hurt you for the world."

She swallowed and brought the rim of the cup back to her lips. There wasn't much she could say to that. She did believe that he wasn't malicious. If she hadn't discovered the truth on her own, maybe he would have never told her. She was quite certain he wouldn't have. Maybe he thought he was doing her a favor by keeping it from her.

He pulled the mug away and then cupped her chin and gently turned her until she looked back at him.

"You'll see, Ash. We'll make this work."

She nodded as she lowered the mug the rest of the way down to the tray in front of her.

"I'll try, Devon. I'll try."

He leaned toward her and pressed a kiss to her forehead. "Get some rest. I'll wake you in the morning."

Twelve

The next morning was a total blur for Ashley. Devon gently woke her and after ascertaining that her headache wasn't better, he arranged a light breakfast, hovered over her while she ate and then all but dressed her and whisked her into a waiting car.

They drove to the airport and once on the plane, he settled her into her seat and gave her another pill. He propped a pillow behind her head, put a blanket over her and then made sure every single window was shut around her.

She drifted into blissful unawareness as the airplane left the island and traveled back to the cold of New York City.

When they landed, once again Devon ushered her into a waiting car, taking the blanket and pillow with them so she was comfortable in the backseat. She dozed with her head on his shoulder until they reached his apartment and then he gently shook her awake.

"We're home, Ash. Wait inside the car while I get out. I'll help you inside."

Home. She blinked as the looming building floated into her vision through the fogged window of the car. A cold rush of air blew over her as Devon stepped out. He spoke a moment with the doorman and then he reached back in to help her out.

"Careful," he cautioned as she stepped onto the curb.

He wrapped an arm around her and guided her to the door the doorman held open for them. Once inside, he didn't loosen his hold. He kept her close all the way up in the elevator until they reached his apartment. Their apartment. It was hard to keep that distinction in her mind.

Their home was already cluttered with her things. She'd moved completely in before the wedding. Devon had suggested having a cleaning lady come in which said to her that he didn't appreciate the somewhat careless way she kept her stuff. She sighed. One more thing she'd have to work on.

When they entered the bedroom, Devon pulled out one of his workout T-shirts and tossed it onto the bed. "Why don't you get out of your travel clothes and into something more comfortable. I'll wake you for dinner so you eat something."

"I'd rather just lie down on the couch," she said, reaching for the T-shirt.

His expression darkened and for a moment she couldn't imagine what she'd done to draw his disapproval. Then it struck her that he assumed she wouldn't be sleeping in his— their—bed.

It wasn't something she'd given any consideration. The thought hadn't even occurred to her. In her mind, if she was staying and making an effort to make their marriage work, she just naturally assumed they'd still sleep together.

Perhaps it wasn't something she should assume at all. She sank onto the edge of the bed, still foggy and loopy from the medication. She rubbed wearily at her eyes before focusing back on him.

"I only meant that when I have a headache, sometimes I'm more comfortable propped on the couch so I'm not lying flat.

However, it does bring up a point that I hadn't considered. I assumed that we'd continue to…" She swallowed, suddenly feeling vulnerable and extremely unsure of herself. "That is, I just thought we'd continue to sleep together. I have no idea if that's something you want."

Devon stalked over, bent down and placed his hands on either sides of her legs so that he was on eye level with her.

"You'll be in my bed every night. Whether we're having sex or not, you'll be next to me, in my arms."

"Well, okay then," she murmured.

He rose and took a step back. "Now, if you're more comfortable on the couch, change into my shirt and I'll get you pillows and a blanket for the couch."

She nodded and sat there watching him as he walked away. She glanced around the room—to all her stuff placed haphazardly here and there—and sighed. When she got rid of this headache, she'd whip the apartment into shape. She'd been away from the shelter more days than she'd ever been away before but the animals were in good hands and they'd be fine while she got the rest of her life in order.

Devon would no doubt be back to work in the morning, which meant she'd have plenty of time alone to figure out things. She wrinkled her nose. Being alone sucked. She was always surrounded by people. In her family she didn't have to look far if she wanted company. There was always someone to hang out with. And aside from her family, her circle of friends was always available even if for a gab session.

But what was she supposed to talk to them about now? How wonderful her marriage was? Her husband? The aborted honeymoon?

Her head was too fuzzy to even contemplate the intricacies of her relationships right this second. She reached for the T-shirt, shed her own clothes and crawled into Devon's shirt.

She started to leave her clothes just where they'd dropped on the floor, but she stopped to pick them up and then deposited them into the laundry basket in the bathroom. It was technically Devon's basket and he might not want her mixing her clothes with his, but she didn't have a designated place of her own yet. One more thing for the to-do list.

She trudged out to the living room to see that Devon had arranged several pillows and put out a blanket for her. As she started across the floor, Devon appeared from the kitchen. She crawled onto the couch and burrowed into all of the pillows while Devon pulled the blanket up to her shoulders. Then he perched on the edge close to her head.

"Are you feeling any better yet?"

She nodded. "Head doesn't hurt as bad. A few more hours and it should be fine. Just fuzzy from all the medication. I've never had to take three in a row like that."

He frowned as if he realized the significance of her having the worst headache of her life after their confrontation.

"Rest for a few hours then. I'll check on you in a bit and see if you're up for some dinner. I thought we'd eat in, of course. I can order anything you like or if you prefer, I can make something here."

She nodded.

"I have some calls to make. I'll let your family know we're back and why. You just concentrate on feeling better."

Her eyes widened in alarm. "What are you going to tell them?"

He frowned again. "I'm only going to tell them that you came down with a severe headache and that we thought you'd feel better if you were back in your own home."

She sagged in relief and the knot in her stomach loosened. "They'll want to come right over, or at least Mom will. Tell her not to bother, please. Let her know I'll call her soon."

"Of course. Now get some rest. I'll sort out dinner later."

He kissed her forehead, pulled the covers up to her chin and then quietly walked away, flipping off all the lights. She heard the door to his office close and she lay there alone in the darkness.

It wasn't anything she hadn't experienced before. In the evenings when Dev got home from work, he often sequestered himself in his office for a time while she watched TV or ordered in their dinner. But she hadn't felt so alone then. Because she'd known he was just in the next room and that in theory she could walk in there at any time. Only now it was as if a gulf had opened between them and he may as well be on the other side of the moon. She didn't feel as though she had the right to interrupt him.

She lay there as the haze slowly began to wear off. She braced herself for the inevitable onslaught of pain, but there was only a dull ache that signaled the aftereffects of a much worse headache than she'd experienced in at least two years.

For that matter, she hadn't been forced to take the pain medication prescribed for her headaches in months. Emotional stress, the doctor had said, was a trigger for her. The last time she'd battled frequent headaches had been when her mom and dad had briefly separated and she'd feared an eventual divorce.

It was the very last thing she or any of their family had ever imagined because it was so obvious her parents loved each other. The separation hadn't lasted long. Whatever their issues had been, they'd worked through them quickly and her dad had moved back into the apartment with her mom and they'd gone back to being the loving couple that Ashley had always witnessed.

But for the entire period of their separation, Ashley had been deeply unhappy and stressed and she'd battled headaches on a weekly basis. The doctor had counseled her on coming up with more effective ways to manage stress but Ashley had laughed. Now she realized she was as guilty as Devon had accused her of being when it came to wearing her feelings on her shoulder. She absorbed too much of the world around her and it affected her. That wasn't something she could change, could she?

She sighed. If she had any hope of not spending the next year in bed knocked out on medication, she was going to have to harden herself. She couldn't go around being a veritable sponge and reacting so emotionally to everything.

Her husband didn't love her? So what. She'd have to find a way to be happy. As Grammy always said, you make your nest now lie in it. Well, Ashley had certainly made the biggest, messiest nest of a marriage and now it was hers to wallow in.

As the medication wore off, she found it impossible to sleep. Her mind was buzzing with a mental list of everything she needed to do. Or not do. The list of things not to do was every bit as long as the list of things that needed to be done.

Learn to cook. That one popped uninvited into her head. She frowned because how did one simply learn to cook? Even Devon possessed rudimentary know-how in the kitchen. He could prepare simple dishes. She wasn't even sure she could boil water if necessary.

Okay that one should be simple enough. Pippa was a first-rate cook and it wouldn't be strange that Ashley would want to learn to cook a fabulous meal for her new husband. She could say she wanted to surprise him with a romantic meal for two.

And cooking shows. There was an entire television network devoted to cooking. Surely there was something she could watch there that would help.

Cleaning. Okay, she knew how to clean. She just didn't possess the organization skills to do it well. But she could muddle her way through it. It simply required discipline and less of a scatterbrain mentality.

She had to curb her tongue and her reactions. That should be simple enough. Smile and nod instead of shriek and wave her hands. Her mother was an expert at all the social graces but then she'd had to be with all the business functions she'd arranged and managed for her husband.

Ashley could certainly draw on the resources around her. She'd never particularly had a desire to be more like her family. She hadn't really considered that she was so different. She hadn't thought much about how she compared. Why would she? But they could help her. She just had to make sure she employed their help in a way that didn't give away the true reason for her transformation.

The door to Devon's office opened and he stepped out, looked her way and then started toward her.

"Can't sleep?" he asked. "Do you need anything?"

She shook her head and pulled the blanket closer to her chin. "I'm fine. Just getting comfortable."

He took a seat in the armchair across from the couch. Their gazes connected but she didn't look away, as tempted as she was. She couldn't keep avoiding him, no matter how desirable the prospect was.

It was hard for her because humiliation crept up her spine every time she had to face him, but eventually that would go away or she'd harden enough that it would no longer affect her. Or at least she hoped so.

"I spoke to your parents. Your mother is naturally concerned for you. She'd like you to call her when you're feeling up to it. Your father wants to see me in the morning, so if you're okay by then, I'll be out for a few hours."

"I'll be fine," she said softly. "Headache's gone. No reason for you to stay home and babysit me."

"If you need anything at all or if you begin to feel bad again, call me. I'll come home."

Hell would freeze over before she'd ever call him at work again, not that she'd tell him that. She nodded instead and sighed unhappily. So this is what her marriage boiled down to. A stilted, awkward conversation between two people who were clearly uncomfortable in each other's presence.

"Do you think you could eat something now?" Devon asked, breaking the strained silence. "What would you like?"

Deciding to take the olive branch, or perhaps create an olive branch out of a dinner offer, she shifted and pushed herself up so that her back was against the arm of the couch.

"You could cook, if you don't mind. I could sit at the bar and watch."

He looked surprised by her suggestion, but his surprise was quickly replaced by relief. He looked almost hopeful.

"That would be nice. Are you sure you're up for the noise and the light?"

Again she nodded. She hadn't talked this little since she'd been a nonverbal toddler. Her parents always swore that because she was late to talk she'd spent the rest of her life making up for lost time.

He stood and held down his hand to her. "Come on then. Bring the blanket with you if you're cold. You can sit on one of the bar stools and wrap it around you."

Hesitating only a brief moment, she slid her hand over his, enjoying the warmth of his touch. He curled his fingers around her wrist and helped her from the couch.

She stood up beside him but he waited a moment for her to get her footing.

"Okay?" he asked. "Fuzziness gone yet? I don't want you falling."

"I'm fine."

He didn't relinquish her hand as he started toward the kitchen. He guided her toward one of the stools and settled her down. He wrapped the blanket around her shoulders and tucked the ends underneath her arms.

"What's your pleasure tonight?"

He walked around to open the refrigerator, surveyed the contents and then glanced back at her.

It was probably another sign of her shortcomings that she had no idea what was or wasn't in the fridge. Heat singed her cheeks and she dropped her gaze. Tomorrow she'd take inventory. After she cleaned the house.

"Ash?"

She yanked her gaze back up. "Uh, I don't care. Honestly. I'll eat whatever."

"Oh, good. I've been dying to cook this cow's tongue before it goes bad."

She blinked for a moment before she realized he was teasing her. The memory of the night he'd first made love to her came back in a flash. The dinner they'd had when he'd asked her if she was a vegetarian.

Unbidden, a smile curved her lips. He smiled back at her, relief lightening his eyes.

"No?" he asked.

She shook her head. "No cow's tongue. But I'd eat his flank. Or his tuchus even."

"So you'll eat cow's ass but not his tongue," Devon said in mock exasperation.

Her smile grew a bit bigger and she leaned forward on the counter, resting her chin in her palm. This pretending felt nice. Who said denial was a bad thing?

If she could effectively put out of her mind the whole debacle that had been her honeymoon and take some time to work on her shortcomings, maybe at some point the pretense could become real. He could love her. He was committed to their marriage. It was a step. He was attentive, caring and he obviously hated to see her hurting. Those weren't the characteristics of a man who loathed her. So if he didn't hate her, and he seemed to like her well enough even if she annoyed him, then eventually, possibly, he could love her.

It was a hope she clung to because the alternative didn't bear thinking about. He didn't want a divorce, but she couldn't remain married to a man who could never love her. If she lost hope that he'd never reciprocate her feelings, it would signal the end of their marriage whether he wished it or not.

Devon tossed a package onto the counter and then returned

to the fridge, where he pulled out an onion, what looked like bell peppers in assorted colors and a box of mushrooms.

"How about I do stir-fry? It's quick and easy and pretty damn good if I do say so myself."

"Sounds yummy."

She watched him in silence and soon the sizzle of searing meat filled the room. While the meat cooked, he sliced the vegetables. He stopped to give the meat a brisk stirring and then returned to the cutting board.

She decided he looked good in the kitchen. Sleeves rolled up, top button undone, his brow creased in concentration. He was efficient, but then he seemed efficient at everything he did. She wondered if there was anything he wasn't accomplished at. Was he one of those people who could pick up anything and do it well?

"Name one thing you suck at," she blurted out.

Then she promptly groaned inwardly because this was precisely what she wasn't supposed to be doing. She had to demonstrate more…control. More decorum. Or at least stop blurting out her first reaction to everything.

He glanced up, his brows drawn together as if he wasn't sure if he'd heard her correctly. "Say that again?"

She shook her head. No way. "It was stupid. Just forget it."

He put down the knife, glanced over at the skillet and then returned his gaze to her. "Why would you want to know something I suck at?"

She closed her eyes and wished the floor would just open up and swallow her. So much for her campaign to become less… everything on his complaint list about her.

"Ash? Come on. Don't leave me hanging here."

She sighed. "Look, it was a stupid question. It's just that you seem like one of these people who is good at everything. You know, a person who can pick up something and just do it and do it well. I just wanted to know one thing you suck at. Gives hope to us mere mortals."

He shrugged. "I suck at lots of things. I'm definitely not one of those people who is good at everything. I've had to work hard for everything I've earned."

This was going from bad to worse. "It didn't come out right, Dev, okay? Can we just forget it? I wasn't insinuating that you haven't worked hard. I think it's evident that you've worked for everything you have. That wasn't what I meant at all. Sorry."

She pushed her hand into her hair and focused her stare down at the countertop. Running out of the room seemed overly dramatic even if it was what she wanted more than anything.

"Then what did you mean?"

There wasn't any anger or irritation in his voice. Just simple, casual curiosity. She chanced a peek back up at him to gauge his expression.

"Well, like cooking. You seem good at that. I just wanted to know something you aren't good at. You seemed to me to be one of those people who have a natural ability to pick up on things. You know, like sports. You ever see kids who just pick up a ball and know how to play? I bet you were one of those."

He groaned. "Oh, man. Clearly you've never watched me try to play basketball. And I say try, but that's probably not even an accurate word to use. Rafael, Ryan and Cam like to torture me at least once a year when they drag me down to play a 'friendly' game of basketball. What it really is is an opportunity for them to pay me back for every imagined slight. And then they don't let me forget it for the next six months."

"So you aren't good at basketball? Is that what you're saying?"

"Yeah. That's exactly what I'm saying."

She smiled. "Oh. Well, that's okay because I'm terrible at it, too."

He smiled back at her and then tossed the vegetables into the pan he'd taken the meat out of. "We can be terrible together then."

"Yeah," she said quietly.

He busied himself finishing up the meal and five minutes later, he set a plate in front of her while he stood on the other side of the bar, leaning back against the sink while he held his plate.

She looked up and frowned. "Not going to sit down?"

"I like watching you," he said as his gaze slid over her face. "I'd prefer to be across from you."

Her cheeks warmed and she quickly looked back down at her plate. She had no response for that. It puzzled her that he'd say such a thing.

But maybe he was trying. Like she was trying. Just as she would be trying as she embarked on her to do list the next day.

It wouldn't happen overnight, but maybe…one day.

Thirteen

Ashley woke with a muggy hangover feeling but then who wouldn't after two days in a medication-induced coma?

Today was the first day in her bid to take over the world. Well, sort of. Or rather it was her attempt to *not* take on the world quite so much. *Reserve* and *caution* were her two new friends.

There would be no more lying around and feeling sorry for herself.

Devon had exited the apartment early. The previous night had been a study in awkwardness.

He'd crawled into bed next to her and they'd lain quietly in the dark until finally she'd drifted off to a troubled sleep. Sometime during the night, he'd drifted toward her, or maybe she'd attacked him in her sleep. Either way, she'd ended up in his arms and had awakened when he'd gotten up early to shower.

He'd kissed her on the head and murmured for her to go back to sleep before leaving her alone.

"Welcome to your new reality," she murmured as she pushed herself out of bed.

She spent her entire time in the shower lecturing herself on how her situation was what she made of it. It could be horrible or she could salvage it. It was just according to how much effort she wanted to invest in her own happiness. Put that way, she could hardly say to hell with it and stomp off.

She winced when she caught sight of herself in the mirror. She looked bad. Not in one of those ways where she really didn't look so bad but said so anyway. She honestly looked like death warmed over. There were dark circles under her eyes. There was a line around her mouth from having her jaw set so firmly. Her unhappiness was etched on her face for the world to see. She'd never been good at hiding any kind of emotion. She was as transparent as plastic wrap.

Thank goodness for Carly and her never-ending list of tips for any type of makeup emergency. This definitely called for the full treatment.

When she was finished with her hair and makeup she was satisfied to see that at least she didn't look quite so haggard. Tired, yes, but that could easily be explained away by the headache. Surely an ecstatic new bride would smile her way through even the worst of migraines.

First stop was her mother's, since if Gloria Copeland didn't soon hear from her chick, she'd move Manhattan to get there to make sure all was well. After that was tackled, she had work to do. A lot of work.

She took a cab over to her former apartment building and smiled when Alex hurried to greet her.

"How are you, Miss Ashley? How is married life treating you?"

It was a standard question that would likely be asked of her a hundred more times before the week was out. Right after the one where most people would ask her why the hell she was back home after only two nights on her honeymoon.

"I'm good, Alex. Here to see my mother. Will you ring up and let her know I'm on my way?"

A moment later, Ashley stepped off the elevator and into the spacious apartment that very nearly occupied an entire floor. It was where she had spent a large portion of her childhood and it still felt like home to her no matter that she'd moved out on her own some time ago.

"Ashley, darling!" her mother cried as she hurried to greet her daughter. "Oh, you poor, poor darling. Come here and let me see you. Is your headache better? I knew there was simply too much excitement going on with the wedding and your moving and all the other plans. I worried it would prove to be too much for you. We should have spaced out the arrangements better."

Her mom enveloped her in a hug and for a long moment, Ashley clung to the comfort that only a mother could offer when her world was otherwise crap.

"Ashley?" her mother asked in a concerned, hushed tone when they finally pulled apart. "Is everything all right? Come, sit down. You don't even look like yourself today."

Ashley allowed herself to be pulled over to the comfortable leather couch. It smelled like home. She settled back and immediately burrowed into the corner, allowing the familiarity to surround her like a blanket.

"I'm fine, Mama. Really. I think you were right. There's been so much excitement and stress that when we finally got to St. Angelo I just crashed. Poor Devon was stuck taking care of me while I was insensible from the medication."

"As he should have. I'm glad he took good care of my baby for me. Are you feeling better now? You're pale and there are dark smudges under your eyes."

So much for Carly's awesome makeup tips.

"I'm better. I just wanted to come over so you wouldn't worry. I have to go back soon. There's a lot I need to do in our apartment to get everything squared away."

Her mom patted her on the arm. "Of course. But first, let me fix you a nice cup of hot tea."

"Spiced tea?" Ashley asked hopefully.

Her mother smiled. "With a peppermint."

Ashley sighed and relaxed into the couch, more than willing to allow her mom to fuss over her and baby her before she crawled back into the real world. If only manufacturers could package a mom's TLC into a box of bandages, they'd make millions.

Think of the marketing opportunities. Life sucks? Slap a mom bandage on and everything's instantly better.

A few minutes later, Ashley's mother returned carrying a tray that she set on the coffee table in front of Ashley. She handed her a cup of steaming tea and then unwrapped a peppermint that Ashley dropped into the bottom.

Ashley studied her mom as she settled back onto the couch, her own cup of tea in hand. "Mom? What happened between you and dad?"

Her mom reacted in surprise and cast Ashley a startled glance as she set her teacup back on its saucer. "Whatever do you mean, darling?"

"When you separated that time. I never asked because honestly I wanted to forget it ever happened. But now that I'm married… I just wanted to know. You two have always seemed so in love."

Her mother's eyes softened and she leaned forward to put her cup down on the coffee table. Then she turned and gathered Ashley's free hand in hers.

"It's natural for you to worry about those things now that you're married yourself. But darling, don't dwell on them."

"I know, but it just seems like that if it could happen to you and Daddy that it could happen to anyone. Was he having an affair? Did you forgive him?"

"Oh, good Lord, no!" She sighed and shook her head. "I know it was difficult for you and Eric, but especially for you. I never imagined that you'd think something like that, though. I should have guessed. I was so determined not to drag you children into our mess and thought I was doing the best thing by protecting you from any of the details. I can see I was wrong."

"What happened then?" Ashley asked softly.

"Oh it sounds so silly now. But back then I was convinced that my marriage was over. Your father was doing what he's always done. The difference was, suddenly it wasn't good enough for me. I began to worry. Maybe it's normal to go through a stage where you question what you want out of a relationship or worry that perhaps your partner doesn't love or value you anymore. Your father was working a lot of long hours. He was traveling constantly. You and Eric were adults and were going your own way and suddenly I found myself feeling quite alone and no longer valuable."

"Oh, Mama. I wish I had known," Ashley said unhappily. "That sounds so very awful for you."

Her mom smiled. "It was at the time but it wasn't entirely your father's fault. He was caught completely off guard when he returned home only to discover that I'd moved his things out and he had to find another place to live. He begged me to tell him what was wrong, what he'd done wrong, how he could fix it. But the truth was, I didn't even know myself. I just knew I was unhappy and that I no longer knew what I wanted from my marriage or my husband. If I didn't know, how could he?"

"What did you do?"

"I refused to speak to him for a week. It wasn't that I was angry. I just didn't know what to say to him. I took that time to think about and articulate what it was I wanted to say to him. And during that time, I realized that it wasn't him that I needed to change. It was me. I needed to find what was going to make me happy and he couldn't do it for me.

"When I finally agreed to see him, the poor man looked like death warmed over. I felt so guilty for the way I'd made him suffer but I knew we'd never last if I couldn't get myself together. I asked him for a period of separation. He was adamantly opposed. It wasn't until I gently reminded him that I didn't need his permission and that we were already separated that he backed off."

Ashley frowned. "I always assumed…I mean I just thought that it was Daddy's decision to move out. I always wondered if there was another woman."

Her mom twisted her lips in a regretful frown. "Yes, it's what Eric thought too, unfortunately. He was furious with your father. It wasn't until I explained things to him that he calmed down. Then I think he was angry with me for making your father move out. Eric is very black-and-white."

"Yes, I know," Ashley said with a grimace. She took another sip of her tea and then looked back at her mom. "So what happened? What made you decide to let him move back in?"

Her mom sighed and a faraway look entered her eyes. "We were separated for six months and in a way, those six months were some of the best times of my life."

Ashley's eyes widened. "But Mama!"

"I know, I know, but listen to me. I didn't say they were easy. They weren't. But those six months outlined to me in clear detail what I wanted my life to be. And who I wanted to spend it with. I had opportunities. There were plenty of men who flirted with me and would have jumped at the opportunity to date or have an affair."

Ashley's mouth dropped open and her mother smiled at her reaction. "Darling, you don't think the need for sex goes away when you hit thirty, do you?"

"Oh, my God," Ashley muttered. "I'm so not hearing my mother talk about all the hot guys she had a chance with while she was separated from my father."

"I had opportunity, yes, but I couldn't do it," her mom said.

"Because you loved Daddy?"

"Because it would have been dishonorable. Your father didn't deserve it. Because I honestly didn't want to be with anyone other than him. And I realized that I'd been blaming him for my own unhappiness. It was easy to say he'd been neglecting me or that he spent too much time at work. But the truth was, after you children grew up and left the nest, I simply didn't know what it was I wanted to do next. And I took out my frustrations on the closest available target because I didn't want to take responsibility for my own failures and feelings of inadequacy."

"Wow, I never realized…"

Her mom smiled and reached up to touch her cheek. "What, that I'm human like everyone else? That your mom isn't perfect?"

"Well, yeah, I guess," Ashley said lamely. "It's a totally shocking discovery. You may not survive the fall from the mom pedestal."

Her mom laughed and tweaked Ashley's nose. "Such a smart alec like your father. I always thought you were so much like him."

"What? I'm nothing like Daddy. He'd probably be horrified to hear you say that. He despairs of me because I have no head for or interest in business."

Her mom smiled indulgently. "But you have a huge heart like your father does and when you love, you love with everything you have. Just like William. He was devastated when I asked him to leave. And even though I knew I absolutely had to do what I did, it was the most difficult decision I've ever made. Our marriage is better for it. When we got back together, I was a stronger, more confident woman. I didn't need him to make me complete. I wanted him. But I didn't need him and therein was the difference."

Ashley set aside her cup and then impulsively threw her arms around her mom in a hug. "I love you, Mama. Thank you for talking to me. It was just what I needed today."

Her mother stroked her hand over Ashley's hair and hugged

her back. "You're welcome, darling, and I love you, too. You know I'm always right here if you need me."

Devon sat across from William Copeland as William completed his order with the waitress. The two had met at William's favorite place to eat lunch, but Devon wasn't in the least bit hungry.

"You not eating, son?" William asked as the waitress looked expectantly in Devon's direction.

"I'll just have a glass of water," Devon said.

After the waitress left, William leaned back and for a moment looked visibly discomfited.

"I wanted to talk to you about some changes in the organization."

Alarm bells clanged in Devon's already aching head. Two nights without decent sleep and the image of Ashley's tearstained face were wearing on him. The very last thing he needed was the old man to renege on their agreement. Wouldn't that be the height of irony?

He must have seen the wariness on Devon's face because he quickly went on.

"It's not what you think. I want you to take over my position at Copeland. I know the merger with Tricorp wasn't supposed to be splashy, that we agreed to keep the Copeland name and that Tricorp would be more of a silent party, but I'm ready to resign and I want you to take my position."

Devon shook his head in confusion. "I don't understand."

William sighed wearily. "I'm sick, son. I've been having health issues. I've been trying to see to matters because I want my family provided for. I want Eric to have a position but he isn't ready to take over. And the thing is, I'm not sure he wants his future locked into the family business. Lately he's hinted that his interests lie in other areas. And Ashley… It's why I pushed so hard for the marriage to take place. I wanted her settled with a man I trusted and whom I knew would take good care of her. If it got out that my health was failing, the vultures would have descended and she would have been easy pickings."

"Sick?" Devon managed to get out. "How sick?"

"I don't know yet. I won't lie. I've been in denial. I haven't even discussed this with Gloria and she's going to hit the ceiling when she finds out. I'm not ready to die yet, though. I want a lot of years with my children and eventual grandchildren. I spent decades working my ass off to get where I am and now I want to retire and enjoy time with my wife and watch my grandchildren play. But in order to do all that, I have to make sure my company is in good hands. I don't want Copeland to die, which is why I wanted this merger so badly. It wasn't Tricorp I was after. To be honest I could have picked a dozen other companies who would bring as much to the table. But I went with Tricorp because of you. You're who I want for my daughter and my company."

"Jesus, I don't even know what to say," Devon muttered. "This is quite the bomb to drop the day after I return from an aborted honeymoon."

"I know you thought I was a crazy old man for making Ashley part of this deal. And that I'm a manipulative bastard. You'd be right on that count. I knew you wanted this partnership. I knew you wanted the Copeland name for the line of resorts you've envisioned. I also knew what I wanted. It just so happened that our wants aligned perfectly. And my children are provided for."

"Everyone but Ashley," Devon said quietly.

William looked up sharply. "What do you mean?"

"She wanted a husband who adores her, who loves her, who is the embodiment of all she's dreamed of."

"So? Any reason you can't be that man?"

It was a good question and one he wasn't sure how to answer. He rubbed his hand through his hair. "How soon are you wanting all of this done?"

"I want to tender my resignation as soon as everything is done. It won't be a secret that I'll want you to take over. Voting won't be an issue. You'll be the most logical person to take over when I retire. I hold a lot of sway over the board. They'll listen to me. I'm going to make a doctor's appointment and then tell my wife so she can rearrange my teeth for me and then drag me to the doctor. After that, she'll take over and I won't be able to scratch my ass without her permission."

The words were said with wry wit, but it was obvious from the warmth in William's eyes that he adored his wife beyond reason and absolutely didn't mind giving up control to her in his retirement.

The older man seemed totally at peace with his actions and decisions and Devon wondered how much he could really fault his father-in-law for taking steps to ensure that his family was provided for. Even if he didn't agree with the methods. Would he have done the same for his son or daughter?

He liked to think that he'd offer them something better than the occasional reminder not to "screw up."

The image of Ashley, round and lush with his child, conjured a powerful surge of emotion. He realized in an instant that he'd do whatever it took to protect a son or daughter.

"Take care of yourself," Devon said gruffly, suddenly unsteady at the idea of something happening to a man who'd seemed so determined to be a second father to him. "I'll expect you to spoil our children."

William's expression eased into a broad smile. "Planning to provide me with them soon?"

Devon shrugged. "Maybe. That'll be up to Ash. I just want her to be happy."

William nodded. "So do I, son. So do I."

They were interrupted by the waitress bringing William's entrée to the table. For a moment, William fussed over his food and then he looked up at Devon again. "I'd like you to plan a cocktail party. It'll give Ashley a chance to play hostess. I'm thinking a couple weeks out at most. I want to go ahead and announce that I'm planning to retire and that you're my choice to succeed me. I want this all to seem like a natural progression of the merger. A changing of the guard with my blessing."

"We can do that," Devon said. Or at least he hoped. Maybe by that time Ashley wouldn't be quite so upset. Right now, asking her to appear happy for an entire night in front of dozens of guests seemed unreasonable at best.

"Good. We'll talk more later and I'll give you a guest list and of course you'll have your own colleagues to invite. I just want to say again how happy I am to have you as my son-in-law. I knew from the moment I met you that you'd not only be the best thing for my company, but for my daughter as well."

Fourteen

When Devon walked into his apartment, he immediately noticed the change. There wasn't any clutter. No magazines strewn about. No shoes littering the floor. No purse hanging from a doorknob. And he could smell cleaning solution.

As he walked farther inside, his stomach knotted because not only was everything picked up, but he also realized that the apartment was completely and utterly devoid of Ashley's presence. All of the things she'd moved in and haphazardly decorated with had been put away. No silly knickknacks on the coffee or end tables.

The apartment looked precisely as it had before she moved in.

Has she packed up and left? Had she decided not to give their marriage a chance?

He experienced a faint sensation of illness. His stomach tightened with dread and the beginnings of panic gripped his throat.

Then he heard a distant sound that seemed to come from

the kitchen. He strode in that direction and realized that a television had been left on. But when he reached the doorway, he had to grip the frame to steady himself.

Relief blew through him with staggering ferocity.

She was still here.

She hadn't left.

She was sitting at the bar, her brow furrowed in concentration as she watched a cooking show. She had a notepad and pencil in front of her and she was furiously taking notes.

As his gaze took in the rest of the kitchen, he realized that she'd evidently spent the day cleaning. The surfaces sparkled. The floor shone. The scent of lemon was heavy in the air.

She was dressed in faded jeans and an old T-shirt. Her hair was pulled back into a ponytail and she wasn't wearing any makeup.

She looked absolutely beautiful.

But she also looked tired. The dark circles under her eyes were more pronounced and she had a delicate fragileness to her that made him instinctively protective of her. But he couldn't protect her from himself and it was he who had hurt her.

Drawn to the vulnerable image she presented, he slid his hands up her arms and then lowered his mouth to kiss her on the neck.

She froze immediately then turned swiftly around. "Hi," she offered hesitantly. "I didn't expect you back quite so soon."

"Technically I'm off this week," he said as he pulled away. "I had lunch with your father. We discussed business and now I'm done."

She made a face but didn't comment, which he was grateful for. Anytime her father and business were mentioned, it was going to be difficult, but the more he did it in passing, maybe it would lessen the sting.

"What happened to all your stuff?" he asked casually as he went around to open the fridge. He pulled out a bottle of water and pushed the door closed.

"Oh, I just organized everything," she said. "I didn't really have time before the wedding. Was too busy with other stuff."

"Mmm-hmm," he murmured. "And the cleaning? Should you have been doing all this today? You just came off a pretty bad headache. I wouldn't think all the cleaning stuff would be good for you to be inhaling."

"It was okay. Headache is gone. Just a little residual achiness."

He frowned. "Why don't you go lie on the couch. I'll figure out dinner and we'll watch some TV or just relax in the living room if you don't want the noise."

She rose from the stool. "No, no, I've got dinner planned. Are you hungry already? What time did you want to eat?"

Perplexed by her sudden agitation, he hastily backed off. It appeared she was at least trying for a semblance of normalcy and that relieved him. Maybe after the initial storm passed and she had time to think she'd see that nothing had changed between them.

In light of today's conversation with William Copeland, Devon was on the verge of accomplishing all his goals. And at a much faster rate than he'd ever planned. Five years down the road was here now. Copeland Hotels would be his. His dream of launching a new luxury chain of exclusive resorts under one of the oldest and most respected names in the business would be realized. He'd have a wife. Children. A family. He'd have it all.

The surge of triumph was so forceful he felt drunk with it.

"I'm in no hurry," he soothed. "Why don't we sit down and have a drink. What are you cooking?"

A dull flush worked over her face. "I'm not. At least not tonight I mean. I will another time. I thought I'd call for takeout. It's almost like a home-cooked meal but they bring it and set it up."

"Sounds wonderful. Thank you. I think a nice quiet dinner at home would be fantastic after the week we've had. We didn't really get to see each other much in the days leading up to the wedding. We can start making up for that now."

Pain flashed in her eyes but she remained quiet, almost as if she was dealing with the sudden reminder of their circumstances. He hated it. Wished he could wipe it from her memory. In time, it would fade. If he showed her that they could have a comfortable relationship, some of the rawness of her emotions would settle and they could go back to the easy camaraderie they'd shared before everything went to hell.

She squared her shoulders as if reaching a decision and then tilted her chin upward. "You go on out and have a seat. Would you like wine? Or do you want me to mix up something for you?"

He opened his mouth to tell her that he'd take care of it, but something in her eyes stopped him. There was a quiet desperation, almost as if she was barely clinging to her composure.

"Wine would be great," he said softly. "You choose something for both of us. I like everything I've stocked here so I'm good with whatever you pick out."

He left the kitchen, his chest tight. The next weeks were going to suck as they found their way in the new reality of their relationship. He had confidence that it would work out, though. He just had to be patient.

A few minutes later, Ashley came into the living room carrying two wineglasses and a bottle of unopened wine. She looked disgruntled as she set the glasses down on the coffee table.

"Can you open the wine?" she asked hesitantly. "I couldn't get the bottle opener to work properly. I'm sure I'm not doing it right."

He reached for the bottle and let his fingers glide over hers. "Relax, Ash. Take a seat. I'll pour."

Reluctantly she backtracked and sank down onto the couch. In truth she still didn't look well and it wouldn't surprise him if her head was still hurting her. Her brow was wrinkled and she looked tired. Maybe a glass of wine would ease some of her tension.

He opened the bottle and then poured a glass for her first. After pouring his own, he set the glass on the table and took a seat in the armchair diagonal to where she sat on the couch.

"Your father wants us to host a cocktail party in a week or two," he said.

"Us?" she squeaked. "As in you and me? Why wouldn't he want Mama to host it? She's awesome at hosting parties. Everyone always talks about how much fun they have when she throws a get-together."

"He's going to be announcing some changes at Copeland soon and this is his way of easing into that. Your father is looking at taking a less active role in the managing of things. He's ready to retire and focus on his family."

She looked despondent.

"Ash, this isn't a big deal. Most of the people who'll attend are people we already know. We'll pick a nice venue, have it catered, hire a band. It'll be great."

She held up her hand. "I'll handle it. No problem. I don't want you to worry about it. I just need to know exactly when. I'm sure you and Daddy will be busy with…whatever it is you're busy with. Mama always handled parties for Daddy. No reason I can't do it for you."

The dismay in her voice troubled him. He thought it rather sounded like she would be planning a funeral, but he wasn't about to shut her down when she was making such an effort. That she was so willing to try when it was obvious he'd crushed her endeared her to him all the more.

"I'm sure whatever you come up with, I and the others will love," he said.

She took a long drink of her wine, nearly draining the glass.

"Want to watch a movie?" he suggested.

She nodded as she put her wineglass back on the coffee table. "Sure. Whatever you want to put on is fine."

He picked up the remote but he didn't return to his own chair. He eased onto the couch next to her and put his arm along the top of the sofa behind her head.

For a long moment she sat there stiffly, almost as if she wasn't sure what she was supposed to do. He cursed the awkwardness between them. Before she wouldn't have hesitated to burrow underneath him and snuggle in tight. She'd drape herself over him when they watched movies. She would have kissed him, hugged him and generally mauled him with affection through the entire show.

Now she sat beside him like a statue, tension and fatigue radiating from her like a beacon.

"Come here," he murmured, pulling her underneath his arm. "That's better," he said when she finally relaxed against him and laid her cheek on his chest.

They were silent as the movie played and he was fine with that. There wasn't a lot he could say. There were only so many times he could apologize or tell her he hadn't meant to hurt her.

It wasn't the movie that captured his attention, though. He sat there enjoying her scent. Her hair always smelled like honeysuckle. Even in winter in the city. She had an airy, floral scent that clung to her. It suited her.

And he loved the feel of her next to him. He hadn't realized how much until he'd spent the last several days with a wall between them.

He touched her hair, idly sifting through the strands with his fingers, savoring the sensation of silk over his skin. By the time the credits rolled, he couldn't have even said what the movie was about. He hadn't cared.

"Ash, are you sure you don't want me to go out for some dinner?" He waited a moment. "Ash?"

He glanced down to see that she'd fallen sound asleep against his chest. Her lashes rested delicately on her cheeks and her lips were tight, almost as if she were deep in thought even at rest.

Gently he kissed her forehead and rested his chin there for a long moment. Somehow, someway, he would make it up to her. He was reaching the high point in his life and career where everything he'd worked so hard and so long for was his. And damn it, he wanted her to be on top of the world with him.

Fifteen

"This is hopeless," Ashley said as her shoulders sagged.

Pippa wrapped her arm around Ashley and squeezed tight. "You're not hopeless. You'll get it down. You're being way too hard on yourself."

"After three weeks, you'd think I'd be able to perform the simplest tasks in the kitchen," Ashley said forlornly. "Let's face it. I'm a culinary disaster."

"Are you all right, hon? You seem really down lately and not just about this cooking stuff. Is everything okay with you?"

Ashley smiled brightly and straightened her stance. "Oh, yeah, fine. Marriage is exhausting work. Who knew? Just trying to get my routine down. I've been spending my mornings at the shelter so I can be at home when Devon gets in from work. I keep hoping one of my meals will actually turn out but I keep having to call in backup."

Pippa laughed. "You're so silly. I don't even know why you're bothering learning to cook. Devon doesn't care if you can cook. The man's obviously crazy about you and you couldn't cook before you got married. I'm sure he's not expecting some miracle to occur."

Ashley bit her lip to keep from crying. The truth was, she was exhausted. Planning that damn cocktail party had turned out to be a giant pain in her ass. She was tempted to call her mother and beg for help but pride kept her from making that call.

The old Ashley would have laughed, thrown her hands up and admitted she was hopeless. The new Ashley was going to suck it up, be calm and get the job done.

"Are you coming to my party?" Ashley asked, suddenly worried she'd be surrounded by a sea of unfamiliar faces.

"Of course I am. I promised you I'd come. I know you're nervous, but really, this is your thing, Ash. You shine at social events. Everyone loves you and you're so sweet."

"Why don't you meet me at Tabitha's place the afternoon before. We'll get our hair done together. I'm aiming for a more sophisticated look for the party. You know, mature and married as opposed to young and flighty."

Pippa snorted. "Flighty?"

Ashley laughed it off but she knew well that Devon considered her a complete ditz.

"I need Carly's makeup skills, too."

"Honey, you aren't holding tea for the queen. You're hosting a cocktail party for friends and business associates. We already love you. And those who don't will. Stop tormenting yourself over this."

"I just don't want to look stupid," Ashley said.

Pippa shook her head. "I swear I don't know what's got into you lately. You're perfect and anyone who doesn't think so can kiss my ass."

"I love you," Ashley said, emotion knotting her throat.

Pippa hugged her fiercely and then pulled away. "Are you pregnant or something? I swear you're not usually so emotional."

"Oh, God, I don't think so. I mean it's possible but I haven't even kept up with my periods. I just remember being thrilled it wasn't going to happen on my honeymoon. You know, the one I ended up cutting short."

"Well, take one of those home pregnancy tests. You're a mess, Ash. Hormones have to be the reason why."

She closed her eyes. No, she couldn't be pregnant yet. Well, she certainly could, but she suddenly didn't want to be. But it was a little too late for that line of thinking. When was the last time she and Devon had made love anyway? Definitely before the wedding. But it was still too soon to tell.

"I'll give it a little more time," she said firmly. "I'm just a wreck over this stupid party. I feel like it's my first big test as Mrs. Devon Carter. I don't want to humiliate myself or him in front of a hundred people."

"Stop it," Pippa chided. "You're going to be awesome. Now, do you want to try this sauce again?"

Ashley sighed. "I'm thinking I should start out with something even easier. Sauces aren't my thing apparently. I keep ruining them."

"Okay, then let's try something different. Name something else you love to eat."

Ashley thought a minute. "Lasagna. That sounds really good right now."

"Perfect! And it couldn't be easier. I'll give you the easy recipe. You can always graduate to fancier once you've mastered the kid-friendly version."

"That's me," Ashley said in resignation. "The kid-friendly version."

Pippa swatted her with a towel. "Grab the hamburger meat from the fridge. I think we're down to the last pack so you better nail this one, girlfriend."

Half an hour later, Ashley put her fist in the air as she and Pippa stood back and closed the oven door on a perfect, if somewhat beleaguered, lasagna.

"I can totally do that on my own," Ashley said as Pippa wiped her hands. "I'm so excited! Maybe I'm not a complete lost cause."

Pippa shook her head. "All it takes is a little time and patience. You're going to be a culinary genius in no time."

Ashley threw her arms around her friend and hugged her tight. "Thanks, Pip. I love you, you know. You're the best."

Pippa grinned. "I love you, too, you nut. Now go home and make your lasagna before your husband gets there. Call me tomorrow and let me know how it went. And take that damn pregnancy test. I'll want to know if I'm going to be an aunt!"

Ashley rolled her eyes. She started to walk toward the door when her cell phone beeped, signaling a received text message. She pulled it out and then frowned as she read it.

"What is it, Ash?" Pippa asked.

"There's a problem at the shelter. Molly is upset but she doesn't give any info. I'll hop over on my way home. It's not too out of the way. See you Friday afternoon at Tabitha's."

"Okay, be careful and call me when you get home so I'll know you made it. You know I hate you going down to the shelter by yourself all the time."

"Yes, mother," Ashley replied. "Later, chickie."

With a wave, she disappeared from Pippa's apartment and headed down to catch a cab to the shelter.

It was later than he'd have liked when Devon entered the apartment. His day had been long and full of endless meetings and his ears were still throbbing from the number of people who'd talked to him.

The only person he wanted to see was Ashley, and he was looking forward to seeing what disaster she'd come up with for dinner.

He grinned as he loosened his tie and headed for the kitchen. The past weeks had been hilarious. Oddly, he hadn't minded the sheer number of ruined meals he'd been served. It had become a contest for him to correctly guess what the meal was *supposed* to have been.

He sniffed as he reached the doorway into the kitchen and the delicious aroma of…something…floated into his nostrils. It didn't smell burned. Or even slightly scorched. It smelled like gooey, bubbly cheese and a hint of tomato.

His stomach growled and he scanned the kitchen area for Ashley. He frowned when he realized she was nowhere to be seen. Deciding he'd better check on whatever was for dinner, he hurried to the oven and pulled open the door.

Inside was what looked to be a perfectly put together and perfectly cooked lasagna. He snagged a potholder and then reached inside to take out the casserole dish.

After setting it on the stove, he turned off the oven and then went in search of Ashley. As he neared the bedroom, he heard the low murmur of her voice.

She was standing by the window overlooking the city and she was on her cell phone. He started to detour into his closet to change when he heard a betraying sniff.

He spun around, frowning as he zeroed in on Ashley. Her back was mostly to him though she was angled just enough that he could see her wipe at one cheek.

What the hell?

It took all his restraint not to walk over, take the phone and demand to know who the hell had upset her.

"I'll see what I can do, Molly. We can't let this happen," she said.

She wiped her cheek with the back of her free hand and then hit the button to end the call. Then she turned and saw Devon. Her eyes widened in alarm and then she closed them in dismay.

"Oh, my God, the lasagna!"

She bolted for the door, gone before he could even tell her he'd already taken care of it. He was more concerned with what had made her cry.

"Ash!" he called as he hurried after her.

He caught up to her in the kitchen to find her palming her forehead as she stared at the lasagna.

"I'm sorry," she said. "I just forgot it. If you hadn't come in, it would have burned."

"Hey, it's okay," he said. He walked over and slipped a hand over her shoulder. "It needs to rest a minute anyway. Let me grab some plates and we'll set the table. Then you can tell me what's got you so upset. Who was that on the phone?"

He steered her toward the table, parked her in a chair and then went back to retrieve plates and utensils. After setting the places, he went back for the lasagna and carried the still piping hot dish to the table.

He sat down, picking up a knife to cut into the lasagna while he waited for her to respond. To his horror, her eyes filled with tears and she buried her face in her hands.

He dropped the knife and bit out a curse. Then he scrambled out of his chair and pulled it around so he could scoot up next to Ashley.

"What's wrong?" he demanded. "Did someone upset you?" Obviously someone or something did but he wanted answers. He wasn't a patient man. His inclination was to wade in and fix things. He couldn't do that if he didn't have the story.

"I've had the most awful day," she croaked out. "And I wanted everything to be perfect. I finally learned how to cook that damn lasagna. But then Molly called. I stopped by the shelter and she had terrible news and I don't know what to do. We've been talking about it all evening."

He gently pulled her hands away, wincing at the flood of tears soaking her cheeks.

"Who's Molly?"

She frowned and lifted her gaze to meet his. "Molly from the shelter."

He looked searchingly at her. Clearly this was a person he was supposed to know, but he was drawing a complete blank.

"She's my boss at the shelter."

"Wait a minute. I thought you ran the shelter."

She shook her head impatiently. "I do, mostly, but she's in charge. I mean she runs it but I do most of the legwork and fundraising. She says I have more connections and am the natural choice to go out and pound the pavement for donations."

Devon scowled. It sounded to him as though this Molly person was taking advantage of Ashley. He wasn't certain of the salary that Ashley drew from her position at the shelter. He assumed that her parents still helped her financially since she didn't have a typical nine-to-five job and she'd been living in her own apartment for a while now. He hadn't concerned himself with her finances because he wanted her to be happy and he knew he'd fully support her once they were married. But he sure as hell didn't want her busting her ass in a job where she was being used.

"So what did Molly have to say?" he gently prompted.

"The grant the shelter had is being pulled and without it, we can't continue to stay open. It pays the basics like the utilities, food for the animals and the salary for the vet we have on retainer. We don't raise enough money to stay afloat without the grant."

Her eyes filled with tears again. "If we don't stay open, all the animals will have to be transferred to a city-run shelter and if they aren't adopted out, they'll be euthanized."

Devon sighed and carefully pulled Ashley into his arms. "Surely there's some way to keep the shelter open. Have you talked to your father about sponsoring it?"

She pulled away and shook her head. "You don't understand. Daddy's all business when it comes to stuff like that. He doesn't make emotional decisions. He's more interested in profit and return or it being a cause he sees the value in. He's not much of an animal person."

Ashley's view of her father was clearly wrong. William Copeland had made an emotional decision. A huge emotional decision when he'd opted to go with Tricorp because for whatever reason he'd decided Devon would be the perfect son-in-law and candidate to take over Copeland.

"How long can you continue running as you are now?"

She sniffed. "Two, maybe three weeks. I'm not sure. We're already at maximum capacity but it's hard to say no when a new animal comes in. We just got in a dog and it was so heartbreaking. The poor thing is the sweetest dog ever but he was horribly neglected. I don't understand how people can be so cruel. Would they dump their child out on the street somewhere? A pet isn't any different. They're just as much a family member as a child!"

Unfortunately, there were people who'd think nothing of tossing out their kid, not that Ashley needed to be reminded of that. It would only upset her further.

He smoothed his hand over her cheek and then leaned forward to kiss her forehead. "Why don't you eat something. The lasagna smells wonderful. There's nothing you can do tonight. Maybe a solution will present itself in the morning."

She nodded morosely and he scooted his seat back. He picked the knife back up and cut into the lasagna, spooning out neat squares onto the plates.

"This looks wonderful," he said in a cheerful tone. He wanted her to smile again. She'd been entirely too serious ever since they returned from their honeymoon and he was becoming impatient for her to return to her usual, sunny self.

He handed her a plate and then took his own. When he bit into the gooey cheese and the perfectly al dente noodles, and the savory sauce slid over his tongue, he moaned in pleasure.

"This is awesome, Ash."

She smiled but it didn't quite reach her eyes. There was still deep sadness in those big, blue eyes and it was twisting his gut into a knot.

As good as dinner was, he was anxious to get through it. He had a sudden urge to comfort Ashley and wipe away her pain.

She picked at her food and it was obvious she had no interest in eating, so he hurriedly gulped his down and then collected their plates to dump into the sink. "Come here," he said, holding his hand out to her.

She slid her fingers into his and he pulled her to her feet. He took her into the bedroom, sat her on the edge of the bed and began taking her shoes off.

Crouching between her legs, he slid his hands along the sides of her thighs until his fingers palmed her hips. He held her there, staring intently at her, unable to believe he was about to make her a promise.

The business side of him balked and demanded to know if he'd lost his damn mind. But the side of him that cringed upon witnessing Ashley's distress was urging him on.

"Listen to me," he said, before he could talk himself out of it. "Let me see what I can do, okay? Don't give up hope just yet. We have a few weeks. I may be able to help."

To his surprise she threw her arms around him and hugged him fiercely. It was the first spontaneous show of affection he'd been treated to since before their marriage.

"Oh, Devon, thank you," she whispered fiercely. "You have no idea how much this would mean to me."

"I have an idea," he said wryly. "You love those animals more than you love people."

She nodded solemnly, not in the least bit abashed to admit it. Then she kissed him full on the mouth.

It was like baiting a hungry lion. He didn't wait for her to pull back in regret. Didn't offer her the chance to change her mind. He'd suffered three long weeks wanting her with every breath and knowing she was emotionally out of reach.

If this was his chance to have her back in his bed without a wealth of space between them, he was going to grab the opportunity with both hands.

He kissed her back, his hands going to her face, holding her there as he fed hungrily on her lips. Tentatively her arms circled his neck and she leaned into him with a soft, sweet sigh that tightened every one of his muscles and made him instantly hard.

He had to force himself to exercise some restraint because what he really wanted to do was tear her clothes off, haul her up the bed and make love to her until neither of them could walk.

"You have far too many clothes on," he said, near desperation as he fumbled with the buttons on her blouse. It was expensive. Probably silk. But ah, hell, he'd buy her another one.

The sound of the material rending and the buttons popping and scattering on the floor only spurred his excitement. He fumbled clumsily with the button on her pants and then began pulling to get them off her. She lifted her bottom just enough that he could slide the material down her legs and then there she was, sitting so dainty and beautiful, clad only in her pale, pink lingerie.

She was the most beautiful sight he'd ever seen. Hair tousled just enough to make her look sexy. Her lips swollen from his kiss. Eyes glazed with passion instead of deep sadness. And her skin. So soft, glowing in the lamplight. Curvy in all the right places. Generous breasts, straining at the lace cups, and hips and behind just the right size for his hands to grip.

He stood only long enough to strip out of his clothes. It wasn't practiced or smooth. He felt like a fifteen-year-old getting his first glimpse of a naked woman. If he wasn't careful, he'd be acting just like one, too.

She stared shyly up at him and he nearly groaned. "Baby, you have to stop looking at me like that. I'm holding on to my control by my fingertips and you're not helping."

She smiled then, an adorable, sweet smile that took his breath away. He forgot all about trying to maintain an air of civility. His inner caveman came barreling out, grunting and pounding his chest and muttering unintelligible words.

He swept her into his arms, hauling her back on the bed.

They landed with a soft bounce and he claimed her mouth, wanting to taste her again and again.

"Love the lingerie," he said hoarsely. "I'll love it more when it's off, though."

She wiggled beneath him and he realized she was trying to work out of her straps.

"Oh, no, let me," he breathed.

He pushed himself off her and then maneuvered himself upward so he straddled her body, his knees digging into the mattress on either side of her hips.

Her gaze slid downward to his groin and her eyes darkened. Tentatively she moved her hands slowly toward his straining erection. Color dusted her cheeks and she glanced hastily upward, almost as if she was seeking his permission to touch him.

Hell, he'd give her anything in the world if she'd touch him. He'd buy her twenty damn shelters if that would make her happy. Right now, it would make him delirious if she just wrapped those soft little fingers…

He closed his eyes and groaned as she did exactly what he'd fantasized about. Her touch was gentle. Light and tentative. Like the tips of butterfly wings dancing over his length.

She grew bolder, stroking more firmly, running the length of him with her palm until he was little more than a babbling, incoherent fool. He was supposed to be in control here. She was the innocent. He was the one with more experience. But she literally and figuratively held him in the palm of her hand.

If he didn't put an end to her inquisitive exploration, he'd find release on her belly and he wanted to be inside her more than he wanted to breathe.

Leaning down, her kissed the shallow indention between her breasts and then nuzzled the swell as he reached up to slide the straps over her shoulders.

He loved the way she smelled. It was one thing he missed about the apartment now. Before she had little bowls of potpourri and little scented candles haphazardly arranged through-out. The entire apartment had smelled like…her. Fresh. Vibrant. Like spring sunshine.

Now that she'd gone through in a mad cleaning rush, it was as if her very presence had been expunged.

The cup of her bra slipped over her nipple, exposing the puckered point to his seeking lips. He sucked lightly, enjoying the sensation of her on his tongue. Underneath him, she quivered and her breathing sped up in reaction.

He slipped one hand beneath her back, reaching for the clasp of her bra. Seconds later, it came free and he pulled carefully until it came completely away. Tossing it aside, he eyed the feast before him.

She had beautiful breasts. Just the perfect size. Small and dainty, much like her, but there was just enough plumpness to make a man's mouth water. Her nipples were a succulent pink that just beckoned him to taste. He knew enough about her now to know her breasts were highly sensitive. And her neck. Up high, just below her ear. It was guaranteed to drive her crazy if he nibbled either spot.

Tonight he wanted to taste all of her, though. He wanted her imprinted on his tongue, his senses. He wanted to be able to fall asleep smelling her, the feel of her skin on his.

Palming both breasts, he caressed, rubbed his thumbs across the tips before lowering his head to suck at one and then the other. He nipped lightly, causing the peak to harden even further. Then he slid his mouth down her middle to the softness of her belly, where he licked a damp circle around her navel.

Chill bumps rose and danced their way across her rib cage. She stirred restlessly, murmuring what sounded like a plea for more.

He thumbed the thin lace band of her panties and carefully eased the delicate material over her hips then down her legs and over her feet. Finally, she was completely naked to his avid gaze.

He moved back over her, his head hovering over the soft nest of blond curls between her legs. Then he stroked his hands over her hips and downward. He spread her thighs with firm hands, opening her to his advances.

All that pink, glistening flesh beckoned. He lowered his mouth, pressed his lips to the soft folds and nuzzled softly until she strained upward to meet him.

"Devon," she whispered.

It had been a while since he'd heard her husky sweet voice murmur his name in what was a blend of pleasure and a plea for more. It made him all the more determined that before he was finished, she'd call out his name a dozen more times. She'd find her release with his name on her lips. There would be no doubt in her mind who possessed her.

He licked gently at the tiny nub surrounded by silken folds, enjoying every jitter and shudder that rolled through her body. She was more than ready to take him, but he held back, enjoying his sensual exploration of her most intimate flesh.

Slowly he worked downward until he tasted the very heart of her, stroking with lazy, seductive swipes of his tongue. She began to shake uncontrollably and her thighs tightened around his head. He pressed one last kiss to the mouth of her opening and then moved up her body, positioning himself between her legs.

He found her heat and sank inside her with one powerful thrust. Her chin went up, her eyes closed and her lips tightened in an expression that was almost agonizing.

He kissed the dimple in her chin and then slid his mouth down her neck and to the delicate hollow of her throat. Her pulse beat wildly, jumping against her pale skin, a staccato against his mouth.

Her slender arms went around him, gripping with surprising strength. Her nails dug into his shoulders like kitten claws.

"Put your legs around me," he said. "Just like that, baby. Perfect."

She crossed her heels at the small of his back and arched into each thrust. Her fingers danced their way across his back, sometimes light and then scoring his flesh when he thrust again. She thrust one hand into his hair, pulling forcefully until he realized she was demanding his kiss.

With a light chuckle, he gave in to her silent demand and found her mouth.

Breathless. Sweet. Their tongues worked hotly over each other, dueling, fighting for dominance. She had suddenly become the aggressor and he was lost, unable to deny her anything.

She was wrapped around him, her body urging him on, arching to meet him and finding a perfect rhythm so they moved as one.

Sex had never been this…perfect.

"Are you close?" he choked out.

"Don't stop," she begged.

"Oh hell, I'm not."

He closed his eyes and thrust hard and deep. And then he began working his hips against hers in rapid, urgent movements. She let out a strangled cry and he remembered his vow.

"My name," he said in a breathless pant. "Say my name."

"Devon!"

She came apart in his arms. Around him. Underneath him. He was bathed in liquid heat and he'd never felt anything so damn good in his life.

"Ashley," he whispered. "My Ashley. Mine."

He unraveled at light speed, his release sharp, bewildering and beautiful. His hips were still convulsively moving against her body as he settled down over her, too exhausted and spent to remember his own name. The one he'd demanded she say just moments ago.

He became aware of gentle caresses. Her hands gently stroking over his back. He was probably crushing her but he couldn't bring himself to move. He was inside her. Over her. Completely covering her. She was his.

He knew this moment was significant. Something had changed. But his mind was too numb to sort out the meaning. Never before had he been so undone after making love to a woman.

It was supremely satisfying and scary as hell.

Sixteen

Ashley surveyed the guests as they filtered into the upscale restaurant she'd rented out for the night and felt the ache inside her head bloom more rapidly. She was so nervous she wanted to puke. She wanted everything to be perfect and for things to go off without a hitch.

She'd spent the afternoon at Tabitha's getting hair and makeup done. Her friends had been skeptical of the look she wanted but in the end they hadn't argued and then told her how fabulous she looked.

Ashley wanted…sophisticated. Something that didn't scream flighty, exuberant or impulsive. This was her night to prove to Devon that she was the consummate hostess and perfect complement to him.

Her dress was, as she'd been assured, the perfect little black dress. Ridiculous as it sounded, it was the first such dress that Ashley had owned. For Ashley, wearing black was the equivalent of going to a funeral. It made her feel subdued and swallowed up. Somber. She much preferred brighter, more cheerful colors.

As for her hair, she never paid much attention to it and wore it down more often than not, or she just flipped it up in a clip and went on her way.

But Tabitha had spent an hour fashioning an elegant knot, without a hair out of place. Pippa had grumbled that it made her look forty and not the young twenty-something she was.

Carly had applied light makeup using muted shades and Ashley wore pale lip gloss instead of her usual shiny pink. The perfect accompaniment to the dress and hair were the pearls her grandmother had given her before she passed away two years ago.

She wore a simple strand around her neck and a tiny cluster at her ears.

Ashley thought she looked perfect. She just hoped everyone else did as well and that she could pull off the evening with a smile.

Across the room, the jazz ensemble played. Waiters circled the room, offering hors d'oeuvres and a choice of white and red wines. Two bartenders manned the open bar and in addition to the appetizers offered by the waiters, there was an elegant buffet arranged by the far wall.

Lights were strung in the fake potted trees, making the room look festive and bright. Flickering candles illuminated centerpieces of fresh flowers on each table.

Ashley had fretted endlessly over all the arrangements until she was sure she was spouting menu choices in her sleep. She'd tasted each and every one of the appetizers, wrinkling her nose at some, loving others. She'd made Pippa accompany her, though, because Pippa's tastes were more refined. Ashley was pickier and more apt to turn her nose up at fine cuisine.

Now the moment had arrived and though she kept telling herself that these people didn't matter to her and that they were her father's and Devon's associates, she couldn't shake the paralyzing fear that she'd make some huge mistake and embarrass herself and her husband in front of everyone.

"Ashley, there you are," Pippa said as she made her way through the growing crowd.

"Oh, my God, I'm so glad you're here," Ashley said. "Thank you for coming. I'm a nervous wreck."

Pippa frowned. "Ash, there's no reason for you to be so worked up over this. It's a party. Loosen up. Have some fun. Let your hair down from that godawful bun."

Ashley let out a shaky laugh. "Easy for you to say. You aren't facing a hundred of your husband's closest business associates."

Pippa rolled her eyes. "Come on, let's go get a drink."

Ashley let Pippa lead her over to the bar but when they got there, Ashley ordered water. Pippa raised an eyebrow and Ashley sighed.

"I have a doctor's appointment tomorrow," Ashley whispered. "Don't you dare say a word to anyone, okay? I haven't told anyone I even suspect I might be pregnant. I took one of those damn home pregnancy tests and it was inconclusive but I haven't had my period yet and I'm sure I'm late. So until I know, I don't want to drink anything."

"What time is your appointment?" Pippa demanded.

"Ten in the morning."

"Okay, then here's what's going to happen. Carly, Tabitha and I are going to wait for you at Oscar's and you're going to come straight over for lunch after your appointment so you can tell us the news one way or another."

Ashley nodded. "Okay. I'll need the support regardless of the outcome. I'm kind of undecided about this whole thing."

Pippa blinked in surprise. "You mean you aren't sure you want to be pregnant?"

"Yes. No. Maybe. I don't know," she said miserably.

"Ash, what the hell is going on with you lately? All you've ever wanted is to have children."

Ashley bit her lip in consternation as she saw Devon making his way toward her. "Look, I can't talk about it now. I'll see you at lunch tomorrow after my appointment. And don't breathe a word! I haven't told anyone. Not even Dev."

Pippa looked at her oddly but went silent as Devon approached.

"There you are," Devon said when he got to the two women. He kissed Pippa's cheek in greeting and then tucked Ashley's hand in his. "If you don't mind, Pippa, I'm going to steal my wife for a bit. There are some people I want her to meet."

Pippa leaned over to kiss Ashley's cheek. "See you tomorrow," she whispered softly. "Take care of yourself."

Ashley smiled her thanks and allowed Devon to lead her away. For the next hour, she smiled and quietly listened as Devon introduced her around and discussed things she had no clue about. But she pretended interest and glued herself to his every word, nodding when she thought it was appropriate.

Her headache had worked itself down her neck until it hurt to even move it. Her cheeks ached from the permanent smile and her feet were killing her.

The old Ashley would have kicked off her shoes, pulled her hair down and found someone to talk with about things she understood. Finding or starting conversation was never difficult for her.

The new Ashley was going to survive this night even if it killed her.

Devon seemed appreciative of her effort. He'd told her she looked beautiful and he'd smiled at her often as he took her from group to group. Maybe she had imagined it or maybe it was wishful thinking on her part but she'd sworn she saw pride reflected in those golden eyes of his.

"Stay right here," Devon said as he parked her on the perimeter of the makeshift dance floor. "I have to find your father. He's announcing his retirement tonight."

She nodded and dutifully stood where he'd left her even

though her feet were about to throb right off her legs and her head hurt so bad her vision was fuzzing.

She was careful to wear a smile and not let her discomfort show. Instead she turned her thoughts to the possibility of her being pregnant.

It was true she'd lived the past week in denial. She hadn't entertained the thought. Hadn't wanted to think about it because if she acknowledged the possibility, then she had to consider the reality of her marriage and whether she was ready to bring a child into such uncertainty.

The previous night with Devon had been… Her smile faltered and she quickly recovered. It had been wonderful. But what was it exactly? Sex? Lust? It couldn't be considered making love. Not when he didn't love her.

He'd been exceedingly tender. She was still embarrassed that she'd lost control of her emotions and cried in front of him. It felt manipulative and she still worried that the only reason he'd had sex with her was because she'd been upset and he wanted to comfort her.

He'd left for work this morning before she'd awakened. She'd overslept—another reason she suspected she was pregnant. She was so tired that some days it was all she could do to remain upright. Twice she'd succumbed to the urge to take a nap simply because she would have lapsed into unconsciousness otherwise.

So she hadn't been able to gauge his mood after they had sex. She had no idea if it changed anything or nothing at all. And she hated the uncertainty. Hated not knowing her place in the world or in this relationship.

Devon had been good to her. He'd been kind. But she didn't want good or kind. She didn't want him to feel sorry for her because he'd broken her heart. She wanted his love.

She could feel the anxiety and rush of anger and confusion crawling over her skin, tightening and heating until the sensation reached her cheeks. She curled and uncurled her fingers at her sides, the only outward reaction she'd allow herself as she sought to calm the turmoil wreaking havoc with her mind.

Maybe it was best she didn't dwell on her possible pregnancy. She was already uptight enough without causing herself full-scale panic.

Her father stepped up onto the elevated platform along with Devon. Ashley's mom stood—just as she always had—by her husband's side. But Devon hadn't wanted Ashley there. He'd wanted her here. All the way across the floor from him. She didn't know if there was any significance to that. Her ego was bruised enough to conjure all sorts of pathetic scenarios that spiked the self-pity meter.

For half an hour her father talked, fondly recounting memories, thanking his staff and his family. She smiled faintly when he singled her out and gave her an indulgent, fatherly smile. Then he went on to say that he was stepping down and that Devon would be succeeding him.

There were surprised murmurs from some. Nods from others who obviously suspected such a thing. A few raised eyebrows but most notably, she noticed that people's gazes found her. There were knowing smiles. A few whispers. Nods in her direction.

Her facade was starting to crack. Her smile was beginning to falter. It was as if the world had put two and two together and said, "Aha! Now we get it."

She just wished she did. She stared around, looking for a possible escape path, but she was surrounded by people. All looking at her. Or between her and Devon. Those damn knowing smiles. The smirks of a few women.

It was the worst night of her entire life. Worse than even her wedding night.

Devon found himself surrounded by a throng of people offering their congratulations. He had only taken one step away from William before everyone had descended. Family members. Staff members. Some offering sincere congratulations. Some clearly wary and uncertain. But that was to be expected. Any time change was announced, fear took hold. It was too early to be offering anyone reassurances. Who knew what would happen over the course of the next few months when a changing of the guard would take place and Devon would be at the helm of what would now be the world's most exclusive line of resorts and luxury hotels.

Tonight, though, Devon was celebrating his own victory of sorts. He'd cornered William before the party had begun and told him that Copeland was going to sponsor Ashley's animal shelter.

William had been opposed until Devon threatened to refuse to take William's place in the company. Devon wanted full sponsorship with a yearly budget allocated to the shelter. He was determined that Ashley wouldn't shed another damn tear over her beloved animals.

His father-in-law grumbled and told Devon he was a besotted fool, but he'd given in, telling Devon he'd just do as he damn well wanted when he took over anyway. Which was absolutely true, but they didn't have that much time and he needed William's cooperation to fund the shelter now so it wouldn't have to close.

Now he just needed the right opportunity to tell Ashley the good news. Tonight in bed after the party seemed perfect. Then he'd make love to her until they were both insensible.

He was yanked from his thoughts when he saw Cam pushing his way through the crowd. He grinned when Cam got to him and he slapped his friend on the back. "Well, we did it. Everything. Copeland. The new resort. Oh, ye of little faith."

Cam ignored Devon's ribbing. His expression was grim and his gaze was focused over Devon's shoulder across the room. "What the hell have you done to her, Dev?"

Devon reared his head back. "Excuse me?" He turned, looking for the source of Cam's attention, but all he saw was

Ashley, standing where he'd left her so she wouldn't be swallowed up by the crowd.

Cam shook his head then turned his gaze on Devon. "You don't even see it, do you?"

Devon's eyes narrowed. "What the hell are you talking about?"

Cam made a sound of disgust. "Look at her, Dev."

Again, Devon followed Cam's gaze to Ashley. He studied her a long moment.

"Really look at her, Dev. Take a long, hard look."

Devon battled a surge of irritation. He was about to tell Cam to go to hell when Ashley rubbed her hand over her forehead. The gesture seemed to make abundantly clear what perhaps he'd missed before. Maybe he'd been missing for a while. Or maybe it just took Cam drawing his attention to it.

She was pale, her face drawn. She looked tired and exceedingly fragile. She looked…different. Not at all like the vivacious, sparkling woman he'd married.

He frowned. "She probably has a headache."

"You're a dumbass," Cam said in disgust.

Before Devon could respond, Cam turned on his heel and walked away, leaving Devon baffled by the anger in his friend's voice.

But he didn't have time to figure out Cam's mood or what bug was up his ass. Ashley looked exhausted. Her forehead was creased in pain and she rubbed the back of her neck. He was more convinced than ever that she had one of her headaches.

He pushed his way through the few people standing between him and where William now stood with his son, Eric.

"I'm going to take Ashley home," he said to William. "Please give our apologies to our guests."

William looked up in concern while Eric frowned and immediately sought Ashley out in the crowd.

"Is something wrong?" William asked.

"Everything's fine," Devon said in an effort to calm the older man. "I think she has a headache."

Eric scowled, his blue eyes flashing as he stared holes through Devon. "She seems to be having headaches quite frequently these days."

Devon wasn't going to stick around to argue the point. He nodded at William and then went to collect Ashley.

He found her conversing with two of the people who worked in the Tricorp offices. Or rather *they* were doing all the conversing. Ashley stood smiling and nodding.

"Excuse us please, gentlemen," Devon said smoothly. "I'd like to steal my wife if you don't mind."

The relief on her face made him wince. She was obviously suffering and she'd had to stand here through her father's speech.

His plans for the evening melted away. His primary concern now was getting her home so he could take care of her. The news about the shelter could wait until tomorrow. They'd have dinner together—another of her experimental concoctions, no doubt—and then he'd tell her that her animals were safe.

He drew her in close, noting again the fatigue etched in her features. But more than that, it was as if the light had been doused from her usually expressive eyes.

He experienced a tightening sensation in his chest but he shook it off and focused his attention on her.

"We're leaving."

She looked up in surprise. "But why? The party will be going on for hours yet."

"You're hurting," he said quietly. "Headache?"

A dull flush worked over her features. "It's okay. I'm fine, really. There's no need for you to leave. I can have Pippa take me home or I can just catch a cab."

"The hell I'll have you leave here in a cab," he bit out. "I've done what I needed to do here. The rest is William's night. I won't have you suffering when you could be at home in bed after taking your medication."

Her shoulders sagged a bit and she nodded her acceptance. He put his hand to her back, noting again just how fragile she felt. It wasn't something he could even describe. How did someone feel fragile? But there was an aura of vulnerability that surrounded her like a fog. He wasn't imagining it.

He guided her toward the door, not stopping to acknowledge the people who spoke as they passed.

She was silent the entire way home. She sat in the darkened interior of the car, eyes closed and so still that he was afraid to move for fear of disturbing her.

Once back at their apartment, he helped her undress and pulled back the covers so she could crawl into bed. He leaned down to kiss her brow as he pulled the sheet up to her chin.

"I'll go get your medication and something to drink."

To his surprise, she shook her head. "No," she said in a low voice. "I don't want it. I hate the way it makes me feel. I just need to sleep. I'll be fine in the morning."

He frowned but didn't want to argue with her. She needed to take the damn medicine. She was obviously in a lot of pain. But her eyes were already closed and her soft breathing signaled that she was relaxing or at least trying to.

"All right," he conceded. "But if you aren't better in the morning, you're taking the medicine."

She nodded without opening her eyes. "Promise."

Seventeen

Devon woke Ashley the next morning long enough to ascertain how she was feeling. Ashley assured him she was fine even though her stomach still churned with humiliation and upset. In truth, she just wanted him gone. The last thing she wanted was a set of eyes on her when she was on the verge of cracking.

After he left for work, she shuffled into the shower and stood for a long time underneath the heated spray. Afterward she didn't linger in the bathroom long. She dried her hair because of the cold, but pulled it back into a ponytail. She was too on edge to worry over makeup and just made do with moisturizer.

She was in turns scared and dismayed over the prospect of pregnancy. At times she firmly hoped she wasn't expecting. Others, she held a secret, ridiculous hope that a pregnancy would... What? She laughed helplessly at just how naive she was. Even as she knew a child would in no way fix a doomed relationship, there was a part of her that wondered if Devon would grow to love the mother of his child.

It angered her that she could even entertain such a notion. Why on earth would she settle for a man loving her because she produced his offspring? If he couldn't love her before that, why would she even care what happened after she popped out a kid?

Unrequited love sucked. There were no two ways about it.

If she had it to do all over again, she'd put a definite "wait and see" on any childbearing. Or at least get through the honeymoon without any life-altering surprises.

She ate a light breakfast to settle her stomach. She couldn't be entirely certain if her queasy morning stomach was due to pregnancy or her rather fragile emotional state of late. Or maybe subconsciously she wanted to be pregnant and so had convinced herself of the possibility. Weren't there women who had false pregnancies?

Her nervousness grew as she got into a cab to go to the doctor's office. The only person who knew what she was doing today was Pippa. And well, now Tabitha and Carly would know as well, but she was counting on them to get her through either scenario. Pregnant or not pregnant.

At the clinic, she filled out the paperwork and waited impatiently for the nurse to call her back. After answering a myriad of questions, she was asked to pee in a cup. They drew blood and then she was asked to wait in the reception area.

For twenty of the longest minutes of her life.

She fidgeted. She flipped through a magazine. Finally she got up to pace as she took in the other women in various stages of pregnancy.

Finally the nurse called her back. Ashley hurried toward the door and was escorted to a private sitting area outside one of the exam rooms.

"Well?" she blurted, unable to remain silent a moment longer.

The nurse smiled. "You're pregnant, Mrs. Carter. Judging by when you say your last period was, I'd say maybe six weeks at most. But we'll schedule a sonogram so we can better determine dates."

Ashley's stomach bottomed out. She broke out in a cold sweat and her head began pounding until her vision was blurred.

"Are you all right?" the nurse asked gently.

Ashley swallowed rapidly and nodded. "I'm fine. Just a little shocked. I mean, I suspected but maybe secretly I didn't really believe I was."

The nurse gave her a sympathetic look. "It takes time to adjust. It can be a little overwhelming at first. The important thing is for you to rest, take it easy. Take a little time to let it sink in. We're doing lab work and will check your HCG levels to make sure they're in an appropriate range. If there's any cause for concern, we'll call you. Otherwise, set up an appointment with the receptionist on your way out for your first visit to the doctor. We'll do your sonogram then."

Ashley walked out of the clinic a little—okay, a lot—numb. Again, it wasn't a huge shock. She and Devon hadn't done anything to prevent pregnancy at all. In fact they'd openly embraced the idea—at her instigation—but now she wondered if he was even as open to the idea as he'd let on. How could she be sure he hadn't said whatever was necessary to get her to agree to marry him?

Her mouth turned down in an unhappy frown as she laid her head back against the seat of the cab. She should have asked the nurse what she could take for a headache now that she was pregnant.

But she doubted even the strongest pain medication would help the roar in her ears and the nerves that were balanced on a razor's edge.

The cab dropped her off half a block from the restaurant where she was meeting her friends and she bundled her coat around her as she pushed through people hurrying by. She ducked into the bright eatery and scanned the small seating area for the girls.

In the corner, Pippa stood up and waved. Tabitha and Carly both turned immediately and motioned her over with a flurry of hands.

Ashley nearly ran, desperate to be surrounded by the comfort of her best friends in the world.

"So?" Pippa demanded before Ashley had even had a chance to shrug out of her coat. "Tell us!"

"Are you pregnant?" Tabitha asked.

Ashley flopped into her chair, wrung out from the events of the past weeks. To her utter horror, tears welled in her eyes. It was like knocking the final stone from an already weakened dam.

Her friends stared at her in shock as she dissolved into tears.

"Oh, my God, Ashley, what's wrong? Honey, it's okay, you have plenty of time to get pregnant," Carly soothed.

Tabitha and Pippa wrapped their arms around her from both sides and hugged her fiercely.

"I *am* pregnant," she said on a sob.

That earned her looks of bewilderment all around. Pippa took charge, taking a table napkin and dabbing at Ashley's tears. Her friends sat quietly, soothing and hugging her until finally she got her sobs under control and they diminished to quiet sniffles.

"What the hell is going on?" Pippa asked bluntly. "You look like hell, Ash. And you haven't been yourself. What the hell was that last night with the weird hair and the dress you wouldn't normally get caught dead in?"

"Pippa!" Tabitha scolded. "Can't you see how upset she is?"

"She's right," Carly said in a grim voice. "Besides we're her friends and we love her. We can get away with telling her she looks like crap."

Tabitha sighed. "I think what they're delicately trying to say is you just don't look happy, Ash. We're worried about you."

"Everything's such a mess," Ashley said as tears welled up all over again.

"We've got all day," Pippa said firmly. "Now tell us what's going on with you."

The entire story came spilling out. Every humiliating detail, right down to the disaster of a wedding night and her decision to make Devon fall in love with her.

The three women looked stunned. Then anger fired in Pippa's eyes. "That son of a bitch! I hate him!"

"So do I," Tabitha announced.

"I'd like to kick him right between the legs," Carly muttered.

"You aren't going to stand for this are you?" Pippa demanded.

"I don't know what to do," Ashley said wearily.

Carly grabbed Ashley's hands. "Look at me, honey. You are a beautiful, loving, generous woman. You are perfect just like you are. The only one who needs to change in this relationship is that jerk you married. I'm so pissed right now I can't even see straight. I cannot believe his nerve. I wouldn't change a single thing about you and moreover he doesn't deserve you."

"Amen," Pippa growled. "You need to tell him to take a long walk off the short end of a pier."

Tabitha pulled Ashley into her arms and hugged her tightly. Then she pulled away and gently wiped at the tears on Ashley's cheeks.

"No one who truly loves you should ever want you to change. And no one who wants to change that essential part that makes you *you* deserves a single moment of your time."

"I love you guys," Ashley said brokenly. "You can't even imagine how much I needed you right now."

"I just wish you'd confided in us sooner," Pippa said. "Nobody should have to endure all of what you've endured alone. That's what friends are for. We love you. We would have kicked his sorry ass weeks ago if we'd known."

Ashley cracked a watery smile. "What would I do without you all?"

"Let's not even consider the possibility since you're never going to be without us," Carly said.

"So what are you going to do, hon?" Tabitha asked, her voice full of concern.

Ashley took a deep breath because until right now, at this very moment, she hadn't known. Or maybe she had but had pushed it aside, unwilling to accept the decision that her heart had already made.

"I'm going to tell him I can't do this," she said softly.

"Good for you," Pippa said fiercely.

"You're leaving him?" Carly asked.

Ashley sighed again. "I can't stay with him. I deserve better. I deserve a man who loves me and doesn't want to change me. I'm tired of trying to be someone I'm not. I liked myself the way I was. I don't like this person I've become."

"That a girl," Tabitha said. "And don't you worry even for a minute about the baby. You have us. You know your parents will support you. We'll be with you every step of the way. We'll babysit. We'll go to the doctor with you. We'll even coach you in the delivery room."

"Oh God, stop before you make me cry again," Ashley choked out.

"Do you want one of us to go with you?" Carly asked anxiously. "I don't want you to have to do this alone. Pippa would be awesome to take with you. She can be scary when people mess with someone she loves."

Pippa grinned.

"No," Ashley said, squaring her shoulders. "This is something I have to do on my own. It's time I regained control over my own life and future. I haven't had it since Devon walked into my life."

"I'm so proud of you, Ash," Tabitha said.

"We all are," Pippa said firmly. "If you need a place to stay until you get everything sorted out, any one of us will be more than happy to let you stay as long as you need."

Ashley looked at her three friends and some of the terrible ache in her chest dissolved at the love and loyalty she saw burning in their eyes. She really would be okay. Things would suck for a while, but she was going to be okay. She'd get through this. She had family and friends—the very best of friends—and now she had a child to focus on.

The moment the nurse had confirmed that she had a life growing inside her, Ashley's entire world had changed. Her priorities had shifted and she'd instantly known that she had to do what was best for her and her child.

It had been a powerful moment of realization.

Calm settled over her. Oh, she was still terrified—and heartbroken. That wouldn't change overnight. But now she knew what she had to do and she couldn't escape the inevitability of the path that for once *she* had chosen instead of it choosing her.

Eighteen

Devon was having a hard time concentrating. He'd already blown three phone calls. He'd sent an email to the wrong recipient and replied to another thinking it was someone else. His focus was completely and utterly shot and he couldn't even pinpoint exactly what had him so out of sorts.

He was concerned for Ashley, definitely. He hadn't wanted to leave her that morning, but she'd insisted she was fine and that he should go into work. Still, he had a nagging sensation tugging at his chest that wouldn't go away.

Something just wasn't right.

He picked up his phone to call Ashley's cell but was interrupted by his door opening. He looked up and frowned. His secretary hadn't announced a visitor and he knew damn well he didn't have an appointment now.

To his surprise, Eric Copeland strode into the room, his expression grim. He stopped in front of Devon's desk and planted his palms down on the polished wood.

"What the hell have you done to my sister?"

Devon pushed back and shot up out of his chair. "What the hell are you talking about? I'm getting damn tired of people asking me what I've done to her. If you're asking why we left the party last night, she had a headache and I didn't want her to suffer needlessly. I took her home and put her to bed."

Eric made a sound of disgust. "You may not know this about Ashley but the only time she gets these headaches with any frequency is when she's stressed or unhappy. I find it pretty telling that she returned from her honeymoon after only two days because of a headache and that since then, she's suffered them on a regular basis."

It was a fist to Devon's gut. He sank back into his chair as Eric stood seething over him.

"My sister looks desperately unhappy," Eric continued. "I don't know what the hell is going on, but I don't like what I see. She's changed and something tells me you have everything to do with that."

"Maybe she's finally growing up," Devon said tightly. "Her family hasn't done her any favors by coddling her and shielding her from the world around her."

Eric gave him a look of pure disgust. The cold fury emanating from the younger man slapped Devon squarely in the face. It pricked at Devon and aroused an instinctive need to defend himself. The idea that his marriage was being picked apart by this outsider roused his ire even as a voice in the back of his mind whispered to him to listen.

"Her family loves her just like she is," Eric bit out. "She is cherished and adored by us all. She is appreciated for the beautiful, warm, loving person she is and we'd damn well never try to change her. Anyone that would doesn't *deserve* her."

He spun around and stalked toward the door but then he stopped and turned back to Devon, his lips curled into a snarl. "I don't know what the hell kind of deal you struck with my father but he was wrong. Dead wrong. You weren't the right man for my sister. The right man would know and appreciate what a gift he'd been given. I'm putting you on notice right now. I'm watching you. If Ashley isn't more herself in very short order, I'm coming after you with everything I've got. I hadn't planned to take over the business for my father, but if the choices are having you as a part of the family and making my sister miserable or me sucking it up and taking over myself, I'll do it."

Devon's lips thinned but he acknowledged Eric's ultimatum with a tight nod.

With another dark look, Eric stalked out of the door.

Devon stared out his window in brooding silence after Eric's abrupt departure. Then he stared down at his phone, suddenly afraid to make the call he'd planned just minutes before.

It also occurred to him that she hadn't called him at work in weeks. Not once. No more silly Tinker Bell chimes that amused his coworkers to no end. Not even a mushy text message like she'd done so often before.

He hadn't given it much thought. Things had been so busy after the wedding, with William wanting to move into retirement and the new resort going up, as well as the endless planning sessions for the future.

He'd honestly just forged ahead, hoping that with time, Ashley would get over her initial upset and see that things really hadn't changed that much between them. But a sick feeling settled into his stomach as he realized—truly realized—that everything had changed. And most notably, *she* had changed.

A ping sounded, signaling the intercom, and Devon raised his head irritably. Now his secretary wanted to talk to him? Giving him a heads-up on Eric's arrival would have been nice. But he forgot all about his irritation when he heard what she had to say.

"Mr. Carter, your wife is here to see you."

Adrenaline surged in his veins.

"Send her in," Devon demanded, rising from his seat.

Ashley hadn't ever set foot in his office. Not even when they were dating. She'd called him. Texted him. Sent him sweet emails. But she'd never actually come into his building.

He was striding across the room, fully intending to meet her, when the door opened and she hesitantly walked in. He stopped abruptly, taken aback by the starkness of her features. She was pale, her face was drawn and her eyes were heavy and dull.

An uneasy feeling crept up his spine as she stared back at him.

"Are you busy?" she asked in a soft voice. "Have I come at a bad time?"

"Of course not. Come, have a seat. Would you like something to drink?"

He was suddenly nervous and he hated that feeling. Somehow she'd managed to completely upend his confidence. Much like she'd upended his life.

She shook her head but took a seat on the small sofa in the small sitting area of his office. "I needed to talk to you, Devon."

It was only natural that any man hearing those words from his wife would dread what followed. But coming from Ashley, they seemed so…final.

"All right," he said quietly. He took a seat across from her and studied the tiredness in her eyes. Those rich, vibrant eyes looked…bleak. Without hope. That was what he'd been reaching for. What had eluded him about the way she looked. He caught his breath, suddenly filled with an impending sense of doom. She looked…hopeless, and Ashley was nothing if not eternally optimistic. Had he ever considered such a thing a flaw? He was ashamed to say he had. Now he just wanted it back.

"I'm pregnant," she said baldly. There was no emotion. No

accompanying excitement. No flash of joy. Frankly, he was bewildered by her reaction.

"That's wonderful," he said huskily.

But her expression said it was anything but wonderful. She looked as though she was battling tears.

"I can't do this anymore," she said in a choked voice.

Alarm blistered up his spine and rammed into the base of his skull. "What do you mean?"

She rose and it was all he could do not to tie her to the damn sofa because he had a sudden sense that she was slipping away from him in more ways than one.

Her hands shook but she exerted admirable control over her emotions as she courageously faced him down.

"This marriage. You asked how long it would take to determine whether it would work. The truth is, it was never going to work. It's taken me this long to realize it, but I deserve more. We both do. You deserve to find a woman you can love and that you won't be manipulated into marrying. I deserve a man who adores me and wants to be married to me. Someone who won't try to change me. Someone who accepts me, faults and all. Someone who loves flighty, impulsive Ashley and isn't embarrassed by her."

Tears clouded her eyes and her voice grew thick with emotion. "I thought… I thought I could make you love me, Dev. It was a mistake from the beginning to even try. It was a hard lesson for me to learn but I can't be someone I'm not even if it meant you'd eventually love the new me. Because it wouldn't be Ashley you loved. It would be someone I made up and all the while the real Ashley would be standing there, unloved. I can't do that to myself. And I can't do it to my child. I want to be a woman and a mother I can be proud of first. Before anyone else. I have to love and be at peace with myself, and you know what? I am. I liked me just fine. Was I perfect? No, but I was happy in my own skin and my family and friends accept that person. Someday there'll be a man who'll accept me, too. Until then, I'd rather be alone and true to myself than with someone who places conditions on his ability to love and accept me."

So stunned was he by her declaration that he stood while she walked quietly toward the door. When he realized she'd already slipped by him, he whirled around, calling her name, the lump in his throat so huge that it came out as a mere croak.

But the door had already closed quietly behind her, leaving him standing there so numb…and broken.

Dread consumed him. The realization, the true realization of just what he'd done threatened to completely unravel him. Oh, God. What had he done?

His legs buckled and would no longer sustain his weight. He staggered back onto the couch and slumped forward, burying his face in his hands.

She was right and so very wrong all at the same time. The realization was as clear to him as if someone had hit him over the head with it.

He'd destroyed something infinitely precious and he'd never forgive himself for it. He didn't deserve forgiveness.

Dear God, was this what he'd done to her? She'd come into his office and delivered the news of her pregnancy in a dispassionate fashion, as if she were telling him that she had a dentist appointment or that she was buying new shoes.

Where she'd once jumped up and down and squealed her joy over her cousin's pregnancy and vowed she'd do the same over her own pregnancy, she'd related the news with dead eyes and a broken spirit.

He'd done that to her. No one else. Him and his high-handed, arrogant opinions of how she should act or not act. He'd taken something beautiful and precious and had spit on it.

He'd suffocated a ray of sunshine and sucked every bit of joy and life from her.

Cam was right. Eric was right. Ashley was right. He didn't

deserve her. They'd seen clearly what he'd blithely ignored. In his arrogance, he'd assumed he was right and that he knew what was best for Ashley.

He had tried to change her. And she was bloody perfect just as she was. He hadn't even realized how much he'd missed all the things he professed to be annoyed over. The random calls at work just to say she loved him. The sudden attacks of affection when she'd throw her arms around him. Her exuberance around others.

She hadn't cleaned and organized their apartment because she felt like it. She'd eradicated every hint of her presence there because she'd thought that's what he wanted. She'd tried to become this image of the perfect wife to please him. He himself had thought he wanted her to.

The cooking. The endless trying to kill herself to please him. She'd gone from a vibrant breath of fresh air to a subdued, beaten-down shadow of her former self.

She no longer sparkled. All because he was the biggest ass on the face of the planet.

His pulse ratcheted up and the sick feeling inside him grew as he realized just how long it had been since she'd said she loved him. Since she'd demonstrated any outward affection for him. Since she'd simply smiled and seemed happy.

Tears burned his eyelids. He'd taken something so very beautiful and he'd crushed it. He'd rejected her love. The very gift of herself. He'd arrogantly told her in essence that she wasn't good enough for him. That he knew better. That she wasn't worthy of him.

A low moan escaped him. Not good enough for him? He wasn't good enough to lick her boots.

In clear and startling detail, he realized what perhaps he'd fought from the very first moment he laid eyes on Ashley. He loved her. Not the new, subdued Ashley. He loved the impulsive, passionate, sparkly Ashley. And the very thing he loved the most was what he'd tried to kill.

Rafe and Ryan had nothing on him when it came to being complete and utter bastards to the women who loved them. Devon had surpassed any amount of sin a man committed against someone they claimed to care for.

How could he possibly expect Ashley to forgive him when he'd never be able to forgive himself?

She was pregnant with his child and she was leaving him.

He didn't deserve her. He should let her walk away and find someone who adored her beyond reason and would never ever treat her as he had.

But he couldn't do it. He couldn't be that selfless. *He* adored her beyond reason and if it took the rest of his damn life, he would make it up to her for every wrong he'd done to her.

But first he had to make damn sure she didn't walk out of his life forever.

Nineteen

Ashley tugged the coat tighter around her as she stepped from the cab in front of her parents' apartment building. She had no desire to face them today but she needed to get it over with and she wanted the comfort only her mother could provide.

Devon had already called her cell a dozen times until finally she'd shut it off so it would stop ringing. She'd expected resistance. She was fortunate that she'd caught him off guard enough that she'd been able to get out of his office without much fuss.

But now he would want to talk to her. No doubt he'd give her another lecture about being impulsive and reckless and whatever other adjectives he'd want to assign to her. Then he'd inform her that there was no reason they couldn't have an enjoyable marriage, blah blah blah.

She wanted more than some damn enjoyable marriage. She wanted…awesome. She wanted a man who loved her and celebrated her for who she was. Maybe she'd never have it. But she damn sure wasn't going to settle for someone her father had bribed to marry her.

Which was another reason she'd come to her parents' apartment. Because first she was going to tell her father to stop interfering in her life. Then she wanted a hug from her mother.

She walked into the apartment and took off her coat. "Mom?" she called. "Daddy?"

Gloria Copeland hurried out of the kitchen and smiled her welcome. "Hi, darling. What brings you over today? I wish you'd called. I would have made sure I had tea ready."

"Where's Daddy?" Ashley asked quietly. "I need to talk to him. To you both, actually."

Gloria frowned. "I'll go get him. Is something wrong?"

"You could say that."

Alarm flashed across her mother's face. "Go sit down in the living room. We'll be right there."

Her mom hurried away and Ashley made her way into the spacious living room. Instead of sitting, she went to the fireplace, grateful for the warmth. She was cold on the inside and it felt as though she'd never be warm again.

A moment later, she heard the footsteps of her parents and she turned slowly to face them.

"Ashley, baby, what's wrong?" her father asked sharply.

Both her mother and her father stood a short distance away, impatient and worried. She drew a deep breath and took the plunge. "I've left Devon and I'm pregnant."

Gloria gasped and put her hand to her mouth. William's eyes narrowed and he frowned. "What the hell happened?"

"*You* happened," she said bitterly. "How could you, Daddy? How could you manipulate us both that way?"

Her father threw up his arm in anger and swore. "Damn it, I told him not to tell you."

"He didn't. I found out on my wedding night. Can you possibly imagine how awful it was to find out on my wedding night that my father had all but bought and paid for my husband?"

"William, what on earth is she talking about?" Gloria asked in bewilderment.

It relieved Ashley that at least her mother hadn't known. She wouldn't have been able to handle the double deception.

"He made me part of the Tricorp deal," Ashley said with more calm than she felt. "He forced Devon to marry me or the deal was off the table."

"Damn it, it wasn't like that," her father bit out. "You make it sound like…" He dragged a hand through his hair and closed his eyes wearily. "I just wanted what was best for you. I thought Devon would take care of you. He seemed perfect for you."

"I can take care of myself. I don't need a man to do that. I want a man who wants me for who I am, not because my father waves a lucrative deal in front of him. I want someone who *loves* me."

"Oh darling," Gloria said, finally finding her voice. She rushed forward and enfolded Ashley in her arms. "I'm so very sorry. How awful for you. I had no idea."

Ashley closed her eyes, absorbing the love and acceptance she'd been denied with Devon.

Her mom pulled away and gently stroked a hand through Ashley's hair. "What about you being pregnant? When did you find out?"

"I went to the doctor this morning. Then I went to see Devon."

"Ashley, are you sure about this?" William asked. "I don't believe for a moment that Devon doesn't care about you. Think about what you're doing here, honey. Do you really want to throw everything away because of the way you met? I understand your anger and I take full responsibility. Devon never wanted to deceive you. It was me from the start."

She had to take a moment as she battled tears. "He doesn't like the real me. He thinks I'm flighty, irresponsible, impulsive, too trusting. He wants to change everything about me.

How can you possibly think this is a man I'd want to be with? Is that really who you'd want your daughter married to? What would that teach my daughter if I stay with a man who doesn't value me? How can I expect her to have any self-respect if her mother doesn't?"

Her mother wrapped an arm around her shoulders and glared her husband down with furious eyes. "I can't believe you did this, William. What in the hell were you thinking? You may as well have told your daughter that she doesn't matter. You've pulled some stupid stunts in your time, but this takes the cake."

William sighed. "Ashley, please don't be angry with me. I only wanted the best for you. You're my only daughter and I just wanted to see your future secured. I thought that you and Devon would make a sound match. I was wrong and I'm sorrier than you can possibly imagine."

"You aren't pulling the plug on this deal," Ashley said in a low voice. "You won't punish Devon because he can't love me. If you think he's the best choice for the business then leave me out of it. I'd appreciate being able to make my own choices in the future, free of manipulation."

"I do love you, baby. Please believe that. I never meant to hurt you. Devon tried to tell me but I wouldn't listen. I thought I knew better. He wanted me to tell you everything. He didn't want to deceive you but I tied his hands and for that I'm sorry."

Tears welled in her eyes. Who knew what may have happened if they'd just been left alone?

William hesitantly pulled her into his arms and hugged her tight. "You know you can count on me and your mother to help you with whatever you need, and we'll be here for the baby when it comes."

"I know," she whispered. "And I love you too, Daddy. Just let me make my own mistakes from now on. Your heart was in the right place but now I've fallen in love with a man who can never love the real me."

He slowly released her and her mom pulled her into another hug. "Do you want me to send someone over for your things? You know you can stay here as long as you like."

Ashley shook her head. "I'm going to stay with Pippa for a bit until I figure out what my next step is. I need to find a better job. I have a child to consider now. Devon is right about one thing. It's time to pull my head out of the clouds and grow up."

How long could she possibly avoid him? Devon paced his office, though he hadn't gotten any work done in the three days since Ashley had walked out on him. He hadn't slept. He'd worn out his phone trying to call her. He'd called her friends, her parents, every family member he had a number for.

The reception had been understandably chilly.

He didn't care. He had no pride where Ashley was concerned. He didn't care if he came across as the most pathetic, lovesick guy who'd ever lived. He just wanted her back. He wanted her stuff strewn all over his apartment. He wanted to be able to smell her as soon as he walked into a room. He wanted her to be happy again. He wanted her to smile.

When he wasn't at the office, he was at the apartment, waiting. She hadn't returned. Not even to get her things. All her clothes were still neatly hung in the closet. Her shoes—and there were a ton of shoes—were stacked in boxes on the shelves in his closet. Ashley never went anywhere without her shoes and the fact that she still hadn't returned to the apartment worried him.

If only she'd answer her damn phone. Or one of the hundreds of texts he'd sent her. He just wanted to know she was all right. Worry was eating a hole in his gut. She was pregnant. What if she had another one of her headaches? Who would take care of her?

Eric had said she had frequent headaches when she was unhappy. Devon had made her miserable. Her medication was also at the apartment but surely she couldn't take it now that she was pregnant. He could at least hold her, rub her head, make sure it was cool and dark in the room.

If she would just talk to him. Just give him a chance to tell her how much he loved her. He hadn't realized how much he missed the sunshine she brought into his life until it was gone. Snuffed out over careless, thoughtless words he'd thrown at her.

His cell rang and he scrambled for it, nearly dropping it in his haste to see if it was Ashley calling. Disappointment nearly flattened him when he saw it was Rafael. With a heavy sigh, he put the phone to his ear and muttered a low hello.

"It's a girl!" Rafael said in a jubilant voice. "A beautiful six-pound, twelve-ounce baby girl. She was born an hour ago."

Devon's eyes closed and he swallowed back the bitter disappointment. He was so envious of his friend in this moment that it took everything he had not to throw the phone at the wall.

"Hey man, that's great. How is Bryony doing?"

"Oh she's wonderful. What a trooper. I'm so damn proud of her. She breezed right through labor. I think she was a hell of a lot stronger than I was. I was ready to fall over by the time the little one made her appearance. But boy, is she gorgeous. Looks just like her mama."

Devon could practically hear Rafael beaming through the phone.

"Give her my love," Devon said. "I'm happy for both of you."

"Is everything okay, Dev? You sound like hell if you don't mind me saying."

Devon hesitated. He didn't want to dump on Rafael on the day his daughter was born, but he was at the end of his rope and he could use any advice he could get.

"No," he said bluntly. "Ashley's pregnant and she left me."

"Whoa. Back up a minute. Holy crap. I thought she was

head over heels in love with you? What the hell happened? And damn, you move fast. How far along is she?"

"I have no idea," Devon said in a weary voice. "I don't know anything. She came to my office three days ago, told me she was pregnant and then announced she was leaving me."

"Ouch. That blows, man. I'm sorry to hear it. Is there anything I can do?"

Devon sank into his chair and rotated around so he could watch the falling snow through the window. "Yeah, you can give me some advice. I have to get her back, Rafe."

There was a prolonged silence. Then Rafael blew out his breath. "Okay, well the first question. Do you love her? Or is this more of a 'you're not leaving me because you're pregnant and we should stay married' type thing?"

Devon swore. "I love her. I screwed up but I love her. Not that she'll ever believe me. I messed up so bad with her, Rafe. I make you and Ryan look like choirboys."

"Oh boy. That's bad. That's really, really bad."

"Tell me about it."

"Well, I'll tell you like a certain gentleman once told me when I was standing around with my thumb up my ass wondering how the hell I was going to get Bryony to forgive me. Either go big or go home."

"What the hell is that supposed to mean?"

"It means you need to pull out the big guns. Do something huge. Make a gesture she can't possibly misunderstand. And then get on your knees and grovel. Trust me. The first time on your knees sucks, but if she takes you back, you'll spend the rest of your life on them anyway so better get used to it now."

"If she'll take me back, I'll gladly stay on them," Devon muttered.

"It pains me that I can't even give you hell about falling hard like the rest of us poor schmucks you liked to rag on. You're too pathetic to pick on right now."

"Gee thanks," Devon said dryly. "Don't you have a daughter to go take care of? She probably needs a diaper change or something."

"She's sleeping with her mama, but yeah, I'm going to get back to my family. It's the best feeling in the whole world, Dev. Get your ass out there and get your family back where they belong."

"I will. And thanks, Rafe."

"Hey, no problem, man. Anytime."

Devon slid the phone back into his pocket and pondered his friend's advice. Go big or go home. Pretty solid advice. Now he just had to figure out how big to go. There was absolutely nothing he wouldn't do to convince Ashley to give him another chance.

Twenty

Ashley sat on Pippa's couch, curled underneath a blanket as she sipped hot tea and watched it snow. It had snowed for the last two days, leaving a heavy blanket over the city. She longed for the comfort of her own apartment...or rather Devon's apartment. She bleakly considered that it had never really been her home. But she missed it all the same. Nights like tonight she and Devon would have snuggled in front of the fire and watched a movie.

"Hey, chickie," Pippa said as she settled down the couch from Ash with a bounce. "How are you feeling? Nausea still a problem?"

It was probably the pregnancy hormones—that was what she was blaming anyway—but she got positively weepy over how protective and caring Pippa had been ever since Ashley had moved in. Or sort of moved in, since Ashley hadn't yet worked up the nerve to get her things from Devon's apartment. Instead she'd been borrowing clothes from Pippa. But soon—as in tomorrow—she was going to have to brave going.

"Yes and no. I honestly don't know if it's the pregnancy or the fact I'm upset. I've been so queasy and nothing sounds good. Even my favorite foods have suddenly lost their appeal."

"I'm sure neither is helping," Pippa said dryly. She hesitated a moment as if deciding whether or not to say what was obviously on her mind. But Pippa wasn't one to hold back. "Have you talked to Devon yet, Ash?"

Ashley put her cup down and sighed. "No. I'm a horrible coward."

"No, you aren't," Pippa said fiercely. "It took guts to go to his office and lay it out to him like you did. I'm so freaking proud of you. I so want to be you when I grow up."

Ashley's eyes got all watery again. "Oh my God. I've got to stop this," she said, sniffling back the tears. "Pippa, you're the most put-together person I know. You've got it all. You're smart. You can cook like a dream. You're gorgeous. And you're the best friend I could possibly hope for."

"And strangely I'm still single," Pippa drawled.

Ashley giggled. "Only because you're a picky bitch, as you should be. I could use some lessons from you."

Pippa shifted forward on the couch, her expression suddenly serious. "Ashley, you have no idea how truly special you are. When the rest of us were struggling to find ourselves, sleeping around and experimenting with all the wrong guys, you were so calm and centered. You knew exactly who you were and what you wanted. You've always known who you were. You valued yourself and you refused to settle for less. Just because Devon turned out to be a prick who tried to change you doesn't mean you did anything wrong. You may have lost your way for a very short time, but ultimately you didn't let him change you."

Ashley smiled but inside she wondered if Pippa was right. Devon had changed her. Irrevocably. No matter that she'd resisted and refused to become someone she didn't like, she'd never truly be who she was before Devon entered her life.

But maybe that was what life was all about. People and circumstances changed you. It was what you did with that change that mattered.

The door buzzer sounded and Pippa made a face. "I swear if that's another salesman I'm going to wet down my steps so they'll freeze and anyone coming up will bust their ass. We've had two already this week."

"Are you expecting a delivery? Maybe it's your groceries."

Pippa grew thoughtful. "No, I'm pretty sure I arranged it for tomorrow. But maybe you're right. I'll be right back."

"You sit," Ashley said as she pushed the blanket back. "You've been on your feet all morning. I've done nothing but sit around and feel sorry for myself."

Pippa rolled her eyes but flopped back on the couch as Ashley padded toward the door. Ashley grinned as she imagined Pippa watering down her steps so they'd become icy. It was something she'd totally do.

She opened the door to the street-level apartment and blinked in shock to see Devon standing on the stoop, snow landing on his hair and wetting it. He wore a coat but had no scarf or cap, and he looked like he hadn't slept in a week.

"Hello, Ash," he said in a quiet, determined voice.

She gripped the door until her fingers went numb. "Uh, hi. What are you doing here?"

He laughed. It was a dry, brittle sound that in no way conveyed true amusement. "I haven't seen my wife in a week. She won't return my phone calls or texts. I have no idea if she's okay or where she's staying and she asks me what I'm doing here when I finally track her down."

She swallowed nervously but she held her ground. It was mean-spirited to make him stand out in the cold, but she didn't want him to come in.

"I was going to come by tomorrow to pick up my things," she said in a low voice that barely managed to hide the tremble. "If that's all right with you."

"No, it's not all right with me," he bit out.

Her eyes widened and she took a step back at the vehemence in his voice.

"Can we go somewhere and talk, Ash?"

She shook her head automatically. "I don't think that's a good idea."

His lips formed a grim line. "You don't think it's a good idea. You're pregnant with my child. We're married. We've only been married a short time. And you don't think we have anything to talk about?"

She closed her eyes and put a hand to her forehead in an automatic gesture.

"Ash? Is everything okay?" Pippa called. Then she came up behind Ashley. "Who is it?"

Ashley turned. "It's okay, Pip. It's Devon."

Pippa's expression darkened, but Ashley held up her hand. Pippa reluctantly turned to go back to the living room but she called back in a low voice, "I'll be right here if you need me."

Ashley returned her attention to Devon. "I know we need to talk. I just don't think I'm up to it right now. This has been hard for me, Dev. I don't expect you to believe that, but this isn't easy."

His expression softened and he took a step forward, snow dusting off his hair as he moved. "I know it's not, baby. Please. There's so much I need to say to you. There are things I need to show you. But I can't do that if you won't talk to me. Give me this afternoon. Please. If you still don't want anything to do with me, I'll take you over to the apartment myself and I'll help you pack your things."

She stared back at him, utterly befuddled by the pleading in his voice. He almost looked as though he were holding his breath. And his eyes. They looked…bleak.

"I—I need to get my coat," she said lamely.

The relief that poured over his face was stunning. His eyes

lightened and he immediately straightened, hope flashing in those golden depths.

"And shoes," he said. "I brought some from the apartment. I wasn't sure you had any you loved here."

She gaped at him. "You brought my shoes?"

He shifted uncomfortably. "Six pairs. They're in the trunk of the car. I chose those I thought would be warm and would protect your feet from getting wet in the snow."

Something loosened in her heart and began to slowly unwind.

"That would be great," she said softly. "Let me go get my coat and my cap. If you brought a pair of boots, that would be perfect."

"I'll be right back. Wait here. I don't want you falling on the ice," he said.

He turned and sprinted back toward the street, where his car was parked. She stood there a moment, staring in bemusement as he popped the trunk and bent over to rummage in the boxes.

He rarely drove his own car. She'd only seen the vehicle once. They always used his car service or hailed cabs.

Realizing she was still standing in the wide open doorway, allowing the bitter chill inside, she hastily withdrew into the apartment and shut the door.

She hurried back into the living room, grabbed a brush from the end table and began pulling it through her hair in short, rapid strokes.

"Ash? What's going on?" Pippa asked cautiously.

Ashley stopped and frowned. "I'm not altogether certain. Devon wants to talk. Asked if I'd give him the afternoon and then he'd take me to the apartment and help me pack if that's what I wanted. He's acting…weird."

Pippa snorted. "Of course he is. You dumped him after telling him you were pregnant with his baby. That has a way of altering your priorities."

"I guess I'll go…talk," Ashley said as she put the brush aside.

"Call me later," Pippa said. "I'll want a full report."

Ashley blew Pippa a kiss and went to the closet to retrieve her coat and scarf. She pulled on a cap and tucked her hair carefully underneath before heading back to the door.

When she opened it, Devon was standing there holding a pair of fur-lined boots. When she would have reached for them, he bent over and said, "Here, let me."

She put a hand on his shoulder to balance herself and stood on one foot while he pulled her boot on the other. After he zipped it up, she switched feet and he put the other one on for her.

When he was done, he straightened to his full height and then took her hand to help her down the steps. He walked her to the car and settled her into the passenger seat.

"Where are we going?" she asked as he pulled away into traffic.

"You'll see."

She wrinkled her nose and sighed. He slid his hand over the center console and tangled his fingers with hers.

"Trust me, Ash. I know it's a big thing to ask and I totally don't have the right to ask it of you, but trust me just this once."

The utter sincerity in his voice swayed her as nothing else could. There was raw vulnerability echoed in his every word and expression. He looked as terrible as she felt, almost as if he'd suffered as much as she had.

It didn't make sense to her. She had no doubt that he wasn't exactly celebrating her departure from the marriage, but with the deal still intact, he was getting precisely what he wanted without the unnecessary burden of a wife.

When they pulled up outside the shelter, Ashley sat there, bewildered. "Why are we here, Dev?"

Devon opened his door, walked around to hers and held out his hand. "Come on. There's something I want you to see."

She allowed him to help her out of the car and they hurried toward the entrance of the older building. As soon as they ducked inside, the sounds and smells of the animals filled her senses. Her heart softened when she saw Harry the cat sound asleep on the reception desk. He was their unofficial mascot and the children who often filtered through the shelter in search of a pet loved to pet him as much as he loved being petted.

To her further surprise, Devon ushered her past the reception area and through the hallway lined with cages. He'd never been here before. How could he possibly know where he was going?

He stopped outside the larger room they used for animal orientation when they'd put pet and new owner together for a period of adjustment before the animal was released to his new home.

He gave her a quick, nervous smile and then pushed the door open. Inside, Molly and the other shelter volunteers stood beaming in a line, and when Devon and Ashley walked fully through the entrance, they let out a loud cheer.

"What's going on?" Ashley asked in bewilderment.

"Say hello to your new staff," he said. "You are now the acting director of the Copeland Animal Shelter."

Ashley's eyes went wide as she stared at Molly and then at the other grinning volunteers. Then she glanced back at Devon. "I don't understand. We aren't closing?"

Molly rushed forward and threw her arms around Ashley. "No, we aren't closing! Thanks to your husband. He gave us the funding we needed to stay running. Not only can we stay open, but we also have the money for improvements and for marketing so we can heighten awareness for the animals we need homes for."

She disentangled herself from Molly's embrace and then turned back to Devon. "You did this for me?"

"I did it before you left," he said gruffly. "I talked to your father about it the night of the party. I threatened to refuse to take his position if he didn't agree to fund the shelter."

Her mouth fell open in shock. She wanted to throw her arms around him so badly, but she knew it wouldn't be what he wanted. But he looked so nervous, as if he worried she wouldn't appreciate what he'd done. How could she not?

"I know how much the animals mean to you, Ash."

Tears blurred her vision and her heart ached. She loved him so much. "Thank you," she whispered. "I can never thank you enough for this. It means the world to me."

"You mean the world to me," he said softly.

Her eyes widened and her heart thumped so hard against her chest that she put a hand over her breast to steady herself.

But before she could question him, he turned to the others and said, "As much as we'd love to stay and celebrate with you, I have to take Ashley one more place."

After saying their goodbyes, Devon ushered Ashley out to the car again. She sat in her seat, bemused and a little hopeful, but for what she wasn't sure. Something was different about Devon. Something that went deeper than simple regret or guilt.

"What did you mean, Dev?" she asked softly as they drove away. "Back there when you said I meant the world to you?"

His hands tightened around the steering wheel and his jaw worked up and down.

"Exactly what I said, Ash. There is so much I need to say to you, but I'm asking you to be patient with me. This isn't a conversation I want to have in a car when I'm driving and I can't look at you or touch you. So I'm asking you to give me a little while. There's a place I want to take you and then I want us to talk and I want you to listen to everything I have to say."

Her mouth went dry at the intensity in his voice. He was tense. Almost as if he feared she'd refuse and demand he take her back. Wanting in some way to alleviate his obvious stress, she reached over to lay her hand on his leg.

"Okay, Dev. I'll listen."

Twenty-One

Devon continuously had to ease up on the accelerator as he headed out of the city. He was impatient and time was running out for him, but the roads were slick and the very last thing he wanted to do was endanger his wife and child.

His wife and child.

The words and the image were powerful. *His* wife and child. The woman he loved and had hurt so terribly. A child resting inside her womb. Their creation. His family. Something that belonged solely to him.

What would he do if he wasn't granted a second chance to make amends?

He couldn't—wouldn't—focus on that possibility. To do so would drive him insane. It was up to him to make her forgive him or at least agree to give him one more chance to make it all right.

She was so beautiful, but there was an aura of sadness that surrounded her. It was as if a light had been extinguished or a black cloud had crawled across the sun and clung stubbornly as the storms rolled in.

He wanted her to smile again. He wanted her to be happy. But more than anything he wanted to be *why* she was happy. He wanted her to be happy with *him*.

The trip to Greenwich, Connecticut, took longer than he'd like. The drive was silent and tense. They both seemed nervous and ill at ease. By the time he turned onto road that would wind around to the front of the sprawling home he wanted Ashley to see, they only had an hour of daylight left.

He pulled to the curb just before the bend in the private lane and shut the engine off. Beside him Ashley's brow furrowed in obvious confusion.

He walked around to her side of the car and opened the door. He pulled her out, carefully arranged her scarf and cap so she'd be warm and then took her hand and tugged her onto the road.

Snow drifted in the ditches and spread out over the landscape, a pristine covering of sheer white. It reminded him of her. Magical, almost like a fairy tale.

He'd once told her that life wasn't a fairy tale, but damn it, she was going to have one. Starting right now.

"It's beautiful here," she said breathlessly.

Enchantment filled her eyes as she stared out over the rolling hills. Her face had softened into a dreamy smile and he felt a stirring in his heart. This was how he wanted her to look every day. Happy. Sparkling. So damn beautiful she made him ache to his bones.

He pulled her up short just as they reached the sharp bend in the road. He kept hold of her hand and pulled her to face him, his heart pounding damn near out of his chest.

Their breaths came out in visible puffs. Snowflakes began to fall again, spiraling lazily down, some sticking in her hair, some melting and absorbed by the splash of sun in the barren white of winter.

"Ash."

It came out as a croak and he cleared his throat, prepared to fight with everything he had to keep the woman he loved.

She cocked her head to the side and sent him an inquisitive glance.

"Yes, Devon?"

Her voice was sweet and clear in the silence that had settled over the area. Only the distant crack of a tree limb disturbed the calm.

He hated that he stood here, tongue-tied, unable to form a single damn word, his heart in knots. There was so much to say he simply didn't know where to start. Finally his frustration got the better of him.

"Damn it, I love you. I'm standing here trying my best to come up with the words to everything I have to say and all I can think, all that weighs on my mind, is that I love you so damn much and I can't live without you. Don't make me live without you, Ash."

Her expressive eyes widened in shock. Her mouth popped open and then snapped shut again. She shook her head wordlessly as if she had no idea what to say to his sudden declaration.

Then hurt entered her eyes, crushing him with the weight of her pain. Her gaze held the memory of all the terrible things he'd said and done. He couldn't breathe for wanting to drop to his knees and beg her forgiveness.

"Then why?" she choked out. "If you love me, really love *me*, then why would you want me to change? You don't love the real me, Dev. You love the image you have in your head of how the perfect wife should be. Well, I've got news for you. I'm not her. I'll never be her."

She was glorious in her anger. Her eyes came to life and sparked darts of fire. Color suffused her cheeks and her lips pinched together as she glared holes through him.

"Trying to change you was the biggest mistake I've ever

made or will make in my life. God, Ash, when I think of how stupid I was I just want to punch something."

He put his hands on her shoulders and stared intently into her eyes. "You are the most beautiful, precious thing that has ever barreled into my life. I didn't see it because I didn't want to see it. When your father suggested the marriage, I was pissed and I resented his interference."

"That makes two of us," Ashley muttered.

"But the thing was, I didn't mind the idea of marrying you. Even when I told myself that I was angry, there was a part of me that didn't at all mind the idea of marriage and settling down. Starting a family. With you.

"I was torn and I was an immature jerk acting out because I felt like marriage was being forced on me instead of when I was ready for it. Even though I didn't mind the outcome, I was resentful on principle. Which is stupid. And then on our honeymoon night I was gutted when you found out because the last thing I ever wanted was to hurt you. I felt cornered. Here you were demanding to know how I felt and my feelings weren't even something I could admit to myself. So I answered out of frustration and I said all that crap about how we could have a good marriage anyway because in my mind I wanted things to go on as they had before but without the vulnerability I felt every time the question of love popped up."

He sighed and released her shoulders, stepping back for a moment as he stared off into the distance. "Your entire family baffles me, Ash. I don't always know how to take them. I'm not used to having this big, huge loving family where dysfunction isn't a way of life. Your dad was always calling me 'son,' and he wanted me to marry you, and all I could think was that I don't fit here. I'm not good enough. I wasn't worthy. And that made me angry because after I left home, I was determined never to feel inferior again."

She was still staring at him like she had no idea what to say.

"You scared me, Ash. You barged into my life, turned it

upside down with your take-no-prisoners attitude. You were the one thing I couldn't control, couldn't put in its proper place, and I tried. Oh, I tried. I was determined that you weren't going to be a threat to me. I hated how rattled you made me feel and how I went soft every time you entered a room. I thought somehow if I covered you up that you wouldn't shine quite so brightly and that maybe I could better control my reaction to you or at least I wouldn't feel like my guts had been ripped out every time you smiled at me."

"Wow," she whispered. "I have no idea what to say, Devon. I had no idea I affected you so badly."

He shook his head. "Oh, God, no, Ash. Don't you see? You are the very best part of me. It wasn't you. It was never you. It was me."

No longer able to keep his hands from her, he stepped forward again and pulled her close so that their faces were almost touching and he could feel the warmth of her breath on his throat.

"You are the very best part of my world. You are my life. I cannot imagine an existence without you. I don't want to. What I did was unforgivable. It was the result of ignorance and stupidity of the highest magnitude. I can only tell you that if you let me back into your life that you'll never have cause to doubt me again. I'll spend every single day proving to you that you are the absolute center of my universe. You wanted a man who adored you beyond reason. Someone who accepted you for the beautiful, amazing woman that you are. Look no further, Ash. He's standing in front of you with his heart in his hands. No man will ever love you more than I do. It isn't possible."

Her eyes were huge in her face. Brilliantly blue, sparkling like the most exquisite gems. Her cheeks were brushed with rose and her throat worked up and down as she swallowed. Tears glittered like diamonds, clung to her lashes but didn't fall. He wouldn't let them this time. If she never cried again, it would be too soon for him.

When she opened her mouth to speak, he simply put his lips to hers and kissed her long and sweet. He was shaking as he crushed her to him. For the last week he'd despaired of ever getting this close to her again and now she was warm and soft in his arms and so very precious.

"Don't say anything yet," he whispered. "There's still something I want to show you."

He pulled away, gathered her hand in his and pulled her along the road. She walked with him haltingly, as if she were in a solid daze. As they rounded the sharp bend, she stopped in her tracks and gazed in wonder at the sprawling house on top of the hill.

In the distance, dogs barked and she turned her head, her brow furrowing as she searched for the source of the noise. And then over the hill, two dogs bounded, making a beeline for Ashley.

"Mac! Paulina!"

She dropped to her knees just as the dogs launched themselves at her, licking and barking excitedly as Ashley tried to hug them.

"Oh my God, where did you come from?" she whispered.

Devon glanced up the hill to see Cam standing there and Devon waved his thanks before turning his attention back to Ashley and the sheer joy in her eyes.

One of the dogs knocked her over and she went laughing to the ground, snow sticking to her coat as she lay gasping for air.

Devon carefully picked her back up and fended off the animals as they tried their best to lick her to death.

"They come with the house," he said solemnly. "Since you're the new director of the shelter, it only stood to reason that some of the animals find their home here."

She brushed herself off and then stared back at the house again. "Is it… Is it yours?" she asked hesitantly.

"No, it's yours."

She turned to stare at him, excitement flashing like fireworks in her eyes. "You mean it? Really? How? Why? When?"

He chuckled indulgently and then because he couldn't help himself, he pulled her into his arms so that he was wrapped solidly around her. They stood staring up at the house as her heart beat solidly against his chest.

"You wanted a home where you could envision children playing and you could be surrounded by your animals. I ignored that because I wasn't ready for anything in my life to change. My apartment was comfortable and I saw no reason we couldn't live there. But the simple truth is, I want to live wherever you are and wherever makes you happy. A good friend told me to go big or go home. I'm going big, Ash. Because I'll do any damn thing in the world to have you back in my life."

"Oh my," she whispered. "I don't know what to say, Dev. You're saying everything I've ever dreamed you saying. I want to believe you. I want it more than anything. But I'm afraid."

He tugged her even closer and rested his forehead on hers. "I love you, Ash. That isn't going to change. I was an ass. I just need a chance to prove to you that you're safe with me and a chance to show you that I'll love and cherish you every day for the rest of your life. You and our children."

"You're okay with the baby?"

"If I was any more okay, I'd burst wide open. I can't think of anything better than this house with you and our son or daughter plus the half dozen or so more we'll fill it with."

"Oh I love that," she said, her eyes lighting up like a thousand suns.

He stroked a strand of her hair away from her face and then he kissed her softly, lingering over her lips as he savored being this close to her again.

"I love you," he said. "I love you more than I ever thought it possible to love another person. I won't lie. It scares the hell out of me, but being without you scares me even more. Give us a chance, Ash. I'll show you that you can trust me again. I swear it."

She wrapped her arms around his shoulders and moved her

forehead down to nestle in the side of his neck. "I love you too, Dev. So very much. You have the power to hurt me like no one else. But you also have the power to make me happier than anyone else in the world."

He inhaled the scent of her hair and hugged her more fiercely. "I want you to be happy. I want you to smile again. I'll do anything to make that happen."

She pulled away and smiled mischievously up at him as the dogs danced around at their heels. "Then why don't you show me my new house?"

He relaxed, going suddenly weak as relief tore through him with the force of a storm. Oh, God. He couldn't even find his tongue because he feared if he tried to speak right now, he'd lose what was left of his composure.

It was several long seconds before he could pull himself together enough to speak.

"The sale isn't final yet but the house has been empty for six months and I've gotten the keys. I'll be happy to show you around."

She threaded her arm through his as they started up the rest of the driveway leading to the house.

"Can't you just imagine our children playing here?" she said wistfully. "And the dogs running after them?"

He pulled his arm loose and wrapped it tightly around her as he leaned down to kiss her temple.

"Know what the best part will be?"

She glanced up at him in question.

"Seeing their mother's smile light up their father's world each and every day of his life."

* * * * *

"If I tried to kiss you right now, you wouldn't stop me."

The thought of Coop leaning over the console and pressing his lips to hers made her heart flutter and her stomach bottom out. But she squared her shoulders and said, "If you tried to kiss me, I'd deck you."

He threw his head back and laughed.

"You don't think I would do it?"

"No, you probably would, just to prove how tough you are. Then you would give in and let me kiss you anyway."

"The depth of your arrogance is truly remarkable."

"It's one of my most charming qualities," he said, but his grin said that he was definitely teasing her this time.

Maybe the confidence was a smoke screen, or this was his way of testing the waters. Maybe he really liked her, but being so used to women throwing themselves at him, the possibility of being rejected scared him.

Weirdly enough, the idea that under the tough-guy exterior there could be a vulnerable man made him that much more appealing.

Dear Reader,

I have a confession to make. I don't like sports.

Yes, you read that right. I don't like them. Baseball, football, hockey, soccer…they all bore me to tears. I don't even watch the Olympics. Which is why it makes no sense that I *love* romance novels with sports-playing heroes, and why I decided, after twenty-eight books, to finally write one myself. And frankly, if Cooper Landon could climb off the page and actually play hockey, I'd probably learn to love the game. Because let's face it, what could be sexier or more heartwarming than a big, tough—and let's not forget clueless—guy falling for a pair of adorable infant twin girls?

That's probably why Sierra Evans, who's not so crazy about sports herself, or men like Coop, can't resist him. Especially when the twins are her own daughters—a fact that she left out when she took the position as their nanny. But the closer she and Coop become, she knows that eventually the truth will have to come out. Still there are some secrets, devastating ones, that must stay hidden away forever or it could mean never seeing her daughters again.

Until next time,

Michelle

THE NANNY
BOMBSHELL

BY
MICHELLE CELMER

Published in Great Britain 2012
by Mills & Boon, an imprint of Harlequin (UK) Limited,
Eton House, 18-24 Paradise Road, Richmond, Surrey TW9 1SR

© Michelle Celmer 2012

ISBN: 978 0 263 89199 7
ebook ISBN: 978 1 408 97195 6

51-0812

Harlequin (UK) policy is to use papers that are natural, renewable and
recyclable products and made from wood grown in sustainable forests. The
logging and manufacturing processes conform to the legal environmental
regulations of the country of origin.

Printed and bound in Spain
by Blackprint CPI, Barcelona

Bestselling author **Michelle Celmer** lives in southeastern Michigan with her husband, their three children, two dogs and two cats. When she's not writing or busy being a mom, you can find her in the garden or curled up with a romance novel. And if you twist her arm really hard, you can usually persuade her into a day of power shopping.

Michelle loves to hear from readers. Visit her website, www.michellecelmer.com, or write to her at PO Box 300, Clawson, MI 48017, USA.

To my granddaughter,
Aubrey Helen Ann

One

This was not good.

As a former defensive center, MVP and team captain for the New York Scorpions, Cooper Landon was one of the city's most beloved sports heroes. His hockey career had never been anything but an asset.

Until today.

He looked out the conference room window in the Manhattan office of his attorney, where he had been parked for the past ninety minutes, hands wedged in the pockets of his jeans, watching the late afternoon traffic crawl along Park Avenue. The early June sun reflected with a blinding intensity off the windows of the building across the street and the sidewalks were clogged with people going about their daily routine. Businessmen catching cabs, mothers pushing strollers. Three weeks ago he'd been one of them, walking through life oblivious to how quickly his world could be turned completely upside down.

One senseless accident had robbed him of the only family he had. Now his brother, Ash, and sister-in-law, Susan, were dead, and his twin infant nieces were orphans.

He clenched his fists, fighting back the anger and injustice of it, when what he wanted to do was slam them through the tinted glass.

He still had his nieces, he reminded himself. Though they had been adopted, Ash and Susan couldn't have loved them more if they were their own flesh and blood. Now they were Coop's responsibility, and he was determined to do right by them, give them the sort of life his brother wanted them to have. He owed Ash.

"So, what did you think of that last one?" Ben Hearst, his attorney, asked him. He sat at the conference table sorting through the applications and taking notes on the nanny candidates they had seen that afternoon.

Coop turned to him, unable to mask his frustration. "I wouldn't trust her to watch a hamster."

Like the three other women they had interviewed that day, the latest applicant had been more interested in his hockey career than talking about the twins. He'd met her type a million times before. In her short skirt and low-cut blouse, she was looking to land herself a famous husband. Though in the past he would have enjoyed the attention and, yeah, he probably would have taken advantage of it, now he found it annoying. He wasn't seen as the guardian of two precious girls who lost their parents, but as a piece of meat. He'd lost his brother two weeks ago and not a single nanny candidate had thought to offer their condolences.

After two days and a dozen equally unproductive interviews, he was beginning to think he would never find the right nanny.

His housekeeper, who had been grudgingly helping him with the twins and was about twenty years past her child-rearing prime, had threatened to quit if he didn't find someone else to care for them.

"I'm really sorry," Ben said. "I guess we should have anticipated this happening."

Maybe Coop should have taken Ben's advice and used a service. He just didn't feel that a bunch of strangers would be qualified to choose the person who would be best to care for the twins.

"I think you're going to like this next one," Ben told him.

"Is she qualified?"

"Overqualified, actually." He handed Coop the file. "You could say that I was saving the best for last."

Sierra Evans, twenty-six. She had graduated from college with a degree in nursing, and it listed her current occupation as a pediatric nurse. Coop blinked, then looked at Ben. "Is this right?"

He smiled and nodded. "I was surprised, too."

She was single and childless with a clean record. She didn't have so much as a parking ticket. On paper she looked perfect. Although in his experience, if something seemed too good to be true, it usually was. "What's the catch?"

Ben shrugged. "Maybe there isn't one. She's waiting in the lobby. You ready to meet her?"

"Let's do it," he said, feeling hopeful for the first time since this whole mess started. Maybe this one would be as good as she sounded.

Using the intercom, Ben asked the receptionist, "Would you send Miss Evans in please?"

A minute later the door opened and a woman walked in. Immediately Coop could see that she was different from the others. She was dressed in scrubs—dark-blue pants and a white top with Sesame Street characters all over it—and comfortable-looking shoes. Not typical attire for a job interview but a decided improvement over the clingy, revealing choices of her predecessors. She was average height, average build...very unremarkable. But her face, that was anything but average.

Her eyes were so dark brown they looked black and a slight tilt in the corners gave her an Asian appearance. Her mouth was wide, lips full and sensual, and though she didn't wear a stitch of makeup, she didn't need any. Her black hair was long and glossy and pulled back in a slightly lopsided ponytail.

One thing was clear. This woman was no groupie.

"Miss Evans," Ben said, rising to shake her hand. "I'm Ben Hearst, and this is Cooper Landon."

Coop gave her a nod but stayed put in his place by the window.

"I apologize for the scrubs," she said in a voice that was on the husky side. "I came straight from work."

"It's not a problem," Ben assured her, gesturing to a chair. "Please, have a seat."

She sat, placing her purse—a nondesigner bag that had seen better days—on the table beside her and folded her hands in her lap. Coop stood silently observing as Ben launched into the litany of questions he'd asked every candidate. She dutifully answered every one of them, darting glances Coop's way every so often but keeping her attention on Ben. The others had asked Coop questions, tried to engage him in conversation.

But from Miss Evans there was no starry-eyed gazing, no flirting or innuendo. No smoldering smiles and suggestions that she would do *anything* for the job. In fact, she avoided his gaze, as if his presence made her nervous.

"You understand that this is a live-in position. You will be responsible for the twins 24/7. 11:00 a.m. to 4:00 p.m. on Sundays, and every fourth weekend from Saturday at 8:00 a.m. to Sunday at 8:00 p.m., is yours to spend as you wish," Ben said.

She nodded. "I understand."

Ben turned to Coop. "Do you have anything to add?"

"Yeah, I do." He addressed Miss Evans directly. "Why would you give up a job as a pediatric nurse to be a nanny?"

"I love working with kids...obviously," she said with a shy smile—a pretty smile. "But working in the neonatal intensive care unit is a very high-stress job. It's emotionally draining. I need a change of pace. And I can't deny that the live-in situation is alluring."

A red flag began to wave furiously. "Why is that?"

"My dad is ill and unable to care for himself. The salary you're offering, along with not having to pay rent, would make it possible for me to put him in a top-notch facility. In fact, there's a place in Jersey that has a spot opening up this week, so the timing would be perfect."

That was the last thing he had expected her to say, and for a second he was speechless. He didn't know of many people, especially someone in her tax bracket, who would sacrifice such a large chunk of their salary for the care of a parent. Even Ben looked a little surprised.

He shot Coop a look that asked, *What do you think?*

As things stood, Coop couldn't come up with a single reason not to hire her on the spot, but he didn't want to act rashly. This was about the girls, not his personal convenience.

"I'd like you to come by and meet my nieces tomorrow," he told her.

She regarded him hopefully. "Does that mean I have the job?"

"I'd like to see you interact with them before I make the final decision, but I'll be honest, you're by far the most qualified candidate we've seen so far."

"Tomorrow is my day off so I can come anytime."

"Why don't we say 1:00 p.m., after the girls' lunch. I'm a novice at this parenting thing, so it usually takes me until then to get them bathed, dressed and fed."

She smiled. "One is fine."

"I'm on the Upper East Side. Ben will give you the address."

Ben jotted down Coop's address and handed it to her. She took the slip of paper and tucked it into her purse.

Ben stood, and Miss Evans rose to her feet. She grabbed her purse and slung it over her shoulder.

"One more thing, Miss Evans," Coop said. "Are you a hockey fan?"

She hesitated. "Um…is it a prerequisite for the job?"

He felt a smile tugging at the corner of his mouth. "Of course not."

"Then, no, not really. I've never much been into sports. Although I was in a bowling league in college. Until recently my dad was a pretty big hockey fan, though."

"So you know who I am?"

"Is there anyone in New York who doesn't?"

Probably not, and only recently had that fact become a liability. "That isn't going to be an issue?"

She cocked her head slightly. "I'm not sure what you mean."

Her confusion made him feel like an idiot for even asking. Was he so used to women fawning over him that he'd come to expect it? Maybe he wasn't her type, or maybe she had a boyfriend. "Never mind."

She turned to leave, then paused and turned back to him.

"I wanted to say, I was so sorry to hear about your brother and his wife. I know how hard it is to lose someone you love."

The sympathy in her dark eyes made him want to squirm, and that familiar knot lodged somewhere in the vicinity of his Adam's apple. It annoyed him when the others hadn't mentioned it, but when she did, it made him uncomfortable. Maybe because she seemed as though she really meant it.

"Thank you," he said. He'd certainly had his share of loss. First his parents when he was twelve, and now Ash and Susan. Maybe that was the price he had to pay for fame and success.

He would give it all up, sell his soul if that was what it took to get his brother back.

After she left Ben asked him, "So, you really think she's the one?"

"She's definitely qualified, and it sounds as though she needs the job. As long as the girls like her, I'll offer her the position."

"Easy on the eyes, too."

He shot Ben a look. "If I manage to find a nanny worth hiring, do you honestly think I would risk screwing it up by getting physically involved?"

Ben smirked. "Honestly?"

Okay, a month ago…maybe. But everything had changed since then.

"I prefer blondes," he told Ben. "The kind with no expectations and questionable morals."

Besides, taking care of the girls, seeing that they were raised in the manner Ash and Susan would want, was his top priority. Coop owed his brother that much. When their parents died, Ash had only been eighteen, but he'd put his own life on hold to raise Coop. And Coop hadn't made it easy at first. He'd been hurt and confused and had lashed out. He was out of control and fast on his way to becoming a full-fledged juvenile delinquent when the school psychologist told Ash that Coop needed a constructive outlet for his anger. She suggested a physical sport, so Ash had signed him up for hockey.

Coop had never been very athletic or interested in sports, but he took to the game instantly, and though he was on a team with kids who had been playing since they were old enough to balance on skates, he rapidly surpassed their skills. Within two years he was playing in a travel league and became the star player. At nineteen he was picked up by the New York Scorpions.

A knee injury two years ago had cut his career short, but smart investments—again thanks to the urging of his brother—had left him wealthy beyond his wildest dreams. Without Ash, and the sacrifices he made, it never would have been possible. Now Coop had the chance to repay him. But he couldn't do it alone. He was ill-equipped. He knew nothing about caring for an infant, much less two at once. Hell, until two weeks ago he'd never so much as changed a diaper. Without his housekeeper to help, he would be lost.

If Miss Evans turned out to be the right person for the job—and he had the feeling she was—he would never risk screwing it up by sleeping with her.

She was off-limits.

Sierra Evans rode the elevator down to the lobby of the attorney's office building, sagging with relief against the paneled wall. That had gone much better than she could have hoped and she was almost positive that the job was as good as hers. It was a good thing, too, because the situation was far worse than she could have imagined.

Clearly Cooper Landon had better things to do than care for his twin nieces. He was probably too busy traipsing around like the playboy of the Western world. She wasn't one to listen to gossip, but in his case, his actions and reputation as a womanizing partier painted a disturbing picture. That was not the kind of atmosphere in which she wanted her daughters raised.

Her daughters. Only recently had she begun thinking of them as hers again.

With Ash and Susan gone, it seemed wrong that the twins would be so carelessly pawned off on someone like Cooper. But she would save them. She would take care of them and love them. It was all that mattered now.

The doors slid open and she stepped out. She crossed the swanky lobby and pushed out the door into the sunshine, heading down Park Avenue in the direction of the subway, feeling hopeful for the first time in two weeks.

Giving the twins up had been the hardest thing she'd ever done in her life, but she knew it was for the best. Between her student loans and exorbitant rent, not to mention her dad's failing health and mounting medical bills, she was in no position financially or emotionally to care for infant twins. She knew that Ash and Susan, the girls' adoptive parents, would give her babies everything that she couldn't.

But in the blink of an eye they were gone. She had been standing in front of the television, flipping through the channels when she paused on the news report about the plane crash. When she realized it was Ash and Susan they were talking about, her knees had buckled and she'd dropped to the nubby, threadbare shag carpet. In a panic she had flipped through the channels, desperate for more details, terrified to the depths of her soul that the girls had been on the flight with them. She'd sat up all night, alternating between the television and her laptop, gripped by a fear and a soul-wrenching grief that had been all-consuming.

At 7:00 a.m. the following morning the early news confirmed that the girls had in fact been left with Susan's family and were not in the crash. Sierra had been so relieved she wept. But then the reality of the situation hit hard. Who would take the girls? Would they go to Susan's family permanently or, God forbid, be dropped into the foster-care system?

She had contacted her lawyer immediately, and after a few calls he had learned what to her was unthinkable. Cooper would be their guardian. What the hell had Ash been thinking, choosing him? What possible interest could a womanizing, life of the party, ex-hockey player have in two infant babies?

She'd asked her lawyer to contact him on her behalf using no names, assuming that he would be more than happy to give the girls back to their natural mother. She would find a way to make it work. But Cooper had refused to give them up.

Her lawyer said she could try to fight him for custody, but the odds weren't in her favor. She had severed her parental rights, and getting them back would take a lengthy and expensive legal battle. But knowing Cooper would undoubtedly need help, and would probably be thrilled with someone of her qualifications, she'd managed to get herself an interview for the nanny position.

Sierra boarded the subway at Lexington and took the F Train to Queens. Normally she visited her dad on Wednesdays, but she had the appointment at Cooper's apartment tomorrow so she had to rearrange her schedule. With any luck he would offer her the job on the spot, and she could go home and start packing immediately.

She took a cab from the station to the dumpy, third-rate nursing home where her dad had spent the past fourteen months. As she passed the nursing station she said hi to the nurse seated there and received a grunt of annoyance in return. She would think that being in the same profession there would be some semblance of professional courtesy, but the opposite was true. The nurses seemed to resent her presence.

She hated that her dad had to stay in this horrible place where the employees were apathetic and the care was borderline criminal, but this was all that Medicare would cover and home care at this late stage of the disease was just too expensive. His body had lost the ability to perform anything but the most basic functions. He couldn't speak, barely reacted to stimuli and had to be fed through a tube. His heart was still beating, his lungs still pulling in air, but eventually his body would forget how to do that, too. It could be weeks, or months. He might even linger on for a year or more. There was just no way to know. If she could get him into the place in Jersey it would be harder to visit, but at least he would be well cared for.

"Hi, Lenny." She greeted her dad's roommate, a ninety-one-year-old war vet who had lost his right foot and his left arm in the battle at Normandy.

"Hey there, Sierra," he said cheerfully from his wheelchair. He was dressed in dark brown pants and a Kelly-green cardigan sweater that were as old and tattered as their wearer.

"How is Dad today?" she asked, dropping her purse in the chair and walking to his bedside. It broke her heart to see him so shriveled and lifeless. Nothing more than a shell of the man he used to be—the loving dad who single-handedly raised Sierra and her little sister Joy. Now he was wasting away.

"It's been a good day," Lenny said.

"Hi, Daddy," she said, pressing a kiss to his papery cheek. He was awake, but he didn't acknowledge her. On a good day he lay quietly, either sleeping or staring at the dappled sunshine through the dusty vertical blinds. On a bad day, he moaned. A low, tortured, unearthly sound. They didn't know if he was in pain, or if it was just some random involuntary function. But on those days he was sedated.

"How is that little boy of yours?" Lenny asked. "Must be reaching about school age by now."

She sighed softly to herself. Lenny's memory wasn't the best. He somehow managed to remember that she'd been pregnant, but he forgot the dozen or so times when she had explained that she'd given the girls up for adoption. And clearly he was confusing her with other people in his life because sometimes he thought she had an older boy and other times it was a baby girl. And rather than explain yet again, she just went with it.

"Growing like a weed," she told him, and before he could ask more questions they announced over the intercom that it was time for bingo in the community room.

"Gotta go!" Lenny said, wheeling himself toward the door. "Can I bring you back a cookie?"

"No thanks, Lenny."

When he was gone she sat on the edge of her dad's bed and took his hand. It was cold and contracted into a stiff fist. "I had my job interview today," she told him, even though she doubted his brain could process the sounds he was hearing as anything but gibberish. "It went really well, and I get to see the girls tomorrow. If the other applicants looked anything like the bimbo who interviewed right before me, I'm a shoo-in."

She brushed a few silvery strands of hair back from his forehead. "I know you're probably thinking that I should stay out of this and trust Ash and Susan's judgment, but I just can't. The man is a train wreck just waiting to happen. I have to make sure the girls are okay. If I can't do that as their mother, I can at least do it as their nanny."

And if that meant sacrificing her freedom and working for Cooper Landon until the girls no longer needed her, that was what she was prepared to do.

Two

The next afternoon at six minutes after one, Sierra knocked on the door of Cooper's penthouse apartment, brimming with nervous excitement, her heart in her throat. She had barely slept last night in anticipation of this very moment. Though she had known that when she signed away her parental rights she might never see the girls again, she had still hoped. She just hadn't expected it to happen until they were teenagers and old enough to make the decision to meet their birth mother. But here she was, barely five months later, just seconds away from the big moment.

The door was opened by a woman. Sierra assumed it was the housekeeper, judging by the maid's uniform. She was tall and lanky with a pinched face and steel-gray hair that was pulled back severely and twisted into a bun. Sierra placed her in her mid to late sixties.

"Can I *help* you?" the woman asked in a gravely clipped tone.

"I have an appointment with Mr. Landon."

"Are you Miss Evans?"

"Yes, I am." Which she must have already known, considering the doorman had called up to announce her about a minute ago.

She looked Sierra up and down with scrutiny, pursed her lips and said, "I'm Ms. Densmore, Mr. Landon's housekeeper. You're late."

"Sorry. I had trouble getting a cab."

"I should warn you that if you do get the job, tardiness will not be tolerated."

Sierra failed to see how she could be tardy for a job she was at 24/7, but she didn't push the issue. "It won't happen again."

Ms. Densmore gave a resentful sniff and said, "Follow me."

Even the housekeeper's chilly greeting wasn't enough to smother Sierra's excitement. Her hands trembled as she followed her through the foyer into an ultra-modern, open-concept living space. Near a row of ceiling-high windows that boasted a panoramic view of Central Park, with the afternoon sunshine washing over them like gold dust, were the twins. They sat side by side in identical ExerSaucers, babbling and swatting at the colorful toys.

They were so big! And they had changed more than she could have imagined possible. If she had seen them on the street, she probably wouldn't have recognized them. She was hit by a sense of longing so keen she had to bite down on her lip to keep from bursting into tears. She forced her feet to remain rooted to the deeply polished mahogany floor while she was announced, when what she wanted to do was fling herself into the room, drop down to her knees and gather her children in her arms.

"The one on the left is Fern," Ms. Densmore said, with not a hint of affection in her tone. "She's the loud, demanding one. The other is Ivy. She's the quiet, sneaky one."

Sneaky? At five months old? It sounded as if Ms. Densmore just didn't like children. She was probably a spinster. She sure looked like one.

Not only would Sierra have to deal with a partying, egomaniac athlete, but also an overbearing and critical housekeeper. How fun. And it frosted her that Cooper let this pinched, frigid, nasty old bat who clearly didn't like children anywhere near the girls.

"I'll go get Mr. Landon," she said, striding down a hall that Sierra assumed led to the bedrooms.

Alone with her girls for the first time since their birth, she crossed the room and knelt down in front of them. "Look how big you are, and how beautiful," she whispered.

They gazed back at her with wide, inquisitive blue eyes. Though they weren't identical, they looked very much alike. They both had her thick, pin-straight black hair and high cheekbones, but any other traces of the Chinese traits that had come from her great-grandmother on her mother's side had skipped them. They had eyes just like their father and his long, slender fingers.

Fern let out a squeal and reached for her. Sierra wanted so badly to hold her, but she wasn't sure if she should wait for Cooper. Tears stinging her eyes, she took one of Fern's chubby little hands in hers and held it. She had missed them so much, and the guilt she felt for leaving them, for putting them in this situation, sat like a stone in her belly. But she was here now, and she would never leave them again. She would see that they were raised properly.

"She wants you to pick her up."

Sierra turned to see Cooper standing several feet behind her, big and burly, in bare feet with his slightly wrinkled shirt untucked and his hands wedged in the pockets of a pair of threadbare jeans. His dirty-blond hair was damp and a little messy, as if he'd towel-dried it and hadn't bothered with a brush. No one could deny that he was attractive with his pale blue eyes and dimpled smile. The slightly crooked nose was even a little charming. Maybe it was his total lack of self-consciousness that was so appealing right now, but athletes had never been her thing. She preferred studious men. Professional types. The kind who didn't make a living swinging a big stick and beating the crap out of other people.

"Do you mind?" she asked.

"Of course not. That's what this interview is about."

Sierra lifted Fern out of the seat and set the infant in her lap. She smelled like baby shampoo and powder. Fern fixated on the gold chain hanging down the front of her blouse and grabbed for it, so Sierra tucked it under her collar. "She's so big."

"Around fifteen pounds I think. I remember my sister-in-law saying that they were average size for their age. I'm not sure what they weighed when they were born. I think there's a baby book still packed away somewhere with all that information in it."

They had been just over six pounds each, but she couldn't tell him that or that the baby book he referred to had been started by her and given to Ash and Susan as a gift when they took the girls home. She had documented her entire pregnancy—when she felt the first kick, when she had her sonogram—so the adoptive parents would feel more involved and they could show the girls when they got older. And although she had included photos of her belly in various stages of development, there were no shots of her face. There was nothing anywhere that identified her as being the birth mother.

Ivy began to fuss—probably jealous that her sister was getting all the attention. Sierra was debating the logistics of how to extract her from the seat while still holding Fern when, without prompting, Cooper reached for Ivy and plucked her out. He lifted her high over his head, making her gasp and giggle, and plunked her down in his arms.

Sierra must have looked concerned because he laughed and said, "Don't let her mild manner fool you. She's a mini daredevil."

As he sat on the floor across from her and set Ivy in his lap, Sierra caught the scent of some sort of masculine soap. Fern reached for him and tried to wiggle her way out of Sierra's arms. She hadn't expected the girls to be so at ease with him, so attached. Not this quickly. And she expected him to be much more inept and disinterested.

"You work with younger babies?" Cooper asked.

"Newborns usually. But before the NICU I worked in the pediatric ward."

"I'm going to the market," Ms. Densmore announced from the kitchen. Sierra had been so focused on the girls she hadn't noticed that it was big and open with natural wood and frosted glass cupboard doors and yards of glossy granite countertops. Modern, yet functional—not that she ever spent much time in one. Cooking—or at least, cooking *well*—had never been one of her great accomplishments.

Ms. Densmore wore a light spring jacket, which was totally unnecessary considering it was at least seventy-five degrees outside, and clutched an old-lady-style black handbag. "Do you need anything?" she asked Cooper.

"Diapers and formula," he told her. "And those little jars of fruit the girls like." He paused, then added, "And the dried cereal, too. The flaky kind in the blue box. I think we're running low."

Looking annoyed, Ms. Densmore left out of what must have been the service entrance behind the kitchen. Sierra couldn't help but wonder how Coop would know the cereal was low and why he would even bother to look.

"The girls are eating solid foods?" she asked him.

"Cereal and fruit. And of course formula. It's astounding how much they can put away. I feel as if I'm constantly making bottles."

He made the bottles? She had a hard time picturing that. Surely Ms. Cranky-Pants must have been doing most of the work.

"Are they sleeping through the night?" she asked him.

"Not yet. It's getting better, though. At first, they woke up constantly." He smiled down at Ivy affectionately, and a little sadly, brushing a wisp of hair off her forehead. "I think they just really missed their parents. But last night they only woke up twice, and they both went back to their cribs. Half the time they end up in my bed with me. I'll admit that I'm looking forward to a good night's sleep. Alone."

"*You* get up with them?" she asked, not meaning to sound quite so incredulous.

Rather than look offended, he smiled. "Yeah, and I'll warn you right now that they're both bed hogs. I have no idea how a person so small could take up so much room."

The idea of him, such a big, burly, rough-around-the-edges guy, snuggled up in bed with two infants, was too adorable for words.

"Out of curiosity, who did you think would get up with them?" he asked.

"I just assumed… I mean, doesn't Ms. Densmore take care of them?"

"She occasionally watches them while I work, but only because I'm desperate. After raising six kids of her own and two of her grandchildren, she says she's finished taking care of babies."

So much for Sierra's spinster theory.

"Is she always so…" She struggled for a kind way to say *nasty,* but Cooper seemed to read her mind.

"Cranky? Incorrigible?" he suggested, with a slightly crooked smile that she hated to admit made her heart beat the tiniest bit faster.

She couldn't help smiling back.

"She won't be winning any congeniality awards, I know, but she's a good housekeeper, and one hel…" he grinned and shook his head. "I mean *heck* of a fantastic cook. Sorry, I'm not used to having to censor my language."

At least he was making an effort. He would be thankful for that in a year or so when the twins started repeating everything he said verbatim.

"Ms. Densmore isn't crazy about the bad language,

either," he said. "Of course, sometimes I do it just to annoy her."

"I don't think she likes me much," Sierra said.

"It really doesn't matter what she thinks. She's not hiring you. I am. And I happen to think you're perfect for the job." He paused then added, "I'm assuming, since you're here now, that you're still interested."

Her heart skipped a beat. "Absolutely. Does that mean you're officially offering it to me?"

"Under one condition—I need your word that you'll stick around. That you're invested in the position. I can't tell you how tough that first week was, right after…" He closed his eyes, took a deep breath and blew it out. "Things have just begun to settle down, and I've got the girls in something that resembles a routine. They need consistency—or at least that's what the social worker told me. The worst thing for them would be a string of nannies bouncing in and out of their lives."

He would never have to worry about that with her. "I won't let them down."

"You're *sure?* Because these two are a handful. It's a lot of work. More than I ever imagined possible. Professional hockey was a cakewalk compared to this. I need to be sure that you're committed."

"I'm giving up my apartment and putting my dad in a home that I can't begin to afford without this salary. I'm definitely committed."

He looked relieved. "In that case, the job is yours. And the sooner you can start, the better."

Her own relief was so keen she could have sobbed. She hugged Fern closer. Her little girls would be okay. She would be there to take care of them, to nurture them. And maybe someday, when they were old enough to understand, she would be able to tell them who she really was and explain why she had let them go. Maybe she could be a real mother to them.

"Miss Evans?" Coop was watching her expectantly, waiting for a reply.

"It's Sierra," she told him. "And I can start right away if that works for you. I just need a day to pack and move my things in."

He looked surprised. "What about your apartment? Your furniture? Don't you need time to—"

"I'll sublet. A friend from work is interested in taking my place and she'll be using all my furniture." Her dad's furniture, actually. By the time Sierra started making enough money to afford her own place, he was too sick to live alone, so she had stayed with him instead, on the pull-out couch of the dinky one-bedroom apartment he'd had to take when he went on disability. She had never really had a place of her own. And from the looks of it, she wouldn't for a very long time. But if that meant the girls would be happy and well taken care of, it was a sacrifice she was happy to make.

"I just need to pack my clothes and a few personal items," she told him. "I can do that today and move everything over tomorrow."

"And work? You don't need to give them notice?"

She shook her head. She was taking a chance burning that bridge, but being with the girls as soon as possible took precedence. As long as they needed her, she wouldn't be going back to nursing anyway.

"I'll have Ben, my lawyer, draw up the contract this afternoon," he said. "Considering my former profession there are privacy issues."

"I understand."

"And of course you're welcome to have your own lawyer look at it before you sign."

"I'll call him today."

"Great. Why don't I show you the girls' room, and where you'll be staying?"

"Okay."

They got up from the floor and he led her down the hall, Ivy in his arms and Sierra holding Fern, who seemed perfectly content despite Sierra being a relative stranger. Was it possible that she sensed the mother-daughter connection? Or was she just a friendly, outgoing baby?

"This is the nursery," he said, indicating a door on the left and gesturing her inside. It was by far the largest and prettiest little girls' room she had ever laid eyes on. The color scheme was pale pink and pastel green. The walls, bedding, curtains and even the carpet looked fluffy and soft, like cotton candy. Matching white cribs perched side by side, and a white rocking chair sat in the corner next to the window. She could just imagine herself holding the girls close, singing them a lullaby and rocking them to sleep.

This room was exactly what she would have wanted for them but never could have afforded. With her they wouldn't have had more than a tiny corner of her bedroom.

"It's beautiful, Cooper."

"It's Coop," he said and flashed that easy grin. "No one but my mom called me Cooper, and that was usually when she was angry about something. And as for the room, I can't take credit. It's an exact reproduction of their room at Ash and Susan's. I thought it might make the transition easier for them."

Once again he had surprised her. Maybe he wasn't quite as self-centered as she first imagined. Or maybe he was only playing the role of responsible uncle out of necessity. Maybe once he had her there to take care of the girls for him, he would live up to his party reputation, including the supposedly revolving bedroom door.

Time would tell.

"They have their own bathroom and a walk-in closet over there," he said, gesturing to a closed door across the room.

She walked over and opened it. The closet was huge! Toys lined either side of the floor—things they had used and some still in the original boxes. Seeing them, Fern shifted restlessly in Sierra's arms, clearly wanting to get down and play.

From the bars hung a wardrobe big enough for a dozen infants. Dresses and jumpers and tiny pairs of jeans and shirts—all designer labels and many with the tags still attached, and all in duplicate. In her wildest dreams Sierra never could have afforded even close to this many clothes, and certainly not this quality. They were neatly organized by style, color and size—all spelled out on sticky notes on the shelf above the bar.

Sierra had never seen anything like it. "Wow. Did you do this?"

"God, no," Coop said. "This is Ms. Densmore's thing. She's a little fanatical about organization."

"Just a little." She would have a coronary if she looked in Sierra's closet. Besides being just a fraction the size, it was so piled with junk she could barely close the door. Neatness had never been one of her strong suits. That had been okay living with her dad, who was never tidy himself, but here she would have to make an effort to be more organized.

"The bathroom is through there," Coop said, walking past her to open the door, filling the air with the delicious scent of soap and man. The guy really did smell great, and though it was silly, he looked even more attractive holding the baby, which made no sense at all. Or maybe it was just that she'd always been a sucker for a man who was good with kids—because in her profession she had seen too many who weren't. Deadbeat dads who couldn't even be bothered to visit their sick child in the hospital. And of course there were the abusive dads who put their kids in the hospital. Those were the really heartbreaking cases and one of the reasons she had transferred from pediatrics to the NICU.

But having an easy way with an infant didn't make a man a good father, she reminded herself. Neither did giving them a big beautiful bedroom or an enormous closet filled with toys and designer clothes. The twins needed nurturing, they needed to know that even though their parents were gone, someone still loved them and cared about them.

She held Fern closer and rubbed her back, and the infant laid her head on Sierra's shoulder, her thumb tucked in her mouth.

"I'll show you your room," Coop said, and she followed him to the bedroom across the hall. It was even larger than the girls' room, with the added bonus of a cozy sitting area by the window. With the bedroom, walk-in closet and private bath, it was larger than her entire apartment. All that was missing was the tiny, galley-style kitchen, but she had a gourmet kitchen just a few rooms away at her disposal.

The furnishings and decor weren't exactly her style. The black, white and gray color scheme was too modern and cold and the steel and glass furnishings were a bit masculine, but bringing some of her own things in would liven it up a little. She could learn to live with it.

"That bad, huh?"

Startled by the comment, Sierra looked over at Coop. He was frowning. "I didn't say that."

"You didn't have to. It's written all over your face. You hate it."

"I don't *hate* it."

One brow tipped up. "Now you're lying."

"It's not what I would have chosen, but it's very… stylish."

He laughed. "You are *so* lying. You think it's terrible."

She bit her lip to keep from smiling, but the corners of her mouth tipped up regardless. "I'll get used to it."

"I'll call my decorator. You can fix it however you like. Paint, furniture, the works."

She opened her mouth to tell him that wouldn't be necessary, and he held up one ridiculously large palm to shush her. "Do you really think I'm going to let you stay in a room you despise? This is going to be your home. I want you to be comfortable here."

She wondered if he was always this nice, or if he was just so desperate for a reliable nanny he would do anything to convince her to take the job. If that was the case, she could probably negotiate a higher salary, but it wasn't about the money. She just wanted to be with her girls.

"If you're sure it's not a problem, I wouldn't mind adding a few feminine touches," she told him.

"You can sleep in the nursery until it's finished, or if you'd prefer more privacy, there's a fold-out love seat in my office."

"The nursery is fine." She didn't care about privacy, and she liked the idea of sleeping near her girls.

He nodded to Fern and said, "I think we should lay them down. It's afternoon nap time."

Sierra looked down at Fern and realized that she had fallen asleep, her thumb still wedged in her mouth, and Ivy, who had laid her head on Coop's enormously wide shoulder, was looking drowsy, too.

They carried the girls back to the nursery and laid them in their beds—Fern on the right side and Ivy on the left—then they stepped quietly out and Coop shut the door behind them.

"How long will they sleep?" Sierra asked.

"On a good day, two hours. But they slept in until eight this morning, so maybe less." He paused in the hall and asked, "Before we call my attorney, would you like something to drink? We have juice and soda...baby formula."

She smiled. "I'm good, thanks."

"Okay, if you're having any second thoughts, this is your last chance to change your mind."

That would never happen. He was stuck with her. "No second thoughts."

"Great, let's go to my office and call Ben," Coop said with a grin. "Let's get this show on the road."

Three

Coop stood outside Sierra's bedroom door, hoping she hadn't already gone to sleep for the night. It was barely nine-thirty, but today had been her first official day watching the girls, so he was guessing that she was probably pretty exhausted. God knows they wore him out.

She had signed the contract the afternoon of her second interview, then spent most of the next day moving her things and unpacking. He had offered to pay a service to do the moving for her, but she had insisted she had it covered, showing up in the early afternoon with a slew of boxes and two youngish male friends—orderlies from the hospital, she'd told him—who had been openly thrilled to meet the great Coop Landon.

Though Coop had tried to pay them for the help, they refused to take any cash. Instead he offered them each a beer, and while Sierra unpacked and the twins napped, he and the guys sat out on the rooftop patio. They asked him about his career and the upcoming season draft picks, leaving a couple of hours later with autographed pucks.

Coop had hoped to be around today to help Sierra and the twins make the transition, but he'd been trapped in meetings with the marketing team for his new sports equipment line all morning, and in the afternoon he'd met with the owner of his former team. If things went as planned, Coop would own the team before the start of the next season in October. Owning the New York Scorpions had been his dream since he started playing for the team. For twenty-two years, until his bad knee took him off the ice, he lived and breathed hockey. He loved everything about the game. Buying a team was the natural next step, and he had the players' blessing.

After the meetings Coop had enjoyed his first dinner out with friends in weeks. Well, he hadn't actually *enjoyed* it. Though he had been counting the days until he was free again, throughout the entire meal his mind kept wandering back to Fern and Ivy and how they were doing with Sierra. Should he have canceled his meetings and spent that first day with them? Was it irresponsible of him to have left them with a stranger? Not that he didn't trust Sierra—he just wanted to be sure that he was doing the right thing. They had already lost their parents—he didn't want them to think that he was abandoning them, too.

When the rest of the party had moved on to a local bar for after-dinner drinks, dancing and skirt chasing, to the surprise of his friends, Coop had called it a night. On a typical evening he closed out the bar, moved on to a party and usually didn't go home alone. But the ribbing he endured from his buddies was mild. Hell, it had been less than a month since he lost his brother. It was going to take him a little time to get back into his normal routine. And right now the twins needed him. He would try to work from home the rest of the week, so he could spend more time with them. After more than two weeks of being together almost constantly, he had gotten used to having them around.

He rapped lightly on Sierra's bedroom door, and after several seconds it opened a crack and she peeked out. He could see that she had already changed into her pajamas—a short, pink, babydoll-style nightgown. His eyes automatically drifted lower, to her bare legs. They weren't particularly long, or slender, so the impulse to touch her, to slide his palm up the inside of one creamy thigh and under the hem of her gown—and the resulting pull of lust it created—caught him completely off guard. He had to make an effort to keep his gaze above her neck and on her eyes, which were dark and inquisitive, with that exotic tilt. Her hair, which he'd only ever seen up in a ponytail, hung in a long, silky black sheet over her shoulders, and he itched to run his fingers through it. Instead he shoved his hands in the pockets of his slacks.

You can look, but you can't touch, he reminded himself, and not for the first time since she'd come by to meet the girls. She was absolutely nothing like the sort of woman he would typically be attracted to. Maybe that alone was what he found so appealing. She was different. A novelty. But her position as the twins' nanny was just too crucial to put in jeopardy.

Maybe hiring such an attractive woman had been a bad idea, even if she was the most qualified. Maybe he should have held out and interviewed a few more people, made an effort to find someone older or, better yet, a guy.

"Did you want something?" she asked, and he realized that he was just standing there staring at her.

Way to make yourself look like an idiot, Coop. He was usually pretty smooth when it came to women. He had no idea why he was acting like such a dope.

"I hope I didn't wake you," he said.

"No, I was still up."

"I just wanted to check in, see how it went today."

"It went really well. It'll take some time to get into a routine, but I'm following their lead."

"I'm sorry I wasn't here to help out."

She looked confused. "I didn't expect you to help."

He felt his eyes drifting lower, to the cleavage at the neckline of her gown. She wasn't large-busted, but she wasn't what he would consider small, either. She was… average. So why couldn't he seem to look away?

She noticed him noticing but made no move to cover herself. And why should she? It was her room. He was the intruder.

And he was making a complete ass of himself.

"Was there anything else?" she asked.

He forced his gaze back to her face. "I thought we could just talk for a while. We haven't had a chance to go over the girls' schedules. I thought you might have questions."

She looked hesitant, and he thought her answer was going to be no. And could he blame her? He was behaving like a first-rate pervert. But after several seconds, she said, "Okay, I'll be out in just a minute."

She snapped the door closed and he walked to the kitchen, mentally knocking himself in the head. What the hell was wrong with him? He was acting as if he'd never seen an attractive woman before. One of his dining companions that evening had worn a form-fitting dress that was shorter and lower cut than Sierra's nightgown and he hadn't felt even a twinge of interest. He needed to quit eyeballing her, or she was going to think he was some sort of deviant. The last thing he wanted was for her to be uncomfortable in his home.

Coop opened the wine refrigerator and fished out an open bottle of pinot grigio. Unlike his teammates, he preferred a quality wine to beer or liquor. He'd never been one to enjoy getting drunk. Not since his wild days anyway, when he'd taken pretty much anything that gave him a buzz because at the time it meant taking his pain away.

He took two glasses from the cupboard and set them on the island countertop. Sierra walked in as he was pouring. She had changed into a pair of black leggings and an oversize, faded yellow T-shirt. He found his gaze drawn to her legs again. He typically dated women who were supermodel skinny—and a few of those women had actually been supermodels—but not necessarily because that was what he preferred. That just seemed to be the type of woman who gravitated toward him. He liked that Sierra had some meat on her bones. She was not heavy by any stretch of the imagination. She just looked…healthy. Although he was sure that most women would take that as an insult.

He quickly reminded himself that it didn't matter what she looked like because she was off-limits.

"Have a seat," he said, and she slid onto one of the bar stools across the island from him. He corked the wine and slid one of the glasses toward her. "I hope you like white."

"Oh…um…" She hesitated, a frown causing an

adorable little wrinkle between her brows. "Maybe I shouldn't."

He put the bottle back in the fridge. Maybe she thought he was trying to get her drunk so he could take advantage of her. "One glass," he said. "Unless you don't drink."

"No, I do. I'm just not sure if it's a good idea."

"Are you underage?"

She flashed him a cute smile. "You know I'm not. I'm just worried that one of the girls might wake up. In fact, I'd say it's a strong possibility, so I need to stay sharp."

"You think one little glass of wine will impair you?" He folded his arms. "You must be quite the lightweight."

Her chin lifted a notch. "I can hold my own. I just don't want to make a bad impression."

"If you drank an entire bottle, that might worry me, but one glass? Do you think I would offer if I thought it was a bad idea?"

"I guess not."

"Let's put it this way: If the twins were your daughters, and you wanted to wind down after a busy day, would you feel comfortable allowing yourself a glass of wine?"

"Yes."

He slid the wine closer. "So, stop worrying about what I think, and enjoy."

She took it.

"A toast, to your first day," he said, clinking his glass against hers.

She sipped, nodded and said, "Nice. I wouldn't have imagined you as the wine-drinking type."

"I'm sure there are a lot of things about me that

would surprise you." He rested his hip against the edge of the countertop. "But tell me about you."

"I thought we were going to talk about the girls."

"We will, but I'd like to know a little bit about you first."

She sipped again, then set her glass down. "You read my file."

"Yeah, but that was just the basics. I'd like to know more about you as a person. Like, what made you get into nursing?"

"My mom, actually."

"She was a nurse?

"No, she was a homemaker. She got breast cancer when I was a kid. The nurses were so wonderful to her and to me and my dad and sister. Especially when she was in hospice. I decided then, that's what I wanted to do."

"She passed away?"

Sierra nodded. "When I was fourteen."

"That's a tough age for a girl to lose her mother."

"It was harder for my sister, I think. She was only ten."

He circled the counter and sat on the stool beside hers. "Is there a good age to lose a parent? I was twelve when my mom and dad died. It was really rough."

"My sister used to be this sweet, happy-go-lucky kid, but after she got really moody and brooding."

"I was angry," he said. "I went from being a pretty decent kid to the class bully."

"It's not uncommon, in that situation, for a boy to pick on someone smaller and weaker. It probably gave you a feeling of power in an otherwise powerless situation."

"Except I went after kids who were bigger than me.

Because I was so big for my age, that usually meant I was fighting boys who were older than me. And I got the snot kicked out of me a couple of times, but usually I won. And you're right, it did make me feel powerful. I felt like it was the only thing I had any control over."

"My sister never picked on anyone, but she was into drugs for a while. Thankfully she cleaned herself up, but when my dad got sick she just couldn't handle it. When she turned eighteen she took off for L.A. She's an actress, or trying to be. She's done a couple of commercials and a few walk-on parts. Mostly she's a waitress."

"What is it that your dad has?" he asked, hoping he wasn't being too nosy.

"He's in the final stages of Alzheimer's."

"How old is he?"

"Fifty."

Damn. "That's really young for Alzheimer's, isn't it?"

She nodded. "It's rare, but it happens. He started getting symptoms when he was forty-six, and the disease progressed much faster than it would in someone older. They tried every drug out there to slow the progression, but nothing seemed to work. It's not likely he'll live out the year."

"I'm so sorry."

She shrugged, eyes lowered, running her thumb around the rim of her glass. "The truth is, he died months ago, at least in all the ways that matter. He's just a shell. A functioning body. I know he hates living this way."

She looked so sad. He wanted to hug her, or rub her shoulder, or do something to comfort her, but it didn't seem appropriate to be touching her. So his only choice was to comfort her with words and shared experiences. Because when it came to losing a parent, he knew just how deeply painful and traumatic it could be.

"When my parents got in the car accident, my dad died instantly. My mom survived the crash, but she was in a coma and brain-dead. My brother, Ash, was eighteen, and he had to make the decision to take her off life support."

"What a horrible thing for him to have to go through. No one should have to make that decision. Not at any age."

"I was too young to really grasp what was happening. I thought he did it because he was mad at her or didn't love her. Only when I got older did I understand that there was no hope."

"I signed a Do Not Resuscitate order for my dad. It was so hard, but I know it's what he wants. Working in the NICU, I've seen parents have to make impossible choices. It was heartbreaking. You have to hold it together at work, be strong for the parents, but I can't tell you how many times I went home and cried my eyes out. Parents of healthy kids just don't realize how lucky they are."

"I can understand how you would burn out in a job like that."

"Don't get me wrong, I really love nursing. I liked that I was helping people. But it can be emotionally draining."

"Do you think you'll miss it?"

She smiled. "With the twins to take care of, I doubt I'll have time."

He hoped she wouldn't eventually burn out, the way she had with nursing. Maybe giving her so little time off had been a bad idea. He knew firsthand how tough it was caring for the twins nonstop. A few hours off on a Sunday and one weekend a month weren't much time. Maybe he should have considered hiring two nannies, one for during the week, and one for the weekends. "You're sure it's not going to be too much?"

"Watching the twins?"

"By taking this job, you're pretty much giving up your social life."

"I gave that up when my dad got too sick to care for himself. He couldn't be alone, so we had a caregiver while I worked, then I took over when I got home."

"Every day? That sounds expensive."

She nodded. "It was. We blew through his savings in just a few months. But I didn't want him to have to go in a nursing home. I kept him with me as long as I could. But eventually it got to the point where I just couldn't provide the best care for him."

"When did you go out? Have fun?"

"I've always been more of a homebody."

"What about dating?"

The sudden tuck between her brows said her love life was a touchy subject. And really it was none of his business. Or maybe she thought it was some sort of cheesy pickup line.

"You can tell me to mind my own business," he said.

"It's okay. Things are just a little complicated right now. I'm not in a good place emotionally to be getting into a relationship." She glanced over at him. "That's probably tough for someone like you to understand."

"Someone so morally vacant?"

Her eyes widened. "No, I didn't mean—"

"It's okay," he said with a laugh. "A few weeks ago, I probably wouldn't have understood."

Dating and being out with other people had been

such an intrinsic part of who he was, he probably wouldn't have been able to grasp the concept of leading a quiet, domesticated life. Since the crash that had taken his brother, his attitude and his perception about what was really important had been altered. Like tonight for instance. Why go out barhopping to meet a woman for what would ultimately be a meaningless and quite frankly unsatisfying encounter when the twins needed him at home?

"Priorities change," he said.

She nodded. "Yes they do. You see things a certain way, then suddenly it's not about what you want anymore."

He wondered if she was talking about her dad. "I know exactly what you mean."

"You really love them," she said.

"The twins?" he found himself grinning. "Yeah, I do. What's not to love? This was obviously not a part of my plans, but I want to do right by them. I owe Ash that much. He sacrificed a lot to raise me. He worked two jobs and put college off for years to be there for me, and believe me, I was a handful. Some people thought that because the twins aren't Ash's biological kids it somehow absolved me of all responsibility. Even their birth mother seemed to think so."

"What do you mean?"

"Her lawyer contacted my lawyer. Apparently she saw on the news that Ash and Susan had died and she wanted the girls back. I can only assume that she thought I would be a failure as a dad."

"And you didn't consider it?"

"Not for a second. And even if I didn't think I could handle taking care of the girls myself, why would I give them to someone who didn't want them to begin with?"

That tuck was back between her brows. "Maybe she wanted them but just couldn't keep them. Maybe she thought giving them up was the best thing for the twins."

"And that changed in five months? She thinks she can give the girls more than I can? With me they'll never want for a thing. They'll have the best of everything. Clothes, education, you name it. Could she do that?"

"So you assume that because she isn't rich she wouldn't be a good parent?" she asked in a sharp tone.

For someone who didn't even know the birth mother she was acting awfully defensive. "The truth is, I don't know why she gave them up, but it doesn't matter. My brother adopted the twins and loved them like his own flesh and blood. He wanted the girls raised by me, and I'm honoring his wishes."

Her expression softened. "I'm sorry, I didn't mean to snap. In my line of work, I've seen young mothers harshly misjudged. It's a natural instinct to defend them."

"Not to mention that you've no doubt heard about my reputation and question my ability to properly raise the girls."

She shook her head. "I didn't say—"

"You didn't have to." It was amazing the people who had strong opinions about his ability to be a good father. Some of his closest friends—the single ones— thought he was crazy for taking on the responsibility. And the friends with families—not that he had many of those—openly doubted his capabilities as a parent.

He intended to prove them all wrong.

"Like I said before," he told Sierra firmly, meaning every word, "priorities change. For me, the girls come first, and they always will."

Four

Sierra could hardly believe how snippy she had gotten with Coop last night.

She replayed the conversation in her head as she got the girls ready for their afternoon nap, cringing inwardly as she placed Ivy on her belly on the carpet with a toy while she wrestled a wiggling Fern out of her jumper and into a fresh diaper.

Antagonize your boss. Way to go Sierra. Was she *trying* to get fired? Or even worse, give him any reason to doubt that she was just the twin's nanny? But all that garbage about him changing his priorities had really ruffled her feathers, and she didn't believe it for a minute, not after the way he was ogling her when she opened the bedroom door in her nightgown. And if he thought she would be interested in a man like him, he was dreaming.

Although she couldn't deny that in a very small and

completely depraved way it had been just the tiniest bit exciting. And to his credit Coop had looked conflicted, like he knew it was wrong, but he just couldn't help himself. Which she was sure summed him up in a nutshell. He would try to change, try to be a good father to the twins, but in the end he would fail because that was just the sort of man he was.

But it had been an awfully long time since someone had looked at her in a sexual way, and what woman wouldn't feel at least the tiniest bit special to be noticed by a rich, gorgeous guy who was known for dating actresses and supermodels? She also didn't let herself forget that he was a womanizer, and she was one of hundreds of women he had looked at in that very same way.

She laid Fern in her crib and turned to pick up Ivy, but she had rolled all the way across the room and wound up by the closet door.

"Come back here, you little sneak," she said, scooping her up and nibbling the ticklish spot on her neck. Ivy giggled and squirmed, but when Sierra laid her on the changing table she didn't put up a fuss. She was definitely the milder mannered of the two, but she had a curious nature. Sierra was sure that left to her own devices, Ivy could get herself into trouble. There was no doubt that Ivy was more like her, and Fern seemed to take after their birth father's side of the family. Sierra was having such a blast getting to know them, learning all their little personality quirks. She realized how fortunate she was to have this opportunity and she wouldn't take it for granted. And if being with her daughters meant putting up with an occasional inappropriate glance, it was worth it.

Speaking of Mr. Inappropriate, Sierra heard the deep

timbre of Coop's voice from his office down the hall. He was on the phone again. He was working from home today, or so he said. Exactly what he was doing in there, or what that so-called "work" entailed, she wasn't sure. Polishing his various trophies? Giving interviews?

Other than basking in the glow of his former fame, she wasn't sure what he did with his time.

She laid Ivy in her crib and blew each of the girls a kiss good-night, then she closed the curtain to smother the light and stepped out of the room…colliding with Coop, who was on his way in. He said, "Whoa!" looking just as surprised to see her as she was to see him. She instinctively held her hands up to soften the inevitable collision and wound up with her palms pressed against the hard wall of his chest, breathing in the warm and clean aroma of his skin. He wore the scent of soap and shampoo the way other men wore three-hundred dollar cologne. And though it was completely irrational, the urge to slide her hands up around his neck, to plaster herself against him, hit her swift and hard.

Touching Coop was clearly a bad idea.

She pulled away so fast her upper back and head hit the door frame with a thud.

Coop winced. "You okay?"

She grimaced and rubbed her head. "Fine."

"You sure? You hit that pretty hard." He reached behind her and cupped the back of her head in one enormous palm, but his touch was gentle as he probed for an injury, his fingers slipping through her hair beneath the root of her ponytail, spreading warmth against her scalp. "I don't feel a bump."

But, oh man, did it feel nice.

Nice? Ugh! This was insane. Knowing the sort of man he was, his touch should have repulsed her.

She ducked away from his hand. "I'm fine, really. You just startled me."

He frowned, tucking his hands in the pockets of his jeans, as if maybe he realized that touching her wasn't appropriate. Or maybe he liked it as much as she did. "Sorry. Where are the girls?"

"I just put them down for their nap."

"Why didn't you tell me? I'd like to say good-night."

Honestly, she hadn't thought it would matter to him. "I thought I heard you on the phone and I didn't want to disturb you."

"Well, next time let me know," he said, sounding irritated. "If I'm here, the girls come first."

"Okay. I'm sorry. They're still awake if you want to see them."

His expression softened. "Just for a second."

He disappeared into their room and Sierra walked to the kitchen to clean up the girls' lunch dishes. Coop really was taking this "being there for the girls" business pretty seriously. But how long would that last? It was probably a novelty, being the caring uncle. She was sure it wouldn't be long before he slipped back into his old ways and wouldn't have the time or the inclination to say good-night to the twins.

"What is this?" Ms. Densmore snipped, holding up the empty bottles from the girls' lunch as Sierra walked into the kitchen.

Was this some sort of trick question? "Um...bottles?"

She flung daggers with her eyes. "And why were they on the kitchen counter and not in the dishwasher?"

"Because I didn't put them there yet."

"Anything you use in the kitchen must be put in the

dishwasher or washed by *you*. And any messes you and the children make are yours to clean."

"I'm aware of that," Sierra said, and only because Ms. Densmore had given her this identical lecture *three* times now. "I planned to clean up after I put the twins down for their nap. Their *care* is my priority."

"I also noticed a basket of your clothes in the laundry room. I'd like to remind you that you are responsible for your own laundry. That includes clothing, towels and bedding. I work for Mr. Landon. Not you or anyone else. Is that clear?"

Sienna gritted her teeth. She was sure it bugged the hell out of the housekeeper that she was forced to feed Sierra, although Coop was right about her being an excellent cook. "The washer was already running so I set them there temporarily."

Sierra had done absolutely nothing to offend her, so she had no clue why Ms. Densmore was so cranky, so inclined to dislike her.

"As I have said to Mr. Landon on numerous occasions, I took this job because there were no children. I am not a nanny or a babysitter. Do not ask me to hold, change, feed or play with the twins. They are *your* responsibility, and yours alone."

As if she'd want her girls anywhere near this nasty old bitch. "I'm pretty clear on that, thanks."

Ms. Densmore shoved the bottles at her and Sierra took them. Then, her pointy, beak nose in the air, Ms. Densmore stalked away to the laundry room behind the kitchen. And though it was petty and immature, Sierra gestured rudely to her retreating back.

"That wasn't very ladylike."

She spun around to find Coop watching her, a wry grin on his face.

He folded his arms across his ridiculously wide chest and said, "I'm glad the girls weren't here to see that."

She bit her lip and hooked her hands behind her back. "Um...sorry?"

Coop laughed. "I'm kidding. I would have done exactly the same thing. And you're right, the girls are your first priority. The dishwasher can wait."

"I have no idea why she dislikes me so much."

"Don't take it personally. She doesn't like me, either, but she's one hell of an awesome housekeeper."

"You would think she would be happy to have me here. Now she doesn't have to deal with the twins."

"I'll have a talk with her."

That could be a really bad idea. "Maybe you shouldn't. I don't want her to think I tattled on her. It will just make things worse."

"Don't worry, I'll take care of it."

Coop walked to the laundry room and over the sound of the washer and dryer she heard the door snap closed behind him. Tempted as she was to sneak back there and press her ear to the door to listen, she put the lunch dishes in the dishwasher instead. Coop was back a couple of minutes later, a satisfied smile on his face.

"She won't hassle you anymore," he said. "If you need me, I'll be in my office."

Whatever he'd said to Ms. Densmore, it had worked. She came out of the laundry room several minutes later, red faced with either embarrassment or anger, and didn't say a word or even look at Sierra. She maintained her tight-lipped silence until dinnertime when she served a Mexican dish that was so delicious Sierra had two helpings.

Sierra was surprised when Coop invited her to eat in the dining room with him. She had just assumed that she would be treated like any other hired help and eat in the kitchen with the girls. Because surely he wouldn't want two infants around making a fuss and disrupting his meal. But he actually insisted on it. While Sierra sat at one end of the table, Ivy in her high chair next to her, he sat with Fern, alternately feeding her then himself. When Fern started to fuss and Sierra offered to take over, he refused. He wiped applesauce from her face and hands with a washcloth, plucked her from her high chair and sat her in his lap while he finished his meal, dodging her grasping hands as she tried to intercept his fork. After their talk last night, maybe he felt he had to prove some sort of point.

When they were done with dinner he switched on the enormous flat-screen television in the living room and tuned it to ESPN. Then he stretched out on the floor and played with the girls while she sat on the couch feeling a little like an outsider.

The girls obviously adored him and it scared the hell out of her. Not because she thought they would love him more. She'd reconciled her position in the girls' lives. She just hated to see the girls become attached to him, only to have him grow bored with parenting. They were a novelty, but his fascination with them would fade. He was still reeling from his brother's death, but that would only last so long. Eventually he would go back to his womanizing, partying ways. And when he did, *she* would be there to offer the stability they needed. She was the person the twins would learn to depend on.

The worst part was that he had flat-out admitted he thought that he could buy their affection by giving them "the best money could buy," but what they really needed, his love and emotional support, he wasn't capable of giving. Not for any extended length of time.

When it was time for the twins to go to bed Coop helped her wrestle them into their pajamas. He gave them each a kiss good-night, then he and Sierra laid them in their cribs.

On their way out of the room Sierra grabbed their soiled clothes from the day and switched off the light. "I'm going to go throw these in the wash."

"You don't have to do the girls' laundry," Coop said, following her down the hall. "Leave it for Ms. Densmore."

"It's okay. I wanted to do a few of my own things, too. Unless you'd prefer I wash the twins' clothes separately."

He looked confused. "Why would I care about that?"

Sierra shrugged. "Some people are picky about the way their kids' clothes are washed."

"Well, not me."

Somehow she didn't imagine he would be. And he probably wouldn't care that she had every intention of washing their "hand wash only" dresses on Delicate in the machine.

Sierra dumped the clothes in the washing machine, noting that the room was tidy to point of fanaticism. There wasn't so much as a speck of dust on the floor or a stitch of clothing anywhere. Ms. Densmore must have been as anal about keeping the laundry done as she was with keeping the house clean.

Sierra opened the cabinet to find the detergents, stain removers and fabric softeners organized neatly by function and perfectly aligned so the labels were facing out. She grabbed the liquid detergent, measured out a cupful and poured it into the machine. She put the cap back on, ignoring the small bit that sloshed over the side of the bottle, then, smiling serenely, stuck it back on the shelf crooked. She did the same with the fabric softener, then gave the stain removers a quick jostle just for fun before she started the machine.

She walked back out into the kitchen and found Coop sitting at the island on a barstool, two glasses of red wine on the counter.

"Take a load off," he said, nudging the other stool with his foot. "I was in the mood for red tonight. It's a Malbec. I hope that's okay."

She wasn't picky. However, she had just assumed that last night's shared wine had been a one-time thing. "You don't have to serve me wine every night."

"I know I don't."

Did he plan to make a habit of this because she wasn't sure if she was comfortable with that. Not that she minded relaxing with a glass of wine at the end of the day. It was the company that made her a little nervous. Especially when he sat so darned close to her. Last night she'd sat beside him feeling edgy, as if she were waiting for him to pounce. Which he didn't, of course. He had been a perfect gentleman. Yet he still made her nervous.

"Maybe we could sit in the living room," she suggested. Far, far away from each other.

Coop shrugged. "Sure."

What she would rather do is take the glass to her room and curl up in bed with the mystery novel she'd been reading, but she didn't want to be rude.

He sprawled in the chair by the window, his long, muscular legs stretched out in front of him, and Sierra sat with her legs tucked underneath her on the corner of the couch. He was yards away from her, so why the tension lingering in the air? And why could she not stop looking at him? Yes, he was easy on the eyes, but she didn't even like him.

Coop sipped his wine, then rested the glass on his stomach—which was no doubt totally ripped and as perfect as the rest of him—his fingers laced together and cupping the bowl. "What do you think of the wine?"

She took a sip, letting it roll around her tongue. She didn't know much about wines, but it tasted pretty good to her. Very bold and fruity. A huge step up from the cheap brands she could afford. "I like it. It tastes expensive."

"It is. But what's the point of having all this money if I can't enjoy the finer things? Which reminds me, I talked to my decorator today. He's tied up with another project and won't be available to meet with you for at least three weeks. If that's not soon enough for you, we can find someone who's available now."

"Three weeks is fine. There's no rush."

"You're sure?"

"Positive. I really appreciate that you want me to be comfortable, though." The truth was, she hadn't been spending much time in there anyway. The twins kept her busy all day, and when she was in her room, she was usually asleep.

"I meant to ask you yesterday—what's going on with your dad? You mentioned moving him to a different place."

"They're taking him by ambulance to the new nursing home Saturday morning."

"Do you need to be there?"

Even if she did, she had a responsibility to the girls. "He's in good hands. I'll be visiting him Sunday during my time off. I can get him settled in then."

"You know, you don't have to wait until Sundays to see him. You can go anytime you'd like. I don't mind if you take the girls with you."

"He's going to be all the way out in Jersey. I don't own a car and taking the twins on the train or the bus would be a logistical nightmare."

He shrugged. "So take my car."

"I can't."

"It's okay, really."

"No, I mean I *really* can't. I don't know how."

His brows rose. "You never learned to drive?"

"I've always lived in the city. I never needed to. And gas prices being what they are, public transportation just makes more sense."

"Well then, why don't I take you? We could go Saturday when he's transferred."

Huh? Why would he want to take time out of his day to haul her to Jersey? Surely he had something better to do. "You really don't have to do that."

"I want to."

She didn't know what to say. Why was he being so nice to her? Why did he even care if she saw her dad? He was her employer, not her pal.

"You're looking at me really weirdly right now," Coop said. "Either you're not used to people doing nice things for you, or you're seriously questioning my motives."

A little bit of both actually, and it was creepy how he seemed to always know what she was thinking. "I'm sure you have other things—"

"No, I don't. My schedule is totally free this weekend." He paused, then added, "And for the record, I have no ulterior motives."

She had a hard time buying that. "You're sure it's no trouble?"

"None at all. And I'll bet the girls would like to get out of the house."

Sierra was going to remind him that she'd taken them for a long walk in the park that morning, but it seemed like a moot point. He obviously wasn't going to take no for an answer, and she really would like to be there when they moved her dad, not only to make certain he was handled respectfully, but also to see that none of his very few possessions were left behind. The pictures and keepsakes. Not that he would know either way. Maybe, she thought sadly, it would be best if she just held on to them now.

"I'll call the nursing home tomorrow and find out when the ambulance will be there. Maybe we could be there a half an hour or so beforehand, then follow them over to the new facility."

"Just let me know when and I'll be ready."

"Thanks."

He narrowed his eyes slightly. "But…you're still wondering why I'm doing this for you. You apparently have this preconceived notion about the kind of person that I am."

She couldn't deny it. He would be surprised by how much she actually did know about him. The real stuff, not the rumors and conjecture. But she couldn't tell him that.

"Believe it or not, I'm a pretty decent guy." He paused then added, "And an above-average dancer."

She would have to take his word on that. "I clearly have trust issues," she said. Fool me once, shame on you, and all of that. Maybe he didn't have ulterior motives, but that was not usually the case. And under normal circumstances she would have told him no on principle alone, but just this one time she would make an exception.

"I guess it will just take time for you to believe that I'm not a bad guy," he said.

Honestly, she didn't understand why he cared what she thought of him. Was he this personable with all of his employees? Granted she had only worked for him a couple of days, but she had never seen him offer Ms. Densmore a glass of wine or heard him offer to drive her anywhere. She was sure it had a lot to do with Sierra being young and, yes, she was what most men considered attractive. Not a raving beauty but not too shabby, either. Then again, she was nowhere near as glamorous as the women she had seen him linked to in the past. But Coop hadn't been born wealthy. Who was to say he didn't enjoy slumming it occasionally?

Well, if he thought doing nice things for her was a direct route into her pants, that just because he was rich and famous and above average in the looks department she would go all gooey, he was in for a rude awakening.

Five

Sierra stood in her dad's new room, resisting the natural instinct to step in and help as the ambulance attendants worked with the nursing home staff to get her dad moved from the gurney to his bed, where he would most likely spend the rest of his life. At least in this new facility the staff was friendly and helpful and she could rest easy knowing that her dad would be well cared for. Unfortunately the ambulance had been an hour late to pick him up and the paperwork had taken an eternity.

Coop had been incredibly patient, taking over with the twins, but that patience had to be wearing thin by now. He was sitting in the rec room with them, and though she had fed them their lunch in the car on the way over, they were about an hour and a half past their nap time and last time she checked were getting fussy. She was thankful to have been around for the transfer, but she felt the crushing weight of guilt for making Coop—her employer—wait around for her.

She would have to make this visit a short one.

Once they got him situated in bed, everyone cleared out of the room. The nurse must have mistaken her guilt for conflicted feelings about her dad because she rubbed Sierra's arm, smiled warmly and said, "Don't worry, honey, we'll take good care of him."

When she was gone Sierra walked over to the bed. The curtain between him and his roommate was drawn, but according to the nurse, the man in the next bed was also comatose. "I can't stay, Dad, but I'll come back tomorrow, I promise."

She kissed his cheek, feeling guilty for cutting her visit so short, and headed to the rec room where Coop and the girls were waiting for her. To look at him, no one would guess that he was a multi-millionaire celebrity. In jeans, a T-shirt and worn tennis shoes, pacing the floor, looking completely at ease with one restless twin in each arm, he looked like just a regular guy. Albeit most "regular" guys weren't six-three with the physique of an Adonis.

She would be lying if she denied it was an adorable sight, the way he bounced the girls patiently. For someone who hadn't anticipated being a dad, and had the duty thrust on him unexpectedly, he had done amazingly well. She couldn't help but wonder if she had been unfairly harsh on him. In the five days she'd worked for him she had seen no hint of the womanizing party animal. So why couldn't she shake the feeling that he was destined to let the girls down?

It was all very confusing.

"I'm so sorry it's taken this long," she told him, plucking a wiggling Ivy from him.

"It's okay," Coop said, looking as though he genuinely meant it. "Is he all settled in?"

"Finally." Ivy squirmed in her arms, so Sierra transferred her to the opposite hip. "Let's get out of here. These two are way past their nap time."

"You don't want to stay and visit a little longer?"

She figured by now he would have been exasperated with the girls' fussing and would be gunning to get back on the road for home. To his credit, though, he hadn't once complained. Not while they sat at the other nursing home waiting for the transport, or when they sat stuck in weekend traffic. But as much as she would love to stay for just a little while longer, to make sure the trip had no adverse effects on her dad physically, she had already taken up way too much of Coop's personal time.

"I'll come by tomorrow on my time off," she told Coop, grabbing the packed-to-the-gills designer label diaper bag and slinging it over her shoulder. Coop commandeered the double umbrella stroller—top-of-the-line, of course, because when it came to the twins Ash and Susan had spared no expense—and they walked out of the building and through the parking lot to his vehicle. Earlier that morning, as she waited on the sidewalk outside his building for him to bring the car around, she'd expected either some flashy little sports car—which logistically she knew wouldn't work with two infants—or at the opposite end of the excess spectrum, a Hummer. Instead he had pulled up in a low-key silver SUV, proving once again that the man she thought she had pegged and the real Cooper were two very different people.

She and Coop each buckled a twin into her car seat, and within five minutes of exiting the lot, both girls were out cold.

"So, where to now?" Coop asked.

Sierra just assumed they would head back into the city. "Home, I guess."

"But it's a gorgeous summer afternoon. We should do something. I don't know about you, but I'm starving. Why don't we grab a bite to eat?"

"The girls just fell asleep. If we wake them up now and drag them into a restaurant, I don't anticipate it being a pleasant experience."

"Good point."

"Besides, don't you need to get home? It's Saturday. You must have plans for later."

"Nope, no plans tonight," Coop said.

He hadn't gone out the night before, either. The four of them had eaten dinner together, then Coop wrestled and played with the twins until their bedtime. After they were tucked into bed, Sierra thought for sure that he would go out, but when she emerged from the laundry room after putting in her daily load of soiled clothes, Coop had been sitting in the living room with two glasses of wine. And though she had planned on reading for a while then going to sleep early, it seemed rude to turn him down after he had gone through the trouble of actually pouring the wine.

One quick glass, she had promised herself, and she would be in bed before nine-thirty. But one glass turned into two, and she and Coop got to talking about his hockey playing days—a subject that even she had to admit was pretty interesting—and before she knew it, it was nearly midnight. Though he did still make her a little nervous and the idea of a friendship with him made her slightly uncomfortable, he was so easygoing and charming she couldn't help but like him.

"On our way in we passed a deli and a small park,"

he said. "We could pick up sandwiches, eat in the car, then go for a drive while the twins sleep."

That actually wasn't a bad idea. If they took the twins home now, the minute they took them out of their car seats they would probably wake up, cutting their nap short by at least an hour, which would probably make them crabby for the rest of the day. But the idea of spending so much time in such close quarters with Coop made her nervous. Not that she was worried he would act inappropriately. If he had wanted to try something, he would have done it by now, and aside from ogling her in her nightie the other evening—which admittedly was her own fault for not putting on a robe—he'd been a perfect gentleman. These feelings of unease were her own doing.

Illogical and inappropriate as it was, she was attracted to Coop, and clearly the feeling was mutual. The air felt electrically charged whenever he was near, and then there was that unwelcome little zap of energy that passed between them whenever they touched, even if it was something as innocent as their fingers brushing when he handed her a jar of baby food. And even though she had no intention whatsoever of expanding the dynamics of their relationship to include intimacy, she couldn't shake the feeling that they were crossing some line of morality.

But what the heck, it was just a sandwich. And it really was the best thing for the girls, and that was what mattered, right?

"I could eat," she said.

"Great." He flashed her one of those adorable grins. The dimpled kind that made her heart go all wonky.

God, she was pathetic.

Though she offered to go inside the deli and order

the food while he waited with the girls, he insisted on going himself and refused the money she tried to give him to cover the expense of her food.

"You shouldn't have to pay for my lunch," she told him.

"If we were at home you would be eating food that I paid for, so what's the difference?"

It was tough to argue with logic like that. Besides, he was out of the car before she could utter another word.

He was in and back out of the deli in five minutes with his grilled Reuben and her turkey on whole grain. He also got coleslaw, a bag of potato chips, bottled water and sodas. They found the park a few blocks away and parked in a spot facing the playground under the shade of a tree. Sierra worried the girls might wake up when he shut the engine off, but they were both out cold.

They spread their lunch out on the console and started eating.

"Can I ask you a question?" she said.

"Sure."

"Besides being a celebrity, what do you do now? For a living, I mean. Do you work?"

Her question seemed to amuse him. "I work really hard actually. I have my own line of hockey equipment coming out, and I started a chain of sports centers a few years ago and they've taken off. We're opening six more by next January."

"What kind of sports centers?"

"Ice rinks and indoor playing fields. Kids sports are big business these days. On top of that I own a couple dozen vacation properties around the world that I rent out. Also very lucrative."

Wow, so much for her theory that he sat around basking in his former fame. It sounded as if he kept himself really busy.

"Where are the vacation homes?" she asked him.

He named off the different cities, and then described the sorts of properties he owned. The list was an impressive one. Clearly he was a very sharp businessman.

"I never realized there was such a market for rental vacation homes."

"Most people aren't in a financial position to drop the money on a home they may only use a couple of times a year, so they rent. Not only is it a lot cheaper, but also you're not locked into one city or country."

She reached into the bag of chips for her third handful.

"I guess you were hungry," Coop teased.

She shot him a look. "Be careful, or you'll give me a complex."

"Are you kidding? I think it's great that you eat like a normal human being. I've taken women to some of the finest restaurants in the city and they order a side salad and seltzer water, or, even worse, they order a huge expensive meal and eat three bites."

"Maybe this is a dumb question, but if it bothers you so much, why do you always date super-skinny women? I mean, doesn't that sort of come with the territory?"

"Convenience, I guess."

Her brows rose. *"Convenience?"*

"They just happen to be the kind of women who hang around the people I hang around with."

"You mean, the kind who throw themselves at you."

He shrugged. "More or less."

"Have you ever had to actually pursue a woman you wanted to date?"

He thought about that for a second, then shook his head and said, "No, not really. In fact, never."

"Seriously? Not once? Not even in high school?"

"Since I was old enough to take an interest in girls I was the team star. Girls flocked to me."

She shook her head in disbelief. "Wow. That's just… *wow.*"

"Can you blame them? I mean, look at me. I'm rich, good-looking, a famous athlete. Who wouldn't want me? I'm completely irresistible."

She couldn't tell if he was serious or just teasing her. Could he honestly be *that* arrogant? "I wouldn't."

That seemed to amuse him. "You already do. You try to pretend you don't, but I can sense it."

"I think you've been hit in the head with a hockey stick a few too many times because I do *not* want you. You aren't even my type."

"But that's what makes it so exciting. You know you shouldn't like me, you know it's wrong because you work for me, but you just can't stop thinking about me."

How did he do that? How did he always seem to know what was going on inside her head? It was probably the third or fourth time he'd done this to her. It couldn't just be a lucky guess.

It was disturbing and…fascinating. And no way in *hell* could she ever let him know just how right he was. "So what you're saying is, all that stuff about you being a nice guy was bull. Everything nice that you've done is because you've been trying to get into my pants?"

"No, I am a nice guy. And for the record, if all I wanted was to get into your pants, I'd have been there by now."

Her eyes went wide. "Oh, really?"

"You're not nearly as tough as you think you are. If I tried to kiss you right now, you wouldn't stop me."

The thought of him leaning over the console and pressing his lips to hers made her heart flutter and her stomach bottom out. But she squared her shoulders and said, "If you tried to kiss me, you would be wearing the family jewels for earrings."

He threw his head back and laughed.

"You don't think I would do it?"

"No, you probably would, just to prove how tough you are. Then you would give in and let me kiss you anyway."

"The depth of your arrogance is truly remarkable."

"It's one of my most charming qualities," he said, but his grin said that he was definitely teasing her this time.

Maybe the confidence was a smoke screen, or this was his way of testing the waters or teasing her. Maybe he really liked her, but being so used to women throwing themselves at him, the possibility of being rejected scared him.

Weirdly enough, the idea that under the tough-guy exterior there could be a vulnerable man made him that much more appealing.

Ugh. What was *wrong* with her?

"Even if I did want you," she said, "which, despite what you believe, I really don't, I would never risk it. I can't even imagine putting my father back in that hell-hole we just got him out of. And without this job I can't even come close to affording the new place. So I have every reason *not* to want you."

Before Coop had time to process that, Ivy began to stir in the backseat.

"Uh-oh," he said, glancing back at her. "We better get moving before she wakes up."

He balled up the paper wrapper from his sandwich and shoved it back in the bag, then started the engine. She thought once they got moving, he might segue back into the conversation, but he turned the radio on instead, and she breathed a silent sigh of relief. She hoped she had made her point, he would drop the subject forever and the sexual tension that had been a constant companion in their relationship would magically disappear. Then they could have a normal employee/employer relationship. Because she feared Coop was right. If he kissed her, she wasn't sure she would be able to tell him no.

And she had the sinking feeling that this conversation, inappropriate as it was, was nowhere close to over.

Six

Sierra didn't hear from her sister very often. She would go months at a time without a single word. Sierra would call and leave messages that Joy wouldn't return, send cards that would come back as undeliverable. Then out of the blue Joy would call and always with the same feeble excuses. She was crazy-busy, or had moved, or her phone had been disconnected because she couldn't pay the bill. But the reality was that Joy was fragile. Watching their mother slowly waste away had damaged her. She simply didn't have the emotional capacity to handle the hopelessness of their dad's illness and dealt with it by moving a couple thousand miles away and cutting off all contact.

Sierra hadn't even been able to reach her when she learned about Ash and Susan's death, and frankly she could have used a bit of emotional support. Which was why Sierra was surprised to see her name on her caller

ID that night after she and Coop put the twins to bed. She had just stepped out of the room and was closing the door when her phone started to ring.

She considered not answering, giving Joy a taste of her own medicine for a change. Sometimes she got tired of being the responsible sister. But after two rings guilt got the best of her. Suppose it was something important? And what if Joy didn't call again for months? Besides their dad and the twins, Sierra had no one else. Not to mention that it was an awesome excuse to skip the post-bedtime glass of wine with Coop. And after what had happened this afternoon, the less time she spent with him the better.

"It's my sister. I have to take this," she said, slipping into her bedroom and shutting the door, pretending she didn't see the brief flash of disappointment that passed across his face.

"Guess who!" Joy chirped when Sierra answered.

"Hey, sis." She sat on the edge of her bed. "What's it been, three months?"

That earned a long-suffering sigh from her sister. "I know, I know, I should call more often. But what I've got to say now will make up for it."

"Oh, yeah?" Somehow she doubted that.

"I'm coming home!"

"You're moving back to New York?"

Sierra's heart lifted, then swiftly plunged when her sister laughed and said, "God, no! Are you kidding? Los Angeles is too fabulous to leave. I'm staying at a friend's Malibu beachfront home and it's totally amazing. In fact, I'm sitting in the sand, watching the tide move in as we speak."

She could just picture Joy in one of her flowing peasant skirts and gauzy blouses, her long, tanned legs folded beneath her, her waist-length, wavy black hair blowing in the salty breeze. She would be holding a designer beer in her hand with one of those skinny cigarettes she liked to smoke dangling between two fingers. She had always been so much cooler than Sierra, so much more self-confident. Yet so tortured. And she was sure that the friend Joy was staying with was a man and that she was also sharing his bedroom.

"Then why did you say you're coming home?" Sierra asked.

"Because I'm flying in for a visit."

"When?"

"A week from this coming Wednesday. They're holding auditions for an independent film that's supposed to start filming this August and my agent thinks I'm a shoo-in for the lead roll. I'll be in town a week just in case I get a callback."

"That sounds promising." Although according to Joy, her agent thought she was a shoo-in for every role he set her up for, or so it seemed.

"I know what you're thinking," Joy said.

"I didn't say a word."

"You didn't have to. I can feel your skepticism over the phone line. But this is different. My new agent has some really awesome connections."

"New agent? What happened to the old one?"

"I didn't tell you about that? We parted ways about two months ago."

And Sierra hadn't talked to her in three months. "Why? I thought he was some sort of super-agent."

"His wife sort of caught us going at it in his office."

"You *slept* with your *married* agent?" Why did that not surprise her?

"A girl does what she can to get ahead, and it was

no hardship, believe me. Besides, you're not exactly in a position to pass judgment."

Technically the twins' father was a married man, but it was a totally different situation. "He and his wife were separated, and it was only that one night."

By the time she realized she was pregnant, he and his wife had reconciled. Not that she would have wanted to marry him. He was a nice guy, but they both knew right after it happened that it had been a mistake.

"So, you said you're coming to visit?" Sierra said, changing the subject.

"For a week. And needless to say, I'll be staying with my favorite sister."

"Oh." That was going to be a problem.

"What do you mean, 'oh'? I thought you would be happy to see me."

"I am. It's just that staying with me is going to be a problem."

"Why? Don't tell me you're living with someone. And even if you are, he damned well better let your baby sister stay for a couple of nights."

"I actually am living with someone, but not in the way that you think. I mean, we're not a couple. I work for him."

"As a nurse?"

"As a nanny."

"A *nanny?* You gave the girls up, what, six months ago? Isn't that, like, a painful reminder?"

"Joy, hold on a minute, I have to check something." She walked to her door and opened it a crack. If she was going to tell Joy what was going on, she didn't want to risk Coop overhearing. From the living room she could hear the television and knew he was probably in his favorite chair, engrossed in whatever sporting event he was watching. She closed her door and walked back to the bed. "Did you get any of my messages about the twins' adoptive parents?"

"I did, yeah. I wanted to call, but...you know..."

She was sorry, but she couldn't deal with it. Same old story. "Well, the girls went to their uncle, Ash's brother."

"Isn't he like some famous athlete or something?"

"A former hockey player. A womanizing party animal. Not exactly the sort of person I wanted raising my girls."

"Oh, Si, I'm so sorry. Have you talked to your lawyer? Is there anything he can do? Can you claim he's unfit and get the girls back?"

She fidgeted with the edge of the pillowcase, knowing this next part was not going to go over well. "My lawyer talked to his lawyer, but he refused to give them up. There's nothing I can do. So I took matters into my own hands."

Joy gasped. "You *kidnapped* them?"

Sierra laughed. "Of course not! I would never do something like that. But I needed to be there for them, to know that they were okay, so when I heard that he was looking for a nanny..."

Another gasp. "Are you saying that *you're* the twins' nanny?"

"You should see them, Joy. They're so beautiful and so sweet. And I get to be with them 24/7."

"And this guy, their uncle, he knows you're their mother?"

"God, no! And he can never know."

"Sierra, that's *crazy*. What are you going to do, just take care of the girls for the rest of your life, with them never knowing that you're their birth mother?"

"I'll stay with them as long as they need me. And maybe some day I can tell them the truth."

"What about your life? What about men and marriage and having more kids? You're just going to give that all up."

"Not forever. I figure once they're in school full-time they won't need me nearly as much. As long as I'm here in the mornings and when they get home after school, they won't really need me to spend the night."

"It sounds as if you have it all figured out."

"I do."

"And this uncle…"

"Coop. Coop Landon."

"Is he really awful?"

In a way she wished he was. It would make this a lot less confusing. "Actually, he seems like a good guy. So far. Not at all what I expected." Almost too good, *too* nice. "He's really committed to taking care of the twins. For now anyway. That doesn't mean he won't eventually revert back to his old ways. That's why it's so important that I'm here for the girls. To see that they're raised properly."

"Suppose he finds out who you are? What then?"

"He won't. The original birth certificate is sealed, and obviously Ash and Susan never told him. There's no possible way that he could find out."

"Famous last words."

She brushed off her sister's concerns. "Just be happy for me, okay? This is what I want."

"Oh, honey, I am happy for you. I just don't want to see you hurt."

"I won't be. It's foolproof." As long as she didn't do something stupid, like fall for Coop. "So anyway, that's why you can't stay with me. I'm living in his Upper East Side penthouse apartment."

"Sounds…roomy."

Not that roomy. "Joy, you can't stay here."

"Why not? You said this Coop is a good guy. I'm sure he wouldn't mind."

"Joy—"

"You could at least ask. Because frankly I have nowhere else to go. My credit cards are maxed out and I have three dollars in my checking account. My agent had to lend me the money for the ticket, which of course is nonrefundable. If I can't stay with you, I'm crashing on a park bench."

She would pay for a hotel for her sister if she could, but there wasn't a decent place within thirty blocks that was less that one-fifty a night. The expense of moving their dad had taken up all of Sierra's cash, and like Joy, her credit cards were maxed out. It was going to take her months to catch up. And though she hated the idea of taking advantage of Coop's hospitality, this could be the perfect opportunity for a dose of emotional blackmail. "I'll ask him on one condition."

"Anything."

"You have to swear that when you're here you'll come with me to see Dad."

She sighed heavily. "Si, you know how I feel about those places. They creep me out."

"Just recently I was able to move him into a really nice place in Jersey. It's not creepy at all."

"It's just the idea of all those old, sick people…ugh."

She fought the urge to tell her sister to grow up. "This is Dad we're talking about. The man who raised you, remember?"

"According to what you told me the last time we

talked, he's not even going to know I'm there. So what's the point?"

"We don't know that for sure. And he probably doesn't have much time left. This could be the last time you see him alive."

"Do you really think that's how I want to remember him?"

And did she think Sierra enjoyed bearing the brunt of his illness alone? Both emotionally and financially. "I'm sorry, but this is nonnegotiable. Either you promise, or it's the park bench for you."

Joy was quiet for several seconds, then she sighed again and said, "Fine, I'll go see him."

"And I'll ask Coop if you can stay." He had already done so much for her, had been so accommodating, she didn't want him to think that she was taking advantage of his hospitality. Yet she had little doubt that he would say yes. He seemed to like to keep up the "good guy" persona. On the bright side, Joy wouldn't be coming in for another week and a half, so Sierra could wait at least another week to ask him. Surely by then she would have worked off the last favor. She couldn't think of anything worse than being indebted to a man like Coop. There might just come a day when he called in the debt and demanded payment.

She would do this one thing for her sister's sake, but after that she would never ask Coop for a favor again.

"Dude, they're Russian models," Vlad said, but with his thick accent, *dude* came out sounding more like *dute*. "These babes are *super hot*. You can't say no."

As Coop had explained to his other former teammate, Niko, who had called him last night, he had turned over a new leaf. His days of staying out all night partying and bringing home women—even if they were *super hot*—were over. Vlad's call suggested that either he hadn't talked to Niko or he didn't think Coop had been serious.

"Sorry dude, you're going to have to count me out. Like I told Niko, I'm a family man now."

"But you find nanny, yes?"

"Yes, but I'm still responsible for the twins. They need me around."

Vlad grumbled a bit and gave him a serious ribbing for "losing his touch," but it didn't bother Coop. He said goodbye and reached down to pick up the toy Ivy had flung onto the sidewalk from the stroller and gave it back to her. The warm morning breeze rustled the newspapers on the table beside them on the café patio, and as he caught a glimpse of Sierra through the front window, standing in line, waiting to order them a cappuccino, Coop felt utterly content.

Besides, if the deal went through and he bought the team, the entire dynamic of his relationship with his former teammates would change. He would go from being their teammate and partner in crime to their boss. But he was ready to make that change.

He stuck his phone back in his shorts pocket and adjusted the stroller so that the twins were shaded from the morning sun. It would be another scorching day as July quickly approached, but at nine-thirty the temperature was an ideal seventy-five degrees. Most days, before the twins, he wouldn't have even been out of bed yet. In his twenties he could have easily spent the entire night out, slept a few hours, then arrived to practice on time and given a stellar performance. Recently though, the late nights out had been taking their toll. Parties and barhopping until 5:00 a.m. usually meant sleeping half the day away.

These days he was in bed before midnight—sometimes even earlier—and up with the sun. He had always been more of a night owl and had figured that the radical change to his schedule would be jarring, but he found that he actually liked getting up early. This morning he had woken before dawn, made coffee and sat on the rooftop terrace to watch the sun rise. He came back down with his empty cup a while later to find Sierra, still in her nightgown, fixing the twins their morning bottles.

She had jumped out of her skin when he said good morning, clearly surprised to find that he was already up. And though he'd tried to be a gentleman and not ogle her, he found himself staring at her cleavage again. And her legs. A woman as attractive as Sierra couldn't walk around half-naked with a man in the house and expect him to look the other way. And the fact that she hadn't tried to cover herself, nor did she set any speed records mixing the formula and filling the bottle, told him that maybe she liked him looking.

He glanced through the front window of the café and saw that she had inched ahead several feet in line and was only a few customers away from the counter. It had been his idea to stop for coffee and also his idea to come with her and the girls for their morning walk. He had just gotten back from jogging in the park as she was walking out the door. And it was an intrusion on her routine that had Sierra's panties in a serious twist. No big surprise considering the way she had been avoiding him the past week. He was sure it had everything to do with their conversation the day they moved her dad into the new nursing home. She could pretend all she liked, but she wasn't fooling him. She wanted him just as much as he wanted her.

A shadow passed over him and he looked up expecting Sierra, surprised to find an unfamiliar young woman in athletic attire standing by the table clutching a bottled water.

"Mr. Landon," she gushed, sounding a little out of breath. "Hi. I just wanted to say, I'm a *huge* fan."

Her long blond hair was pulled back in a ponytail and a sheen of sweat glazed her forehead. She must have been jogging past and noticed him sitting there. He wasn't really in the mood to deal with a fan, but he turned on the charm and said, "Thank you, Miss…"

"It's Amber. Amber Radcliff."

"It's nice to meet you, Amber."

Short and petite, she could have easily passed for seventeen, but he had the feeling she was closer to twenty-five. Just the right age. She was also very attractive, not to mention slender and toned. In fact, she was exactly the sort of woman he would normally be attracted to, yet when she smiled down at him, he didn't feel so much as a twinge of interest. She didn't even seem to notice that there was a stroller beside him with two infants inside.

"I've been a hockey fan, like, my *whole* life," she said, slipping uninvited into the empty seat across from him. "My dad has season tickets and we never missed a home game. I know you probably hear this all the time, but I am truly your number-one fan."

Her and a couple hundred thousand other fans. "Well, then I'm glad you stopped to say hi."

"The team just hasn't been the same since you retired. Last season was such a disappointment. I mean, they didn't even make the championships."

"I'm sure things will turn around next season." Because he would be in charge. Negotiations were currently at a standstill, but he was confident the current owner would come around and accept Coop's very reasonable offer.

Sierra appeared at the table, holding two cappuccinos and looking annoyed, not that he blamed her with some strange woman sitting in her chair. "Excuse me."

Amber looked up, gave Sierra a quick once-over, flashed her an oh-no-you-didn't look and said, "Excuse *me,* but I saw him first."

Seven

Sierra's brows rose, and Coop stifled a laugh. It was like that sometimes with fans. They figured just because they'd shelled out the cash to watch him bang a puck around the ice, they had some sort of claim on his personal time.

"Sierra," he said, "this is Amber. She's my biggest fan."

Sierra set the drinks down on the table with a clunk. "Charmed to meet you, Amber, but you're in my seat."

"Oh…sorry." Amber flushed a vivid shade of pink and awkwardly stood. "I didn't realize…"

"It's all good," Coop said, smiling up at her. "Give my best to your dad, and tell him I said thanks for being such a loyal fan. And don't give up on the team. They'll come back strong next season, I guarantee it."

She mumbled a goodbye, tripping on the wheel of the stroller in her haste to get away.

"Well, that was interesting," Sierra said, sliding into her seat.

"It's the price you pay as a celebrity, I guess."

"Are all your fans that rude?"

"Some are a bit more aggressive than others, but no harm done. Besides, without the fans, I wouldn't have had a job. There wouldn't be a league, and I would have no team to buy." He took a sip of his cappuccino. "Delicious. Thanks."

"Were the twins okay?"

"Fine. Although Ivy keeps tossing her toy on the ground."

"Because she knows you'll pick it back up again."

"They do have me wrapped," he admitted, smiling down at them. And he would no doubt continue to spoil them until they were all grown up.

Sierra was quiet for a minute, a furrow in her brow as she gazed absently at her cup, running her thumb around the edge. She had seemed distracted all morning, as if there was something on her mind. Something bothering her. He would like to know if it was something he had done.

"Penny for your thoughts," he said.

She looked up. "You don't want to know."

Whatever it was, it looked as if it wasn't pleasant. If she was about to tell him she was quitting, after so adamantly vowing her dedication to the girls, he was going to be seriously pissed off. "Is there a problem?"

"Not exactly, no."

"Then what is it exactly?"

"I need a favor. A really big one. And I want you to know that you are under absolutely no obligation to say yes. But I promised I would at least ask."

"So ask me."

Ivy started to fuss, so Sierra reached into the diaper bag for a bottle of juice and handed it to her, and when Fern saw it and began to fuss, she gave her one, too. "The thing is, my sister has an audition in New York so she's coming to visit."

"Do you need time off?"

She shook her head. "No. Anything we do together we can take the girls with us. The thing is, she would normally crash at my place. Unfortunately, I hadn't actually gotten around to telling her about my new job, so she just assumed she could stay with me. I guess she had to borrow money from her agent for the plane ticket, which is nonrefundable of course, and she doesn't have money for a hotel."

"So you want to know if she can stay with us."

"I wouldn't even ask, but Joy is a master at making me feel guilty. She threatened to sleep on a park bench."

"When? And how long?"

"She's flying in around noon tomorrow and staying a week. Which I know is a really long time."

He shrugged and said, "That's fine."

"You're sure you don't mind? Because you shouldn't be expected to invite complete strangers into your home."

"But she's not a stranger. She's your sister. And for the record, it's not a very big favor. If you asked me for a kidney, or a lung, that would be a big deal."

"But she's a stranger to you, and I feel like a dork for putting you on the spot."

He drew in a breath and sighed. Would she ever learn that he wasn't the ogre she seemed to have pegged him for? "Because we both know that deep down I'm a big fat jerk who would never do something nice for someone if not forced."

She shot him a look. "You know that isn't what I mean."

Sometimes she made him feel that way, as if she always expected the worst from him, despite the fact that in the two weeks he had known her, he had been nothing but courteous and accommodating and he hadn't once complained about anything. Someone must have done a serious number on her to make her so wary of trusting him. And trusting her own instincts.

"She's welcome to stay. And I'm not saying that because I feel obligated or because I'm trying to get into your pants."

Sierra bit her lip and lowered her eyes. "I didn't think that."

Not that he didn't want to. Get into her pants, that is. But not at the expense of losing her as the twins' nanny, and certainly not if she felt she owed him out of some sense of duty or repayment.

Ivy tossed her bottle this time, so far that it hit the chair leg of the elderly woman sitting at the next table. She leaned down to pick it up, carefully wiped it off with her napkin, then gave it back to Ivy, who squealed happily.

"What beautiful little girls," the woman said with a smile. "They look just like their mommy, but they have their daddy's eyes."

There didn't seem any point in trying to explain the situation, so Coop just smiled and thanked the woman. When he turned back to Sierra, she looked troubled. Did the idea that someone might mistake the twins for their children disturb her so much? There were an awful lot of women out there who would be happy to earn that distinction. Clearly she was not one of them.

She leaned in and whispered, "You don't think they look like me, do you?"

"I can see why someone might think you're their mother."

"What do you mean?"

"You have similar skin tone and dark hair. But do you actually look alike?" He shrugged. "I don't really see it. And other than the fact that they have two eyes, the similarities between them and me pretty much stop there." He paused then said, "However, to see you with the twins, one would naturally assume they are yours."

She cocked her head slightly. "Why is that?"

"Because you treat them like a mother would treat her own children."

"I'm not sure what you mean. How else am I supposed to treat them?"

"Susan once told me that before she and Ash adopted the girls, she would sit at the park on her lunch break and watch the kids on the playground, hoping that some day she could watch her own kids playing there. She said she could always tell which of the adults were parents and which were nannies or au pairs. The parents interacted with their kids. She said you could just tell that they wanted to be there, that they cared. The caregivers, however, stood around in packs basically ignoring the kids and talking amongst themselves, occasionally shouting out a reprimand. She said that she made her mind up then that if she ever was blessed with a baby, she would quit working and stay home. And she did."

"It sounds like she was a really good mom," Sierra said softly.

"She was. So I'm sure you can imagine how I must have felt, knowing I had to hire a nanny, when Susan was so against the idea. Knowing that there was no way I could manage it alone, be both a mom and a dad to them. Feeling as if I was letting them down, as if I had failed them somehow. But then you came along, and in two weeks time you have surpassed my expectations by leaps and bounds. I can rest easy knowing that even when I can't be around, the twins are loved and well cared for. And even though they don't have a mom, they have someone who gives them all the love and affection a real mom would."

Sierra bit her lip, and her eyes welled up. He hadn't meant to make her cry. He just wanted her to know what an important part of their lives she had become and how much he appreciated it. And that it had nothing to do with wanting to get into her pants.

He reached across the table and wrapped his hand around hers, half expecting her to pull away. "So when I do something nice for you, it's because I want you to know how much we appreciate having you around. And I want you to be as happy with us as we are with you. I want you to feel like you're a part of our family. Unconventional as it is."

She swiped at her eyes with her free hand. "Thank you."

Ivy shrieked and threw her bottle again, and this time Fern followed suit. Coop let go of Sierra's hand to pick them up. "I think the natives are getting restless."

She sniffled and swiped at her eyes again. "Yeah, we should probably get moving."

Leaving their barely touched cappuccinos behind, they gathered their things and left the café. Coop had the overwhelming desire to link his fingers through hers, but with both her hands clutching the stroller handle he couldn't have anyway.

It defied logic, this irrational need to be close to her. To do things like skip meetings and ignore his friends just to spend time with her and the twins. He could have practically any other woman that he wanted. Women who showered him with flattery and clawed over each other for his attention. Women willing to be whatever and whoever he wanted just to make him happy.

Didn't it just figure that he had to fall for the one woman who didn't want him?

While the girls napped Sierra did laundry, wishing that this morning at the coffee shop had never happened.

Did Coop have to be so darned nice all the time? That stuff about her taking care of the girls was hands down the sweetest and kindest thing anyone had ever said to her. He was making it really hard for her to not like him. In fact, when he'd taken her hand in his… oh, my God. His hand was big and strong and had a roughness that should have been unpleasant, yet all she could think about was him rubbing it all over her. If they hadn't been in a public place, she might have done something completely insane like fling the table aside, plant herself in his lap and kiss him senseless. And then she would have divested him of the tank top and running shorts and put *her* hands all over *him*. The fact that he was still sweaty, unshaven and disheveled from his run should have been a turnoff, yet when she imagined touching his slick skin, feeling the rasp of his beard against her cheek, tasting the salty tang of his lips, she'd gone into hormone overload. She didn't even like sweaty, disheveled, unshaven men.

Why was she even thinking about this?

As good as it would be—and she *knew* it would be

good—it would be a mistake. She still wasn't sure why he was attracted to her in the first place. Was it convenience—because he said himself that was how he normally chose his women? And what could be more convenient than a woman living right under his roof? Or was it the thrill of the chase fueling his interest? And if she let him catch her, just how long would it take before he got bored?

Probably not very long. And after he dumped her, she would find herself heartbroken, out of a job, homeless, and, worst of all, ripped away from her children. She simply had too much to lose. She had to do what was best for them.

The spin cycle ended and she tossed the damp linens into the dryer along with a dryer sheet and set it on High, then she dumped hers and the girls' dirty clothes in the washing machine.

She poured a scoop of detergent over the clothes, then realized she was still wearing the shirt that Fern had flung a glob of pureed carrots all over at lunch. Ms. Densmore was at the market and Coop had left an hour ago for a meeting that he said would drag on until at least dinnertime, so figuring she could make it from the laundry room to her bedroom undetected in her bra, she pulled the shirt over her head, spritzed the spot with stain remover and tossed it in, too.

She shut the lid, started the machine and headed out of the laundry room…stopping dead in her tracks when she realized that Coop was in the kitchen.

For a second she thought that her mind must be playing tricks on her. No one's luck could be *that* bad.

She blinked. Then she blinked again.

Nope, that was definitely Coop, his hip wedged against the island countertop, his eyes lowered as he sorted through the mail he must have picked up on his way in. And any second now he was going to look up and see her standing there in her bra.

She could make a run for her bedroom, but she couldn't imagine doing anything so undignified, nor would she run back to the laundry room. Besides, Coop must have sensed her there because he looked up. And *he* blinked. Then he blinked again. Then his eyes settled on her breasts and he said, "You're not wearing a shirt."

She could have at least covered herself with her hands or grabbed the dish towel hanging on the oven door, but for some weird reason she just stood there, as if, deep down she *wanted* him to see her half-naked. Which she was pretty sure she didn't.

"Ms. Densmore is at the market, and I didn't think you would be home so soon," she said.

"My lawyer had to cut the meeting short," he explained, his gaze still fixed below her neck. "For which I plan to thank him *profusely* the next time I see him."

The heat in his eyes was so intense she actually thought her bra might ignite. "That explains it then."

"Out of curiosity, do you always walk around in your bra when no one is home?"

"My shirt had carrots on it from the girls' lunch. I threw it in the washing machine." When he didn't respond she said, "You could be a gentleman and look the other way."

He tossed the mail on the counter, but it hit the edge, slid off and landed on the floor instead. "I could. And I would if I thought for a second that you didn't like me looking at you."

There he went, reading her mind again. She really wished he would stop doing that. "Who says I like it?"

"If you didn't you would have made some attempt to cover yourself or leave the room. And your heart wouldn't be racing."

Right again.

"Not to mention you're giving off enough pheromones right now to take down an entire professional hockey team. And you know what that means."

She didn't have a clue, but the idea of what it might be made her knees weak. "What does it mean?"

"It means that I *have* to kiss you."

Eight

"Coop, that would be a really bad idea," Sierra said, but her voice was trembling.

Maybe it was, but right now, Coop didn't care. He crossed the room toward her and she held her breath. "All you have to do is tell me no."

"I just did."

He stopped a few inches from her and he could actually feel the heat radiating from her bare skin. "You said it would be a bad idea, but you didn't actually say don't do it."

"But that was what I meant."

"So say it."

She opened her mouth and closed it again.

Oh, yeah, she wanted him. He reached up and ran the pad of his thumb up her arm, from elbow to shoulder, then back down again. Sierra shivered.

"Tell me to stop," he said, and when she didn't say

a word, when she just gazed up at him with lust-filled eyes, her cheeks flush with excitement, he knew she was as good as his.

He cupped her cheek in his palm, stroked with his thumb, and he could feel her melting, giving in. "Last chance," he said.

She blew out an exasperated breath. "Oh, for heaven's sake just shut up and *kiss* me already!"

He was smiling as he lowered his head, slanting his mouth over hers. When their lips touched, and her tongue slid against his, desire slammed him from every direction at once.

Holy hell.

Never in his life had he felt such an intense connection to a woman just from kissing her. Of course, he'd never met a woman quite like her. And he knew without a doubt that a kiss was never going to be enough. He wanted more…*needed* it in a way he had never needed anything before.

She slid her arms around his neck, trying to get closer, but his arm was in the way. She broke the kiss and looked down at his crotch, which he was cupping in his free hand, then she looked up at him questioningly.

"Just in case I was wrong and you followed through on your threat."

"Threat?"

"You said that if I tried to kiss you I would be wearing the family jewels for earrings."

She laughed and shook her head. "You do realize, the fact that you thought I might actually do it makes you about a million times more appealing."

He grinned. "I told you, I'm irresistible."

"Coop, this is so wrong," she said.

He slid his hands across her bare back. Sierra sighed and her eyes drifted closed. "Nothing that feels this good could be wrong."

She must have agreed because she wrapped her arms around his neck, pulled his head down and kissed him. He might have taken her right there in the kitchen—he sure wanted to—but Sierra deserved better than sex on the counter or up against the refrigerator. She wasn't some woman he'd picked up in a bar or at a party. She was special. She wasn't in it for the cheap thrill of being with a celebrity. This would mean something to her, something profound. She deserved tenderness and romance, and when he did make love to her—which he would do, there was no longer any doubt about that—he wanted to take his time. He didn't want to have to worry about things like the twins waking up from their nap, which they were likely to do pretty soon. And though he could be content to stand there kissing and touching her until they did, Ms. Densmore could walk in at any moment. Not that he gave a crap what *she* thought, but he didn't want Sierra to feel embarrassed or uncomfortable. He really *cared* about her, which was just too damned weird.

Could he possibly be falling in love with her?

He didn't *do* love. Hell, he usually didn't do next week. To him women were nothing more than a way to pass the time. And not because of some psychological wound or fear of commitment. He hadn't been profoundly wounded by his parents' death or dumped by his one true love. He hadn't been double-crossed or cheated on. He had just been too focused on his career to make the time for a long-term relationship. He also hadn't met anyone he'd cared so deeply for that he couldn't live without them. But it was bound to happen eventually, wasn't it? What was the saying? There was someone for everyone? Maybe Sierra was his someone.

It took every bit of restraint he possessed to break the kiss, when there was really no guarantee she would ever let him kiss her again. He was giving her time to rethink this, to change her mind. But that was just a chance he had to take.

He took her hands, pulled them from around his neck and cradled them against his chest. "We should stop before we get too carried away."

She looked surprised and disappointed and maybe a little relieved, too. "The girls will be up soon."

"Exactly. And unless you want Ms. Densmore to see you half-naked, you might want to put a shirt on."

She looked down, as though she had completely forgotten she wasn't wearing one. "It might almost be worth it to see the look on her face."

From behind the kitchen they heard the service-entrance door open. If she wanted to see the look on Ms. Densmore's face, this was her chance. Instead she turned tail and darted from the room, ponytail swishing.

He chuckled at her retreating back. Not so tough, was she?

Ms. Densmore appeared with two canvas shopping bags full of groceries. He'd told her a million times that she could just order the groceries and have them delivered, but she insisted on walking to the market and carrying the bags back herself nearly every day.

When she saw him standing there she said, "I didn't expect you home so soon."

She looked tired, so he took the bags from her and set them up on the countertop. "Meeting ended early."

While she put her purse away he poked through

the bags, finding a variety of fresh vegetables, several jars of baby food and a package of boneless, skinless chicken breasts. "Chicken for dinner tonight?"

"Chicken parmesan," she said, looking curiously at the mail on the floor and stooping to pick it up. "We need to talk."

He could see by her expression, which was more troubled than sour, that there was a problem. "What's up?"

She put the chicken in the fridge, closed the door and turned to him. "I'm afraid I can't work for you any longer."

He knew she wasn't thrilled with having the twins around, but he didn't think she was miserable enough to quit. She may not have been a very nice person, but she was a good housekeeper and he hated to lose her. "Is there a specific problem? And if so, is there anything I can do to fix it?"

"I took this job because it fit certain criteria. First, there were no children and not likely to ever be any, and second, you were rarely here. I like to be alone and left to my own devices. Since you brought the twins here everything has changed. I have to cook all the time and I hate cooking." She paused and said bitterly, "Not to mention that your nanny has been *tormenting* me."

He couldn't help laughing, which only made her glare at him. "I'm sorry, but *Sierra?* She's not exactly the tormenting type."

"She plays tricks on me."

"What kind of tricks?"

"She moves things around just to irritate me. She takes the milk off the door and puts it on the shelf and she rearranges things in the laundry room. She's petty and childish."

"I'll have a talk with her."

"It's too late for that. Besides, as long as the twins are around I won't ever be happy working here again."

He was sorry she felt that way, but neither did he want an unhappy employee. Or one who couldn't appreciate two sweet and beautiful infants. "So is this your two-week notice?"

"I got a new job and they need me to start immediately, so today is my last day."

Today? He couldn't believe she would leave him in a lurch that way.

"Let's not pretend that you wouldn't have eventually fired me. *She* would have insisted."

"Sierra? That's not her call."

"When she becomes the lady of the house it will be, and you know that will be the eventual outcome."

Coop had no idea that his feelings for Sierra were so obvious. And she was right. If he and Sierra did ever get married, she would insist that he get rid of Ms. Densmore, and of course he would because he would do practically anything she asked to make her happy.

"Don't worry," Ms. Densmore said. "You'll call a service and have a replacement before the week is out."

She was right. He just hated the idea of training someone new. "Do you mind my asking who you're going to be working for?"

"A diplomat and his wife. Their children are grown and they spend three weeks out of every month traveling. I'll pretty much be left alone to do my job."

"That sounds perfect for you."

"With the exception of the past month, it really has been a pleasure working for you, Mr. Landon. I just can't be happy here any longer. I'm too old and set in my ways to change."

"I understand."

"I'm sure Sierra can handle things until you find someone new."

He'd seen Sierra's bedroom. Housekeeping was a concept that seemed to escape her completely. Besides, with two infants to care for, she wouldn't have time to cook and clean, too. He needed someone within the next few days at the latest.

"Dinner will be ready at six-thirty," she said. "And I'm making a double recipe so there will be some left over. You can warm it for dinner later this week."

"Thanks."

She turned and busied herself starting dinner as Coop went to look for Sierra, to tell her what he was sure she would consider very good news. The nursery door was closed, meaning the girls were still asleep, so he knocked on Sierra's bedroom door instead. She opened it after a few seconds, and he was sorry to see that she had changed into a clean shirt.

"Have you got a minute?" he asked.

"Of course." She stepped aside and let him in. The bed was unmade, there was a bath towel draped over the chair, the desk was piled with papers and junk, and there was a pile of books and magazines on the floor next to the bed.

"Excuse the mess," she said. "I just can't ever seem to find the time to straighten up. After being with the girls all day I'm usually too exhausted to do much of anything."

Which meant doubling as housekeeper would be out of the question. "It's your room. If you want to keep it messy, that's your choice."

"I know it drives Ms. Densmore crazy, but she won't set foot in my room."

"Funny you should mention her. She's the reason I came to talk to you."

A worry line bisected Sierra's brow. "She didn't see me without my shirt on, did she?"

"Nope. But the way I hear it, you've been tormenting my housekeeper."

Uh-oh. Someone had tattled on her.

Sierra put on her best innocent look and asked, "What do you mean?"

Coop folded his arms, and though he was trying to look tough, there was humor in his eyes. "Don't even try to pretend that you don't know what I'm talking about. You know I can always tell when you're lying."

It was that mind-reading thing that he did. *So* annoying. "To call it 'torment' is an exaggeration. They were just...*pranks.* And you can't tell me that she didn't deserve it. She's so *mean.*"

"She just quit."

She gasped and slapped a hand over her heart. "She didn't!"

"She did, just now in the kitchen. This is her last day."

"Oh my gosh, Coop. I'm so sorry. I wanted to annoy her, not make her leave. This is all my fault. Do you want me to talk to her? Promise to behave from now on?"

He grinned and shook his head. "You may have accelerated the process, but she would have left eventually anyway. She said she's been unhappy since the girls moved in. It wasn't what she signed on for. I hired her five years ago, when I was still playing hockey and barely ever here. She liked it that way."

"I still feel bad."

"Don't," he said, and gestured to a framed photo on the dresser. "Is that your mom?"

She smiled and nodded. It was Sierra's favorite shot of her. It was taken in the park, on a sunny spring afternoon. Her mom was sitting cross-legged in the grass on the old patchwork quilt they always used for picnics or at the beach, and she was looking up at the camera, smiling. "Wasn't she beautiful?"

He walked over and picked it up. "Very beautiful."

"She was always smiling, always happy. And it was infectious. You could not be in the same room and not feel like smiling. And she loved hugs, loved to snuggle. She and I would curl up on the love seat together every Sunday and read books or do crossword puzzles all day long. She was so much fun, always thinking up new adventures, trying new things. And my dad loved her so much. He never remarried. He didn't even date very often. I don't think he ever got over losing her. They never fought, never bickered. They had the perfect marriage."

"She was Asian?" Coop asked.

She nodded. "Her grandmother was Chinese. I used to wish that I looked more like her."

"You do look like her."

"I actually favor my dad more. Joy looks more like she did."

"You really miss her."

She nodded. "Every day."

He walked over to where she stood, took her hand and tugged her to him. She didn't put up a fight when he pulled her close and looped his arms around her, and it felt so *good* to lay her head on his chest, to listen to the beat of his heart. He was so big and strong and he smelled so yummy. And kissing him...oh, my. It was a little slice of heaven. And now it was just going to be the two of them, alone in the house—with the girls, too, of course. The idea made her both excited and nervous. She knew that kissing Coop had been a bad idea and that letting it go any further would be a mistake of epic proportions. But couldn't she pretend, just for a little while, that they actually had a chance? That an affair with Coop wouldn't ruin everything?

No, because for whatever reason, and though it defied logic, he seemed to genuinely like her. If all he cared about was getting her between the sheets, that's where they would be right now. And if she believed for a second that his feelings for her were anything but a passing phase, she wouldn't hesitate to drag him there herself. Unfortunately, she and Coop were just too different. It would never work.

She untangled herself from his arms and backed away. "We need to talk."

"Why do I get the feeling that I'm not going to like this?"

"What happened earlier, it was really, *really* nice."

"But...?"

"You and I both know that it's not going to work."

"We don't know that."

"I don't want to have an affair."

"I don't, either. I know this will be hard for you to believe, but I want more this time. I'm ready."

If only that were true. "How can you know that? You've known me what? Two weeks?"

"I can't explain it. All I know is that I've never wanted anyone the way I want you. It just...feels right."

His expression was so earnest, she didn't doubt he believed every word he said, and oh how she wished she could throw caution to the wind and believe him, too. But there was too much at stake. "I want you, too, Coop. And I don't doubt that it will be really, really good for a while, but eventually something will go wrong. You'll be unhappy, and I'll be unhappy, then things will get awkward, and though you'll hate to have to do it, you'll fire me because it will be what's for the best."

"I wouldn't do that."

"Yes, you would. You wouldn't have any other choice. Because think about it—what are you going to do? Dump me, then bring other women home right in front of me?"

"You're assuming it won't work. But what if it does? We could be really good together."

"That isn't a chance I'm willing to take." And there was no way to make him understand why without telling him the truth. And if she was looking for a way to get fired, that was it.

"So, the job is more important than your feelings for me?" he asked.

"The girls need me more than you do. And, if I lose this job, my father goes back into that hellhole he was in. I won't do that to him."

She could tell by his frown that he knew she was right, he just didn't want to accept it.

"I could fire you now," he said. "Then you would be free to date me."

She raised her brows at him. "So what you're saying is, if I don't sleep with you, you'll fire me?"

His frown deepened, and he rubbed a hand across his jaw. "When you say it like that it sounds really sleazy."

"That's because it *is* sleazy. It's also sexual harassment." Not that she believed his threat was anything but an empty one. He just wasn't used to not getting his way, but he would have to *get* used to it.

In her jeans pocket, the cell phone started to ring and she pulled it out to check the display. When she saw the number of the nursing home her heart skipped like a stone on a very deep, cold lake. That always happened when someone called about her dad because her first thought was inevitably that he had passed away. But they had lots of other reasons for calling her. So why, this time, did she have an especially bad feeling?

"I have to take this," she told Coop. "It's the nursing home."

She answered the phone, pulse pounding, her heart in her throat.

"Miss Evans, this is Meg Douglas, administrator of Heartland Nursing Center."

"Hi, Meg, what can I do for you?" she asked, hoping she said something simple, like there was a form that needed to be signed or a treatment they needed authorization for.

"I'm so sorry to have to inform you that your father passed away."

Nine

Coop changed the twins' diapers, wrestled them into their pajamas, then sat in the rocking chair with them, one on each arm, but neither made it even halfway through their bottle before they were sound asleep. It had been a busy afternoon of going first to the nursing home so Sierra could see her dad one last time, then to the funeral home to make the final arrangements. By the time they finally got home it was well past the twins' bedtime.

Ms. Densmore had left dinner warming in the oven and, in a show of kindness that surprised both him and Sierra, a note on the refrigerator expressing her sympathy for Sierra's loss. She wasn't so sorry that she offered to stay on a few days longer, though. Not that he expected her to.

He got up and carried the twins' limp little bodies to their cribs, kissed them and tucked them in. For a minute he stood there, watching them sleep, feeling so…peaceful. At first he'd believed that once he hired someone to care for the twins, life would go back to the way it had been before he got the girls. Two months ago, if someone had told him he would enjoy being a parent and be content as a family man, he would have laughed in their face. He figured he would be happy playing the role of the fun and cool uncle, showering them with gifts and seeing that they were financially set while someone else dealt with the day-to-day issues. The feedings and the diapers and all the messy emotional stuff that would later come with hormonal teen-aged girls. He realized now that they deserved better than that. They deserved a real, conventional family.

Shutting the nursery door softly behind him, he took the half-finished bottles to the kitchen and stuck them in the fridge, just in case one or both of the girls woke up hungry in the middle of the night. His and Sierra's dinner dishes were still in the sink, so he rinsed them, stuck them in the dishwasher and set it to run, recalling the days when he and his brother hadn't even been able to afford a dishwasher, and doing them by hand had been Coop's responsibility. He'd had to do his own laundry and cook three days a week, too. Maybe he was spoiled now, but he had no desire to return to those days, even temporarily. And with caring for the twins, her sister's visit and planning her dad's memorial service, Sierra definitely wouldn't have time to clean and cook. He didn't even know if she *could* cook.

He made a mental note to call a service first thing tomorrow and set up interviews for a new housekeeper as soon as humanly possible.

Though he normally drank wine in the evenings, a cold beer had a nice ring to it tonight, so he grabbed two from the fridge. He switched out the kitchen light, hooked the baby monitor to his belt and walked to the rooftop terrace where he'd sent Sierra while he got the twins settled for bed. She'd balked, of course, and gave him the usual line about how he had done enough already and she needed to do her job, but with a little persuasion she'd caved. It was strange, but lately he'd begun thinking of her as not so much a nanny, but the two of them as partners in raising the girls. And he liked it that way.

The sun had nearly set, so he hit the switch and turned on the party lights that hung around the perimeter of the terrace.

Sierra looked up from the lounge chair where she sat, her knees tucked up under her chin. When they got home she had changed into shorts and a tank top, and her feet were bare. He half expected her to be crying, but her eyes were dry. The only time she had cried today was when she'd gone into her dad's room.

"Are the twins in bed?" she asked.

"Out cold before their heads hit the mattress," he said, holding up one of the two beers. "Can I interest you in a cold one?"

"That actually sounds really good, thanks."

He twisted the tops off and handed her one of the bottles, then stretched out in the chair beside hers.

She took a long, deep pull on her drink, sighed contentedly and said, "That hits the spot. Thank you for helping me with the twins today and for driving me all over the place. I'm not sure how I would have managed without you."

"It was my pleasure," he told her, as he had the dozen other times she had thanked him during the day. He took a drink of his beer and cradled the bottle in his lap between his thighs. "How are you doing?"

"You know, I'm okay. I'm not nearly as upset as I thought I would be. I mean, I'm sad and I'm going to miss him, but the man who was my dad has been gone for a while now. No one should have to live that way. For his sake I'm relieved that it's over, that he's at peace." She looked over at Coop. "Does that make me a terrible person?"

"Not at all."

"I'm worried about Joy, though."

"She didn't take the news well?"

"No, she took it a little too well. She hasn't actually seen our father in almost four years. That's why I thought it was so important she see him when she was here. Now she'll never get the chance. I'm worried that she's going to regret it for the rest of her life. I asked if she wanted them to hold off on cremating him, so she could at least see him, but she said no. She doesn't want to remember him like that."

"It's her decision."

"I know." She took another swallow of beer and set the bottle on the ground beside her.

"Is there anything I can do? Do you need anything for the memorial? I know money is tight for you and your sister."

"I'm not letting you pay for my dad's memorial, so don't even suggest it."

"So what will you do?"

She shrugged. "I haven't quite figured that out yet."

"Is there insurance? If you don't mind my asking."

"There's a small policy. But after the medical bills and the funeral costs, there won't be much left. It's going to be at least a couple of weeks before I get a check."

"How about I give you an advance on next week's salary? Or more if you need it."

She hesitated, chewing her lip.

"I don't mind," he said. "And I'm pretty sure I can trust you to stick around."

She hesitated, picking at the label on her beer bottle. He didn't get why she was so wary of accepting his help. Isn't that what friendship was about? And he definitely considered her a friend. He would like to consider her much more than that if she would let him.

"You're sure it's not an imposition?" she asked.

"If it was, I wouldn't have offered."

"In that case, I would really appreciate it."

"I'll have the money wired into your account first thing in the morning."

"Thank you."

She was quiet for several minutes, so he said, "Penny for your thoughts."

"I was just thinking about the twins and how sad it is that they won't remember their parents. At least I got fourteen years with my mom. I have enough wonderful memories to keep her alive in my mind forever. Or maybe, if the girls had to lose their mother and father, it was better now than, say, five or ten years from now. That way they don't know what they've missed. There was no emotional connection. Or maybe I'm totally wrong." She shrugged. "Who knows really."

"Losing Ash and Susan doesn't mean they won't have two loving parents."

She looked confused. "What do you mean?"

"The twins shouldn't be raised by an uncle. It's

not good enough for them, either. They deserve a real family."

Her face paled. "Are you saying you plan to give them up?"

"No, of course not. I love them. I'm ready to settle down and be a family man. So I've decided to adopt them."

Sierra bit down hard on her lip, blinking back the tears that were welling in her eyes. She had wanted to believe that Coop had changed, that he would be a good father, but until just now she hadn't been sure. It felt as if an enormous weight had been lifted off her shoulders, as if she could breathe for the first time since she heard the horrible news of the crash. She was confident that no matter what happened between her and Coop, the twins would be okay. He loved them and wanted to be their father.

She looked over at Coop and realized he was watching her, worry creasing his brow. "I hope those are happy tears you're fighting," he said. "That you aren't thinking what a terrible parent I'll be and how sorry you feel for the girls."

More like tears of relief. "Actually, I was thinking how lucky they are to have someone like you." She reached for his hand and he folded it around hers. "And how proud Ash and Susan would be and how grateful."

"Come here," he said, tugging on her arm, pulling her out of her chair and into his lap. She curled up against his chest and he wrapped his arms around her, holding her so tight it was a little hard to breathe. And though she couldn't see his face, when he spoke he sounded a little choked up. "Thank you, Sierra. You have no idea how much that means coming from you."

She tucked her face in the crook of his neck, breathed in the scent of his skin. Why did he have to be so wonderful?

"You know the girls are going to need a mother," he said, stroking her hair. "Someone who loves them as much as I do. We could be a family."

"You hardly know me."

"I know how happy I've been since you came into our lives. And how much the twins love you." His hand slipped down to caress her cheek. "I know how crazy you make me and how much I want you."

Did he really want her, or was it that she was convenient? She fit into his new "family plan." And did it really matter? They could be a family. That was what the girls needed, and isn't that was this was about? "And if it doesn't work?"

He tipped her chin up so he could see her face. "Isn't it worth it to at least try?"

Yes, she realized, it was. They were doing it for the girls.

She turned in Coop's lap so she was straddling his thighs, then she cupped his face in her palms and kissed him. And he was right about one thing. Anything that felt this good couldn't be wrong.

She circled her arms around his neck, sliding her fingers through the softness of his hair, and as she did she could feel the stress leaching from her bones, the empty place in her heart being filled again. After what had been a long, stressful and pretty lousy day, he'd made her feel happy. In fact, she couldn't recall a time in her life when she had been as happy and content as she was with Coop and the twins. That had to mean something, didn't it? She had been trying so hard not to fall for him, maybe it was time to relax and let it happen, let nature take its course. Besides, how could she say no to a man who kissed the way he did? In no time his soft lips, the warm slide of his tongue, had her feeling all restless and achy.

Although she couldn't help noticing that kissing was *all* they were doing. She was practically crawling out of her skin for more, and he seemed perfectly content to run his fingers through her hair and caress her cheeks, but not much else. And when she tried to move things forward, tried to touch him, he took her hands and curled them against his chest.

Now that he had her where he wanted her, had he suddenly developed cold feet? Had he decided that he didn't want her after all? He was aroused, that much was obvious, so why wasn't he moving things forward?

She stopped kissing him. "Okay, what's the deal?"

He looked confused. "Deal?"

"You do know how to do this, right? I mean, it's not your first time or anything?"

One brow arched. "Is that a rhetorical question?"

"You're not doing anything," she said.

"Sure I am. I'm kissing you." He grinned that slightly crooked smile. "And for the record I'm thoroughly enjoying it. Is there something wrong with taking things slow? I want you to be sure about this."

Could she really blame him for being cautious? She was sending some pretty major mixed signals. Coop, though, had been pretty clear about what he wanted from the get-go.

"I want this, Coop," she told him. "I'm ready."

"Ready for what, that's the question," he said. "Am I going to get to second base? Third base? Am I going to knock it out of the park?"

She couldn't resist smiling. Were they really using

sports euphemisms? "You can't hit a home run if you don't step up to the plate."

He grinned. "In that case, maybe we should move this party to my bedroom."

Ten

Watching Coop undress—and taking off her own clothes in front of him—was one of the most erotic and terrifying experiences of Sierra's entire life. He had insisted on keeping the bedside lamp on, and she couldn't help but worry that he wouldn't like what she saw. But if he noticed the faint stretch marks on her hips and the side of her belly, or that her tummy wasn't quite as firm as it had been before the twins, he didn't let it show. She was sure that he'd been with women who were thinner and larger busted and all around prettier than she was, yet he looked at her as though she was the most beautiful woman in the world.

Coop seemed completely comfortable in his nudity. And why wouldn't he? He was simply *perfect*. From his rumpled hair to his long, slender feet, and every inch in between. She'd never been crazy about hairy men, so the sprinkling of dark-blond hair across his pecks and the thin trail bisecting his abs was ideal. And all those muscles…wow.

"I've never been with anyone so big," she said.

One brow arched up as he glanced down at his crotch. "I always thought I was sort of average."

She laughed. "I meant muscular."

He grinned. "Oh, *that*."

But he wasn't *average* anywhere. "I just want to touch you all over."

"I think we can arrange that." He pulled back the blankets, climbed into bed and laid down, then patted the mattress beside him. "Hop in."

Feeling nervous and excited all at once, she slid in beside him. And though she wanted this more than he would ever know, as he pulled her close and started kissing her, she found she couldn't relax. Not that it didn't feel good. But he'd been with a lot of women, and she was willing to bet that compared to most of them she was, at best, a novice. Her experiences with her high school boyfriend had been more awkward than satisfying, and the handful of encounters she'd had while she was in nursing school hadn't exactly been earth-shattering. Her last sexual experience sixteen months ago with the twins' father had at most been a drunken *wham, bam, thank you ma'am* that they both regretted the minute it was over.

She wanted sex to be fun and satisfying. She wanted to feel that spark, that…*connection*. The sensation of being intrinsically linked—if such a thing really existed. Yet every new experience left her feeling disappointed and empty, faking her orgasms just to be polite, wondering if it was something she was doing wrong. What if the same thing happened with Coop? What if she couldn't satisfy him, either? What if she didn't live up to his expectations?

She had herself in such a state that when he cupped a hand over her breast, instead of letting herself enjoy it, she tensed up. He stopped kissing her, pushed himself up on one elbow and gazed down at her. "Now who's just lying there?"

Her cheeks flushed with embarrassment. She was naked, in bed with a gorgeous, sexy man and she was completely blowing it. "I'm sorry."

"Maybe we should stop."

She shook her head. "No. I don't want to stop."

"You have done this before, right?" he teased. "I mean, it's not your first time or anything."

If he wasn't so adorable, she might have slugged him. Instead she found herself smiling. "Yes, I've done this before. But probably not even close to as many times as you have."

He stroked her cheek, a frown settling into the crease between his brows. "And that bothers you?"

"No, of course not. I'm just worried that I won't measure up. That I'm going to disappoint you."

"Sierra, you won't. Trust me."

"But I *could.*"

"Or I could disappoint you. Have you considered that? Maybe I've been with so many women because I'm such a lousy lay no one would sleep with me twice."

She couldn't help it, she laughed. "That is the dumbest thing I've ever heard."

"And for the record, I haven't slept with *that* many women. And not because I haven't had the opportunity. I'm just very selective about who I hop into bed with."

His idea of *not that many* could be three hundred for all she knew. And maybe that should have bothered her, but it didn't. Because she knew it was different this time. He was different. This actually meant something to him.

"What can I do to make you more comfortable?" he asked. "To assure you that your disappointing me isn't even a remote possibility."

"Maybe you could give me some pointers, you know, tell me what you like."

"You could kiss me. I like that. And you mentioned something about touching me all over. That sounds pretty good, too." He took her hand and cradled it against his chest, brushed his lips against hers so sweetly. "We'll take it slow, okay?"

She nodded, feeling more relaxed already. He had a way of putting her at ease. And good to his word he was diligent about telling her exactly what he wanted and where he liked to be touched—which was pretty much everywhere and involved using her hands and her mouth. And after a while of his patient tutoring, she gained the confidence to experiment all on her own, which he seemed to like even more. And Coop was anything but a disappointment. The man knew his way around a woman's body. He made her feel sexy and beautiful.

By the time he reached into the night table drawer for a condom, she was so ready to take that next step, she could barely wait for him to cover himself. He pressed her thighs apart, and she held her breath, but then he just looked at her.

"You're so beautiful," he said.

"Coop, please," she pleaded.

"What, Sierra? What do you want?"

Him. She just wanted him.

But he already knew because he lowered himself

over her, and the look of pure ecstasy as he eased himself inside of her almost did her in. He groaned and ran his fingers though her hair, his eyes rolling closed, and she finally felt it, that connection. And it was even more intense, more extraordinary than she ever imagined. This was it. This was what making love was supposed to feel like. And whatever happened between them, as long as she lived, she would never forget this moment.

Everything after that was a blur of skin against skin, mingling breath and soft moans and intense pleasure that kept building and building. She wasn't sure who came first, who set whom off, but it was the closest thing to heaven on earth that she had even known. Afterward they lay wrapped in each other's arms, legs intertwined, breathing hard. And all she wanted to be closer. They could melt together, become one person, and she didn't think that would be close enough.

In that instant the reality of the situation hit her like a punch to the belly. She hadn't planned it, hadn't expected it, not in a million years, but now there was no denying it. She was in love with Coop.

Coop was a disgrace to the male gender.

In his entire life he had never come first. Not once. He prided himself on being completely in control at all times. Until last night.

Watching Sierra writhe beneath him, hearing her moans and whimpers, had pushed him so far past the point of no return, a nuclear explosion wouldn't have been able to stop him. She made him feel things he hadn't realized he was even capable of feeling. For the first time in his life, sex actually meant something. He had reached a level of intimacy that until last night he hadn't even known existed. It should have scared the hell out of him, but he had never felt more content in his entire life.

"She's grabbing her suitcase right now," Sierra said from the passenger's seat, dropping her phone back in her purse. "She said to meet her outside of Terminal C."

Joy's flight had been a few minutes late, so they had been driving around in circles while Joy deplaned and collected her luggage.

"I'm glad I fed the twins their lunch early today," Sierra said, looking back at them, sitting contentedly in their car seats. "And thank you again for picking Joy up. She could have taken the bus."

"It's no problem." He reached over and took her hand, twining his fingers through hers. "Besides, I owe you for last night."

She blew out an exasperated breath and rolled her eyes. "I don't know why you're making such a big deal out of this. It couldn't have been more than a few seconds before me."

That was a few seconds too long as far as he was concerned. "I don't lose control like that."

"I didn't even *notice*. I wouldn't have even known if you hadn't said something."

"Well, it's not going to happen again." And it hadn't. Not the second or third time last night, or this morning in bed, or in the shower. Not that there hadn't been a couple of close calls.

She shook her head, as if he were hopeless. "Men and their egos. Besides, I sort of like knowing that I make you lose control."

"That reminds me, we need to stop at the pharmacy on the way home. We blew through my entire supply of condoms."

"We don't have to use them if you don't want to."

He glanced over at her. "You take birth control pills?"

"IUD."

Sex without a condom…interesting idea.

From the time he reached puberty Ash had drilled into Coop the importance of always using protection. Years before Coop became sexually active, Ash had bought him a box of condoms and ordered him to keep one in his wallet at all times, just in case. A thing for which Coop was eternally grateful, ever since one fateful night his junior year of high school when Missy Noble's parents were out for the evening and she jumped him on the den couch right in the middle of some chick movie whose title escaped him now.

Being the stickler for safety that Coop was, not to mention the very real likelihood of being trapped into a relationship with an *accidental* pregnancy, he'd actually never had sex without one. But the idea was an intriguing one.

"I've been told that it feels better for the man that way," she said.

"Who told you that?"

"The men who tried to get me to do it without one, so I'm not sure if it's actually true or not. But logistically you would think so."

He looked over at her and grinned. "I guess we'll have to put that theory to the test, won't we? Just so you know, I get tested regularly."

"As a nurse I have to," she said.

"How's tonight looking for you?" he asked.

"With my sister here?"

"What we do in the privacy of our bedroom is our business."

"*Our* bedroom?"

"She's going to be sleeping in your room, so it just makes sense that you sleep in mine. And continue to sleep there when she's gone."

"You don't think we should take things a little bit slower?"

"You didn't seem to want to go slow last night."

"Having sex and me moving into your bedroom are two very different things."

"We're living together, Sierra. Where you sleep at this point is just logistics." He gave her hand a squeeze. "We're together. I want you to sleep with me."

She hesitated for a second, then nodded and said, "Okay."

Coop steered the SUV up to the C terminal and spotted Joy immediately. She was a taller, slimmer version of her big sister, with the same dark hair, though Joy's was wavier and hung clear down to her waist. Gauging by her long gauzy skirt, tie-dye tank, leather sandals and beaded necklaces, she was the free-spirit type. A total contrast to Sierra, who couldn't be more practical and conservative.

"There she is!" Sierra said excitedly.

Coop pulled up beside her and before he could even come to a complete stop Sierra was out the door.

He turned to the twins and said, "I'll be right back, you two," then hopped out to grab Joy's bag. By the time he made it around the vehicle the sisters were locked in a firm embrace, and when they finally parted they were both misty-eyed.

Sierra turned to him. "Coop, this is my sister, Joy. Joy, this is Coop, my...boss."

Joy offered him a finely boned hand to shake, but her grip was firm. "I can't thank you enough for giving me a place to stay while I'm here. And for picking me up."

"I hope you don't mind squeezing in between the girls," he said.

"It beats takin' the bus."

He opened the door for Joy, and when both women were inside he grabbed the suitcase, heaved it into the back, then got back in the driver's side. Sierra was introducing her sister to the twins.

"That's Fern on the right and Ivy on the left," she said.

Joy shook each one of their tiny hands, which the twins seemed to love. "Nice to meet you, girls. And it's a pleasure to meet the man who my sister can't seem to stop talking about. Are you two a couple yet or what?"

"Joy!" Sierra said, reaching back to whack her sister in the leg. Then she told Coop, "You'll have to excuse my sister. She has no filter."

Joy just laughed and said, "Love you, sis."

Coop had known Joy all of about two minutes, but he had the distinct feeling that he was going to like Sierra's sister, and he didn't doubt that her visit would be an interesting one.

"You're sleeping with him," Joy said when the twins were down for a nap and they were finally alone in Sierra's bedroom...or Joy's bedroom as the case happened to be now.

"Yeah," she admitted. "As of last night."

"I kinda figured. There was a vibe." Joy heaved her suitcase onto the bed and unzipped it. "I knew he had to be hot for you to let your sister crash here."

"You don't pack light," Sierra said as she emptied the contents of her case onto the duvet.

"The guy I've been staying with is getting his place

fumigated while I'm gone, so it just made sense to bring it all. Have you got a few extra hangers?"

Sierra pointed to the closet door. "In there."

Joy crossed the room and pulled the door open. "Holy mother of God, this closet is *huge*."

"I know. It's twenty times the size of the dinky closet in my apartment."

"I didn't realize that hockey players made so much money," she called from inside the closet, emerging with a dozen or so hangers.

"He's also a successful businessman. And he does tons of charity work. He sponsors teams in low-income areas and donates his time to hold workshops for young players. For someone who had no interest in having kids of his own, he sure does a lot for them." She took note of the hippie-style clothing in a host of bright colors piled on the bed and asked Joy, "Did you bring something to wear to the memorial?"

Joy made a face. "I don't do black."

Sierra sighed, watching her hang her clothes and lay them neatly on the bed to be put in the closet. "It doesn't have to be black. Just not so…bright. If I don't have anything that fits you, we can go shopping tomorrow after your audition."

"You know I don't have any money."

"But I do. Coop advanced me a month's pay so I could pay for the memorial service."

"That was nice of him." She paused then said with a grin, "I suppose it had nothing to do with the fact that you put out."

She glared at her sister. "Not that it's any of your business, but he offered it *before* I slept with him. And only because I refused to let him pay for the memorial himself. He's always trying to do things like that for me."

"Wow, that must be rough. I know I would hate having a rich, sexy man try to take care of me. How can you stand it?"

Sierra leaned close to give her sister a playful swat on the behind. "I almost forgot what a smart ass you are."

Joy smiled. "I've been told it's one of my most charming qualities."

It could be. But then there were the times when it was just plain annoying.

"You know I like to take care of myself," Sierra said, and now that she no longer had to pay for their father's care, she could build herself a nice nest egg.

But how would that work exactly? Now that she and Coop were a couple, would he keep paying her, or would he expect her to care for the girls for free?

It was just one of many things that they would have to discuss. Like how far he wanted to take this relationship. Would she be his perpetual live-in girlfriend, or was he open to the idea of marriage some day? Would he want more kids, or were the twins going to be it for him? And if being with the twins meant sacrificing a little, wasn't it worth it?

She still wasn't one-hundred percent sure that moving into his bedroom at this early stage in their relationship was a good idea. Yes, technically they were living together, but sleeping in the same room after being lovers for less than twenty-four hours seemed to be pushing the boundaries of respectability.

"You know you're going to have to tell him the truth," Joy said.

And there lay her other problem—telling Coop she

was the twins' birth mother. But what would be even more difficult would be telling him about the birth father. "I'll tell him when the time is right."

"Honestly, I'm surprised he hasn't figured it out on his own. They look just like you."

"We were at a café yesterday morning and the woman at the next table assumed we were the twins' parents. She said they looked just like me, but have their daddy's eyes."

"What did Coop say?"

"He doesn't see it, I guess."

"If you want this thing with Coop to go anywhere, you have to be honest with him."

"I'm in love with him."

Joy looped an arm around her shoulder. "Si, you can't start a relationship based on lies. Trust me. I know this from personal experience."

She laid her head on her sister's shoulder. "How did I get myself into this mess?"

"He'll understand."

"Will he?"

"If he loves you he will."

The trouble was, she didn't know if he loved her or not. He hadn't said he did, but of course, neither had she. It was one thing to feel it, but to actually put it out there, to leave herself so vulnerable...it scared her half to death. Especially when she was pretty sure that for him, his affection for her was in part motivated by his desire to do right by the twins. Was it her that he cared about, or was it the idea of what their relationship symbolized? His mental image of the perfect family.

If she did tell him the truth—*when* she told him— would his feelings for her be strong enough to take such a direct blow? And what if she didn't tell him? Would it really be so bad? What if knowing the truth changed his perception of his relationship to the girls? What if it did more damage than good? There was no way that he could ever find out on his own.

Joy took her hand and grasped it firmly, and as if she were reading Sierra's mind said, "Si, you have to tell him."

"I will." Probably. Maybe.

"When?"

"When the time is right." If it ever was.

Eleven

Sierra and Coop had just gotten the girls settled for the night and into bed, and he had slipped into his office to answer the phone, when Joy exploded through the front door of the apartment in a whirl of color and exuberance and announced at the top of her lungs, "I got it!"

She'd had her audition that morning and had been waiting all day for a callback, pacing the apartment like a restless panther, whining all through dinner that if she hadn't heard something by now, she wasn't going to and that her career as an actress was over. When Sierra couldn't take it a minute longer, she'd given her money and sent her out to find a dress for the memorial. Apparently she'd found one.

"That was fast," she said, setting the girls' empty bottles in the kitchen sink. "Let's see it."

"See it?" Joy said, looking confused.

"The dress." She turned to her sister, realizing that Joy wasn't holding a bag.

"I didn't get a dress. I got the *role*."

Confused, she said, "I thought if they were interested, they would have you in for a second audition."

"Normally they would, but they were so impressed with my performance and thought I was so perfect for the role, they offered me the part!"

"Oh my gosh!" Her baby sister was going to play the leading role in a movie! "Joy, that is so awesome!"

She threw her arms around her sister and hugged her, and that's how Coop found them a second later when he came out of his office.

"I heard shouting," he said.

"Joy got the part," Sierra said.

"Hey, that's great!" Coop said, looking genuinely happy for her. "I hope you'll remember us little guys when you're a big Hollywood star."

Joy laughed. "Let's not get ahead of ourselves. Although this could open some major doors for me. And honestly, I'm just thrilled to have a job. I had to give up my waitressing job to come here. If it wasn't for my friend Jerry letting me stay at his place, I would be out on the streets until filming starts."

"When is that?" Sierra asked.

"Early August in Vancouver, and we wrap in September."

"I've played in Vancouver," Coop said. "You'll love it there."

"Oh, my God!" Joy said, practically vibrating with excitement. "I can't believe I actually got it!"

Joy was usually so negative and brooding, it was nice to see her happy for a change. Sierra was about to suggest they celebrate when the doorbell rang.

"That's Vlad and Niko," Coop said, heading for the

door. "Former teammates. They called to say they were stopping by."

He pulled the door open and on the other side stood two very large, sharply dressed Russian men. One looked to be around Coop's age and the other was younger. Early twenties maybe. Both men smelled as if they had bathed in cologne.

Sierra heard Joy suck in a quiet breath and say, "Yum."

"Ladies, this is Vlad," Coop said, gesturing to the older man, "And this is Niko. Guys, this is my girlfriend, Sierra, and her sister, Joy."

Neither man could mask his surprise. Sierra was assuming that men like Coop didn't usually have "girlfriends."

"Is good to meet you," Vlad said with a thick accent, addressing Sierra, but Niko's eyes were pinned on Joy, and she was looking back at him as if he were a juicy steak she would like to sink her teeth into. If she weren't a vegetarian, that is.

"You come out with us," Vlad told Coop. "Big party at the Web's place. You bring girlfriend. And sister, too."

"The Web?" Sierra asked.

"Jimmy Webster," Coop told her. "The Scorpions goalie. He's known for his wild parties. And thanks for the invitation, guys, but I'm going to have to pass."

"You must come," Vlad said. "I don't take no for answer."

Coop shrugged. "I have to be here for the twins."

"But you have nanny for twins," Vlad said.

"Actually, I'm the nanny," Sierra said, which got her a curious look from both men. She could just imagine what they were thinking. How cliché it must have appeared. The starry-eyed nanny falls for the famous athlete.

Sierra turned to Coop. "You go. I'll stay here and watch the girls."

"See," Vlad said. "Is okay. You come with us."

Instead of darting off to change, Coop looped an arm around her shoulder and said, "No can do. Sorry."

Sierra wasn't exactly crazy about the idea of him going to a party where there would be women more beautiful and desirable than her lobbying to be his next conquest, but it was something she would just have to get used to. She couldn't expect him to give up his friends and his social life just because she lacked the party mentality. "It's really okay. Go be with your friends."

"Web's parties are really only good for two things—getting wasted and picking up women. I'm well past my partying days, and the only woman I want is standing next to me."

If he was just saying that to keep from hurting her feelings, she couldn't tell. He looked as though he meant it, and it made her feel all warm and fuzzy inside.

"How about you?" Niko said, his gaze still pinned on Joy. "You come to party."

It was more of a demand than a question, which would have annoyed Sierra, but Joy smiled a catlike grin and said, "I'll go grab my purse."

"Do you think she'll be okay?" Sierra asked after they left, Joy draped on the younger player's arm. Not that she didn't think Joy could hold her own, but she didn't know the Russian guys, and she was still Sierra's baby sister. She would always feel responsible for her.

"Those guys are harmless," Coop assured her. "It

looks as though she already has Niko wrapped around her finger."

"Men have always been helpless to resist her beauty." And usually got way more than they bargained for. Joy was beautiful and sexy, but she was also moody and temperamental. It would take a special kind of man to put up with her antics. In the long term, that is.

"Why don't you come sit down?" Coop said, nudging her toward the couch.

"Let me finish up in the kitchen real quick." She had been doing her best to keep things tidy until Coop found a new housekeeper, but she'd been tied up a good part of the day finalizing the details for the memorial, and already clutter was beginning to form on every flat surface and the furniture had developed a very fine layer of dust.

"Leave it for tomorrow," he said, trying to steer her toward the couch, but she ducked under his arm. She already had a full day tomorrow.

"Five minutes," she said, heading into the kitchen.

Coop stretched out in his chair and turned on ESPN as she finished loading the dishwasher and wiped down the countertops. Ms. Densmore had kept them polished to a gleaming shine, but under Sierra's care they were looking dull and hazy. She poked through the cleaning closet for something to polish them, but after reading the label decided it was too much work to start tonight. She fished out one of those disposable duster thingies instead, but as she started to dust the living room furniture Coop looked up from the sports show he was watching and said, "What are you doing? Come sit down and relax."

"The apartment is filthy," she said.

"And we'll have a new housekeeper in a few days."

He reached over and linked his hand around her wrist, pulling her down into his lap. He took the duster and flung it behind him onto the floor, creating an even bigger mess of the room. Then he pressed a soft kiss to her lips. "This should be our alone time."

And she still felt guilty for making him stay home or making him feel as though he had to. "Are you sure you're not upset about missing the party? Because you can still go."

"I didn't want to go. If it had been one of the married guys having a party, then sure, but only if we got a sitter and you came with me."

"I'm really not the party type."

"You wouldn't like a party where the couples are all married and instead of getting hammered and hooking up, they talk about preschools and which diapers are the most absorbent?"

"They do not."

"They do, seriously. I used to think they were totally insane. What could be more boring? Now I totally get it."

"I guess I wouldn't mind a party like that," she said.

"The married guys on the team are very family oriented, and I think you would like the wives. They're very down-to-earth and friendly. Everyone gets together for barbecues during the summer. We should go sometime."

That actually sounded like fun. There was only one problem. "You said it's the players and their wives, but I'm not your wife."

"Not yet. But there are girlfriends, too. The point is, it's not a meat market."

Sierra's breath backed up in her chest. Did he really just say "not yet," as in, someday she would be? Was he actually suggesting that he intended to make her an honest woman?

"We don't have to go," Coop said.

"No, I'd like to."

"Are you sure? Because you just had a really funny look on your face."

"It wasn't that. I just didn't know… I didn't realize how you felt about that. About us."

His brow wrinkled. "I'm not sure what you mean."

"I said 'I'm not your wife,' and you said 'not yet.'"

His frown deepened. "Are you saying that you wouldn't want to be my wife?"

"No! Of course not. I just didn't know that you would *want* me to be. That you ever wanted to get married. You strike me as the perpetual bachelor type."

"It's not as if at some point I decided that I would never get married. To be honest, I was jealous as hell of Ash. He found the perfect partner for himself, and they were so happy. I just haven't had any luck finding the right one for me. I may not be ready for a trip down the aisle right now, but eventually, sure. Isn't that what everyone wants?"

The question was: Did he want to take that trip with her? That was definitely what he was implying, right? And how long was eventually? Months? A year? Ten years? She'd never been in a relationship serious enough to even consider marriage, so how long did it take to get to the wedding? Or the proposal? After he got down on one knee, how long before they said *I do?*

"You know," he said, nuzzling her cheek, nibbling her ear, sending a delicious little shiver of pleasure up her spine. "You came to bed so late last night we never got to test out that condom theory."

She and Joy had sat up until almost three last night

talking, and Coop had been sound asleep by the time she slipped into bed beside him. "But we have the place all to ourselves now," she said, turning in his lap so she was straddling him. She reached down and tugged at the hem of his T-shirt, pulling it up over his head. He was so beautiful, it was still a little hard to believe that a man like him would want someone like her. But she could feel by the hard ridge between her thighs that he did.

She pulled her shirt up over her head and tossed it on the floor with his. He made a rumbly sound in his throat and wrapped his big, warm hands over her hips.

"You are the sexiest woman on the planet," he said, sliding his hands upward, skimming her bra cups with his thumbs. He sure made her feel as if she were. So why did she have the nagging feeling that it wasn't destined to last, that she was a novelty, and at some point the shine would wear thin? That he was going to miss the parties and the running around.

Either way, it was too late now. She was hooked. She loved him, and maybe someday he would learn to love her, too. They could make this work. She would be such a good wife, and keep him so happy, he wouldn't ever want to let her go.

For the twins' sake she had to at least try.

Holy freaking hell.

Coop lay spread-eagled on his back in bed, the covers tangled around his ankles, sweat beading his brow, still quaking with aftershocks from what was hands down the most intense orgasm he'd ever had. Making love to Sierra without the barrier of latex, to really feel her for the first time, was the hottest, most erotic experience of his life.

"So is it true?" Sierra asked, grinning down at him, still straddling his lap, her skin rosy with the afterglow of her own pleasure. Looking smug as hell. "Is it better without a condom?"

He tried to scowl at her, but he felt so good, so relaxed, he couldn't muster the energy. "You're evil," he said instead, and her smile widened. He should have known, when she insisted on being on top, that she was up to something. That she intended to humiliate him again. But even he couldn't deny it was the most pleasurable humiliation he'd ever had to endure.

"You beat me by what, five seconds?" she said.

No thanks to her. He had obviously been having trouble holding it together, but instead of giving him a few seconds to get a grip, she had to go and do that thing with his nipples, which of course had instantly set him off.

For someone who claimed not to have much experience with men, she sure knew which buttons to push.

"It's the principle of the thing," he told her. "The man should never come first."

"That's just dumb."

"Yeah, well, as soon as I can breathe again, you're in trouble." He wrapped his arms around her and pulled her down against his chest, kissing the smirk off her face. Sierra slid down beside him, curling up against his side. It felt as if that was exactly where she belonged. Beside him. It was astounding to him what adding an emotional connection could do to crank up the level of intimacy. He had never felt as close to anyone, as connected to another person. He had no doubt that she would be the perfect wife. A good mother, a good friend and an exceptional lover. And he knew that once she met his friends, and trusted them enough to drop her guard a little, she would fit right in.

Yeah, she wasn't much of a housekeeper, and her expertise in the kitchen was pretty much limited to things she could heat in the microwave, but he could hire people to do that. In all the ways that counted, she was exactly the sort of woman he would want as a companion. She was predictable and uncomplicated…what you see is what you get. And she was as devoted to the twins, to taking care of them, as he was. Never had he imagined finding someone so completely perfect. He'd never been one to believe in cosmic forces, but he was honestly beginning to think that fate had brought them together. She had been thrust into some pretty rotten circumstances, and like him she had come out swinging. In fact, in a lot of ways they were very much alike.

So why couldn't he shake the feeling that she was holding something back? That she didn't completely trust him. He was sure it had more to do with her own insecurities than anything he had done. She just needed time. Time to trust him and believe him when he said that he wanted to make this work. That he wanted them to be a family.

But as her hand slid south down his stomach, he decided that he had plenty of time to worry about that later.

Twelve

When Sierra got back from her morning walk with the twins the next day, Joy was awake—a surprise considering she didn't wander in until after 4:00 a.m.—and she was dusting the living room dressed in yoga pants and a sport bra. And she somehow made it look glamorous.

"You don't have to do that," Sierra told her, taking the twins from the stroller and sitting them in their Ex-erSaucers.

"Someone has to do it."

"I'll get around to it."

Joy shot her a look. "No you won't. You hate cleaning."

She couldn't deny it. People would naturally think that Joy, being such a free spirit, would be the one with the aversion to cleaning, and Sierra, the responsible one, would be neat as a pin, but the opposite was true.

"If you decide to have anyone come back here after the memorial tomorrow, it should at least be tidy," Joy said.

"Well, thank you. I'm sure Coop will appreciate it."

"Consider it payment for letting me stay here. And introducing me to Niko. He's too adorable for words."

"How was the party?"

"Wild. Those hockey dudes really know how to have a good time."

Sierra walked into the kitchen to fix the twins' bottles and nearly gasped when she realized that it was spotless and the granite had been polished to a gleaming shine. "Oh my gosh! It looks amazing in here!"

Joy shrugged, like it was no big deal. "I like cleaning. It relieves stress."

She took after their dad in that respect. And Sierra was like their mom, who was more interested in curling up with a book or taking a long, leisurely walk in the park or working in the local community garden. Their home had been messy but happy. Even when they found the cancer, it hadn't knocked her spirits down, or if it had, she never let it show. Not even when she had been too sick from the chemo to eat or when the pain must have been excruciating. She had taken it in stride up until the very end.

It would be twelve years in September, and though the pain of losing her had dulled, Sierra still missed her as keenly as she had that first year. She missed her warm hugs, and her gentle voice. Her playful nature. Why sit inside cleaning bedrooms and doing homework when there was a world full of adventures to explore? Sierra only hoped that she would be as good a mother, as good a wife as her mom had been.

She poured juice into bottles and carried them to the

living room for the twins. "Do you still miss her?" she asked Joy.

"Miss who?" she asked, though Sierra had the feeling she knew exactly who she meant.

"Mom. It'll be twelve years this fall."

Joy shrugged. "I guess."

"You *guess?*" How could she *not* miss her?

"You were always closer with her than I was."

"What are you talking about? Of course I wasn't."

Joy stopped dusting and turned to her. "Si, come on. Half the time she didn't even know we were there, and the other half she spent doting on you. You two were just alike, she used to say."

"Yes, she and I were more alike, but she didn't love you any less."

"Didn't it ever bother you that the entire world seemed to revolve around her? Dad ran himself ragged working two jobs, and half the time she wouldn't even have dinner fixed when he got home. We would end up eating sandwiches or fast food."

"Not everyone is a good cook," Sierra said.

"But she didn't even try. And the apartment was always a mess. It was as if she was allergic to cleaning or something. Dad got one day a week off, and he would have to spend it vacuuming and picking up all the junk she and you left all over."

Sierra couldn't believe she would talk about their mom like that, that she even felt that way. "She was a good wife and mother. Dad adored her."

"She was a flake, and dad was miserable. My bed was right next to the wall and I could hear them fighting when they thought we were asleep."

"All couples fight sometimes."

"Sure, but with them it was a nightly thing."

Sierra shook her head. "No, they were happy."

"Look, believe me or don't believe me, I really don't care. I know what I heard. I don't doubt that Dad loved her, but he *wasn't* happy."

Maybe their mom could be a little self-centered at times, but she loved her family, all of them equally, despite what Joy believed. She did her best. If that wasn't good enough for Joy, that was *her* problem.

Joy's cell phone, which was sitting on the coffee table, started to ring and she dashed over to grab it.

"It's Jerry!" she said excitedly, who Sierra remembered was the "friend" she had been staying with. "Did you get my message? I got the part!" She flopped down on the couch and propped her feet on the coffee table. "I know! Isn't it awesome... No, not until August. Maybe you can come visit me there."

There was a pause, and Joy's smile began to disintegrate. "No, I don't have anyone else I can stay with until then. Why?" Joy sat up as outrage crept over her features. "What do you mean she's moving back in? You told me that you're getting divorced!"

Another married boyfriend? What was Joy's fixation with unavailable men? Why couldn't she find a nice, single guy? One who wouldn't screw her over and break her heart.

Joy jerked to her feet, shouting into the phone, "You sleazy-ass son of a bitch. You've been planning this since before I left, haven't you? You were never going to fumigate. You just wanted my stuff out so you could move her back in. I could have had a totally hot Russian guy last night, but I was being faithful to you, you big jerk! He was young and hot and I'll bet he doesn't have any of your *performance* problems."

Whoa. Maybe this was a conversation best kept private. Not that she thought Joy gave a damn if Sierra heard. She liked that element of drama. *Clearly*.

Joy listened, looking angrier by the second, then growled, "Take your apologies and shove them, you heartless bastard." She disconnected the call, blew out a frustrated breath and said, "Well, *crap*."

"You okay?" Sierra asked.

Joy collapsed back onto the couch. "It's official, I'm homeless."

"I meant about Jerry. You were dating him?"

She shrugged. "I don't know if you would actually call it dating. He gave me a place to stay and I kept him company."

Sierra could just imagine what that entailed.

"I mean, I liked him, but it's not as if we had some sort of future. He's kind of old to be thinking long term."

"How old?"

"Fifty-two."

Sierra's jaw dropped. "He's *thirty* years older than you?"

"Like I said, I didn't want to marry the guy. It was just…convenient."

Sierra raised a brow.

"For *both* of us. He liked having a much younger companion to flaunt, and I liked having a roof over my head."

"You liked him enough to be faithful to him," Sierra said.

Joy shrugged. "He was a nice guy. Or so I thought."

Sierra had the feeling Joy cared about him more than she wanted to admit. "So, what are you going to do?"

"I have no idea. I gave up my waitressing job for this trip and the film doesn't start shooting until the end of

August. Even if I could find another job it would be a month before I could afford first and last months' rent."

"Can't you get some sort of signing bonus?"

She shook her head. "It's very low budget. My salary will barely cover living expenses."

"So what are you going to do? Stay with another friend?"

"When you mooch off everyone you know, eventually you run out of people to mooch off. But don't worry," she said, pushing herself back up off the couch and grabbing the duster. "I'll figure something out. I always do."

Sierra was a little surprised that Joy hadn't asked if she could stay with her and Coop. Maybe she knew Sierra would say no. It was one thing to have her stay for a short visit, but for more than a month? If she had her own place, no problem, but she would never ask Coop for that kind of favor.

Joy was a big girl. She was going to have to figure this one out on her own.

Coop sat at the conference table in his lawyer's office, fisting his hands in his lap, struggling to keep his cool, to keep his expression passive.

"We agreed on a price," he told his former boss, Mike Norris, the current owner of the New York Scorpions. A price that had been a couple million less than what he wanted today.

The arrogant bastard sat back in his chair, an unlit cigar clamped between his teeth, wearing a smug smile. Flanking him were his business manager and his lawyer, both of whom were as overweight, out of shape and devoid of human decency as Mike.

"My team, my terms," Mike said. "Take it or leave it."

He knew how badly Coop wanted it, and he was trying to use it to his advantage. The paperwork had been drawn up and Coop came here thinking that they would be signing to lock in the terms. But Mike had gotten greedy. Coop should have seen this coming, he should have known the son of a bitch would pull something at the last minute.

At the price they had agreed on last week, buying the team would have had its risks, but it was still what he considered a sound investment. At the price Mike was demanding now, Coop would be putting too much on the line. His conservative nature with money was responsible for his healthy portfolio. If it were just his financial future hanging in the balance, he might say what the hell and go for it, but he had the twins to consider now. Sierra, too, although he doubted his money was a motivating factor in her feelings toward him. In fact, he was pretty sure she was intimidated by it. It was one of her most appealing qualities.

"Why the hesitation, Landon?" Mike said. "You know you want it, and we all know you can afford it. If you're hesitating because you think I'm going to back down, it ain't gonna happen." He leaned in toward the table, his belly flab preventing him from getting very close. "Just say yes and we've got a deal."

Even if he had planned to say yes, to give Mike what he wanted, that would have killed the deal.

He wanted that team, wanted it more than anything in his life, and giving it up would be one of the hardest things he would ever have to do, but it would be for the best. He glanced over at Ben, whose expression seemed to say that he knew what was coming, then Coop pushed back from the table and stood. "Sorry, gentleman, but I'm going to have to pass."

He started for the door and Mike called after him, sounding a little less smug now. "This deal is only good this afternoon. After today the price goes up again."

Mike thought Coop was bluffing. He wasn't. And though Coop wanted to tell him to shove his threat where the sun don't shine, he restrained himself. He was dying to see Mike's expression as he left, but he resisted the urge to turn and look as he walked out the conference room door and down the hall to Ben's office.

He sat down, taking long, deep breaths, fisting his hands in his lap when what he wanted to do was wrap them around that smug bastard's throat.

Ben walked in the office several minutes later, presumably after seeing the other men out.

"Coop, I'm sorry. I had no idea they were going to pull that."

Coop shrugged. "It's not your fault."

"You have every right to be furious. I know how much you wanted this."

It wasn't just about owning the team and the money that it would bring in. He cared about those guys. Mike was an old-school businessman who, until he bought the team five years ago, had never even been to a hockey game. For him it was nothing more than an investment. He knew nothing about the game and had been running the team into the ground since he took over. He didn't care about the players—his only goal was to pad his pockets. And the players knew it. They also knew that when Coop was at the helm, things would change. They would be back on top.

He felt as if he was letting them down.

"I don't know what I'm going to tell the guys."

"You're going to tell them exactly what happened.

Norris screwed you. But don't consider this over. Not yet. You should have seen Norris's face when you walked out. He really thought he had you. I wouldn't be too surprised if we get a call from him in a day or two backing down on his price."

"If he does, make it clear that I'm not paying him a penny over what we originally agreed on."

"There's something else we need to talk about," Ben said, and the furrow in his brow made Coop think that whatever it was, it wasn't good. "I didn't want to say anything before we signed the deal, and now probably isn't the best time after what happened in there…"

Whatever it was, it couldn't be much worse than what he'd just gone through. "Just tell me."

"A source at the National Transportation Safety Board has informed me that the official report on the plane crash is going to be released Monday."

Coop's heart clenched in his chest, then climbed up into his throat. "Did this source tell you what's in the report."

"They're calling it pilot error."

"No way!" Coop shot up from his seat. "No way it was pilot error. Your source must have it wrong."

"According to the report there were narcotics recovered from the scene."

"Which wouldn't surprise me in the least. Susan hurt her back a week before the trip. She ruptured a disc. It was so painful she couldn't even pick the twins up. I'm sure her doctor can confirm that. And she wasn't flying the plane."

"He said they found narcotics and marijuana in both Susan and Ash's systems."

No way. He knew that Ash and Susan smoked occasionally, but Ash would *never* take anything and then operate a plane. "I don't believe it. I know my brother, Ben. Ash would never take drugs and fly."

"We'll know more when we get a copy of the report, but if it's true, all hell is going to break loose and the vultures are going to descend. You might even want to get out of town for a few days, or even a week or two. Until things die down."

With the deal falling through he had nothing pressing to keep him in town, and frankly, he could use a vacation. "We have the memorial for Sierra's dad tomorrow, but after that there's nothing keeping me in the city. I think a trip to my place in Cabo might be in order."

"How is it working out with Sierra?"

Coop scrubbed a hand across his jaw. "Um…well, better than I anticipated, actually."

Ben narrowed his eyes. "Oh, yeah, how much better?"

A smile tugged at the corners of his mouth. "She moved into my bedroom two nights ago."

"I distinctly recall you telling me that you weren't going to sleep with her."

"It wasn't something I planned. But she's just so… extraordinary."

"So it's serious?"

"Yeah, I think so. She's everything I didn't realize that I wanted in a woman."

Ben grinned and shook his head. "I had no idea you were such a romantic, Coop. You should needlepoint that on a pillow."

"Who'd have thought, right? But she's smart and funny and beautiful, and the twins love her. And she doesn't seem to give a damn about my money."

"Should I start drafting the prenup?"

"Let's not get ahead of ourselves." Besides, he couldn't imagine making Sierra sign one of those. It would be the same as saying that he didn't trust her. He was a pretty good judge of character and as far as he could tell, she didn't have a deceitful bone in her body.

Ben eyed him warily. "You do plan to have a prenup, right? Assuming that you're going to marry her eventually."

"I'm definitely going to marry her. Eventually. But as far as a prenup…I don't think that's going to be necessary. She's not after my money."

"Not now, maybe…"

"I trust her, Ben."

"It's not about trust. It's about protecting you both in the case of a divorce."

"That would never happen. She's it for me. I know she is."

"One of my partners specializes in divorce, and the horror stories he could tell you—"

"That wouldn't happen to me and Sierra. We both come from very stable, loving homes. We aren't products of divorce. Her parents were happily married and so were mine. Whatever problems we might have, we would work them out."

"You're rationalizing."

"I'm being realistic."

"So am I."

"To even ask would feel like a betrayal. It would be like saying that I don't trust her."

"If the two of you have such a great relationship, I would think she would understand. The least you could do is ask. If she balks, I might reconsider my position on the matter."

"She won't."

"Promise me that you'll at least consider it."

"I will. And like I said, we have no immediate plans to get hitched. I haven't even proposed yet."

"Just keep it in mind when you do."

In a way Coop wished he hadn't said anything to Ben about marrying her. What with the sour deal, the accident report and Ben's prenup lecture, Coop left his office feeling downright depressed.

But on the bright side, things couldn't get much worse.

Thirteen

Coop caught a cab back home, getting out a block early so he could pick up a bouquet of flowers for Sierra from a street vendor. Remembering that they had never really had a chance to celebrate Joy's new job, he got her one, too. He walked the rest of the way home, the sun's heat beating down on his shoulders and back, melting the tension that had settled into his bones. Which made a week or two in a sunny locale sound even more appealing. If they left Sunday, they would be long gone before the backlash from the NTSB report hit the media.

The doorman greeted Coop as he headed inside and he had the elevator all to himself on the ride up. He opened the apartment door and the scent of something delicious tantalized his senses. Something that smelled too good to have come from a microwave. He dropped his keys on the entryway table and walked into the living room, realizing that not only was someone cooking, but also someone had cleaned. The apartment was spotless.

Sierra appeared from the hallway, jerking with surprise when she saw him standing there. "Hey! Hi, I didn't hear you come in."

At the sight of her, his heart instantly lifted, a smile tugged at his lips and all the crap that happened today, all the rotten news, didn't seem so terrible any longer. "I just got here."

"I just put the girls down for a nap." Her eyes settled on the bouquets he was carrying. "Nice flowers."

"One for you," he said, handing her the larger of the two.

"Thank you!" She pushed up on her toes and kissed him. "I can't even remember the last time someone gave me flowers."

"This one is for Joy," he said of the second bouquet. "To say congratulations. Is she here?"

"She ran down to the market. She should be back soon. In the meantime why don't I put them in water? They look like they're starting to wilt."

"It's hot as blazes out."

"I know. It was pretty warm and sticky when we took our walk this morning. Do you have a vase?"

He shrugged. "I recall Ms. Densmore setting out fresh flowers, but if there is a vase I have no idea where it would be."

He followed her to the kitchen, where she began to search for something to put the flowers in.

"Whatever you're making, it smells delicious."

"It's some sort of Mexican casserole, but I can't take credit. Joy said she was tired of carryout. But I'll warn you that it's vegetarian."

He didn't care, as long as it tasted good. Because

frankly, he was tired of carryout, too. He'd been spoiled by Ms. Densmore's home-cooked meals and the five-star dinning that he'd grown used to.

He opened the fridge and grabbed a beer, noticing that someone had even cleaned out the food that had begun to spoil. "The apartment looks great, by the way."

"Also thanks to Joy," she said, rising up on her toes to peer in the cabinet above the refrigerator. "She went through here like a maniac this morning."

He twisted the cap off his beer and took a long pull. "She doesn't strike me as the type who would like to clean."

"You wouldn't think it to look at her, but Joy is far more domestically gifted than I am," she said, going through another cupboard with no luck. "She says it relieves stress. And she was pretty stressed out today."

"Is she nervous about the film role?"

"No, apparently the much older guy that she was living with decided to move his wife back in, so she's got nowhere to live and no job when she goes back to L.A."

"What is she going to do?"

Sierra shrugged. "Joy is twenty-two. It's time she started taking responsibility for herself. She can't be the reckless kid any longer."

Joy may have been a bit irresponsible, but she was still family. He knew from personal experience that pursuing dreams took sacrifice, and it sounded as if this film role was the break she had been working toward. He knew Sierra wasn't in a position to help her out, and though he knew she would never ask him to help Joy, he could. In fact, he had a pretty good idea how he could do it, without actually appearing to do it.

Sierra finally found the vases in the very back of one of the lower cabinets and pulled out two. "These should work."

She set them on the countertop, then turned to him. "I almost forgot, how did your meeting go?"

"The deal fell through."

"What! What happened?"

He told her how Norris had raised his price and that he had turned him down. "Ben seems to think that he'll come around, but I'm not holding my breath."

"I'm so sorry, Coop. I know how much you wanted this."

"I'm more concerned about the guys on the team. Since Norris took over he's been running the team into the ground. They were counting on me to turn things around."

"They're your friends. They respect you. I'm sure they'll understand."

"I hope so."

As she was filling the vases with water the front door opened and Joy stepped inside, weighed down with more plastic grocery bags than one person should carry. Coop set his beer down and rushed over to help her. "I hope Sierra gave you money out of the house account for all this," he said, carrying several bags to the kitchen.

"Since I'm broke and my shoplifting days are over—" she set her bags down on the granite with a thunk "—she had no choice."

"Look what Coop got you," Sierra said, dropping Joy's bouquet into a vase.

"Well, damn, wasn't that sweet of you." Joy leaned close and inhaled the scent of the blooms. "They're lovely. Thanks."

"Originally I bought them to say congratulations, but I think they work better as a thank-you for cleaning the apartment and cooking dinner."

"It's the least I can do. Besides," she added, shooting Sierra a wry smile, "you've probably noticed my sister isn't much of a housekeeper. Or a cook."

Sierra gave her a playful jab in the arm. "And let's see you balance a checkbook or pay your rent on time."

"Gotta find a place to live before I can pay rent, don't I?"

She had just given him the perfect segue. "Sierra mentioned that your living arrangements have changed, and I wondered if that meant you might not be going back to L.A."

She collapsed on one of the stools, looking thoroughly frustrated. "Honestly, I'm not sure what I'm going to do. I want to go back to L.A., but I might have a better chance finding a job here."

"Can I offer a third option?"

She shrugged. "I'm open to pretty much anything at this point."

"Then how do you feel about Mexico?"

"You think you're pretty sneaky, don't you?" Sierra called to Coop from bed later that night when they were in their room with the door closed. It was still a little strange to think of it as *their* room, but she was feeling more comfortable there. It was decorated in warmer colors than the spare room, with traditionally styled cherrywood furniture, including a king-size bed so huge she could get lost in it. Though there wasn't much chance of that happening, considering that Coop was a cuddler. She was used to sleeping alone, so sharing a bed would take a bit of getting used to, but she couldn't deny the pleasures of waking spooned with a warm, naked and aroused man.

Coop stuck his head out of the bathroom, a toothbrush wedged in his mouth. "If brushing one's teeth can be considered sneaky," he said around a mouthful of toothpaste.

She shot him a look. "Two weeks in Mexico?"

He grinned. "Oh, *that*."

He was gone again, and she heard the water running, then he walked out of the bathroom.

"You knew Joy didn't have anywhere to go," she said. "And rather than making her figure this out on her own—"

"In my defense, I had already planned to take the trip, and I would have invited her to come with us even if she did have a place in L.A. to go back to." He sat on the edge of the mattress to untie his shoes. "But yes, I'm trying to help her. Is there something wrong with that?"

"I just worry that she's never going to learn to be responsible, to take care of herself."

"She seems to have done okay until now. And following your dream takes sacrifice. That I know from personal experience."

Maybe he had a point. Besides, this way she would get to spend a little more time with Joy because who knew when she would talk to her again?

He kicked his shoes off, peeled off his socks, then stood and pulled his shirt over his head. His jeans went next, then his boxers.

Nice.

He looked so good naked, it was a shame he couldn't walk around like that all the time.

He gathered his clothes and dropped them in the

hamper, then he pulled the covers back and slipped
into bed beside her. But instead of pulling her into his
arms and kissing her, like he normally would, he rolled
onto his side facing her, wearing a troubled expression. He'd been unusually quiet all night, and she had
a pretty good idea what was on his mind. He'd mentioned the accident report being released and what his
lawyer's source had said it contained. And though he
had clearly been disturbed, he'd seemed hesitant to discuss it. Maybe because Joy had been there, or maybe he
just hadn't been ready to deal with it. But maybe now
he was.

She rolled onto her side facing him and asked, "Are
you thinking about Ash and Susan?"

He drew in a deep breath and blew it out. "I just keep
thinking, there has to be some sort of mistake."

She hated to believe that the people she had en-
trusted her children to could be so irresponsible, but
facts were facts. If the report said there were drugs in
their systems, then there probably were.

"I *know* Ash," Coop said. "He just wouldn't do
something like that."

And she knew for a fact that he didn't know everything about Ash. Everyone had secrets and did things
that they weren't proud of. Everyone made mistakes.

"If it had been faulty equipment or turbulent
weather…" He shook his head. "But pilot error? It just
seems so senseless. How could he do that to Susan and
the girls?"

"And you?"

"*Yes,* and me. After all we went through losing our
parents, why would he put me through that again? I'm
just so damned…*angry.*"

"I felt the same way about my mom."

"But she got sick. She couldn't help that."

"Actually, she could have. Joy doesn't know this, and I don't ever want her to know, but I overheard my dad talking to his sister a few months after the funeral. My mom had a cyst in her breast a couple of years earlier but it turned out to be benign. So when she found another lump, she assumed it was a cyst again."

"But it wasn't."

She shook her head. "By the time she went to the doctor, it had already metastasized. It was in her lungs and her bones. There really wasn't much they could do."

"And if she had gone in as soon as she found the lump?"

"Statistically, there's a seventy-three-percent chance she would be alive today. I was *so* angry at her, but being mad wouldn't bring her back. It just made me really miserable." She reached over and touched Coop's arm. "I'm sure your brother didn't get into that plane thinking that something like this would happen. People make mistakes."

"Come here," he said. She scooted closer and he wrapped his arms around her, pulling her against him chest to chest, bare skin against bare skin. Nice.

She closed her eyes and laid her head in the crook of his neck.

"I just want this to be over, so I can get on with my life," he said.

"It doesn't always work that way."

"I miss him."

"I know."

He buried his face against her hair, holding on so tight it was hard to breathe. "He was all I had left."

"You have the twins. They need you."

"And I need them. I never realized how much having

a child could change a man. I'm a better person because of them."

She pulled back so she could see his face. "You said before that you were worried you would let Susan and Ash down, but you've done such an awesome job with the twins. They would be so proud of you." She couldn't imagine being separated from the girls, but if that ever happened, she felt confident that they would be well taken care of. Coop would be a good dad. All the more reason for him not to know the truth. She didn't want to risk changing the way he felt about the girls. And yes, her, too.

"This is probably a really weird time to ask this," he said. "But what are your feelings on prenuptial agreements?"

The timing was a little weird. And it was the second time that week that he'd brought up the subject of marriage. "I haven't really given it much thought," she said. "I've never come close to getting married, and even if I had, the men I date aren't exactly rolling in money."

"But if someone asked you to sign one?"

He looked conflicted, as if he didn't really want to be talking about this. He had seen his attorney that morning, so she could only assume the subject had come up. Which meant he was discussing marrying her with other people now. That had to be a good sign, right?

She hadn't wanted to let herself believe it could really happen. She didn't want to get her hopes up only to have them crushed. But it was looking as though he was seriously planning to marry her. Why discuss a prenup with his attorney if he wasn't?

"I guess it would depend on who was asking," she said.

"What if *I* was asking?"

She shrugged. "I would say sure."

"You wouldn't be upset or hurt?"

"Considering what you're worth, I would think you were a moron if you didn't ask for one. I know you would be fair. And maybe you haven't noticed, but I'm not interested in your money."

A slow smile crept across his face. "Have I ever mentioned what an amazing woman you are?"

If he knew the truth, he may not think she was all that amazing. Learning that his brother may have been under the influence of drugs while flying would be nothing compared to the bombshell she could drop on him. And in this case, what he didn't know really couldn't hurt him. So what was the harm in keeping a secret that he had no chance in ever learning? Why, when things were so good, would she risk rocking the boat?

And if she was so sure it was okay, why did she feel so guilty? Would she ever be able to completely relax with Coop, or would she always feel the nagging feeling of something unsettled between them?

But then Coop pulled her closer, trailed kisses from her lips to her throat and down to her breasts, awakening a passion that she'd felt with no one before him. Like he said before, nothing that felt this good could be wrong. And some things were better left unsaid.

The last month had been the most blissful, most relaxing of Sierra's life. Coop's beachfront condo in Cabo San Lucas was like an oasis. And being out of the States and away from the media seemed to soften the blow of the NTSB report, which was just as bad as Ben's source had predicted.

She and Coop spent their days walking along the

beach or lounging by the pool, and the twins were like little mermaids in their matching swimsuits and floating rings. They *loved* the water, howling pitifully whenever she and Coop took them out. But with all the sun and activity, they were so exhausted by evening, they began to sleep peacefully through the night, leaving the adults plenty of alone time.

They spent their evenings out on the patio sipping wine and snacking on the local fare, and after dark they built bonfires. A few days after they arrived they met a young couple from Amsterdam, Joe and Trina, who were renting a neighboring condo and had a son close to the twins' age. For the next week both the kids and the parents became inseparable. Coop and Joe went golfing together while Sierra and Trina played with the kids by the pool or took them into the village to shop. The week flew by, and everyone was disappointed when Joe and Trina had to leave.

Sierra had hoped that the trip would mean spending some quality time with her sister, but Joy being Joy, she met a man and spent a considerable part of her time with him at his condo about a quarter of a mile down the shore.

When their two weeks were drawing to an end, no one felt ready to leave, and because Coop had no pressing business back in New York, he suggested they stay a third week. Then three weeks became four, and by the time they flew home—with Joy remaining in Mexico until she had to leave for Vancouver—July was practically over.

Everyone missed the sun and the beach and especially the pool. The twins were so despondent at first that Coop suggested they consider looking for a home upstate. Maybe something on a lake with a huge yard for the girls to play in and of course a pool. Sierra hadn't been sure if he was completely serious, but then he disappeared into his office and came out an hour later with a stack of real estate listings that he had printed out.

Life with Coop was more perfect than she could have imagined, and she was happier and more content than she'd ever been. But as close as she and Coop had become, she knew that deep inside she was holding something back. She loved Coop, but she still hadn't said the words. Of course, he hadn't said them, either, or brought up the subject of marriage again, but he'd shown his affection for her in a million other ways. She couldn't expect a man like Coop, who had never even had a steady relationship, to go all gooey and lovesick in his first few months out of the gate. These things took time. Maybe she was holding back because she didn't want to rush him, didn't want to make him feel as though he had to commit to feelings he wasn't quite ready to express. Or maybe she was holding back because of the secrets she couldn't bring herself to tell him.

"What do you think of this one?" Coop asked the week after they returned from their trip. The twins were down for their nap and Coop had called her into his office. He pulled her down into his lap so she could see the listing on his ginormous computer monitor.

"It just went on the market yesterday, and the Realtor thinks it's a great price for the area and probably won't be available for long."

The house itself was gorgeous. Big and beautiful and modern, with all the amenities they were looking for, and when she saw the listing price she practically swallowed her own tongue. "It's so expensive."

He shrugged. "It's half of what this place cost me. And after we settle into the house I'll put this place on the market. So technically I'll actually make money. The Realtor can take us through this afternoon. Maybe Lita can watch the kids for a couple of hours and we can go just the two of us.

Lita was the housekeeper Coop had hired right before they left for Cabo. She had taken care of the apartment while they were gone, and since they returned the twins had taken an immediate shine to her. Even better, she absolutely adored them. Her English wasn't the best, but she kept the apartment spotless, she was a decent cook, and most important, she had a very pleasant disposition. And having raised six kids of her own, she was also an experienced babysitter.

"Unless you don't like the house," Coop said, "In which case we'll keep looking."

"It looks really nice, but what I think doesn't really matter. You're buying it, not me."

"No, *we're* buying it. It's going to be your house as much as mine."

She wished that were true, but until they were married, it was his dime. No community property, no alimony if it didn't work out.

Coop shook his head and rubbed a hand across his jaw. "You don't believe me."

"It has nothing to do with me believing you."

"Then you don't trust me."

"It's not about that, either. We're living together, but technically we're still just dating. If you buy a house, it's going to be *your* house."

"Because we're not married."

She nodded.

"Well, maybe we should get married."

It took a second to process the meaning of his words. Had he really just asked her to marry him? She opened her mouth to reply, but no sound came out. She didn't know what to say. Was he seriously asking, or just throwing out suggestions?

"Is that a no?"

Oh, my God, he was asking, and he expected an answer. "Of course it isn't, I just—"

"Look," he said, turning her in his lap so he could look into her eyes, taking her hands in his and holding them gently. "I know this is hard for you. I know you have trust issues, and I've been trying really hard to give you space, to not overwhelm you, but I'm getting tired of holding back. I love you, Sierra. I know it's only been two months, but it's been the happiest two months of my life. I want to marry you and spend the rest of my life with you. I want us to adopt the girls together and be a real family. If it happens next week, or next year, I don't care. I just need to know that we're on the same page, that you want that, too."

More than he could imagine. "I do want that, and I had no idea you felt that way. I fell in love with you the first time you kissed me. I just didn't say anything because I didn't want to overwhelm *you*. I might have trust issues but not with you."

He grinned, sliding his arms around her. "Sounds like we had a slight breakdown of communication."

She looped her arms around his neck. "I guess we did."

"Let's promise that from now on, we tell each other exactly what we're feeling, that we don't hold anything back."

"I think that's a good idea."

He gave her a soft, sweet kiss. "So, if your answer isn't no…"

"Yes, I'll marry you."

He pulled her close and held her tight.

She loved Coop, and she wanted this, more than anything in her life. She thought about what Joy said, that they couldn't base this relationship on lies. But the truth could tear them apart forever.

Fourteen

Things were moving fast, but Coop liked it that way.

He rolled over in bed and reached for Sierra, but her side of the bed was cold. He squinted at the clock and was surprised to see that it was almost nine, which meant Sierra and the twins were probably taking their morning walk. And he needed to get his butt out of bed. They had a long, busy day ahead of them. After a week of negotiating, they would find out this morning if the sellers of the house they wanted had come back with a reasonable offer. After lunch they had a meeting planned with a wedding coordinator—one who came highly recommended from several of the players' wives—and after that Coop and Sierra were going ring shopping. They had been scouring the Internet for a week, trying to find the perfect one with no luck. She decided that if she was actually seeing them in person, putting them on her finger, something might click. They had a list of a dozen or so places in the city to look, including Cartier, Verdura and of course Tiffany's.

Coop pushed himself out of bed, showered and dressed, then wandered out to the kitchen, surprised to find Lita sitting on the living room floor playing with the twins.

"Good morning, Lita. Where is Miss Evans?"

"Morning, Mr. Landon. She have appointment. She say she leave note for you, on your desk."

"Thanks."

He gave the twins each a kiss on the tops of their heads, then poured himself a cup of coffee and carried it to his office.

He found Sierra's note on his desk by the phone. It said that Ben had called and needed him to call back ASAP. He had been drafting a prenup, even though Coop was still opposed to the idea, but Sierra had insisted.

He sat at his desk and dialed Ben's number.

"Are you sitting down?" Ben asked.

"Actually, yeah, why?"

"I got a call from Mike Norris's lawyer this morning. He wants to talk deal."

Coop's heart stalled in his chest. "You told him I won't budge on price?"

"He knows. Apparently Mike just wants to sell. It would seem that the players have been giving him a bit of a hard time lately."

Coop smiled. He had been worried that they would be angry, but instead they had rallied around him. They knew exactly what Norris was doing and they were pissed.

"When do they want to meet?" Coop asked.

"Tomorrow at three."

"Make it eleven—that way, when the deal is locked in, you and I can go out for lunch to celebrate."

"I'll let him know. Maybe you can come a little early and look over the final draft of the prenup. We made all the changes you asked for, although I still think you're being a little too generous."

"I know what I'm doing."

"I hope so."

He hung up wearing a grin. He had a hunch that Norris would come around, but until just now he hadn't let himself get his hopes up. He still didn't want to count his chickens, but it did sound as if Norris was ready to accept his offer. Everything was falling into place. Personally and professionally. It was almost too good to be true.

He glanced over at the boxes lining one wall of his office. Susan's mother had sent them over after she packed up Ash and Susan's belongings. Things she thought Coop would want. He hadn't been ready to deal with what he would find inside them, especially after reading the NTSB report. But Sierra had been right—being angry at Ash was irrational and counter-productive.

He walked over, grabbed one of the boxes and carried it to his desk. He took a slow, deep breath, telling himself it's like a Band-Aid. You just have to rip it off.

He grabbed the edge of the packing tape and ripped. He opened the flaps, and inside he found a stack of wrapped photo frames. One by one he pulled them from the box and extracted them from the packing. He found photos of Ash and Susan and the girls together. Photos of Ash and Coop with their parents from holidays and vacations, and a 5x7 of Ash and Coop at Coop's high school graduation—Coop in his cap and gown and Ash standing beside him, beaming like a proud parent.

Swallowing back an acute sting of sorrow, he set the photo aside to hang on his office wall.

At the very bottom of the box he found the twins' baby book. Smiling, he lifted it out and flipped through the pages. At the front there were pages and pages of prebirth information, filled in, he was assuming, by the birth mother. Then there was a section record-ing the events of the girls' first few months, and that was in Susan's handwriting. It contained their growth charts, their sleep and eating schedules, the date of their first smile and the first time eating cereal. A couple of months ago he would have seen keeping such details as a silly waste of time, but now he found himself en-grossed.

He sat at his desk sipping his coffee and reading the pages Susan had filled in, which ended abruptly after the girls turned five months. He was assaulted by guilt for not continuing on the tradition, realizing that some day the twins would probably want to look back at it, maybe even show it to their children.

He vowed that, starting today, he would go back and fill in as much information as possible from those missed months, then keep the book up to date from now on. He was sure Sierra would help him. She would re-member the finer details he'd forgotten or overlooked.

Curious about the woman who gave birth to the girls, he flipped back to the beginning. He couldn't find her name, which was no surprise, and though there were a few photos of her pregnant belly, they were all from the chest down. Yet as he thumbed through the pages, reading the pregnancy milestones, he was over-whelmed with an eerie sense of déjà vu. He was sure he'd read this before. It just looked so...familiar. He racked his memory, wondering if maybe he'd seen the baby book at Ash and Susan's place. But he was sure he hadn't. Even if it had been sitting right in front of him he wouldn't have thought to pick it up. So why did it look so familiar?

Realization hit him like a stick check to the gut, knocking the air from his lungs. No way. It wasn't possible.

He snatched the note Sierra had left him from the trash beside his desk and compared it to the writing in the baby book, and the coffee he'd just swallowed threatened to rise back up his throat. It was identical. Completely and totally identical.

Sierra, the woman he loved and planned to marry, was the girls' birth mother.

Sierra opened the apartment door, her hair clinging to her damp forehead. It was a hot, sticky morning headed toward a blistering hot afternoon. She went right to the kitchen, poured herself a glass of cold water from the fridge and guzzled it down. Then she went down the hall in search of Lita and the girls. She found them in the nursery in the middle of a diaper change.

"I'm back, Lita. Is Mr. Landon still here?"

"He in his office," she said, concern furrowing her brow. "I go to talk to him, but he look angry."

Which probably meant that their offer on the house had been turned down. Well, shoot. They had seen a dozen different places in the past week, but that was by far their favorite. Coop was going to be so disappointed.

The past week, since she said she would marry him, had been a bit of a whirlwind. He seemed determined to get them married and settled into a house as fast as humanly possible. As if he were trying to make it official before she had a chance to get away. He had even mentioned that if they were going to have more children, he wanted to do it soon, so they would be close in age. She already had her hands pretty full with the twins, but he seemed to want it so badly she didn't have the heart to say she wanted to wait a while.

She felt a little like she was on a speeding train, and even if she wanted off, it was moving too fast to jump.

Sierra walked to Coop's office. The door was closed so she rapped lightly.

"Come in."

She opened the door and stepped inside. Coop was standing by the window, looking out, hands wedged in the pockets of his jeans.

"Hey, is everything okay? Lita said you looked angry."

"Close the door," he said, not looking at her.

Something definitely was wrong. She snapped the door shut and asked, "Coop, what's the matter? Did the Realtor call? Did they turn down our offer?"

"They didn't call yet. I finally started going through one of the boxes of Ash's things."

No wonder he was upset. "Oh, Coop. That must have been really hard."

"I found a whole bunch of photos, and the twins' baby book. It's on my desk."

She walked over to his desk. A stack of framed photographs sat on one corner, and next to it, the baby book she hadn't seen in almost seven months.

"I bookmarked my favorite page. Have a look."

She picked it up and thumbed through it until she found the page, marked with the note she'd written him this morning. She saw the writing on the note and the writing on the page, and her stomach bottomed out. Side by side they were clearly identical. Her knees went so limp she had to sink down into the chair.

She looked up to see that Coop had turned and was glaring down at her, his eyes so cold she nearly shivered.

"That's your handwriting. You're the twins' birth mother."

She closed her eyes and drew in a shaky breath. Joy was right. She should have told him.

"Nothing to say?" he asked, and the anger simmering just below the surface made her heart skip.

"I can explain."

"Don't bother. Here's what I think happened. You wanted them back, but I refused to give them up and you knew you didn't have a shot in hell in court. So instead you decided to infiltrate my home, to prove me unfit."

"No, Coop—"

"But then you looked around and realized what a sweet life you could have as my wife, so you seduced me instead."

"It wasn't like that at all. I just needed to know that they were okay. Your reputation… I didn't know what kind of parent you would be. I was scared. I thought they needed me. I swear, I never intended to act as anything but their nanny. And I never wanted anything from you. You know that."

"Did you ever plan to tell me the truth?"

She could tell him she did, that she was waiting for the right time, but that would be a lie. "I was afraid to."

"Because you thought I would be angry? And feel betrayed? Well, you were right."

"It wasn't that. At least, not entirely. I was afraid

it would change the way you felt about the twins. You're so good with them, and you love them so much. I thought it might change your feelings toward them. And yes, toward me."

"So you just planned to lie to me, what, for the rest of our lives?"

"You'll never know how hard it's been keeping the truth from you. And if I thought for a second that you would understand, I would have told you that very first day. But look at it from my point of view. I didn't know you. All I knew is what I read in the papers and heard on the news. I didn't even know that you had any interest in taking care of twins who you believed you weren't technically related to."

His eyes narrowed. "What do you mean, who I *believed* I wasn't related to?"

Damn it. Had she really just said that?

"Sierra?"

Damn, damn, *damn*.

It was one thing not to tell him and another to lie about it. Besides, he was bound to ask about the birth father some day, and not telling him would be another lie. "Coop, you're the girls' uncle."

"I know that."

"No, I mean that you are the girls' *biological* uncle. Ash wasn't just Fern and Ivy's adoptive dad. He was their birth dad."

The room seemed to tilt on its axis and Coop clutched the edge of the desk for support. "You *slept* with my brother."

"Yes, but it's not what you're thinking."

"You have *no idea* what I'm thinking."

"Please," she said, looking desperate, "give me a chance to explain."

Nothing she could say could take away the sick feeling in his stomach, in his soul. Ash had cheated on Susan. On top of being responsible for killing himself and his wife, Ash, who Coop had considered beyond reproach, had committed adultery. It was as if everything he knew about his brother was a lie.

"I met Ash in a bar."

"Ash didn't hang out in bars."

"And neither did I, but I had just put my father in a nursing home and I felt horrible, and I didn't feel like sitting home alone, so I stopped in for a drink. I just happened to sit beside him at the bar, and we were both drinking vodka tonics, and we got to talking. He said he was there because he and his wife were separating. He told me that they had been having fertility issues for years and after another failed IVF attempt, it was just too much."

Coop knew they had been trying to get pregnant for a while, but Ash never said anything about any negative effects on his marriage. If he and Susan had been separating, he would have said something to Coop. "I don't believe you."

"It's the truth."

"So why didn't he tell me?"

She shrugged. "I don't know. Maybe he was embarrassed? Maybe it was easier to talk to a stranger. All I know is that he had come from his lawyer's office, and they were going to sign papers the next morning. If you don't believe me, I'm sure his lawyer could confirm it. I'm sure with them gone he would waive privilege."

He would be sure to check that. "So you met in a bar…"

"We talked for a long time and had a few drinks too many, and we ended up back at my place. It was a mistake. We both knew it right afterward. He called me the next day to apologize and to tell me that what happened between us had knocked some sense into him. He and Susan had talked and were going to try to work things out. He begged me not to say anything to her, and of course I wouldn't. He was a great guy, and I was really happy for him. But a couple of weeks later I found out I was pregnant. I called him, and of course he was stunned and heartbroken. He wanted a child so badly, but to be in the baby's life he would have to admit to Susan what he'd done, and that would ruin his marriage."

"He would never do that. He would never refuse to take responsibility for his own child."

"He wanted to, but how would he explain the missing money? He said that Susan handled all of their finances. Things were already really tight. The fertility treatments were draining them financially."

If things were that bad, why hadn't he asked Coop for help? Coop *owed* him. He could have been the one to pay the support. Ash had made a mistake, and he should have owned up to it.

"It was a really terrible time for me to be having a baby. I was barely scraping by as it was, and I would have had to put the baby in day care while I worked seventy hours a week. I started to think about adoption, and when I found out I was having twins, I knew I couldn't keep them. I couldn't give them the sort of life they deserved. But I knew who could. I figured if the twins couldn't be with their mother, they could at least be with their dad."

"So why did Ash have to adopt his own kids?"

"He came up with the adoption idea so Susan wouldn't know about the affair. He was so afraid of losing her."

"And you just went along with this. You just gave up your babies to save a virtual stranger's marriage."

"I didn't have a choice. It was an impossible situation. Without his help, I couldn't keep them, and he couldn't give me any financial help without ruining his marriage. Giving them up was the hardest thing I ever had to do, but I did it because it was best for them."

"You must have been pretty happy when you heard about the crash, knowing you would get the chance to be with them again."

Tears welled in her eyes. "That's a terrible thing to say. And it's not true. If I didn't think they would have a good life with Ash and Susan, I never would have suggested the adoption. I would have given them to some other family who was desperate for children."

"You know what I find ironic? All this time I knew something wasn't right. I chocked it up to you having trust issues, when all along you were the one lying, the one who couldn't be trusted."

"I know it was wrong to lie to you, but I didn't have a choice. I didn't expect to fall in love with you. It's not something I planned, and I fought it. You know I did."

"Or that's what you wanted me to believe."

"It's the truth."

"What difference does it make now? It's over. I won't ever be able to trust you again."

She lowered her eyes, wringing her hands in her lap. "I know. And I'm sorry."

"And to think I was willing to marry you without a prenup. That's the last time I question my lawyer's advice." And he didn't doubt for a second that her insistence in signing one was all a part of her scheme. And what if he had married her? What if they'd had a child? The thought made his stomach ache.

"You didn't deserve this," she said. "And I know you won't believe this, but I do love you."

"You're right. I don't believe you."

She rose to her feet, her face pale, looking like she might either be sick or lose consciousness. "I'll go pack."

He laughed. "You don't seriously think I'm going to let you off that easy, let you leave your daughters?"

She blinked, confusion in her eyes. "But...I thought..."

"I may think that you're a miserable human being, but they need you. Do you really think I would rip them away from the only mother they have? But don't think for a second that you are anything but an employee."

"You want me to stay? *Here?*"

"Obviously you're moving back into your bedroom. And I'm going to treat you like the servant that you are. And you're going to take a substantial pay cut."

"You don't think it will be awkward, me staying here?"

"Oh, I'm counting on it. It's going to be that nightmare scenario you mentioned when you were telling me all the supposed reasons why you didn't want to get involved. You are going to live here, day in, day out, watching me get on with my life. Watching me exercise that revolving bedroom door."

"And if I say no? If I quit?"

"You never see the twins again. And you have to live with knowing you abandoned them twice."

She swallowed, tears welling in her eyes again, but he couldn't feel sorry for her. He flat out refused. She'd made him suffer, and now he was going to return the favor.

"Well then," she said, squaring her shoulders, trying to be strong. "I guess I have no choice but to stay."

Fifteen

Coop had given it considerable thought and had come to the conclusion that he was an idiot.

He sat in his office, staring out the window at nothing, without the motivation to do anything but feel sorry for himself. The past two weeks had been the longest and most miserable of his life. If he thought making Sierra suffer would bring him some sort of satisfaction, he'd been dead wrong. He just wanted her to feel as miserable and betrayed and as *hurt* as he was. But knowing that she was unhappy and hurting was only making him feel worse.

He couldn't concentrate, couldn't sleep. When he was out with friends he wanted to be home, but when he was home he felt as restless as a caged animal. He didn't want to upend the twins' lives, but living in the same house with Sierra, seeing day to day how guilty and unhappy she felt, was killing him.

The worst part was that this was just as much his fault as hers. Probably more.

Deep down he had known there was something wrong, that something was just slightly…off. And instead of bothering to try to identify its real source, he'd passed it off as her shortcoming and left it at that, thinking that as soon as she accepted how wonderful he was she would be the perfect companion. When, in reality, he was the one with the bigger problem. He had lousy vision. He saw only what he wanted to see. He had pursued her with a single-minded determination that was almost manic. She'd resisted, and he'd ignored her. She pushed back, he insisted. He hadn't *let* her tell him no.

Looking back, he couldn't help but wonder what the hell he'd been thinking. Moving her into his bedroom after two weeks and planning a wedding six weeks after that. If she'd been pregnant he maybe could have understood the urgency. And speaking of that, the stretch marks should have tipped him off that there might be something she wasn't telling him. He had just assumed that she had been a little overweight at some point and they were the result. It wasn't the sort of thing a man could ask a woman. Not without getting slugged. Or so he wanted to believe. He never really asked her about her past. The truth was, he didn't want to know. It had been easier just to pretend that she was perfect, that her life didn't really begin until she met him.

What a selfish, arrogant jerk he'd been.

Though it had taken a little time to realize it, it wasn't even Sierra who was making him so angry. How could Ash, who had drilled into Coop the virtues of being a responsible adult and a good man, be so careless and self-centered? He should have supported

Sierra, his marriage be damned. He should have owned up to the responsibility, so she could keep the babies, so they could be with their mother, where they belonged. Instead he had ripped them from her arms and taken them for himself. Coop didn't think he would ever understand it or ever be able to forgive him for what he'd done.

Yes, Sierra had lied to him but only because she thought she was doing what was best for her children. They were her number-one priority, as they should be. She was a good mother. She'd made more sacrifices for those girls than most women would ever consider. And he intended to make sure they knew it.

Ironically, now that he knew who Sierra was, warts and all, he loved her more than he had two weeks ago when he had her built up in his mind as the perfect mate. But after the way he'd treated her, why would she ever want him back? He told her that he loved her, that he wanted to spend the rest of his life with her, and at the first sign of trouble, he'd bailed on her. How could she love someone who had failed her so completely? And how could she ever trust that he wouldn't do it again?

He had really hoped by now that she would have come crawling to him on her knees begging for forgiveness, in which case he wouldn't have to admit what an utter jerk he'd been. Clearly that wasn't going to happen. He needed her a whole lot more than she needed him. Or maybe she just believed it was hopeless and didn't want to risk being rejected again.

He heard the doorbell ring and knew that it was Vlad, Niko and a few other guys from the team. Coop had met with Norris, who after some balking had agreed to their original terms. The deal was in place, and in just a few weeks Coop would officially be the new owner, so the guys wanted to celebrate. This deal had been all he could think about for months, yet now that he'd gotten what he wanted, he couldn't work up the will to be excited about it. It was as if losing Sierra had sucked the life right out of him.

Lita poked her head in his office. "Your guests is here, sir."

"Serve them drinks and I'll be right there."

She nodded and backed out.

He had no choice but to go out there and pretend as if everything was fine. But it wasn't, and wouldn't be, until Sierra was his again. And she would be. He would get her back. He just didn't have a clue how to go about it.

Sierra ignored the doorbell and read the girls their bedtime story. She had overheard Coop telling Lita—who seemed hopelessly confused by Sierra's abrupt switch from lady of the house to employee—that he was having a few guys from the team over. Was this him finally getting on with his life? Because she had been waiting, and other than a night out with friends in which he came home alone at an unimpressive nine-thirty and a couple of business meetings, he'd spent most of the past two weeks holed up in his office.

When it came to dishing out revenge, he wasn't very good at it.

That didn't mean she wasn't miserable and unhappy, and she missed him so much every cell in her body ached with it. Yet she couldn't deny the feeling that some enormous, cloying weight had been lifted from her, and for the first time in months she could actually breathe again. She realized now that if she had married

Coop with that secret between them, she never would have been able to relax. She would have forever felt as though she didn't deserve him because everything that he knew about her was essentially a lie.

Unfortunately, the one thing that could have saved their relationship, *the truth,* had been the thing that killed it. Just like her pregnancy, it had been a lose-lose situation from the start, and she had been a fool for letting herself believe that it would work. For thinking that he wouldn't eventually learn the truth. And that it would end in anything but total disaster.

If he could ever find a way to forgive her, she would never lie to him again. But it seemed unlikely that would ever happen. He hated her, and that really sucked, but at least he knew the truth.

From the other room she heard men's voices. No doubt they would go up on the roof, drink and talk about what a waste of time she had been and the compromising position he had managed to trap her into.

Because she was in no mood for a confrontation with Coop's pals, she read the twins a second then a third book, realizing halfway through that they were out cold. She laid them in bed, grabbed their empty bottles and walked to the kitchen. Lita had already left for the night, and the dishwasher was running, so she dropped the bottles in the sink and washed them by hand.

She was setting them on a towel to dry when she heard the sound of footsteps behind her, but the cloying scent of aftershave tipped her off to the source. She turned to find Niko standing behind her.

"I need beer," he said, setting an empty beer bottle on the counter.

Was he just stating fact, or was he expecting her to

wait on him? She was the nanny, not Coop's hostess. His friends could serve themselves, which Niko did.

"Coop tell us it's over," he said, walking past her to the fridge and pulling out a beer. Normally she didn't feel threatened by the younger Russian, but there was something in the way he looked at her tonight. His eyes roamed over her in a way that made her feel dirty.

"That's right," she said.

He stepped closer. "I like sister, maybe I like you, too."

Oh, yuck. "I'm not interested."

She turned to the sink and felt a very large palm settle on her butt. Repulsion roiled her stomach. And she couldn't help wondering if Coop had put him up to this, if that was part of her humiliation. But before she could turn and slap his hand away, it was gone. She spun around to see Coop pulling the Russian away from her, then he drew his arm back and punched him square in the jaw. Actually *punched* him.

Niko's head snapped back and he lost his balance, landing on his ass on the ceramic tile floor.

If he put Niko up to it, then why punch him?

Niko muttered something in Russian that Sierra was guessing was a curse and rubbed his jaw. He looked more annoyed than angry.

"What the hell is wrong with you?" Coop said.

"You say you and her is finished. So I think, why not?"

Coop glared at the Russian, then looked over at Sierra and said, "Are you okay?"

"Fine." Just mildly disgusted.

Coop turned back to Niko, jaw tight, and said, "I'm only going to say this once, so listen clearly and spread the word. The only man who's going to be touching this woman's ass is *me*."

Niko shrugged and pulled himself to his feet. "Okay, fine, jeez. I look but I don't touch."

"No, you don't get to look, either. Or *think* about looking."

Sierra planted her hands on her hips. "Excuse me, but do I have any say in this, since it is *my* ass we're talking about."

He pointed to Niko. "You, back to the terrace." He turned to Sierra. "You, bedroom, *now*."

What did he think, he could just order her around? And if he couldn't, why, as he stomped down the hall to his bedroom, was she following him? Maybe because the fact that he would punch someone to defend her honor was just a tiny bit flattering. But what she didn't appreciate was the part about him basically owning her. He'd lost that right when he dumped her.

He opened the bedroom door and gestured her inside, and she dumbly complied, but she wasn't a total pushover.

"Look. I don't know who you think you—"

That was as far as she got before Coop spun her around, slanted his mouth over hers and kissed away whatever she'd been about to say. His arms went around her, pulling her hard against him, and instead of fighting it and asking what the heck he thought he was doing, it felt so amazingly wonderful, and she had missed him *so* much, she couldn't help but kiss him back.

So much for not being a pushover.

He kicked the door closed.

"I have been such a jerk," he said. "A miserable excuse for a man. I am so sorry."

She tucked her face against his chest, breathed in deep the scent of him, knowing that she was home. Any reservations that she had been feeling before their fight were gone. "I deserved it."

"No you didn't. And when I saw him touch you…" He squeezed her so hard it was difficult to breathe. "Tell me you didn't like it."

"God, no! It was revolting."

"I don't want another man to ever touch you again. Only me, for the rest of our lives."

She cupped his face in her hands. "You're the only man I want, Coop. The only man I'll ever want. And I am so sorry for what I did. It was killing me having to lie to you. I should have told you the truth from the beginning."

"Sierra, it's okay."

"It's not. I should have come to your door, told you I was the twins' mother and asked you if I could be a part of their lives."

"You never would have made it to my door. The doorman would have to let you up, and he wouldn't have done that without permission from me, and I wouldn't have let you near the twins."

"So you're saying it was okay to lie to you?"

"Maybe not okay, but necessary. If I were in your position, and I thought the twins were in danger, I would have done anything to keep them safe. And what my brother did to you…" He shook his head, as if it was almost too painful to say. "It was so wrong, Sierra. He never should have taken the twins from you. He should have owned up to his responsibility."

"But his marriage—"

"To hell with his marriage. He made a mistake and he should have been man enough to admit it. I love my brother, and I appreciate all the sacrifices he made for me, but I just can't excuse the things he did. I'll never believe it was okay. And I will always take care of you and the twins, the way that he should have."

Her heart sank. She didn't want him to see her as some debt he had to repay. That just wasn't good enough for her anymore. "Because you feel guilty," she said.

He cradled her face in his hands. "No, because I *love* you. I asked you to marry me, and you put your faith in me and the first time things got a little hard I bailed. But it isn't going to happen again. I'm dedicated to making this work. I don't have a choice. I need you too much, love you too much to let you go."

"I love you, too," she said.

"And just so you know, I'm calling my lawyer first thing tomorrow and telling him to tear up the prenup."

Not this again. "But, Coop—"

"I don't need it. And I'm going to tell him to get the ball rolling on having your rights as the twins' mother fully restored."

She sucked in a soft breath. The most she had hoped for was to someday be their adoptive mother. She never thought that she would ever be recognized as their biological mother. "Are you sure, Coop?"

He touched her cheek. "They're your daughters. Of course I'm sure. Then after we're married, I'll adopt them. They'll belong to both of us."

It sounded almost too good to be true, and this time she wasn't going to take a second of it for granted. "I'm going to be the perfect wife," she told him. "I'll figure out how to cook a decent meal and learn to clean if that's what it takes."

He shook his head. "Nope."

She blinked. "What do you mean?"

"I don't want the perfect wife."

"You don't?"

He grinned down at her, with that sweet, crooked smile—the one she would get to look at for the rest of her life—and said, "I only want you."

* * * * *

So you think you can write?

Mills & Boon® and Harlequin® have joined forces in a global search for new authors.

It's our biggest contest yet—with the prize of being published by the world's leader in romance fiction.

Look for more information on our website:
www.soyouthinkyoucanwrite.com

So you think you can write?
Show us!

A sneaky peek at next month...

PASSIONATE AND DRAMATIC LOVE STORIES

2 stories in each book – only £5.49!

My wish list for next month's titles...

In stores from 17th August 2012:

☐ The Temporary Mrs King – Maureen Child

& The Paternity Proposition – Merline Lovelace

☐ A Perfect Husband – Fiona Brand

& A Scandal So Sweet – Ann Major

☐ Relentless Pursuit – Sara Orwig

& Ready for Her Close-up – Katherine Garbera

☐ Unfinished Business – Cat Schield

& The Ties that Bind – Emilie Rose

Available at WHSmith, Tesco, Asda, Eason, Amazon and Apple

Just can't wait?

Visit us Online

You can buy our books online a month before they hit the shops! **www.millsandboon.co.uk**

0812/51

MILLS & BOON® Book Club

2 Free Stories!

Get your free stories now at

www.millsandboon.co.uk/freebookoffer

Or fill in the form below and post it back to us

THE MILLS & BOON® BOOK CLUB™—HERE'S HOW IT WORKS: Accepting your free stories places you under no obligation to buy anything. You may keep the stories and return the despatch note marked 'Cancel'. If we do not hear from you, about a month later we'll send you 2 Desire™ 2-in-1 books priced at £5.49* each. There is no extra charge for post and packaging. You may cancel at any time, otherwise we will send you 4 stories a month which you may purchase or return to us—the choice is yours. *Terms and prices subject to change without notice. Offer valid in UK only. Applicants must be 18 or over. Offer expires 31st January 2013. **For full terms and conditions, please go to www.millsandboon.co.uk/freebookoffer**

Mrs/Miss/Ms/Mr (please circle)

First Name

Surname

Address

Postcode

E-mail

Send this completed page to: Mills & Boon Book Club, Free Book Offer, FREEPOST NAT 10298, Richmond, Surrey, TW9 1BR

Find out more at
www.millsandboon.co.uk/freebookoffer

Visit us Online

0712/D2YEA

The World of Mills & Boon®

There's a Mills & Boon® series that's perfect for you. We publish ten series and, with new titles every month, you never have to wait long for your favourite to come along.

Blaze®
Scorching hot, sexy reads
4 new stories every month

By Request
Relive the romance with the best of the best
9 new stories every month

Cherish™
Romance to melt the heart every time
12 new stories every month

Desire™
Passionate and dramatic love stories
8 new stories every month

What will you treat yourself to next?

Ignite your imagination, step into the past…
6 new stories every month

INTRIGUE...

Breathtaking romantic suspense
Up to 8 new stories every month

Medical Romance

Captivating medical drama – with heart
6 new stories every month

MODERN™

International affairs, seduction & passion guaranteed
9 new stories every month

nocturne™

Deliciously wicked paranormal romance
Up to 4 new stories every month

RIVA™

Live life to the full – give in to temptation
3 new stories every month available exclusively via our Book Club